THE QUEEN OF LIES

Architects of the Grand Design, Book One

Jacob,
Thank you
for reading. We
survived a house
of horrors

Michael J. Bode

5/4/15

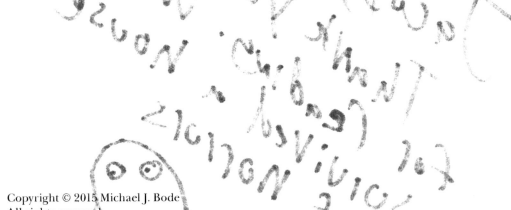

ISBN 13: 9781507862971
Library of Congress Control Number: 2015902016
CreateSpace Independent Publishing Platform
North Charleston, South Carolina

To J. Michael Wilbanks, for being the best friend ever.

"The strong devour the weak. So it can be said that weakness is the source of strength."

"I don't know what's worse to believe—that life is random and meaningless or that it was deliberately designed to be shitty."

CONTENTS

ACKNOWLEDGMENTS

I'd like to thank my parents, sister, and friends for their support. I also want to thank the team at CreateSpace, particularly my editor Angela, for their support in making this book.

I give a particular shout-out to the inventor of wine and the cast of drunks who inspired me.

Also special love to my D&D group (Logan, Will, David, Erin, Dreama, Dan, Jason) who allowed me to develop some of the characters in this book. And of course… my Facebook friends whose likes actually did make a difference in making this book a reality.

SERRA

Serra floated up the stairs to the eastern wing of Landry Manor, her long black robes billowing behind her. City Inspector Berringer followed, never closer than ten paces behind, torn between his fear of dealing with the Invocari and his desire to see that his case was cleared of foul play. There were six bedrooms in each wing of the house—twelve total, not including the servants' quarters.

Serra was a slight girl, but the robes of the Invocari and her levitation were designed to give her an air of menace. Her face was deeply shadowed under her heavy cloak, and her sleeves covered all but her fingertips. She was the dark specter of Rivern's law, ever vigilant against all threats physical and metaphysical. Today was her first time assisting in an investigation.

"The master bedroom is at the end of the hall," Inspector Berringer said, clearing his throat.

Serra didn't reply. Her silence was as much a badge of office as her robes or her starmetal rings.

It was a vast, well-appointed room, dominated by a large four-poster mahogany bed draped in purple silks. An ornate armoire was crowded into one corner. Serra noted the old nobility were loath to part with any of the ugly antiques from the days of the monarchy. So they crammed the little used spaces of the manors.

She lingered in the doorway and looked to the ceiling. Inscribed above the bed was a circular warding seal of moderate complexity. It looked intact as far as she could tell. Warding wasn't really her specialty, but the Cabal was short on wardens.

The coroner, one of the few practicing necromancers in Rivern, was already on the scene along with one of the wizards from the college—a blood mage in red robes who wore gold-rimmed spectacles. The abbess was present as well. She wore

1

long robes and a white veil that masked all but her eyes. Serra could tell she was dark of skin but could make out little else about her.

"There are no eyes," Isik the necromancer grumbled. He had a thick Volkovian accent and the surly demeanor to match.

The body of Lord Landry and his wife were still in bed, their eyes burned out, their lifeless faces contracted in terror. The tableau was horrifying in the context of the ornate furnishings and exotic purple silk bedding. Black veins spidered out from the orbits of their eyes and corners of their mouths. Lady Landry was twenty years the junior of her husband and probably quite fetching while alive.

Isik complained, "I can't recover the final moments of a corpse that has no eyes."

"Can you at least confirm it was an attack by Harrowers?" the abbess inquired.

Isik shrugged. "It fits. You didn't need to drag me all the way across town to say this."

"We're just being thorough," Serra said. "We've never heard of two attacks occurring at the same time. And we still need you to confirm the time of death."

"Bah," Isik said, shaking the wrists of the Landry corpses. "Midnight…ish."

The chance of having one's soul carried off in the night, Serra knew, was vanishingly small. More people died by falling into one of the three rivers each year than those who died by the hands of the Harrowers, but the arbitrary and grisly nature of these deaths (the eye sockets burned out, leaving the skull completely empty) made the danger greater in peoples' imaginations. With three of these deaths in as many months within the city proper, the people of Rivern were panicking.

Achelon the Corrupter had unleashed the Harrows upon creation five hundred years prior. When they finally were banished, their echoes remained in dreams to return each night to claim twelve souls, one for each of the twelve Harrowers (the thirteenth abstained for some reason). With twelve people dying out of everyone in the world, every night and in different nations, the chances were extremely remote of it happening to multiple individuals in the same city.

"Cause of death," Serra said, "harrowing. This investigation is closed."

⟨⟨⟩⟩

After finishing her reports at the Invocari tower, Serra walked home, exhausted. The sun was little more than an orange sliver on the horizon. Now that her shift was over, she wore civilian attire: a burgundy dress with black laces up the front. No one gave her a second glance as she jostled through the flow of people to her apartment. The Invocari were everywhere in Rivern; you just didn't always see them.

When they did appear like dark sentinels floating over the streets, people gave a wide berth. Even Serra didn't recognize most of them in their hoods, but when they cast their gaze toward her, she placed two fingers to her collarbone in a salute of respect. The dark watchers sometimes returned the gesture by curling all but those same two fingers into the folds of their sleeves.

The Invocari were terrifying because they had to be, but beneath their robes they were the best men and women Serra ever had the honor of knowing. She loved all of them like family. Like her, most had been orphaned or abandoned. The Cabal had given them a home in order to gain their unwavering loyalty, but it was loyalty well deserved.

Serra stopped outside her apartment building.

An old man in tattered gray robes stood across the street, watching with milky eyes. His face betrayed no emotion, and he stood eerily still amid the people jostling by. As an Invocari, Serra had become accustomed to the unnerving, so the sensation of unease was doubly troubling to her.

She regained her composure and marched toward him.

He looked Genatrovan, and she guessed he was eighty or ninety; it was difficult to tell. "Excuse me, sir," she said. "Do you need any assistance? I can guide you somewhere if you need. It's no trouble."

He sighed and smiled kindly to her, the warmth in his face suddenly breaking through his stoic facade. His eyes were white from cataracts. "No dear. I have nowhere to be but here."

"It's just," she continued, "this isn't a very good part of town for beggars. There have been a few disappearances lately, and with all the talk of Harrowers, it's really better for you to sleep somewhere warded."

The old man took Serra's hand. "Whatever is meant to happen will happen. I'm too old to spend what little time I have left worrying about what might or might not be. Death comes for us all when it is our time. What matters isn't when, but *what* we did before those moments. You should spend time with friends and people you love. Surely there's another man you'd rather be talking to. There's one watching us from the window now." He pointed at her building.

She turned in time to see a pair of curtains on the second floor shutting abruptly.

Serra blushed. It was Warder Vernor's apartment. She'd been sweet on him for the last few months and suspected he harbored similar feelings. Had he been waiting up for her? It was strange how they always seemed to meet in the hallway.

"My vision is better than it appears." The old man released her hand and winked. "I'll be fine. You should run along."

"Okay. Be safe!" She smiled and turned to her apartment building.

She beamed as she entered the cramped lobby. Behind the desk, Loran the watchman was scribbling in his logs. He had a round, kindly face and a bushy red mustache. "Who were you talking to?"

"That man out front." Serra motioned over her shoulder. "He seems harmless. He's just standing in front of the building and didn't seem particularly interested in moving. If he's a spy, he's either terrible at concealing himself or brilliant at making it look like he's terrible at it."

"I noticed him earlier," Loran said. "What did he say to you?"

"That life is short and we should make the most of it." Serra grinned. "Shorter for some of us than others."

"It's bad luck to joke about that—I'm a week away from retirement," Loran scolded her playfully. He was only in his fifties but much senior to the other warders living in the building.

Serra turned and ran up the stairs, half expecting to see Vernor coming out of his room. Her heart sank a little when his door didn't fly open. He was probably embarrassed that he'd been spotted watching her. She readied her hand to knock but lost her nerve at the last second.

No, it would be too strange after she'd caught him spying. She'd see him in the morning and maybe ask him to get a drink after her inspections. She chuckled to herself. If people knew the Invocari had silly romantic entanglements, their image as the menacing enforcers of law would be ruined.

She went to her room and prepared a sleeping draught. If she got up early enough, she could catch Vernor before he went to the tower. She picked out her prettiest blue dress and laid it across the top of her dresser. She didn't have many eye-catching fashions, but this one complemented her more so than her others.

Serra prepared for bed then lay down on the mattress, anxious for the possibility of tomorrow. Even the daunting workload of ward inspections didn't bother her. She waited for the draught to take effect and drifted off to sleep.

She had nearly dozed off when a gentle knock sounded at her door. She gathered her night-robe and opened the door, just a crack at first.

Vernor stood outside, looking timid and anxiously planning what he was going to say. He hesitated then said, "I had to see you. I had to tell you…"

Serra beamed. "I've dreamed of this."

His expression darkened. "You're still dreaming."

Serra stepped away from the door. Suddenly everything felt very wrong. Her room no longer seemed familiar. Vernor stared with cold blue eyes from the doorway, his mouth opening slowly.

She glanced over her shoulder and saw herself fast asleep under her covers.

A part of her knew that if she looked back at Vernor, it would be the last thing she ever saw. A cold hand gripped her shoulder.

She never awoke.

THE BINDING (MADDOX)

A glyphomancer, a necromancer, and an alchemist walk into a bar. The bar mage asks them, "What can I conjure you?"

The glyphomancer provides a detailed schematic and says, "I want one perfect drink that only needs to be made once and keeps me drunk for life."

"Done." The bar mage claps his hands, and the drink appears exactly as described. "What will you have?" he asks the necromancer.

The necromancer communes with his dead granny's ghost for a moment then rasps, "I'll have a pink-raspberry lemon cocktail that turns to ash in my mouth. And I'd like two cherries as well."

"Done." The bar mage claps his hands, and the drink appears exactly as described. He turns to the alchemist. "How about you, sir?"

The alchemist hems and haws for a while before he asks, "Do you have anything bitter and foul tasting, made from poisonous plants, that won't actually do much of anything?"

The bar mage looks at him and says, "What do I look like, an alchemist?"
—old Archean joke (origin unknown, likely mid-Second Era)

Maddox ducked behind the statue of Armadel and sneaked a quick drink from his flask while the rest of the students were preoccupied with inscribing the circle. The long-dead old magus would have been rightly horrified, but the statue kept lookout with its implacable, sober expression as the junior Adepts busied themselves setting up chairs and preparing the space. Maddox knew he could complete the ritual blindfolded; a few sips wouldn't kill him.

There wasn't much in the drawing room to detract from the Circle, a massive set of concentric rings and arcane inscriptions inlaid with metal into the mirror like polish of the granite floor. Standard stuff for any binding and conjuration, but it was one of the largest in the Free Cities. Chairs and benches were being set up around the periphery. Behind them the likenesses of the revered magi stared out from alcoves that were just barely large and private enough to squeeze into for a quick drink.

"Maddox. There you are!"

He quickly made to conceal his flask, but his fingers fumbled, and it went tumbling to the floor. His blood quickened with panic, but he managed to levitate it seconds before it struck the floor. He turned, startled at first, but then his expression returned to its brooding scowl. "Torin. Shouldn't you be setting out appetizers?"

Maddox's nemesis, "Lord" Torin Silverbrook, was easy to despise. His family came from old money and title—his aunt was the richest woman in Rivern. So of course when young Torin, dense as a brick, had decided to study magic, he had been breezed into the Lyceum with a generous endowment to repair their stupid planetarium. And he was blond. And vexingly handsome, which didn't help matters.

Torin looked at the floor then directly at Maddox with his obnoxiously vivid blue eyes. "Hey. I know we don't get along, but…today is a big deal for you. For the school. No matter what my personal feelings are, I just want to say that all the other students and I are wishing you good luck." He put his hand out.

Maddox made like he was going to return the handshake but at the last minute ran his fingers through his midlength chestnut hair. "Fuck off."

Torin grimaced and shrugged before turning and rejoining the others. "You're welcome, asshole."

Maddox reached out his hand and willed his flask into it so he could quickly tuck it into his sash. People like Torin were a perfect example of the mediocrity that was ruining the reputation of the Lyceum. Yes, Torin did have three seals, which technically made him an Adept.

So far Maddox had attained only the Seal of Ardiel, also known as the Seal of Movement. He had completed the entire inscription and binding in less than ten minutes, which was unheard of. It was that bit of confidence that had set him back two years from Torin as he prepared himself physically and mentally to attain the ultimate seal: Sephariel, also known as the Seal of Vitae, the Seal of Life.

The doors to the drawing room swung open, and Magus Tertius marched in, his white robes flowing behind him energetically. He paused briefly to survey the room before seeing Maddox walking toward him, a spring in his step despite his advanced years. Behind him trailed Magus Turnbull, an effete, fat, sneering slug of a man with a bored expression, and a woman he'd never seen before.

She had fiery red hair and wore a plain violet blouse and indigo trousers. Her face was pretty but in a plain, middle-aged sort of way. She could have easily been mistaken for a commoner on the street if not for the simple gold-and-silver sash across her chest. Maddox didn't need Tertius to explain who she was.

"Scholar Maddox Baeland, may I present"—Tertius genuflected to her slightly—"High Wizard Petra Quadralunia, preceptor of the Archean Academy, here to witness the first inscription of the Seal of Vitae at the Lyceum in nearly half a century."

This was a big fucking deal for the Lyceum. It had been nearly five decades since any students had been offered an apprenticeship at the Archean Academy. The preceptors didn't even bother sending representatives but once every lunar conjunction, and even then it was a transparent excuse for them to load up on duty-free nonperishables. Meat was apparently a rare commodity for the floating city.

Maddox had rehearsed his acceptance to study at the Academy many times in his head, but actually seeing this woman here was intimidating. She probably knew more about theurgy than every magus in the college.

Taking his awkward silence in stride, she said, very formally in her Archean tongue, "Your magus regards you highly, and I was bemused with the quality of the scribble things he sent to the Academy. The registrar sends his regards that he could not be here, but it is my…you know, honor…to serve as attestator to your thing today."

Or at least that was what he understood. Although he read Archean proficiently, speaking it wasn't his strong suit.

Maddox cleared his throat and answered in broken Archean, "Thank…you."

Petra replied in very fluent Thrycean, with barely a hint of an accent, "The augurs have foreseen a favorable confluence. Their accuracy is…um…better these days, so I'm hopeful as well. You certainly have the capacity for success in this." She had a brilliant, motherly smile.

"Really?" he said, then quickly added, "I mean, of course. How hard can it be?"

It was extremely difficult. Not only was the inscription exacting, but drawing it incorrectly was potentially fatal. Some of the failures for this seal had been spectacular—everything from spontaneous aging, to necrotic ailments, to even an unstoppable reversal of the aging process had ended the careers of many promising mages.

Petra grinned slightly. "Remember that confidence is only part of the Circle."

"Comprehension and competence complete the ring," Maddox finished for her.

"Exactly so." She nodded then turned to Tertius. "But imparting wisdom is traditionally the role of your preceptor. I'll leave you two to discuss."

"Come, Archwizard," Turnbull said cattily to Petra. "I'll show you to the buffet. I've taken the liberty of having some food packed. I imagine you'll be leaving very shortly...with our most promising student of course."

"How are you feeling, my boy? Are those arms loosened?" Magus Tertius wrapped his arm around Maddox's shoulders and gave him a fatherly squeeze. The older man was practically bubbling over with enthusiasm.

"Yes, Magus." Maddox took a deep breath. He'd spent the better part of the morning warming up his shoulders and wrist for the inscription, although he didn't find it made much of a difference. He had drawn the glyph hundreds of times from memory, each of them perfect. His hands remembered.

"Good, good," Tertius said, hastily fishing a box from a fold in his white robes. "I wanted to give you a present." He barely could contain his excitement as he handed it to Maddox. "Go on! Open it."

Maddox looked at the small wooden box and, using his Seal of Movement, caused the latch to open and the lid to flip back. The bound magic within him functioned like an extension of his own limbs; with barely a conscious thought, he could move objects as if he were holding them.

Inside, a long golden stylus with a rune-inscribed shaft and a ruby tip rested on a pillow of black velvet. The stylus floated out of the box and spun slowly in front of Maddox's face. "This is beautiful. It's a fucking piece of art."

Tertius grinned with obvious satisfaction. "I had Aurius fabricate it to the most exacting specifications, measured to your grip."

Maddox was blown away. The tip looked irregular, but each facet had been cut to produce a specific kind of line. He let the stylus fall into his hand and tested the weight. It shifted slightly—a mercury core. "This is beautiful, but I haven't practiced with it—"

Tertius waved his hand dismissively. "It's for after the inscription. You'll need a new stylus."

After he completed the seal he was attempting today, he would be expected to relinquish his current stylus to the archive, to sit framed beside his portrait. The thought of giving up his first stylus was bittersweet, but he was already eager to practice with the new one. "Thank you," he said.

"I knew when you first came to this school you would bring great honor to this institution. Now go out there and show the Archeans what Genatrovan mages are capable of."

Maddox hugged Tertius. "I won't let you down."

He took a deep breath and entered the Circle. Already he sensed the thrum of power on his fingertips. Above him was a skylight, the clouds outside providing a diffuse overcast but more than enough illumination. He took a seat in the center and laid out his instruments: a book of diagrams, a parchment, and an incense burner, which was purely for show.

From his tool kit, which contained styluses, rulers, and compasses, he selected his plain black beginner's stylus. As worn and simple as this stylus was, his hand knew its quirks. Most students threw their first styluses away when they could afford better instruments, only to waste months relearning tension and release.

Magus Tertius had taken his seat next to High Wizard Quadralunia, who donned a pair of wire-framed spectacles with lenses made out of polished prismite. The material flickered with soft, shifting illumination, making her eyes appear to glow. She seemed to be in good spirits.

The red-robed Magus Quirrus took a seat toward the back. This was turning out to be quite the event if the dean of Blood Sages was in attendance. Maddox felt the sudden gravity of the occasion as Magus Aurius floated into the chamber behind Quirrus. The artifact mage inhabited a golden sphere no larger than a man's head. The Grand Invocus followed after, shrouded completely in his black cloak. This current Grand was rarely seen outside of the tower.

All the magi of Rivern were here. It made sense; after Maddox attained the seal, he would be awarded the honorific of magus and join their ranks on the council. It was tantamount to mastery. If he pulled this off, he would bypass decades of required study and become the youngest magus in the history of the Lyceum.

"I'm ready," Maddox announced.

Tertius looked at him gravely. "Are you certain?"

He couldn't back out now if he wanted to. Half of Rivern was in the drawing theater, with more filing in. Maddox knew in his bones that he could do this. He was born to do this. The liquor from earlier was helping him relax, which was good.

More were still coming in. The room was so full that the alchemist magi in their blue tunics had to stand toward the back. Maddox smiled in satisfaction at that. His first degree from the Lyceum was in alchemy, a discipline he was proficient in but utterly despised. It was the only scholarship available, however, and he'd gotten it only because he had worked in his father's alchemy shop. He didn't have the good luck to be born a Silverbrook. He'd had to earn his dues.

"I'm certain," he said, projecting confidence.

"Close the doors." Tertius waved his hand before addressing the room. "Friends, the Seal of Vitae is the height of mastery for our discipline. The extension of life is the pinnacle of theurgical achievement in our era and in the eras that have come before us. No one at the Lyceum has attained it in nearly half a century, and all but one out of a hundred who attempt it either fail or perish in their efforts." He paused for dramatic effect.

He directed his voice to the room but spent more time announcing to the archwizard than anyone else. "I've watched Scholar Baeland grow from a frightened, skinny boy from the downriver district to a Scholar and draftsman of unparalleled proficiency. Under my tutelage he has mastered the fundamentals of our craft and today has reached the culmination of those years of study.

"I also would like to take this opportunity to welcome an esteemed colleague from the Archean Academy, Archwizard Petra Quadralunia, who is here as an envoy to the Archean senate."

Petra cleared her throat. "I'm a representative, not an envoy. All Archeans with the rank of archwizard have votes in the senate."

Tertius grinned broadly. "How marvelously progressive! Female senator Quadralunia graces us with her presence. And Scholar Baeland takes the ultimate risk to become the fourth youngest to ever attain the seal and the first to attempt it as his second inscription. I couldn't be prouder of any student than I am today." Tertius smiled and took a seat. "You may begin," he said. "May the Guides direct your hand."

Maddox began.

The task of the inscription was twofold. The seal of the Guide Sephariel would be drawn in the center of a circle, surrounded by the words of Maddox's own True Name binding them together as one. The diagrams were exacting and required perfect precision.

The tip of his stylus glowed as he focused his will into it. The seal wasn't created with ink but with the pure concentration of the caster. He drew the initial circle freehand with a flourish. There was a collective gasp; it was nearly perfect. Even Turnbull looked mildly impressed. Torin was mesmerized. Tertius leaned back smugly, enjoying their reactions.

The archwizard was absolutely stoic.

Maddox waved his hand and watched the paper crumple and fly to the side of the circle. It was a nearly perfect inscription. His next one, drawn more deliberately, was perfect. He made a few checks with one of the compasses and, satisfied, continued the seal.

He drew the lines and curves from memory, imagining them on the surface of the parchment and tracing as he had done in his practice sessions. He had done it so many hundreds of times that it came as naturally as breathing. There were 123 specific points of detail in the seal that needed to be done perfectly.

Sweat poured down Maddox's forehead as he worked at a feverish pace. He practiced each stroke with his hand just once before he committed it. As the details of the seal—its stylized lines—came into focus, he felt the chamber surge with theurgy. The Seal of Movement was child's play compared to the energies that coalesced around him.

The Guides appeared slowly at first. They were motes of twinkling lights that descended gracefully from the heavens, like little lanterns on strings blowing gently back and forth in the breeze. Maddox counted nearly twenty. Each point of light was supposedly a fragment of Sephariel; he'd need fifty to adequately power the seal.

Each stroke was perfect. He always had been skilled, but he'd never been as focused as he was now. The room disappeared, and it was Maddox alone with his drawing as he completed the forms and ligatures.

Above him massive balls of glowing white light had formed in the dome of the skylight. Hundreds of smaller glimmers reached all the way to the floor, swimming playfully across his field of vision, sometimes alighting at the end of his stylus, other times timidly investigating his seal before darting away.

It was nothing short of miraculous.

As he placed his final stroke, an agonizing thirty minutes later, he admired the seal and felt the energy build and surge through his body. He gazed up at the marvel of lights and completed his invocation. "*Sephariel, Azzailement, Gesegon, Lothamasim, Ozetogomaglial, Zeziphier, Josanum, Solatar, Bozefama, Defarciamar, Zemait, Lemaio, Pheralon, Anuc, Philosophi, Gregoon, Letos. Anum! Anum! Anum!*"

He waited, arms to his side, head toward the sky, as the first mote of light floated to his mouth. He sighed with relief.

And then the light hesitated. With growing horror Maddox watched as it started to ascend, and then all around him the motes gathered themselves and moved upward. It was as if they were…rejecting him.

"No!" he screamed.

"Say the invocation again!" Tertius whispered insistently.

"This is remarkable," Petra said, adjusting her glasses, "for so many to have come all this way just to meet your student."

Maddox knew differently. He was being judged. And for what? He'd been a good person, unselfish mostly. He'd never been intentionally cruel to anyone who didn't deserve it. It would have been better to die than to live with the shame of failure and Tertius's disappointment.

His green eyes returned to the inscription. Maybe he'd missed something. Everything looked perfect, but he began to panic. He reached out with his mind for his magnifying glass and pored over the seal.

The room started to darken.

Maddox returned to his schematic. The image didn't look right. It drew and redrew itself on the page hundreds of times in rapid succession. Something had made it indecipherable. The outer wheel of the diagram spun as the lines bounced off it, and slowly the lines fell into place and locked. The wheel stopped, and the sigil appeared to him.

There! He'd missed a crucial ligature between two halves of the design. It was a symmetrical construction, but he'd forgotten to join it with a small vertical bar in the lower quarter of the central parallel.

With a single desperate stroke, he created the line and repeated the invocation.

The lights splashed to earth at once with an ear-splitting shriek, shaking the room with the force of raw theurgy as they struck. The floor cracked beneath Maddox as the light poured into his body.

Immediately he rejuvenated, as if he had been dying slowly from a wasting illness and suddenly had been cured. It was a feeling he'd known so long that he didn't have a word for it, but the closest thing that came to mind was *rot*. He had been rotting for as long as he could remember, and now he was clear of it.

Maddox ripped off his tunic, revealing his narrow, wiry frame. His new seal was opposite his first, above his heart. It looked like a tattoo done in shining liquid gold. It was absolutely stunning to look at.

"What the fuck?" Petra gasped, literally causing every person in the room to stare at her.

Turnbull sighed. "Well, this has been a colossal waste of a morning."

"Leave us!" Tertius stood abruptly. His voice trembled with fury. "All of you!"

The attendees didn't waste a second getting out of their seats and filing toward the exit. No one would look at Maddox directly, but he caught many of them staring and whispering as they walked out. He was still smiling, but the slow, cold realization that something had gone amiss started to dawn on him.

Oh, Guides! Maybe I'm dead. Maybe they can't see me.

He cleared his throat and said, "But I did it! The seal bound!"

"Bound *what* exactly? There's no central ligature in the schematic," Turnbull said. "And it wouldn't kill you to get some sun. Or at least put your shirt back on."

He heard one of the junior apprentices say to Torin, "Couldn't have happened to a nicer guy."

Torin punched the apprentice in the shoulder. Hard. "How would you feel if that was you?"

"No, no, no...It was right here." The book containing Maddox's diagram flipped toward him. The fat fucker was right. The schematic had a symmetrical design divided in half with nothing joining them.

This was bad. Really bad. If he went off book...a seal mage never went off book deliberately. He had done something that never could be undone.

The book fell to the floor, and he dropped to his knees next to it. Trying to make the line reappear, he rubbed his finger on the diagram until the ink started to smudge.

THE BACKWASH
(HEATH AND SWORD)

If the Inlet District is the face of Rivern, then the Backwash is her stinkin' arsehole. Like a great painted whore squatting on a chamber pot, the city sits astride the Trident Falls, her legs spread wide to the majestic river in the east and her ass to the rest of the Protectorate. Above the falls, she's a right marvel of engineering and architecture. But all those fancy shitters and aqueducts have only one place to go.

Wander down the granite switchbacks sometime, past the beggars and the cripples, to the Spray, and you'll see what she's really about. Away from the leering eyes of the Chillers and Fodders, you'll find her warren of creaking boardwalks and claptrap shanties. There's gambling, drugs, and a thug on every corner. Alchemists dump their waste right into the water, breeding all manner of monstrosities.

Lore has it they threw men over the falls as a method of execution in the old days. They're still sending us down here to die, but they do it more subtle like—with vagrancy laws and voting precincts. We can't get representation in the Assembly to ask for more representation in the Assembly. And most of the poor fucks are too busy trying to survive to give two shits about politics.

Those who do manage to claw their way back to Rivern's teat never look back. Everyone loves a story about a boy from the Backwash made good. Gives 'em peace of mind. The rest of us is just lazy fucks who like livin' in their shit.
—Assemblyman Cameron, Twenty-Fifth-District representative, in a groundbreaking ceremony for the restoration of the Inlet District Viaduct

Heath sipped a glass of wretched cormieu at the bar as a group of shifty thugs leered at him from a corner of the Broken Oar. The place was the kind of shit hole that you went to when you wanted to get mugged. It was Cordovis's turf to boot; the man had been Heath's mentor in his formative years, so Heath knew how shit went down. He was pretty much guaranteed to get jumped the second he stumbled out the front door drunk.

He wore a ridiculous getup of purple velvet finery that would pass for extravagant to the eyes of the Backwash thugs, with a hooded cloak and golden half mask frequently worn by Bamoran nobility to hide from their indiscretions. He looked every bit the part of a dark-skinned Bamoran noble looking for excitement in the seedy ghettos of Rivern. Being one of the few black men in Rivern who would deign to wander the impoverished districts, he quickly earned a reputation. The clothes, the mask…they hid his athletic physique enough that Cordovis's goons wouldn't recognize him.

He had Sword out next to him. Even in its humble scabbard, it was a fine piece of cutlery. The hilt was simple, but the steel gleamed in the flickering lamplight of the smoky tavern. Large, impractical, ruby-colored gems rested in the pommel and cross guard.

"Is this seat taken, sir?"

Heath spun in surprise, one finger sliding to the trigger of his springblades. He heaved a sigh of relief when he saw a portly man with a red mustache that looked like walrus tusks scoot out one of the stools and sidle up next to him.

"I'm working a job, Loran," Heath said with a smile, not moving his lips. "What do you want?"

"Heath," Loran said smiling.

"Don't use my name here," Heath cautioned.

Loran slid a folded sheet of parchment to him. "My friends in the tower are looking for someone who's proving hard to find."

Cryptic of course. Loran never said which of the two towers his friends were in, but he doubted they were in the Assembly. Heath unfolded the parchment as he watched the thugs from the corner of his eye. Half of them were Fodders, probably mercenary muscle who had turned to crime after being discharged or deserting the army. They were whispering among themselves.

"Did you draw this?" Heath asked, looking at the picture. It was a good pencil rendering of an elderly man with milky-white eyes. A cold shudder of recognition coursed through him as he placed the man's face. Fire, screaming, and a shitload of spiders.

"Nay," Loran said. "One of my plainclothes saw him standing outside the place where the Harrowers struck. Asked around, and he's been seen at the other spots too. No one knows who he is. We've exhausted standard channels for this sort of thing."

"What do I do if I find him?" Heath discreetly folded the parchment and slipped it into his sleeve. "If he's involved, he could be the most dangerous man in Creation."

Loran shook his head. "I don't know. Improvise. See if he knows anything. Try to get him to come in, but if you can't, just take care of him. My friends want the situation handled, and they're leaving it to your discretion."

Heath flashed an ivory smile and sipped more wine. "I need everything you've got on this guy plus double my standard advance. Leave it at the drop spot, and I'll pick it up by sunrise tomorrow. Now if you'll excuse me, I have to find my business partner. Don't follow me no matter what you hear outside."

Heath grabbed Sword, chugged the last of his wine, and headed for the door. The moment he stepped outside, he heard the scoot of chairs and the sound of boots clomping to the door. In the open night air, he threw his hood back and let the mist of Trident Falls cool his skin. The boardwalk was deserted at this time of night. Anyone with somewhere else to be was there a long time ago.

"Hey!" one of the Fodders yelled from the door as three more guys poured out. You couldn't tell Fodders apart, but he didn't recognize any of the other men. A woman with fiery red hair hung toward the back, her dagger already drawn. It was five on one, with three of them highly trained in the Patrean Army.

"Can I help you?" Heath asked plainly.

"That's a nice sword," a scar-faced Fodder said. "I bet this little queer can't even use that thing."

The others chuckled. Heath couldn't help chuckle too. Mainly because the Fodder was unknowingly right about two important facts: Heath was queer, and he couldn't use Sword. But he couldn't just hand the thing over. There were rules as to how it worked. He threw it on the ground in front of him. "Try to take it."

The scarred Fodder motioned to two of the other thugs, who went to grab Heath on either side.

Heath stretched out his hands and clicked the trigger for his springblades. The abraveum knives shredded his velvet sleeves and struck each man in the stomach. From each blade a razor-thin filament of liquid silver trailed back to the twin mechanisms mounted on his arms.

He gave the strings a quick tug, and they retracted, pulling the blades out of his opponents and back into their resting mounts before the men hit the boards. Blood pumped out of their stomachs, through the cracks in the boardwalk, and into the roiling river below. Heath tossed his golden mask aside.

"It's Heath!" The redheaded girl screamed. "Cosgrove! Heath fucking killed Cosgrove, the fucking fuck! Fuck!"

The other two men, one Fodder and another guy with a gnarled beard, drew their weapons and moved around him slowly. They were jumpy. He looked over to the scarred man, whom he guessed was their leader, and met his gaze. Fodders were tough fighters if one lacked the element of surprise. They were strong and quick, and most had been trained to fight from the moment they could walk.

Heath tumbled to the side, slashing at the bearded man's legs as he rolled past him. He jumped to his feet and hit the trigger to draw his blades back to their gauntlets. The springblade wound around the man's ankles as it retracted, digging the filament into his flesh and pulling the blade along its course. The man kicked wildly and toppled over, his leather armor shredded and blood gushing. Heath then shot his other blade into the man's skull to silence his screaming.

Heath then shot a springblade toward Mr. Scar, aiming for the space between him and Sword. It thunked into the boardwalk, hitting nothing. Scar didn't wait for the blade to retract; he jumped for Sword and grabbed it by the hilt.

Heath backed away as the Fodder chucked off the sheath and let the blade free. It was polished to mirrorlike perfection. The Fodder admired his face in the surface of the blade, lost in it for a second.

The girl started to run. "What the fuck are you fucking waiting for? Let's get the fuck—"

Sword swept through the night air, reflecting moonlight into the mist like a ghostly halo as the scarred Fodder spun it in a wide arc. It looked particularly majestic in the hands of a trained warrior. One almost could hear the tone of the steel, the sound of the finest drops of water being split on its edge, as it made its way through the girl's neck and came to rest in his remaining compatriot's heart.

Sword was ancient and intelligent. You could touch it as long as you didn't intend to use it as a weapon or steal it. But if you tried either of those things, the Geas took control, permanently consuming the soul of its wielder, until either the host died or he or she was too far separated from the blade (which was also fatal). Sword had been Heath's partner through ten incarnations, each one distinctly Sword but heavily seasoned with the mannerisms and experience of its current "owner."

There were many stories of cursed items that influenced their owners' behavior. Sword was the opposite—he was an intelligent artifact that was influenced by his wielders.

"I call that maneuver Heart and Soul," the scarred Fodder said, admiring his new countenance once in the surface of his blade. "Get it? You do one in the head and the other in their—"

"I get it." Heath retracted his blade. "Please tell me giving cute names to your killing blows isn't your new quirk."

"Nah, I don't think I'm that witty," Sword said. "We should get out of here before the Invocari decide to investigate a noise disturbance. I'm pretty sure they heard that screaming bitch all the way up in the Overlook."

"Was that really necessary?" Heath indicated the head on the boardwalk, the girl's mouth and eyes frozen wide in a perpetual shriek of horror.

"She was no saint." Sword grabbed his scabbard off the ground and shoved his blade inside. "You know how you always said you'd put me in people who deserved it? Well, this asshole's a part of me now, and the lot of them deserved much worse than a quick death. And he worked for Cordovis, which is several orders of magnitude worse."

Heath held his hand over the bodies. "In the name of Ohan, Lord Father and bringer of Illumination, I command your return to the Light Eternal. May you shine forever." This was called the battle eulogy because it the whole rite consisted of exactly twenty-three words, a holy number of life, and it could be said quickly over a mass grave during the heat of combat or a hasty retreat.

Sword rolled his brown Fodder eyes. "You know doing four seconds of priesty shit doesn't make up for the fact that three out of these four kills were yours, right? If he existed, your god would be right pissed at you over this carnage."

Heath turned away. "You didn't grow up down here. No one will give a shit about poor old Cosgrove, except the eight-eyed piranhas that live in the alchemical waste pools or the shadow urchins who'll pick their pockets clean when we head out of here. This place made them the way they are. They deserve at least a small measure of humanity."

Heath tore off his bloody doublet and tossed it into the river, revealing reinforced black leather armor strapped with hidden throwing knives. He then paused, doubled over, and puked in the river. It came on without warning. Sword's meaty hand rubbed his back.

Sword scrunched his brow. "You don't get sick."

Heath wiped his mouth and dismissed Sword's concern. "It was probably that rancid wine I had at the Oar. Forget about it."

"I hate it when you get all serious," Sword moaned as he followed him.

"Me too." Heath sighed. "I do have just the thing to lighten the mood, however."

"Oh?" Sword placed his hands on Heath's. "That's riiiight...I'm a man now. A big rough-and-tumble Patrean bloke with scars and everything. And nothing gets me more worked up than a good fight. Or a really one-sided fight. Any fight actually…"

"Let's keep it professional." Heath picked up Sword's bloody hands, raised them off his shoulder, and casually released them to the air behind him. "I meant that I have a job for us that you might find interesting. Do you know anything about Harrowers?"

Sword froze. His eyes lit up like a little boy unwrapping his first training sword. "Are they back?"

Heath shook his head. "There's been a rash of harrowings lately, all in Rivern and sometimes more than one a night. That's never happened, as far as I know. And what's more, someone's been spotted at the scenes of the deaths."

"The fuck?" Sword said. "The killings are supposed to be random."

Heath unfolded the parchment Loran had given him. "This is who we're looking for. Recognize him?"

"The fucking shepherd from Reda," Sword said.

"He's back."

DEPOSED (JESSA)

Though I am distant relation to the Empress Iridissa, I'd never imagined being called before the Coral Throne. The circumstances of my birth are ignominious, and all that needs be said is that the man who begat me was a Stormlord of a minor lineage who abandoned my mother and me to squalor.

The first tremor came when I was ten. I didn't know what was happening to me—I seized with pain as if my whole body were vibrating. It lasted only a few seconds, but it happened three times during the night. Much, much later I would coincide the event with the traitor Stormlord Renax and his family's assassination in Rivern.

There were other fits spread so many years apart that I forgot them entirely until they came upon me. Then on a fateful windy Krackensday in Low Tide, my birth father died in a port a hundred miles from Sargasso. The pain was excruciating beyond anything I'd felt before. But as with all the others, it passed in an instant. To the great surprise of my loving wife, my eyes had turned bright silver.

She wept with joy as she pressed my head beneath the waters in our little bath, and I calmly breathed the soapy water. My children squealed with delight as I blasted seagulls from the sky with arcs of lightning. I exulted in the rains that once chilled my very bones. By the pure accident of my birth, I had become the newest and last in line for the Coral Throne, an heir to the glory of the Thrycean Dominance.

—excerpt from the diary of Stormlord Melicor, ninety-ninth in the line of succession for the Coral Throne, Baron of Fang Island, and captain of the *Wailing Siren*

Satryn preened in the mirror, fixing her long silver hair with scrimshaw-and-onyx hairpins. She could have passed for Jessa's older sister, a fact she was fond of telling nearly everyone. Jessa had inherited some of her mother's features but none of her presence. Whereas Satryn's silver eyes smoldered with intensity, Jessa's were pensive.

Jessa stared out the window panes at the Rivern Patrean guards and shadowy Invocari gathered on the lawn below her third-story guest quarters. She counted fifteen Patrean soldiers and two Invocari.

"They don't trust us, Mother," Jessa said nervously.

Satryn sighed. "If the soldiers are there for our protection, it's unnecessary. And if they're there to detain us, it's an insult. Either way I would pay them no mind."

"Should we have brought our own guard from Amhaven?" Jessa worried.

"Honestly," Satryn said reaching for her powder, "you could kill those guards with a flick of your wrist." Like her mother, Jessa had been born with the power to control lightning and water.

Jessa spun toward her. "I don't think that will be necessary. Muriel is my cousin. I'm sure she's just ensuring our safety."

"She underestimates us," Satryn corrected. "Either way."

"The countess has been nothing but gracious in receiving us," Jessa said.

"Don't be fooled by our hosts' hospitality," Satryn cautioned. "The countess appears generous because she believes we're weak. This veneer of civility will crack like an eggshell if these negotiations go poorly, and they would gladly see us strung up in the tower so all the toothless city folk could gawp at our moldering, naked corpses. Now fetch me a necklace that accentuates my neckline."

"Are you trying to negotiate or seduce her? I'd have thought the countess was a bit old for you." Jessa rummaged through her mother's jewelry box for something tasteful.

Satryn played with the button on her silk blouse, which she wore open to her bosom, beneath her embroidered crimson naval doublet. Like all highborns in the Dominance, she was the nominal admiral of a fleet in the empress's armada. She wore a pair of long boots made of black eel skin.

"No, I suspect the countess's cunt has seen fewer fingers than a rusty bear trap. But my appearance will let you bond with your cousin over your shared passion for feeling morally superior."

"Then this would be the last thing I'd wear with that." Jessa passed her mother a ruby drop-pendant necklace and took an ivory cameo choker for herself. "I'd hate for you to feel like you weren't the center of attention."

Satryn laughed as she draped the necklace and let the long ruby shard rest in her bosom. It brightened and flickered softly as she lightly electrified the filaments in the gold chain, causing the tungsten backing to glow. "Perfect. Let's remind them what harnessed electricity looks like."

Jessa braced herself for another wistful recollection of the wonders in Thrycea. *"Limitless energy," my mother would exclaim. "The city of Thelassus is lit at every hour. The factories and forges run without need for wood or coal. Can you imagine what would be possible here if we could harness that?"* Jessa had visited Thrycea once as a child, and it seemed a dreadful place to live for common folk. The Everstorm kept the city in perpetual darkness save for the storm lights and the constant flashes of lightning. Rain poured constantly as shivering work crews fought a constant battle to maintain the buildings against the onslaught of the elements.

Satryn appraised her daughter, her silver eyes moving from the hem of her dress to the pearl embroidery around her collar and sleeves. Jessa impatiently waited for her mother's snide remark.

"It favors you," Satryn offered. "These Genatrovans like their brides to be virgins for some reason, and you certainly look the part…in a prim, forgettable sort of way."

Jessa forced a smile. "Thank you, Mother…I think."

"Let's just get through this," Satryn said. "The countess has had ample time to find you a suitor. If all goes well, you're to meet him and let us work out the arrangements. You'll be married and coronated within the week, and all this foolishness with Duke Rothburn will be over."

Duke Rothburn controlled the eastern half of Amhaven and waged a merciless guerilla campaign against her supporters, burning homes and fields. It was all-out civil war. "And you'll return to Thelassus, never to trouble me again," Jessa said. The prospect of a blindly arranged marriage might have bothered her, but nothing could spoil her excitement about finally being free of Satryn.

Jessa was the rightful queen of Amhaven, but her mother had seized the regency after Jessa's father had died. Though the law stated the ruler must be male, there were no such limitations on regents. But now Jessa was of an age to marry, and she couldn't wait.

Satryn grabbed Jessa's arm and glared at her. "I have given you everything! Do you think my mother, the *empress*, picked out my clothes for me? Do you imagine that she dried my tears when my father passed away? Did she run to protect her darling baby daughter from the cruelty and scheming of my sisters? Do think she even *once* showed me a single shred of maternal kindness in all the seventeen years I lived in the Sunken Palace? If I *ever* spoke to her in such a way, do you know what she would have done to me?"

Jessa shrugged free of her mother's grip. "Isn't that why she exiled you and married you off to my father?"

"You ungrateful little bitch!" Thunder rumbled outside as Satryn struck her across the cheek.

Jessa laughed in surprise as she wiped blood from her lip. "I don't care if this suitor is fat and ugly. He could be old and want me to engage in degenerate acts that would make the bards blush. There's no prospect more loathsome and insufferable than the idea of spending the rest of my life under the dark cloud of misery you travel with. When I am queen, you will not strike me again."

"Good." Satryn nodded calmly. "That's exactly the kind of focus you'll need to pull this off. Now shall we meet your Lord Silverbrook?"

Jessa forced a smile.

DEATH SENTENCE (MADDOX)

As of this writing, the youngest to attempt the Seal of Vitae was thirty-eight-year-old Lester Dumand of Bamor College. A prodigy known for his intricate illuminated manuscripts, he had attained seven seals in a short time, made even more impressive by a late start to his study. What led a man, at so young an age, to attempt then mistranscribe the seal is pure speculation.

Over the next fortnight of observation, Scholar Dumand exhibited a shocking transformation. Piebald and graying at the temples, with a midsection typical of a Scholar who did not engage in strenuous exercise, he began to regrow hair and slim at a startling rate. By the fourth day, he had recaptured both the figure and appearance of his younger days, when his profession had been that of a sellsword. By the eighth day, he was a young man in peak physical condition.

Had the process stopped there, Lester Dumand would have made the discovery of the ages. Who among us doddering old magi would not wish to spend our extra centuries in the prime of our respective youths? But Scholar Dumand's trajectory continued backward toward infancy. He retained his faculties through his teenage body, but as he reentered childhood, his mind lost the capacity for higher reason.

As he degenerated into infancy, his lungs could not support him, and he perished from asphyxiation on the thirteenth day.

—entry in the Unabridged Codex Hamartia for Lester Dumand

Despite its name, the Mage's Flask wasn't frequented by anyone respectable and certainly not by anyone from the Lyceum. Even prostitutes were a rarity. Sawdust covered the creaking floor and its many probable bloodstains. The crudely hewn stools wobbled no matter which way you turned them.

Maddox pounded a glass of firebrandy. It had been two days. He hadn't shaved or changed his clothes, which reeked of alcohol and sweat.

The bartender, and possibly owner of the establishment, Cassie, was a plump black woman with a perpetually stoic expression. Despite her size she was surprisingly quick and could clear the counter faster than you'd think possible to beat the shit out of customers who tried to sneak out on their tabs. She polished what was probably the only clean glass in the bar.

The good news for Maddox was that one way or another he was going to make history. When you mistranscribed the Seal of Vitae, you got your own chapter in the accounts of the magi and an entry in the Codex Hamartia. His name would be a cautionary tale for ambitious young Scholars for centuries to come. People may not have remembered the name of the dean of the Academy when Lester Dumand had inverted the third inner curvatures across the median lineation of his seal, but everyone knew Lester's story.

"Hit me with another one, Cassie," Maddox called from his usual seat.

She sighed as if she'd been asked to shoulder the weight of the world as she brought a bottle over and filled Maddox's glass. "Your dad came in here a few nights ago," she said.

"And?"

"He ran out on his bar tab." She raised her eyebrows, clearly expecting Maddox to pay.

"It was your mistake for serving him." Maddox raised his glass. "He'd only come into this shit hole if every other place had thrown him out."

"In Bamor a son repays his father's debt," Cassie said as she poured him another shot. She went back to polishing her glass. She knew better than to push it. Having an actual mage frequent the establishment was handy, and no one could break up a fight or toss someone out like Maddox.

His dreary ruminations returned. The best-case scenario would be if his seal killed him in his sleep. His promising career—and all the hard work he had poured into it—had been irrevocably marred with a single impulsive stroke of his stylus. What could he possibly look forward to…a teaching position in the alchemy department? He would kill himself before that ever happened.

He felt something on the back of his neck, something soft and hot, like breathing.

Maddox turned slowly and nearly leapt out of his seat. A lanky, unshaven man was looming inches from the back of his neck with a shit-eating grin and blazing green eyes. Before the man could even speak, Maddox dragged him up several feet in the air by the collar of his black jerkin. The man's arms clutched at the fabric, his boots kicking frantically as the power of the seal suspended him midair.

"Riley," Maddox said, regaining his composure. "Do not fucking do that. Ever."

Riley was alternating between gasping for breath and laughing his ass off. The guy was certifiably nuts—creepy but without really being scary. Maddox released Riley, and he plopped down to the floor, still gasping and chuckling. "Should've seen yer face. Priceless!"

"Not a good time, Riley," Maddox said, suppressing the desire to cause bodily injury.

Riley's shoulders sank. "You look bummed. T'fuck happened? I were always able to get a smile from you back in the old days."

Riley had developed a one-sided kinship with Maddox, a fictional narrative in which they'd been friends rather than passing acquaintances when they were in the Lyceum together. Riley's unfortunate Amhaven accent had marked him for ridicule early on, and he washed out before he'd even chosen a specialty. Maddox, who generally regarded everyone as inferior, ignored him but never went out of his way to be cruel either. But on a bad day, he sadistically had allowed Riley to cheat off his theurgy exam. The source of Riley's sudden brilliance was obvious to everyone and had led to Riley's expulsion. However, in Riley's mixed-up head, that caper had made them something like blood brothers.

Maddox rolled his eyes. Riley was like a stupid dog—you couldn't hate him without feeling guilty. And you could pretty much tell him anything, and he wouldn't judge. "I tried to inscribe the Seal of Sephariel, and I fucked it up. And I bound it anyway. So I'm not really in much of a laughing mood. And you aren't that funny."

"Whoa!" Riley's eyes got huge. "You fuckin' madman! I knew you was gonna be a big shot one day, but holy fuck! Can I see it?" Riley enthusiastically reinvaded Maddox's personal space.

"No!" Maddox pushed him back with his seal.

"So they kicking you out of the school then? That's what happens if you mess up, innit?" Riley asked, with unseemly enthusiasm.

"I don't fucking know!" Maddox shouted, and slammed his hand on the bar. More calmly he continued, "Turnbull wanted me gone yesterday, but Tertius is the dean. As long as he's around, I think they'll find something for me to do. Fuck, there's a backlog of administrative shit, and they need someone halfway competent to do it, providing I don't spontaneously turn into some putrifactcd corpsc."

"Fuck Turnbull and Tertius!" Riley spat on the floor, which in any other place would have been met with a reprimand from the management. Riley's hatred of Tertius was understandable; he was the one who had ordered his expulsion, to make him an example for the other students.

"Can I tell you a secret?" Riley whispered.

"If I say no, are you going to tell me anyway?"

Riley sat himself next to Maddox and rolled up his sleeve. He had pale, veiny arms, and some of the veins had turned black, which could have come from impurities common to any number of illicit substances. "I been practicin' a little meself...Got us a school of sorts even. I made this a few nights ago when I was right fucked on dragonfire."

Maddox recoiled slightly as Riley revealed a mark on his arm.

It wasn't even an attempt at one of the thirteen seals. It was drawn inside a triangle. The lines squiggled like worms, some of them falling outside the edges. The intersects were all wrong as well. The geometry was utter nonsense—and it seemed to be moving. "What...the...fuck?"

"You know there're mages who say there was more than thirteen seals. Before the Long Night."

"That's...kind of a seal, Riley." Maddox winced. "What does it do?"

He shrugged. "Dunno. But it ain't killed me yet. My point is there's all kinds of knowledge outside what those old buggers teach in that stupid school. They spend all those years fillin' your head with rituals and rules so you don't know what's actually real anymore. The seals ain't there to bind the Guides—they're there to bind *you*."

"That's deep, Riley." Maddox remembered that he had a drink and downed it.

Maddox looked away from Riley's "seal." To inscribe something without knowing what it was required a specific type of stupidity. The seals were specific to the Guides themselves, so how that nonsense even had been bound in the first place made no sense. On the other hand, Riley seemed like his normal self, which was by no means a good thing, but not any worse than usual.

"Hey." Riley perked up suddenly. "You should come hang out wit us. I've got meself a study group of sorts. Nontraditional students and the like. We could really use someone like you—you're the smartest guy I know, in fact."

"As much as I love an intellectual challenge, I'm going to have to pass on explaining the Principia Magica to a bunch of downriver hedge wizards." Maddox tapped the rim of his shot glass to get Cassie's attention.

"Yeah, well…" Riley looked down. "I understand—you probably don't need nobody to teach you nothin'. You was always smart like that. But if you change your mind or just want to say hello, we're squatting in a brown two-story at the end of Langley Pier. You can't miss it. There's big red writs of condemnation on the door."

Maddox waited for Cassie to pour his shot; her urgency fell somewhere between slow and geological. "Maybe I will," he said, immediately regretting it.

"Yes!" Riley beamed as he pumped his fists. "You'll be my guest of honor, you will. And we've got a bedroom set up that's real nice. Homey like."

Maddox paused uncomfortably, unsure if that was an invitation or just some random thing that popped into Riley's drug-addled brain. "I don't need to see your bedroom, Riley."

Riley stood and brushed his wrinkled jacket. "Well. Gotta be going. I've a bit of business to attend to."

Maddox raised his eyebrow. "You're leaving?"

"Yeah." He smiled at Cassie and slapped five ducats on the table. "Me boy here—drinks, whatever he wants…on us." He raised his arms triumphantly and bounded out the front onto the boardwalk outside.

"I've never seen that boy put his own money on my counter." Cassie walked over to collect the ducats. "You want some of the good shit or the cheap shit so you can pass out on my floor?"

Maddox pondered the question for a second. "Cheap shit."

Cassie thunked a bottle in front of him. "Saves me a trip."

A SUITABLE ARRANGEMENT (JESSA)

Thrycea is a nation of slaves, yet the Stormlords are masters of deception, and the shackles are subtle. It is true that no one goes hungry in Thrycea; salt-rations are in every public forum open for the taking. Indigence is illegal; one sees many slaves on the streets of Thelassus, but there are no beggars. Those too sick to work are made whole by the ministrations of the Blood Priests and sent back to work.

Certainly corruption and abuse are rampant (as they are here and elsewhere), but the Stormlords have a dictum, "Might makes right." If a lord fails to keep his thralls complacent and obedient, he is perceived as weak and replaced by a rival. Only the strongest and smartest survive long enough to hold their positions.

Barring the miraculous ascension of a compassionate Stormlord to the Coral Throne, it is difficult to see such a system ever changing. Not so for our experiment in democracy. With each generation the will of the Assembly drifts further from the will of the people and the lofty ideals of freedom and welfare for its constituents. I see how readily people are willing to trade their independence for personal security, as if freedom were merely one means to an end.

It is not with admiration that I describe the workings of our enemy, but resignation and disappointment. It is my hope that democracy will reign eternal, but if we are to see our nations suborned once again to the interests of powerful men, we could do worse than follow our enemy's example.

—*A Treatise on Comparative Politics,* by Dorian Brand, written in the hundredth year of the Protectorate's founding but still widely read

Jessa and Satryn walked down the circular wooden staircase to the marble foyer of Silverbrook Manor. The curving banister was a single piece of Maenmarth timber polished to a glassy finish.

Bronze automatons, like men in polished armor, moved about the foyer, tirelessly cleaning the floors and dusting the furniture. Jessa couldn't begin to hazard how much each of those must have cost as she made her way to the sitting room through the foyer's eastern set of double doors. The doors parted automatically, triggered by a pressure plate.

Countess Muriel was an aficionado of clocks. Different mechanical timepieces, in various states of working order, sat in alcoves and adorned the walls. Jessa read that the old nobility of Rivern displayed wealth by craftsmanship and quality rather than art and precious substances.

Countess Muriel Silverbrook was an elderly but sprightly woman in her seventies. She wore a bold green dress with a hard leather corset like one might wear on a hunt. One hand rested on the armrest of her chair, absently fingering what looked to be a large air-compression crossbow that leaned against it.

Behind her, two men in black cloaks floated by the wall of books. Invocari. Jessa could see only their pale hands, folded in front of them. They appeared every bit as menacing as people said. The shadowy enforcers were a feature of Rivern that visitors tended to like the least. Mother had dismissed them entirely, which only made Jessa more uneasy.

"Your Majesty," Muriel said with a hint of sarcasm. She did not rise.

"Muriel," Satryn cooed as she took a seat on a plush couch opposite the countess. "You're looking well."

Muriel made a dismissive wave. "Try not to sound so disappointed."

Satryn laughed. "I'm learning that the stories of your wit weren't an exaggeration."

"And you, Satryn, are…much as I imagined." The countess moved her gaze from Satryn to Jessa. "Please dear, have a seat. You're making the Invocari twitchy. And your lip appears to be bleeding. Let me call for the healer." She reached for a tiny bell on the side table.

"Please don't waste the Light on my expense. I bit too hard trying to loosen the clasp of a necklace." Jessa chose a chair off to the side and sat primly, her hands folded.

"Before we begin," Muriel said, "can I offer you any refreshment? A Lowland clover tea perhaps?"

"Do you have anything stronger?" Satryn leaned back, crossing her leg and luxuriously draping her arm over the back of the couch. Jessa half expected her to prop her boots on the mahogany table, but thankfully she abstained.

"I suppose it's late enough in the morning." Muriel nodded knowingly and produced a flask from a concealed pouch in her dress. She poured a generous two fingers of brown liquid into her own glass before passing it to Satryn.

Jessa watched for Muriel's reaction when Satryn drank directly from the flask. Long ago the Stormlords had been corsairs, and when they had taken rulership of Thelassus, they imposed many of their uncouth behaviors as etiquette for the ruling class. The older woman gave no indication that she was fazed by it.

"Now that we've survived the pleasantries," Muriel declared, "I was hoping we might discuss the occasion for this royal visit to my humble estate."

"Indeed." Satryn looked around the library and turned over one of the pillows next to her before addressing Muriel. "So where is he hiding?"

Muriel smiled. "Torin is at the Lyceum on some important business. Apparently another student is attempting something very dangerous or some such and his attendance is mandatory."

"Another student?" Satryn mused archly. Jessa could tell by her mother's tone that she was less than pleased.

Muriel said, "My grandnephew is a student of glyphology in his third year. He's of good pedigree, close enough to Jessa in age, and amenable to the possibility of the arrangement. You see, his parents squandered their fortune in a series of poorly timed business endeavors. They need the prestige as much as they need the money."

"Which other prospects have you considered? Perhaps there's a highborn bastard working in your stables who would be able to attend this meeting on short notice," Satryn scoffed. "I come on behalf of the empress to negotiate a peace between the Protectorate of the Free Cities and the Thrycean Dominance, and you offer me…a student with a poor family?"

"Really?" Muriel sipped her drink. "Many in the Assembly are of the impression that you're here because you were deposed. It wouldn't be the first time Amhaven has driven out the Dominance."

"A momentary inconvenience," Satryn explained. "Jessa's claim is rightful. Out of respect for our sovereignty, I've asked my mother to abstain from intervention, something Rothburn's supporters in the Assembly haven't done. Amhaven needs a king who can shut down this nonsense. I doubt a student of glyphology possesses the necessary political capital to secure a bloodless succession."

Muriel let out a loud uncomfortable sigh then gently began. "Satryn, dear, there's no delicate way to put this, so I'll simply say it. There are no other prospects. Of the eligible gentry, few would have an interest in giving up a life in

Rivern for the...rustic simplicity of Amhaven. Then there's the unfortunate history of nobles who have married into the imperial family and met untimely ends. People still talk about Renax."

"With the signature of this peace treaty, Amhaven will be a new center of trade. Thrycean trade guilds will flood the rivers with goods from the Mazatar and the Gold Coast, not to mention timber from Maenmarth," Satryn declared. "Surely someone more pragmatic must realize the benefit to this arrangement. Lord Hale, for instance, has experience in the lumber trade. Have you considered him?"

"Hale is confirmed bachelor." Muriel waved her hand limply to dispel the idea from the air. "And while I'm impressed by your due diligence, I'll assure you that I've researched this exhaustively. Those who would seek the prestige of Jessa's title are too lowborn. Those who would profit by it are too prudent. But I'm sure we can round up some greedy merchants from the Assembly or bastard stableboys, if that's what you'd prefer."

"There's no harm in meeting him," Jessa blurted. "This marriage is about more than wealth and title. It's about bringing peace between two empires and settling our disputes at home in Amhaven."

Satryn shot Jessa a withering look that seemed to say, *I hope he's fucking hideous.* She turned to Countess Muriel. "The empress empowered me to broker this marriage on her behalf. An impoverished student from a fallen house is an insult to the Dominance. You simply must find another candidate."

"It was worth a try." Muriel shrugged and rose from her chair. "But if Jessa is too good for Torin, there's little I can do. The ongoing war is unfortunate, but the Assembly feels confident that the Dominance has once again overreached itself and is willing to let this conflict play itself out. I won't keep you any longer. I'm certain you'll want to get back to Weatherly and deal with your situation with Duke Rothburn. Give him my regards."

"No!" Jessa stood abruptly.

The Invocari at the back of the library raised their hands with palms outstretched. Satryn flinched and readied her own hands in response, pointing to each of them. Muriel's eyes widened like pale green saucers, but the old woman remained outwardly calm.

Jessa smiled. "My mother speaks for the empress, but I speak for the people of Amhaven. Our nation has suffered from generations of exploitation by the Dominance and neglect from the Protectorate. Only when a Stormlord is poised to take the crown does the Assembly bother to funnel money, and they do so to start an insurgency. I can't let these talks fail."

"Entertaining this proposal is a humiliation, Jessa." Satryn rested her hands on her lap. "The countess only presses us because she thinks she can. Let this war rage and see how the Assembly feels when Thrycea commits the full fury of the Red Army to its bordering nation."

"You forget that my blood is Silverbrook as well as Stormlord," Jessa said. "These people are my father's kin, and it is you who offers insult."

Satryn threw her hands in the air and swallowed her words. "My daughter didn't inherit the fiery temperament of a Stormlord, which in this situation may prove beneficial. If this Torin is of noble birth, I'm sure the empress can be swayed to offer her blessing. Provided of course that there are reasonable concessions."

Muriel returned her gaze with flinty eyes. "The offer is marriage and consideration of a treaty. I hardly think you're in a position to ask for more."

Satryn smiled. "Perhaps Rivern and the Protectorate are well funded enough to afford the services of the Patreans. But the mercenaries, supplies, and warmaster aren't a trivial expense for any nation. If some of that coin went to reestablishing Torin's *rightful* position, which was lost through no fault of his own, then he'd be the equal of any of the other suitable prospects, would he not?"

Muriel sat back down. "A dowry…for a *husband?* That's highly unusual."

"An investment."

"I'll need to discuss it with the usury board." Muriel said. "They might be convinced, if the numbers align."

"Jessa's happiness and security are my only concerns. For her sake I'll work with you on this."

Muriel sighed. "Then we're in agreement. Tomorrow I'll arrange a formal introduction between Torin and Jessa. If he finds her as agreeable as I do, we should be on our way to forging a new alliance."

"Have we not already agreed to the match?" Jessa asked plaintively.

"Arranged marriages may be the rule of law in the border nations, but we haven't officially had one for centuries," Muriel explained. "I've done my best to persuade Torin, but there's nothing to be done if he doesn't agree to it. He's *ambivalent* about the prospect, but…in fairness, the portrait you sent does not do you justice, cousin."

"Mother painted it," Jessa stated.

"I'm sure Jessa will do everything in her power to bring him around," Satryn said. Her ruby necklace was pulsing hot from the electricity on her skin.

"Let's hope so," Muriel agreed. "A lot rides on the potential affections of our young lovers to be."

THE LONG WAY DOWN (MADDOX)

The High Wizards can lift a whole city into the air to protest an ancient import tax; you'd think they could come up with a better way to transport ingots than having a bunch of guys load them into retrofitted flying sailboats. But that's Archean efficiency for you: "We could do everything with magic if we wanted to, but then we'd be depriving people of their livelihoods…and just feeding everybody is beneath us."

The hours are shit, and the work is backbreaking, but going to the ground is worth every second of bullshit. Groundfolk practically roll out carpets and throw flowers when you step off that ship. You can trade a single prism for a hundred metal coins. Tell someone how an Archean privy reconstitutes food, and they'll be asking you questions about it all night.

Moving streets, fabrication centers, and projection theaters are all they seem to care about. Some even beg you to smuggle them in. I guess the sky is always bluer on the other side. They have no appreciation for how cheap food is or how mages and common men are equals under law.

A lot of us get tempted to jump ship when we go to the ground. Save enough prisms and a guy can get himself started; and someone always needs crates moved after he's blown his scratch on fresh fruit and fish.

But it's true what they say—the ground is cursed. People still die in their sleep every night from Harrowers trying to come through. It's only a matter of time before one of them does.

—an account from an interview with an Archean laborer

"How did you find me?" Maddox sighed as he looked out over the parapets of the Lyceum's observation tower. It was shorter than the twin towers that rose on either side of the falls, but it afforded a dazzling view of the city at night. The sky was clear, and amid the stars, he made out the twinkling light of Archea, just under the kraken's eye.

"One of the Invocari told me you were up here," Tertius said, walking over to Maddox. The medallions representing his seals seemed to jingle louder. "You look like you've been taking a swim in the Backwash. Care to tell me what's happening with you?"

Maddox's eyes started to sting. "I disappointed you. I made a fool of myself, and I know the other magi see that as a reflection on you…You were the only person who ever gave a shit about me, and I failed you. And now I'm going to be expelled. I wish I'd died right then and there so I wouldn't have to know what it's like to be a fucking failure."

A bottle of golden liquid floated over to the stone railing where Maddox leaned, along with a glass. It poured itself as Tertius spoke softly. "It's century-aged Archean brandy. It doesn't have the same kick as the stuff they sell in the Backwash, but I think you'll appreciate the subtleties. Everyone should try it once in their life."

Maddox wanted to chug the glass, but bottles like this were passed down through generations like heirlooms, so he sipped. The taste was smooth and indescribably complex. It evoked memories more than it did flavor—swimming in the river on a hot summer day, being kissed in the middle of winter as snow fell all around him on an empty street…and an odd hint of elder nettle.

Tertius laughed to himself. "From the moment your aunt dropped you on our doorstep, I knew you were special. It isn't our practice to take students on the word of their parents, but you were sharper than some of my best pupils. And you weren't modest about it either."

Maddox forced a smile. "I'm still smarter than those assholes. I just made one fucking mistake…" He finished his glass and poured another.

"That's one more than any Master of the Seal can afford to make." Tertius sighed as he looked out onto the horizon. "When you decided to study glyphology, I was so…proud, but I was also blind. You have more than the necessary skill, and you're a perfectionist, but you always lacked the right temperament. The seals are the art of cautious men, Maddox. You could have excelled in a discipline where risk taking is rewarded."

"You mean like fucking alchemy?" Maddox took another swig from the bottle and let the liquor warm his throat. He'd learned how to mix potions before he could read, when his father's hands were too shaky from drinking to measure properly. They weren't pleasant memories.

"It's a noble discipline in need of more brilliant minds to bring it into the modern era. You were a prodigy with elixirs." Tertius's voice sounded ragged.

"It was my own selfish desire for a legacy that nudged you into glyphomancy. As surely as if I inscribed that seal with my own hand, I destroyed you, Maddox."

"I wish you had. Destroyed me." Maddox shook his head, and the motion made him suddenly dizzy. His body felt numb from the brandy. It was hitting him a lot harder than it should have. *Maybe I should take it easy on the Archean stuff.*

Tertius placed a hand on his shoulder. "If any student from the Lyceum were going to receive an invitation from the Academy, it would have been you. It…it should have been you. The archwizard was very impressed, although it's unlikely a woman would have the authority to make a decision either way."

"I think I need to sit," Maddox said as he plopped himself to the floor.

"How it tempts us, that jewel in the sky. While we struggle to patch together scraps of forgotten lore, the High Wizards tempt us with table scraps of their arcane principia," Tertius continued, as he looked onto the horizon toward the twinkling glimmer of Archea.

"Maybe my seal isn't bad. Maybe it's something new. And when they see what it can do, they'll want to have me in their school," Maddox said, feeling warm and peaceful. "Maybe it's still okay, and I can send you correspondence and even have you visit me up there."

Tertius shook his head. "If it is something new and not a permutation, then it's something dangerous. To experiment with things beyond our knowledge would open the door to dark avenues best forgotten. We can't afford to compound one error with one potentially more grievous."

"Did they put actual tincture of elder nettle in this brandy?" Maddox shut his eyes and slurred, "You know, if it's mixed with alcohol in the incorrect proportions, it can become a potent narcotic. You want to reduce it to half volume before introducing it to another solution. That's basic fucking alchemy…"

Not that Maddox minded the sensation. He felt as if his body were floating weightlessly, without sensation or a care in the world. His fingertips were numb, and his brain was steeped in a heavy fog. He licked his lips, but every movement seemed to happen hundreds of miles away in slow motion. He estimated he was about as close to a fatal dose as one safely could get.

"Turnbull is calling for an investigation." Tertius's voice sounded muffled and distant. "The Council of Deans will meet to discuss your fate. They'll demand answers I can't give them. And I can't protect you. As you said, it would be better for both of us and this institution if you did pass away gently. It's easier doing this, knowing that you see that as well."

Wait. What? Maddox struggled to open his eyes as the floating sensation seemed to lift him off the ground into a spinning vortex of numbness.

That last part sounded important, so Maddox forced his eyes open. He was floating, literally. Below him he saw the courtyard of the Lyceum and its great tree. He was being suspended over the edge, cradled in Tertius's magic. "What the fuck?"

Tertius stood on the edge of the tower, his hand extended. "Let the mixture work, Maddox. It's better this way. It'll be quick, and you'll feel no pain. The accounts will remember that you chose to end your life, as Sephariel's Seal intended."

Maddox plummeted.

He reached out with his mind to grab on to something, anything, as the wind whistled past him. But it was hopeless. The Seal of the Hand was anchored to his position but not connected. He couldn't use it to grab on to a passing branch or windowsill any more than he could lift himself off the ground by pulling his own hair.

He turned to look at the ground as it rose to meet him. His last vision was the cobblestones of the courtyard where he'd spent so many early years sweeping, playing, and studying.

He managed to say, "Oh, sh—"

He struck the ground, and the pain lasted an instant, like smashing through a wall, and then it was over. He was cold and it was dark, but only because his eyes were shut. Tentatively he opened them and glanced at an intricate lattice of copper tubing that had been affixed to the ceiling.

⊷ ⊶

Maddox found himself on a metal slab, feeling slightly groggy but otherwise fine. He was naked, faceup, on an operating table in Quirrus's lab. Vats of blood with copper tubes lined the walls, along with books and anatomical diagrams. One wall was entirely glass, holding countless gallons of blood behind it. The table was covered in a thin coat of blood, and he saw organs in jars and dishes on another table beside him. A slimy dead heart sat on a scale.

"Gross," Maddox said, sliding off the operating table. Surprisingly he felt fine, not even bruised. It must have been the tincture in his system—maybe it had relaxed his muscles enough that he survived the fall. If the magus of the blood mages had found him, he probably had removed the toxin and accelerated the healing process somehow.

He paused at a jar that contained a scrap of skin. It was a square with the Seal of Vitae etched into it. His seal to be exact. He shuddered uncomfortably. Blood mages sometimes grew new skin out of humors to replace flesh. Disgusting shit is what it was.

Maddox didn't know a great deal about blood magic—besides the fact that Quirrus was renowned for grafting parts to make strange new animals at the menagerie. He always equated it with necromancy in terms of its purview and general creepiness. Still he had a newfound respect for the art as he looked around the lab for his clothing.

His cock was fully hard from a morning erection, which made it all the more imperative that he find something to cover himself. The grisly implements of the blood mages lab did nothing to soften him. His clothes were missing, but he found a cabinet stocked with white linen aprons. He slipped one on and tied it behind his back.

His ass was still showing, but it was a short walk to his dormitory, and if he took the back hallways, he could make it without being seen.

He felt sick to his stomach with fear as he marched through the hallway. The place was empty. Usually when he was wandering halls that were this empty, it was a precursor to a very bad recurring dream. The lecture halls were abandoned, but light was pouring in from the windows.

Someone I considered a father tried to fucking kill me. Again. His world went from crumbling around him to completely disintegrating. His goals and dreams were gone. His routine life was effectively over. His mentor had abandoned any hope of helping him. He had nowhere to turn to.

Maybe Tertius was right. This is no way to live. I should just mix up an elixir and finish the job. First things first. I need to get my clothes. I need a fucking drink. I need time to figure this out.

"By the Guides…Maddox?"

He didn't need to turn around to recognize the voice. Next to Tertius, he was one of the last people he wanted to deal with right now. He turned, not too quickly, to face him. "Magus Turnbull."

He was standing in the hallway, his books forgotten in a pile in front of him. Usually he had a controlled, sneering sense, but now he simply looked terrified. He raised one hand and called on a sphere of crackling fire. "Stay back, abomination!"

Maddox raised his own hand defensively.

Turnbull didn't waste a moment unleashing a massive plume of red-hot flames that stretched toward Maddox, who flicked his wrist in response, creating a defensive barrier out of the priceless lore books Turnbull spilled on the floor.

The accumulation of centuries of knowledge, though dry and extremely flammable, averted the worst of the blast.

The air wavered, and the hallway was hotter than an oven. Turnbull meant to kill him.

"What the fuck? It's me, Maddox!"

Turnbull waved his arm, and the scorched remains of the floating volumes scattered into ash. His expression soured. "You're telling the truth…or at least you think you are."

The Veritas Seal was one almost all the faculty had attained and one of the more lucrative services provided by the Lyceum. A licensed Veritas notary could make very decent money, although the seal came with a hefty drawback. It was constantly active.

"First Tertius, and now you're trying to kill me too. When have you two ever agreed on anything?" Maddox demanded. He was still ready for a fight. Magus Turnbull had five seals to Maddox's one, but the Seal of Movement was versatile enough on its own in a fight. It didn't really help to detect lies or have an eidetic memory when shit was getting thrown at you.

Turnbull lowered his hands cautiously. "I have good reason. You were, as of this morning, dead from an apparent suicide that shattered your head open like an overripe melon. I don't need to explain to you the profoundly disturbing implications of seeing you parade your pasty buttocks around the hallowed halls of our institution. For all I knew, you were a revenant or a prank from one of the necromancers."

"I was dead?" Maddox echoed.

"Quite." Turnbull sniffed. "I saw your broken body and your lifeless eyes, and had it been anyone else, I might have been moved to tears. But murder is a line too far—even in your case—and Tertius's actions will need to be answered for in front of the full faculty. Get some clothes on and meet us in the drawing room in twenty minutes."

"I came back from the dead."

"Yes," Turnbull said with a heavy sigh. "Twenty minutes."

Maddox shook his head. "Wait—you're calling a faculty meeting in twenty minutes?"

Turnbull rolled his eyes. "Twenty minutes is how long it'll take you to run to your room, get dressed, and hurry back to the drawing room. Everyone else is already there. Magus Tertius died in his sleep last night, and we need to elect a new dean."

TWIN SHIELDS
(HEATH AND SWORD)

Imagine you have a beautiful gown only to discover every lady at the ball is wearing the same thing. Suddenly it's no longer beautiful. The stitching hasn't changed; the emerald satin remains the highest quality; the playful pearl embroidery about the décolletage continues to shimmer in its intricate dance with the candlelight… but what was intended to catch the eye now has become lost in a sea of monotony.

Such it is also with the Patrean face. His bone structure—the square jaw, the straight nose, the determined brow—such a man should be stunning. The woman is nearly his equal with her raven hair and soft, earthy features. Yet those faces are worn by every guard in Thelassus, every soldier in the Red Army, and in the armies of all the lesser nations. The eye grows familiar and learns to disdain it, just as a man cannot feast on whale sausage and plum wine for every meal and still enjoy it.

Whatever ancient magician crafted such features clearly had an eye for beauty, but I'm always puzzled—why the one face? Could they not all be made handsome or beautiful in different ways? Beauty and rarity are intertwined. I'm often asked which is more important. There is no answer to this question, but I always say if one is presented with the choice, always be unique.

—Messer Pisclatet, royal stylist to Princess Sireen of Thrycea

The entrance to the Twin Shields Longhouse was straddled by a painting of a warrior woman holding two bucklers at chest level to cover her tits. They'd mounted real shields with long points in the center to drive home the subtle meaning of the image. Depicted behind her was a phalanx of oiled men wearing loincloths and holding spears with tips shaped like dicks.

"This is my kind of place!" Sword pumped his fist as he swaggered up to the entrance. "Your 'friends' in the tower are covering expenses, right?"

"Classy." Heath chuckled as he stepped forward and pushed his way inside. "Just keep your hands to yourself unless there's trouble."

The main room of the Longhouse had been done up to resemble a warmaster's pavilion; maps with battle plans hung on the walls beside battered shields and an arsenal of melee weapons. The blades weren't just decorative; most of them looked like they'd seen combat. A couple of female Fodders reclined on cushioned benches in skimpy leather styled after Rivern battalion uniform.

A one-eyed Fodder with a full blond beard and intricately tattooed arms stood guard by the door. He wore a black leather jerkin, and two longswords hung on his belt. "Brother"—the man nodded to Sword—"looking for work or action?" That's what Sword would look like in ten years, if he could keep his current body alive that long.

"Information," Heath said.

"Talk to Red. She's in back through the door on the left." The Fodder didn't even attempt to look like he gave a shit.

Sword halfheartedly saluted the bouncer as he followed Heath to the back. Under his breath he muttered, "What kind of asshole uses two longswords? A longsword isn't an offhand weapon. Frankly I find it offensive."

"Remind me what kind of sword you are again." Heath grinned.

"Technically…the term 'bastard sword' comes from my impressively large hilt, which allows me to be held with one or two hands," Sword said hastily. "It's no reflection on my character."

Heath reached the door and knocked a couple times. "You're the biggest bastard I've ever met. Technically."

"Well, you're…the stupidest person I've ever met." Sword grumbled and thumped the side of his head. "Except for this meat suit. You couldn't put me in someone smarter? This tiny brain is killing my witty repartee."

The door flung open. A statuesque Patrean woman in her late forties stood majestically at the door, her posture straight as an arrow. There was no question, based on the red leather armor or the crimson dye in her hair, as to her identity. "I'm Red, commander of this establishment. Welcome to the Twin Shields." She saluted them formally. "What are you gentlemen in the mood for?"

"Information." Heath didn't bother playing his usual "Orthodoxy business" angle. Most Fodders weren't religious, and the ones who had served in the Hierocracy didn't remember their assignments fondly. The priests preferred spending the coin to pay death gratuities for fallen soldiers to spending their Light to heal the unfaithful.

"I could also use a whore," Sword said.

"It's the same rate whether you want to talk or fuck," Red said matter-of-factly. "Twenty ducats an hour, one hour minimum. More if you want to play rough. I've got green cadets, seasoned warriors, drill sergeants if you like to take orders, and a couple of night wrestlers if you like to take it up the ass."

"Night wrestlers are what they call their queers," Sword whispered to Heath. "They have special training at night in hand-to-hand where the blokes can blow off steam."

Heath sighed and pulled out the parchment, which he handed to Red. "I understand this man was seen near your establishment the night one of your customers died in his sleep. I'd like to talk to whomever may have spoken to him and to whomever was with the client that night."

"Really?" Red asked defensively. "The guard and the creepers already took statements."

"I'm a concerned citizen."

"I know who you are, dark-skinned one," Red said. "The rumors say you're a spice merchant with black-market connections. You live in the Inlet District, so I doubt you're *that* concerned."

"I came up on these boardwalks with Cordovis."

"I heard that too." She smiled. "You two had a falling out?"

"A lot of people are under the mistaken impression that I work for Cordovis's people." He motioned to the bar. "Not many customers here. The attacks can't have been good for business."

Red let out a sigh. "Since the attack the only people who come in are Fodders, most of them looking to enlist. People are afraid we're not warded, but I salt those sheets every morning. The guy who died wasn't even a client. He was a boatman sweet on Hilta. Her contract was almost up, and I didn't see the harm in letting them have the room."

Salted sheets? That's a new one. Heath pointed to the parchment. "Did you see this man that evening? He may have been directly responsible for your recent decline in revenues."

Red nodded. "Yeah. The creepers asked about him too. I talked with him, but he was never anywhere near Hilta's room. Why? What does he have to do with the deaths?"

"I'll talk to Hilta," Sword volunteered, and darted off. Over his shoulder he called out, "Pay the lady."

"Step into my office." Red motioned for Heath to follow. The room was Spartan and well organized with shelves of neatly lined ledgers and lockboxes. Red gingerly set herself down in a chair by her desk, pressing her hand against her back. It looked painful. "Your friend is very odd…He has Protectorate markings, but he speaks like an outsider."

"Fortunately there's only one of him." Heath sat in the chair opposite her. "Are you hurt?"

"Old injury that never healed right," she explained. "You see a lot of that here. I provide a line of work for those of us who no longer can take on mercenary contracts and don't fancy growing pumpkins in the veteran farmsteads. But you didn't come here for my service record."

"You've got a fine establishment." Heath smiled. "I suppose it helps when the girls know three ways to break an arm."

"There's more than three, young man." Red looked at the parchment. "Verge, the bouncer, didn't remember seeing him come in. When homeless show up, we send them away gently and tell them to come back in the morning for a handout around the back. A lot of them served beside us in the Protectorate's wars, but Genatrovan vets don't get farmsteads they can go to. War is just a lot harder on them mentally. No offense."

"None taken," Heath said. "Our peoples experience fear differently."

She continued, "He didn't make a fuss. He was just sitting in a corner by himself. I don't even know how long he was there. I thought maybe he was trying to get a free show, but his eyes were white as snow. I told him he had to leave but said to come back the next day for some rations."

"Did he?" Heath knew this from Loran's reports, but he suspected there was more to the story; there always was when authority was involved.

"Leave? Eventually. Haven't seen him since," Red said. "Old Milk Eyes said he could pay, but he phrased it really strangely. 'I can't afford to justly compensate you,' he told me, 'but if you permit me to linger here a while, I have something small you may find pleasing.' Then he handed me this."

Red reached down the front of her leather corset and drew out a small black velvet pouch about an inch and a half long. She opened the bag slowly, and Heath recognized instantly what it was by the soft glow that came from within. She pulled out a slender crystal that pulsed with soft, coruscating light. Strands of ultravivid hues appeared and floated through it before fading into diffuse forms.

"He gave you *that*?" he whispered.

"I thought it was pretty." She suddenly looked concerned. "Is it dangerous?"

"That's an Archean shard," Heath said. "Worth about thirty prisms, which is probably enough to buy this place—staff contracts included—three times over. Hard to find buyers, though. I could help broker something for a percentage."

Red tucked the prism into the pouch and slid it down her bra. "Thank you for the offer."

Heath shrugged. He had a couple of them himself, and he understood. They were almost too beautiful to sell. "You didn't show that to the Invocari, did you?"

"I didn't even realize both things happened on the same night until you brought it up today," Red said. "When the creepers came back a few weeks later, I thought they were looking for the shard. I knew if I told them, they'd have confiscated it."

"They probably would have," Heath said, "but they weren't looking for it. That man's been at the near the scene of every killing that's happened. From what I hear, he hasn't been sneaky about it either."

"Could he have killed all those people?" Red asked. "Why choose Hilta's boyfriend? He was nobody special."

Heath shrugged. "I have no clue, which makes this guy very, very dangerous."

"Curious he would pick this establishment. Patreans aren't susceptible to the sleeping death."

Heath cocked his head. "Really?"

"The warmasters keep extensive archives of every death. Millions of troops over the centuries, camped out for months at a time. Never a single death showing the telltale signs. Most of us think it's because we don't have dreams when we sleep. It must be so strange to hallucinate every night."

"I never knew that," Heath said. He'd known a lot of Fodders in his time, but they never made mention of that fact. Of course when you were running in street gangs, the topic of dreams rarely came up in conversation. For all he knew, Patreans never cried either.

"Most people never ask." She shrugged. "Our creators probably didn't see the point in giving us dreams. Like fear, it seems they'd be a distraction to a warrior."

"When did Milk Eyes finally leave?" It seemed a fitting enough name for the mysterious man.

"I don't know." Red said. "I let him stay in that corner as long as he liked. Told the troops to give him his privacy. At some point I stopped even noticing him, and then the corner was empty. It was a couple hours from dawn when I realized it, but he could have been gone longer. That's all I know. No one else spoke to him, as far as I know."

Heath smiled and stood. "Thank you for your time. If I may…"

He put his hand on her shoulder. She recoiled at first, her fist ready to strike, but then she felt his Light. His hand glowed golden where his dark fingers touched her dusky skin. The energy flowed through her body, tracing along her veins in gentle pulses of illumination. She gasped and shut her eyes as the energy cycled through her. She clenched the edge of her chair then moaned softly. Heath removed his hand, and her head lolled forward.

Red placed a hand on her back and looked at him in disbelief. "The pain—it's gone."

"It'll come back. Like you said, the injury wasn't properly treated. But I did remove the inflammation between your spinal discs. It should be a lot easier to manage. Don't tell anybody I did this," he said, placing a finger over his lips.

"Secrets are my trade, Mr. Heath," Red said proudly.

"Mine too." He bowed slightly and let himself out of the office.

Sword was buckling his trousers when he came out of Hilta's room. Heath had been waiting only a couple of minutes, and Red had informed the boys to keep his cup full, but he projected total impatience. His friend was acting more impulsive than usual in his new skin, and Heath was considering giving this vessel an early retirement.

"You fucked her," Heath stated, feeling slightly sick to his stomach. It was the second time he felt nauseated in as many days.

Sword plopped himself down next to Heath and threw his arm around his shoulder. "Don't get jealous. There's plenty of this big hilt to go around. These Fodder bodies have some fucking stamina."

"I appreciate the irony of *me* lecturing *you* on morality." Heath sipped some more wine. "But her boyfriend just died. That's low, Sword."

"You forget that I've spent roughly half my existence as a woman. I was very empathetic and respectful in the manner in which I fucked her," Sword said solemnly. Heath missed Sword's last incarnation. Catherine's voice and mannerisms had a way of making his boorishness seem charming.

"I almost believe you," Heath said.

Sword grabbed the wine from Heath's hand and tasted it. He made a disgusted face. "So get this. Her boatman boyfriend, Jerron, who was twenty-two, was a student at the Lyceum a few years back. He had a Hamartia, which is a—"

Heath cut him off. "I know what a fucking Hamartia is." He knew more about seal magic than he ever wanted to.

"Oh, right. Touchy, touchy!" Sword scooted away. "Anyway he fucked up the Seal of Communication. Made him totally illiterate—like letters would run around on the page like little wriggly worms. Real sad story, because Hilta said he was supposedly the most promising pupil to ever join the college."

"Or he said he was. Maddox would have dropped the kid's name if he was even a contender. So he talked a big game and washed out of the Lyceum." Heath grabbed his wine back from Sword. "Milk Eyes was carrying an Archean shard on him. Did you learn anything that might connect him and the kid?"

"High Wiz, you think?" Sword seemed uncertain.

Heath set the glass down beside him. "Could be. A shard is rare as hell and a lot of money for a deckhand to bring on shore leave, when he can trade prisms. And then to just hand it over to Red—well, if Milk Eyes was a wizard, he might not care. But then what's the interest in Hilta's boyfriend?"

"Maybe he just likes pulling the wings off insects. I don't know much about the Archeans. They typically don't involve themselves in terrestrial affairs," Sword said. "But I do know the Harrowers have a favorite snack: unstable magicians. With the right combination of untapped power and cockiness, they could find themselves another Achelon and then…*boom*. All the wizards in Creation go crazy and the world plunges into another Long Night."

"So far we have six deaths: two nobles, the magic-school dropout, a drug addict, a clerk at the temple, and an Invocari," Heath mused. "Two out of the six could fit the pattern, but the paper pusher, nobles, and junkie don't…that we know of."

"I say we check out the junkie next." Sword grinned. "I've been itching to fill this body with some drugs. He got himself a pretty bad dragonfire habit before I took over."

Heath massaged his temples. "I can never tell if you're kidding."

"You can fix an addiction with a little touch of those glowy fingers, can't you?"

Heath slapped Sword's cheek gently. "Come on. We have work to do."

FIRST IMPRESSIONS (JESSA)

I must confess that my most satisfying deceptions over the years came from being underestimated. When I was new to court at Thelassus and presented to the emperor, the other Stormlords thought me a callow ingenue, an act I maintained for several years before I gained my reputation for intrigue.

I can't in good faith claim that all my initial blunders were intentional, but my reputation as a poor liar eventually led people to trust me as if I were an honest person. And of course being as seemingly clueless as I was made me the perfect "pawn" in the schemes of others.

For a time I was suspected of being in league with Lord Calatax in his bid for the Bleak Atoll shipping contract. I protested to everyone that it wasn't the case, which only made them more certain of it. Then I started to deny the rumors (which I'd invented) about Lord Calatax's plans and capabilities in order to convince the armadas to destroy him. And that was just the first of three Upheavals.

I entreat you to consider all those around you: your friends, your enemies, and especially your blood. The next Lord of Lies is already among you, and it's the person you least suspect. It might even be you.

Enjoy the game. Trust no one.
—foreword to *The Sea of Deception*, allegedly written by Lady Alessandria, "Queen of Lies," and published after her reported death

Jessa's husband-to-be wasn't ugly, but he certainly left much to be desired otherwise. His wavy blond hair sat like a bird's nest atop his head, somewhat hiding his dark-blue eyes. He was completely shaven on the face, giving his jawline a girlish quality Jessa found distasteful. His build was short and modest. He wore an ill-fitting coat over a wrinkled shirt and a large gold chain with two clunky medallions, along with a pair of leather sandals.

He waited for Jessa at a table on the wine barge under the canopy section. An Invocari hovered behind him, hands folded. Jessa had started to recognize the Silverbrooks' Invocari bodyguards—this one had a bit of a gut and ginger hair on his knuckles. A few other couples drank and talked at other tables, but they made a good show of not staring as the hostess brought Jessa to his table.

She wore a modest white gown that seemed old-fashioned compared to the other women on the barge, who bared their shoulders.

He stood up sharply and stuck out his hand. "Lord Torin the Fourth."

Did he really expect her to shake his hand? Clearly he was unschooled in refinements, but then again manners in Rivern were curious when it came to women. She actually had seen the countess sporting a pair of trousers in public.

"It's a pleasure to finally meet you." Jessa awkwardly placed her fingers in Torin's hand as if they might pinch them off. He squeezed them for a moment then released her.

"Will you sit?" He awkwardly motioned to a chair, suddenly realizing he probably should have pulled it out when he had greeted her. It scooted back a foot or so.

Jessa giggled as she took a seat. "Impressive trick."

"It's no trick," Torin said. "I'm a Master of the Seal of Ardiel. And a Master of the Seal of Veritas, which I'm required by Rivern law to inform you of." He took a deep breath. "I hope you don't mind that I started us off with a bottle of Lowland red cuvée from 560."

Jessa and Torin both took their seats.

"Oh, not at all. I don't drink," Jessa said. *Mother does enough of that for the both of us.*

"Oh." Torin's brow furrowed under that mass of hair. He was so close to her that Jessa could have reached out and quickly brushed it to the side, but she resisted the urge. "I guess this was a bad choice for a first date then. We can go somewhere else—"

"It's fine. I enjoy being on the water and watching the people." Jessa looked out across the railing of the wine barge's deck. All around her small boats and gondolas plied the massive fork of the Trident River while people bustled back and forth between tall stone buildings on its banks. The deck hummed from the vibration of some sort of mechanized propulsion that she felt slicing through the current.

"Oh, right." He gave a sigh of relief.

The waitress appeared with a bottle in her hand and set it down along with two glasses. "Lowland red cuvée. A blend from Barstea County. The grapes are grown on the north bank on the site of the old city, which is said to be haunted. The wine is aged in Maenmarth timber for twelve years. It's a personal favorite of mine. Please enjoy."

Torin smirked and waited till she walked away before saying, "She's lying. It's probably terrible."

"How does that work? Your Veritas Seal?" Jessa asked. She'd never met a mage with a seal, outside of the occasional notary Mother brought in for important affairs of state.

"Lies sound different," he explained. "When someone says something that's not true, their voice reverberates. You hear what they're saying, but you can also barely make out what they aren't telling you. It's not intelligible speech, but it's louder when what they say differs from what they know to be true. And she was practically screaming when she said this was her favorite."

"It must be horrible," Jessa gasped.

"It can be." Torin shrugged. "It's a little awkward at times to know when people aren't telling the truth, especially about personal stuff. And it can be lonely when people stop talking to you because they're afraid you'll tell their secrets."

"I meant the wine must be horrible," Jessa hastily clarified. "I would love nothing more than to know when people are being honest with me. Can you ever turn it off?"

"Once a seal is bound, it never turns off. The arcane force is contained in a perfectly closed construction. That's why seal magic doesn't have a limit as to how often it can be used. What about you? Does a Stormlord's magic draw from a source or is it self-contained?"

Jessa shrugged. "What's the difference?"

Torin cocked an eyebrow. "Sourced magic requires something to fuel it, so mages might feel tired after casting, or they may run out of power and need time to recharge. But they also can create massive bursts of power. Self-contained magic is inexhaustible, but it never gets weaker or stronger."

"I never really thought about it," Jessa said. "I don't think my magic makes me tired, but I don't know what the limits are. We measure power based on our blood relation to the Coral Throne. The person next in line for it is always stronger than the one after them."

"So you never had to study the Principia Arcana or pass the Trials of Focus?" he said, shaking his head. "You're so amazingly lucky."

"When I was a little girl, I always wanted different powers. People don't really like storms, and you're always blamed when there's awful weather. I wanted to be like the witches who lived in the Maenmarth and be able to change my form. I never had any opportunity to study magic anyway. Amhaven has no colleges, which is why we haven't prospered like Rivern."

Torin's wine bottle poured itself into the glass while he pondered.

"Maybe I could start a college." He blushed and quickly added, "That is…if I decide to become king. It sounds so strange to hear myself say it."

"Not at all!" Jessa insisted. "We badly need institutions of learning. My people aren't backward by choice—the empires on both sides have withheld their knowledge from us for centuries. Even with just a few more glyphomancers, we could meet them on even footing."

Torin added more confidently, "I also think Amhaven needs a parliamentary body where people could have a say in their governance. No leader should have unlimited power simply by the accident of birth. And the fate of a kingdom shouldn't rest on two total strangers hitting it off."

Are we hitting it off? Jessa laughed as she considered it. "It's not a terrible idea. The Protectorate has prospered under such a system, and you're right—if the monarchy falls, there needs to be something in place to maintain order. We would need to consider the dukes of course…but I think the people would love it."

"You know"—as Torin spoke, his wineglass levitated and swirled the liquid against the edges of the crystal, "I wasn't sure I could go through with this, but you're nothing like I expected. And forgive me for saying this—you're beautiful."

Jessa smiled bashfully. He was full of ideas and maybe a bit idealistic—like her father might have been, if he hadn't been beholden to centuries of tradition. She giggled. "Since I can't lie to you, I think you need a haircut, but your virtues outweigh your flaws."

"Is it that bad?" He peered at his reflection in his floating wineglass. "It's been insane at the Lyceum. The dean passed away last night. I just—" He cut himself off and sipped his wine. His eyes seemed to darken.

"The wine…is it terrible?" Jessa asked, trying to veer the subject back to something more pleasant.

"It's quite good. It's got a fruit-forward flavor with a smoky finish that's very nicely balanced. There's even a slight hint of something…vegetal but that balances the berry flavors nicely. In a few years, I think this vintage will be drinking wonderfully. Are you sure you won't have at least a taste?"

"What the hells? I think this calls for a celebration." Jessa sighed as she reached for a glass. It slid into her hand, and then the bottle floated and poured a bit into the glass. She raised it delicately and clinked it against Torin's.

She inhaled the bouquet and tasted the wine. The first drop exploded with bitterness. *One must cultivate a refined palate, Jessa. As queen you'll be expected to attend state dinners and preside over feasts where all manner of delicacies will be proffered. Food and drink are the perfect vehicles for toxins, so we'll be tasting them all.*

Jessa spat the wine and knocked the glass from Torin's hand. "It's poison! Someone find a healer!" She looked around the barge. Couples were staring wide-eyed in shock.

Torin fell back in his chair, confused. He was breathing heavily.

Her eyes met with those of the waitress at the other end of the wine barge and saw her reach for something beneath the counter. The woman jerked a crossbow from under the bar and drew it on Jessa with nearly lightning-quick reflexes. If her reflexes *had* been lightning quick, Jessa might have died.

Before she even knew what she was doing, Jessa stood and threw her right hand in front of her. A flare of blinding light exploded from her palm as a crackling trail of electricity struck the waitress in the chest and sent her crashing limply against the wine rack behind her. Glass bottles tumbled and crashed to the deck of the ship. The waitress didn't move.

Screaming and chaos ensued as the couples dove under tables. A young man abandoned his date and plunged into the Trident River.

Jessa looked to Torin, who was breathing shallowly. His body wasn't moving or speaking, but his blue eyes searched hers fearfully. The Invocari hovered by his side, trying to loosen his collar, but it almost seemed as if Torin were pushing him away. On the table a shard of glass cut into the wood of its own accord, scratching a final message.

"THIS SUCKS."

The shard of glass fell over, and Torin's eyes stopped moving. The tip of Jessa's tongue felt cold with the paralytic as she spoke. "Torin?"

Desperately she pressed her hands to his chest. She never had used her lightning to revive someone from the brink of death. She had no sense of how much power to apply. She shocked his chest, but he remained motionless, his rib cage silent of rumblings of life.

The Invocari rushed over to her. "We need to get you to safety. I'll carry you to the riverbank."

Jessa shrugged off his hands and gathered her skirt. "It's fine…" She stepped off the edge of the boat onto the river, letting the surface of the water support her. "I'll walk."

The Invocari followed her as he signaled to the city guards on the bank. People gaped in open amazement as Jessa stepped across the river. Her heart was racing. Overhead she felt the skies start to darken.

EXPULSION (MADDOX)

XIII. Forbidden Arcana

I. Any mage who seeks to alter the course of past events through chronomancy will be made to relive the memory of her greatest anguish for the rest of her natural days.

II. Any mage who seeks to traffic with beings from the other realm of existence by planar summoning will be stripped of his power and given unto the chimera to devour.

III. Any mage who seeks to undo Creation through the practice of annihilation magic will be tortured to death over the course of a fortnight.

IV. Any mage who seeks to become a god through the Rituals of Apotheosis will be offered to the Primal Titans in a blood sacrifice appropriate to the element.

V. Any mage who seeks immortality will be made to live with her mistake for all eternity.

—the Thirteenth Table of Archean Law

Maddox stood in the center of the drawing room as the Scholars and Masters took their seats. Torin's face was thankfully missing from the crowd. Magi Lidora and Turnbull sat front and center, a grim scarecrow of an old woman and a bald man who looked like a giant fat baby. Maddox scanned the faces for any sign of the Archean High Wizard, Petra, but she wasn't present.

Turnbull spoke first. "Once again we find you here, Scholar Baeland, and under circumstances most dire."

"Speak before those who bear the Seal of Veritas what happened last night," Lidora intoned.

"Magus Tertius threw me off the observation tower," Maddox said, not seeing any point in trying to conceal it.

"Truth," the assembled scholars with the Veritas Seal muttered in unison, although some of their voices said it more like a question. There were gasps and whispers.

"He poisoned me first." Maddox paced back and forth leisurely as he recounted the events. "I don't really blame him. Deaths from the Vitae Seal are a fucking lousy way to go. I just wish he'd maybe waited. Anyway he lifted me into the air and dropped me onto the pavement, where I lost consciousness and half my brain matter. I awoke in Magus Quirrus's laboratory next to what I'm told were my removed organs."

"Truth."

"And do you have any idea how you came back from your apparent demise?" Lidora asked.

"No," Maddox said.

The chorus of notaries chimed back whispers of "Evasion" and "Uncertainty."

"Obviously I *think* it has to do with my seal," Maddox clarified, "but since I don't know that, I can't testify as to its nature. You can't ask me what I think after making open-ended speculation."

"Tell us about the seal," Turnbull said. "Why did you draw it that way? Did you know this would be the result?"

"I...I had a vision. I didn't know what would happen, just that it felt right."

"Truth," the mages said.

"Do you have to keep doing that?" Maddox snapped at one of the notaries. "Both the magi and record keepers have the Veritas Seal. And I know if I'm telling the truth. No one needs you to keep telling everyone."

Turnbull nodded. "Let it be known that Scholar Baeland foregoes his rights to know the results of the Veritas in regard to his testimony. Now...you were saying you had a vision. Have you had visions before?"

"No."

"Have you studied any arts that would grant you the power of visions? I didn't see any in your records." Turnbull indicated a leather folio stuffed with parchment that rested next to him.

"No."

"Did you have anything to do with Magus Tertius's untimely death? Even so much as a desire for it to happen during those final moments?" Lidora asked pointedly.

"No," Maddox said, suddenly angry. "I didn't have time to think about re-venge. I was pissed as hell when I woke up because the man was like a father to me and the only person in this entire institution I considered a friend, but I never once wanted him to die."

"But you must agree," Turnbull said in his high, lispy voice, "the timing and nature of his death are highly suspicious. We've never had a harrowing inside the wards of the Lyceum, yet the very man who tried to end your life winds up dead the same night. And to compound the suspiciousness, you're miraculously restored to life within hours, if not minutes, of another life being taken."

Maddox waited before folding his arms. "I didn't hear a fucking question."

"Watch your tone, Scholar." Turnbull rolled his eyes. "Tertius may have found humor in your antics, but that doesn't apply to the remaining faculty. It's not cute."

"Truth," one of the mages said under his breath. The one next to him hit him in the side.

Lidora continued, "Have you had any contact with the Harrowers last night or ever, either directly or through one of their agents or through any area of study not sanctioned by the Lyceum? An answer of yes must account for anything remotely suspect—anything from agreeing to a pact or as innocuous as handling an artifact from one of the dark dolmens."

"Absolutely not."

Maddox paused. The mages were staring at him intently, almost leaning out of their seats. It was a loaded question, and Turnbull was clearly out for blood.

"I know justice is a legal gray area in this situation, but I'm not even going to get a fucking apology? Tertius killed me rather than risk his own reputation." Maddox was furious. "What is wrong with you?"

"Magus Tertius exceeded his authority as dean of the college," Lidora said. "It's a regrettable coda to an exemplary life of scholarship. I speak for everyone when I say we all feel deeply betrayed by his actions."

"Actions you inspired," Turnbull added quickly.

"So it's my fucking fault?" Maddox couldn't believe his ears. He couldn't even look at the bastards. He turned his back to them and stared at the drawing table.

"You're a troubled, unstable individual, Maddox Baeland." Turnbull raised his voice slightly. "You're a drunk and a bully. Exactly the sort of person who has no business learning the Grand Art, and we're seeing firsthand the conse-quences of having allowed it."

Lidora offered sympathetically, "You may spend the time you have remain-ing here in the special annex for observation and study, where you'll be made comfortable. Since no one at this school aside from Tertius has attained the Seal of Life, we must bring in an expert from one of the other colleges to determine whether your seal is in fact pact magic."

"You can't do this." Maddox turned red. The special annex was a euphemism for the arcane loony bin—for people whose magic or minds were too shattered for them to return to a normal life.

"It's already done," Lidora said. "Magus Turnbull has been elected dean, and it's his decision. With your death the school is legally under no obligation to offer you any further services. The annex is a generous offer, not a punishment."

Turnbull added, "And your meager wealth has been remanded to the Lyceum, as per your last will. It won't cover even a fraction of the damage to the conjuration circle incurred during your attempt to bind the seal. Obviously your license to practice any magic outside the school is revoked."

"Hell. No." Maddox pointed his finger accusingly. "You can all shit flaming centipedes! I'm not going to the annex, and you can't keep me here to study me. I'm done. Go fuck yourselves." He stormed toward the side door, but it shut firmly as he approached.

"You should really reconsider," Turnbull said mildly. "If you leave we'll have to turn this investigation over to the Hierocracy. I'm sure the inquisitors will be…thorough."

"Tell the Hypocrisy they can choke on it. I've broken no laws."

Maddox yanked at the door with his mind. It rattled as he and Turnbull wrestled with it. For a Master of Five Seals, the giant baby didn't have much muscle behind his magic. The door burst open.

"Might want to get that door looked at," Maddox said. "It sticks a little."

"Go with Ohan, Maddox Baeland," Turnbull called after him, as he stomped down the hallway.

Three Invocari hovered by the door and followed him like a flock of dark angels. More appeared from alcoves on either side, joining their brethren in formation as he marched off the premises into the afternoon light of Rivern.

He took one last look at the Lyceum. On the marble steps, ten or twelve black-cloaked figures formed a phalanx in front of the door. His eyes looked to the dome over the drawing room and the seals inscribed over the walls. The sun had just passed behind the observation tower, leaving him in a long shadow. "Fuck it," he muttered, as he ripped off his gold medallion with its lone seal and chucked it at the steps.

As Maddox made his way through town, he noticed many stores were closed, and the markets were empty save for a few vegetable stands and silk-wrapped

Turisian women peddling protective trinkets. People looked exhausted as they trudged down the pavement. Hand-painted signs advertised evening hours; people were starting to sleep during the day to avoid the nocturnal death.

A harrowing happened once a decade at most in Rivern. Two deaths within the same year happened once a century. Now the total was five, and people were panicking. The bars seemed to be doing a brisk trade—people were spilling out onto the street by the Wolf & Owl. A bottle of Shyford County bourbon sounded great, but it was a little out of his price range.

He walked past a sad, rickety cart selling day-old meat pies, the merchant too ashamed of his wares to even make eye contact. Maddox couldn't remember the last time he'd eaten anything. It was at least three days ago, and his stomach didn't so much as grumble as he sniffed the stale bread.

He made his way down to the falls and took the switchback road to the Backwash. The streets were livelier as people went about their daily business. Five deaths in a month wasn't even news in this part of town, or at least people were more accustomed to taking their chances.

"Hand job, ser?" A kid who couldn't have been more than fifteen and looked to be fresh off the farm from some backward corner of the province walked beside him, looking scared and pathetic. "Five ducats for a wank. I haven't eaten in days, ser. Please…I gots real soft hands."

"And I bet you have real sticky fingers—it's easy to grab a coin purse and run, leaving a man's trousers around his ankles."

"Been caught with your pants down a lot before, ser?" the kid said sarcastically.

"I grew up here," Maddox said as he left him behind. The kid yelled some profanity, but with the rush of the waterfall so close, his words disappeared into the mist.

Even if the offer had been at all interesting to him, five ducats was more than Maddox could afford for a hand job. He had made a small stipend as Tertius's assistant, but most of that had gone toward his tuition. All his possessions were at the Lyceum in his room, which he was now banned from entering.

That left him fifteen ducats to his name. He immediately regretted tearing off his Scholar's emblem—it was real gold, mostly. He had nowhere to sleep. *Fuck, I might have to start giving hand jobs.* It wouldn't be such a bad gig, considering the only other thing he was qualified to do was work on Alchemists' Row.

Maddox made his way to the wharfs and to the familiar comfort of the Mage's Flask. It was a special kind of shit-hole establishment: a haven for outcasts, constantly teetering on the brink of financial insolvency, which somehow had lasted over the years because it was too stubborn to die. He swung open the door and stepped inside. His barstool waited for him, like a loyal dog greeting him when he came home.

Cassie set a bottle of his usual on the counter along with a cracked glass that probably hadn't been washed since the last time he was here. He took his seat and drank straight from the bottle. He fished two coins out of his pouch and slid them across the bar.

He pulled out his tool pouch and unbuckled it on the counter. Magus Tertius's gold-and-ruby tipped stylus stood out in stark contrast to the other plain instruments. There was his original black stylus, a couple of midlevel models he rarely used, an assortment of compasses, some rulers, and half a pencil. The gold stylus was the only thing he had of any real value.

Maddox picked it up and felt its weight in his hand. He felt the fine inscription with his finger around the grip, the way the back was weighted so it rested more firmly in the back of his hand. The core contained mercury to maintain the momentum of each stroke.

Absently he began to draw on the bar's scratched, rough surface. The finish was spotty, and the lumber had turned gray in places, making it a terrible writing surface. He started with a perfect circle then filled it in with lines and geometric forms. It wasn't an actual seal—just a practice exercise based on common forms to test the stylus.

"You're pretty good with that." A Patrean sailor with a mug of ale looked over at his drawing. The man was older, scruffy, his arms covered in cuneiform glyphs denoting his military record. "You do any tattoo work?"

Maddox took another shot and pulled up his shirt. "Just these babies."

The man got up from his seat, sat next to him, and placed his hand on the golden Seal of Vitae. His rough fingers brushed along the lines of the seal delicately. "I've never seen anything like this—is this liquid-gold ink? It's almost shining."

The man's knee was pressed against Maddox's thigh. He saw the tenting in the Fodder's breeches as his own dick responded to the touch. "Maybe we should go somewhere private…"

Maddox led the man out back to a hidden boardwalk between the Flask and an adjoining warehouse. The sailor had his cock out and ready before they'd even stepped into the alley. *Even their dicks look exactly the same.* Maddox fell to his knees as he freed his own prick from his trousers. He kissed the tip of the Fodder's penis, tasting the salty precum in his mouth.

"You like to suck it, faggot?" The soldier grabbed his dick and slapped Maddox's cheek with it. "Say, you want to know what a real man tastes like, you little cocksucker?"

Maddox already was working his own rock-hard prick. "Please. I want to fucking take your manly load in my worthless mouth."

"That's right," the sailor grunted as he rammed his dick down Maddox's throat. "All that mouth is good for is serving Patrean dick. I should take you with me—make you my cabin slave and rent you out to my mates. You'd like that wouldn't you?"

Maddox grunted with approval as he worked the man's dick, using his tongue to lick the shaft while applying gentle suction. He had to stop, or he'd explode. He took his hands and slid them under the man's jerkin, feeling the taut, perfect abdomen of a physically superior species.

"Fuck, mate…" The Fodder gripped Maddox's brown hair and pressed him down on his cock as he shot his juice into Maddox's throat. The moment over, he let his hand release.

Maddox slid off the dick and back onto his heels. He pumped his cock with a few quick strokes and grunted as he blew his load.

Without a word, the man turned and walked out of the alley, casually adjusting the front of his breeches. He looked twice before exiting to the main thoroughfare and, assuming the coast was clear, headed off in the direction of the docks.

"Hey! Whatever your name is!" Maddox called after him. "You dropped something." A handful of coins were scattered on the boardwalk. Maddox saw three ducats, a pair of intricately pressed Karthantean fillers, and half a Thrycean crown.

He picked up one of the coins, and after the man didn't return, he gathered them into his coin purse.

He stood and headed back toward the bar. Riley was standing in the doorway, mouth agape. "Cassie said you was out back." His voice was quiet with shock. He had stumbled upon the whole sordid encounter and, being Riley, probably had watched it. The subject of Maddox's sexual proclivities never had come up because Maddox found Riley mildly to extremely revolting.

"This isn't what it looks like," Maddox said. "He dropped the money. And I can't tell Fodders apart, so I don't have a way to return it."

"Then why was his cock in your mouth?"

"Because I like to suck cock. Do you have a problem with that, Riley?" Maddox secretly hoped he did. Amhaven folk took a dim view on homosexuality, and it would be a quick and easy way to sever the tie of "friendship."

"Nah," he said after a while. "Less competition for the ladies, right? It's a bit of a relief actually. You bein' so good-looking and smart and everything." He punched Maddox in the arm.

"There's nothing I could ever do to get rid of you, is there?"

"Nothing in the world." Riley bear-hugged him and whispered in his ear, "I accept you for who you are."

In a bizarre way, it was touching. The last person to say that to him was Tertius, followed by a lecture on discretion. The mages at the Lyceum were expected to follow a code of morality that precluded most casual sex, but it wasn't strictly enforced. He still remembered working up the nerve to express his attraction to Torin only to feel the sting of rejection and ridicule.

Riley pulled away. "Look, I know you're going through a rough patch. If there's anythin' you need—anythin' at all—just ask."

And that was it. Maddox broke down. The raw nerves of his emotions kicked into high gear, and he sobbed, "I don't have anywhere to go. I don't have any money. I don't have anything."

"Shh, shh, shh." Riley put Maddox's head on his shoulder. "You have me. You can stay with us. I got everything you'd ever want. Come on…"

At best Maddox had only ever tolerated Riley. He certainly hadn't done anything to earn his loyalty or devotion. He was generally a dick to the guy, and Riley never got angry or complained. Stupid, annoying Riley was the only person in all Creation who actually gave a shit about him. And he realized he didn't deserve even that.

"Okay."

APOSTASY (HEATH AND SWORD)

The Will and the Wanderer

1.1. In the village of Tarinth, three of every ten were stricken by a virulent pox, and the village elders sent for a priest from the temple at Felice. The Hierophant decreed that Brother Lathan should travel to Tarinth and minister to the ill.

1.2. Brother Lathan was a luminary of the Third Order who never had set foot outside the Temple since completing his Vow and taking his Name. He yearned to travel Creation and perform the good works of our Father Ohan.

1.3. Upon arriving in Tarinth, Brother Lathan was dismayed to find all but a handful dead from their affliction. "We have been forsaken," the village elder declaimed, and Brother Lathan wept for the dead infants who had been burned last in the Rite of Reunification.

1.4. "What is Ohan's will in all this?" the villagers cried. "We must know how a god that is just and righteous can allow such misery to befall our innocent children." And Brother Lathan, who'd never set foot into the world as a priest, found he had no answer.

1.5. Brother Lathan returned to Felice and secluded himself in prayer and fasting. In his despair he demanded the Father of All give account for his supernal reasons. "Lord of Illumination, I must know whether you are unable or are unwilling to stop the needless suffering of innocent babes."

1.6. To wit the Father of All appeared to Brother Lathan in a sphere of all-consuming light. "My reasons are not within your ability to know, but if you truly desire answers, I will give you the power to understand them."

1.7. And Brother Lathan understood but found the knowledge did not satisfy him. "I see now, All Father and Lord of Light, the necessity and intention of your design, but knowing your Truth is worse than ten times the pain of grief. You suffer for this more greatly than all of mankind!"

1.8. "It is my burden to bear alone," Ohan said. "It is my gift and my mercy that you shall not understand my will. But while I will not give you answers, I will remove your pain."

1.9 And the Father of All struck Brother Lathan with his Light, smiting him where he knelt and thereby raising him to Sainthood.
—excerpt from *The Trials of Faith,* Book Three, Canto 16

The Temple of Ohan sat in the center of four large obelisks that stood in the corners of a well-manicured garden filled with circular paths. The structure itself was three stories of marble and glass, adorned with bas-relief suns. Above the main entryway stood the god himself, depicted as a man in his youth holding a baby in his arms. Heath knew the statue wasn't Ohan's true form, but he felt justified in admiring it for different reasons.

Sword was getting a lot of strange looks due to the long weapon slung across his back. The church frowned upon carrying weapons into the sanctuary, but there was no concealing a bastard sword. "I should probably go to confession while I'm here," Sword said.

"You couldn't afford absolution. Murder starts at a hundred ducats for self-defense, and it only goes up from there." Heath checked the springblades under his sleeves to ensure the mechanisms were ready.

"That's it? It's a little steep, and I'd rather spend it on something practical… like drugs."

"If you get that body addicted to anything, I'm not healing you," Heath warned. During one of his incarnations, Sword had figured out that if Heath removed the toxins from his body, he could start his initial high all over. Thankfully that body had died quickly.

"This one's in the early stages already," Sword scratched his arm. "I feel kinda itchy."

The templars in white, lacquered armor guarding the vestibule made no effort to stop Heath as he and Sword made their way into the sanctuary.

A long luxurious carpet of gold led from the vestibule to the altar, behind which was a massive stained-glass mural of Ohan creating the world from light. All laughable bullshit, of course, but undeniably the work of master artisans. The pews were relatively full of people praying for protection. The dream killings were good for business, Heath noted, as a young cleric hauled a donation cask to the undercroft.

Heath and Sword followed. In contrast to the white marble and gilded finery of the temple above, the lower level was stark and gray like a dungeon. Narrow corridors and locked doors led them past the morgue, where junior clerics anointed the corpses of the recent dead before shipping them off to the holy incinerator.

Daphne's office was a moderate-size cell dominated by a large desk carved from a single piece of lacquered timber. Atop it lay papers and books along with the obligatory statue of Saint Lathan, better known in some circles as the patron saint of *not asking questions that can get you killed.*

"The prodigal brother returns." Daphne smiled warmly as she looked up from her paperwork. She was a middle-aged woman who took very good care of herself. She had dark skin and wore a floor-length white cloak trimmed with spotted fur. It had two long slits for her arms but otherwise completely covered her body. Long gloves covered her arms past the elbows.

"Daphne," Heath said, "this is Sword, whom you've met before."

"The Patrean suits you," she said to him very politely.

Heath took a deep breath. He'd been dreading this moment since he'd started the investigation, but there was no way around using his connections. "I need information on the clerk who died from the dream killing. Was she a mage?"

"I'm doing wonderfully. Thank you so much for asking." Daphne stonewalled with her characteristic fake grin and deadpan gaze. "And how have you been enjoying your sabbatical? I hear you've been quite busy running up your debt with Cordovis. What's it up to—ten thousand ducats?"

"I don't owe Cordovis shit," Heath said.

"Then let me at least pay it off so he stops grousing about it." Daphne indicated a sheet of parchment on her desk. "The donations this month have been exceptionally generous, and I'd be happy to do it. Just take the money."

"I'll take it if he doesn't want it." Sword offered. "I mean…whatever you can spare."

"I'm not here for your ducats. I'm working an independent investigation on the harrowings, and I need for you to answer a simple question. Friend to friend."

Daphne shrugged. "Yes, the clerk used to be a mage. She had a Hamartia of the Seal of Memory; she couldn't remember anything for longer than two weeks. That level of confidentiality and discretion will be very hard to replace. Does that help?"

"Of course you know why I'm here." Heath slid the picture of Milk Eyes across Daphne's desk. "What *haven't* you told the Invocari about this man?"

"You won't find him unless he wants to be found," Daphne said, glancing at the parchment. "I told the Invocari the same thing when they asked *us* to go on this wild-goose chase they have you going on."

Heath shoved the paper in her face. "Who is he?"

She rolled her eyes and swatted the paper away. "He's called the Harbinger. He's a like vulture circling above a cow as it crawls to its death in the desert. He appears whenever chaos or destruction is imminent. He doesn't interfere; he just watches. He's been around as long as we've kept records: plagues, wars, upheavals. He's a symptom, not the cause."

"What is he?" Heath demanded.

Daphne shook her head. "We don't really know. For lack of a better term, we call him a Traveler, although sometimes the Cantos refer to them as saints; the Prophet James seems to be loosely based on him."

Sword scratched his head. "You mean the First Mages? That's what we used to call them back in the old days, Second Era and whatnot. Mostly they kept to themselves and their own crazy hobbies, like collecting one of every kind of bug or teaching squirrels witchcraft. Last time I saw one was in the Shadow War—when they got off their arses and helped us. The Long Night wouldn't have ended without their help."

"Indeed," Daphne said. "They're Creation's defense against forces of cosmic potency. If the Harbinger is here, it could be a sign that they're taking interest. And until he deigns to make contact with us, his investigation is above our pay grade."

"But he does know something about the killings," Heath said.

"I'm sure he knows everything"—Daphne gestured to the air—"but he's not going to tell you anything useful. These people trade in impossibly cryptic half-truths about the future that are only made clear in retrospect. It's worse than useless. But you're welcome to try."

Sword nodded. "Getting a straight answer out of one of those blokes is like trying to eat your own teeth."

"I wish I could be more help, old friend." She took a folio of papers from her desk and slid them over to Heath. "But while we're engaging in the friendly exchange of information, I did come across something unusual. Do you still talk to your 'friend,' Maddox Baeland?"

"Ancient history," Heath said. "Why?"

"Fucking barmy tosspot." Sword got ready to spit on the ground to emphasize his distaste, but a sharp glance from Daphne stopped him cold. He covered his mouth and gulped.

Daphne slid the bundle of parchments over to Heath. "According to the Lyceum, he has a flawed Seal of Vitae that's not reacting as expected. The new dean claims Maddox died and came back to life, and they have four confirmations of multiple witnesses under the Veritas Seal. He's floating out there, and I'd like to have a conversation with him."

"Four?" Heath asked. The seal wasn't as infallible as the mages wanted to believe, but beating it took a rare talent for deception.

"You can imagine my concern if this is true," Daphne said bluntly.

"If I see him, I'll tell him you're looking." Heath smiled.

She laughed. "I doubt he'd come see me willingly."

Sword asked, "What's the bounty then? The little bastard is a telekinetic ball of needy rage."

"We're not doing this, Sword!" Heath shouted as he threw the papers off the desk. This is what Daphne did—reasonable requests but always pushing the limits of what he was willing to do. Pushing and pushing until he broke, and there was always just a little bit less of the person he used to be. Not this time.

"He fucking subverted the fucking natural order," Sword insisted. "Now you may not have much experience with immortal psychopaths, but trust me, if ever there was a wizard to lose his shit, it's that boy, and you don't want to see what he becomes in a thousand years. And might I further add that it's awful convenient timing that he does this thing and people start ending up in the river, if you get my drift."

Heath glared murderously at Sword, who looked back at him and flashed his eyes emphatically.

"We used to be friends, Heath." Daphne's voice dripped with false pleasantness. "I trained you to use your Light, to be a killer. I had high hopes for you. But when you asked to leave, I allowed you to have your freedom. I don't hold you to your vows. And when I ask you to do a favor, you're free to decline. But I'm not asking this time.

"You'll always be a member of this Order, and I'm sorry the terrible things we have to do to preserve the lives of millions keeps you up at night. You know why it must be done. You've seen the darkness behind the Light, and that isn't something you get to walk away from when you want to *pretend* you have principles."

Sword interjected, "He does have some principles, actually...sometimes."

"If I see him"—Heath mastered his emotions—"I'll take care of it...out of respect for the deep kindness you've shown to me. I wouldn't be who I am without you, and if this is important, I can set aside my feelings."

"I also trained you to lie, remember?" Daphne smirked. "Send his body to the Invocari. They have a secure cell in their tower that's warded with old magic. It's the best we have."

Sword nodded. "Just to be clear, that's ten thousand *each*."

Daphne leaned back in her chair and steepled her fingers. "Of course it is. Just bring him to me."

THE CAGE (SATRYN)

Cherished older sister Satryn,

You were missed terribly at the gala; even Nasara admitted your absence was regrettable. It was the event of the season, to be certain. I had Mssr. Pisclatet craft me a bodice of living crabs that was utterly stunning. It was all any of the ladies could talk about for weeks.

Boromond even challenged Glasyr to a duel over my affections. It was quite the spectacle, if you can imagine portly Boromond trying to hit Glasyr over the head with his rapier like it was a piece of driftwood. You or I could have handled both of them with one arm, sister. I hope you've stayed in practice—I imagine being the queen's regent leaves little time for amusement.

How is Amhaven, by the way? I was worried the food there might ruin your appetite, but you looked very healthy during your last visit. I only wonder when I'll finally get to lay eyes on my niece. Even here in Thelassus, people say Jessa's grown more beautiful than her mother. You must be so proud—remember when you used to receive such attention all those many years ago?

But enough with pleasantries. The wheels are in motion on our end. Regardless of what everyone says, I have every confidence in you. I tell Nasara it's such a simple task that even an idiot could be trusted to perform it, but you know what a bitch she can be.

Thinking of you always brings me laughter,
Sireen

"Are these manacles really necessary?" Satryn rattled her chains impatiently as the metal cage rose through the gloomy stone shaft toward the peak of the Invocari tower. Two cloaked Invocari and a female magister in brown rode with her, their shadowed gaze facing the doorway to the clanging metal box as it raised them. The woman's black hair was short, her expression severe.

"That depends on you, Your Majesty. Did you have knowledge of the assassination of Torin Silverbrook and the attempted assassination of Princess Jessa?"

"Think for a moment—how would that make *any* sense?" Satryn laughed. "You should question Duke Rothburn's relations. They have more to lose from this union than I do."

"We have." The magister turned to her. "And they were exonerated under the Veritas Seal. If you would do the same, none of this would be necessary."

"I'm a sovereign ruler and duly appointed emissary negotiating a matter of national importance on commission from the Coral Throne to your Assembly. You know I can't testify before a seal, per your own article of legislation, article thirty, subsection 4-A."

"Your daughter waived her rights under that article and was cleared of suspicion," the magister said. "It's a simple question, not a matter of state security."

"Jessa knows nothing useful, so that's hardly surprising."

"And you do?"

"I won't answer that one way or the other."

The metal cage ground to a halt, and the doors slid open. The entire center of the tower was taken up with a glass cylinder etched with runes that glowed slightly green. It reminded Satryn of a vivarium in the Sunken Palace, a pocket of protected air that allowed air breathers to access the submerged portions of the castle. It even had a small vestibule that could serve as an airlock. It was sparsely furnished and spacious, with enough room for her jailors to watch her every movement from any direction.

The airlock hissed open. "It will open to refresh the air once a day. If you find it difficult to breathe, signal one of the Invocari by pressing on the glass. The wards are soundproofed and proof against all theurgy. Please...step inside." The magister waved her hand, and Satryn's mostly decorative manacles opened and flew off her wrists.

One of the Invocari escorted her into the cage.

"Marvelous." Satryn admired the mechanical intricacy of the airlock. The door behind her hissed closed, and the vault door before her slowly retracted.

She ran her fingers along the battered wooden dresser as she paced the confines of her new accommodations. It was simply furnished with a bed and a privy behind a tattered changing curtain. The Invocari were far more generous in appointing their dungeons than the Stormlords.

"Are you going to watch me constantly?" She glanced over her shoulder at the dark hooded Invocari who floated in front of the iron door to her cell. Beneath the shadow of his hood, she made out the strong jaw of a young man in his prime.

"It's for your safety as well as ours," he said.

"Good." She smiled. "I feel more secure already." Satryn faced the wall and unbuttoned her blouse. She let the white silk slide sensuously off her shoulders and turned to her guard, bearing her naked breasts to him. She ran her fingers down her abdomen and unfastened her belt with a flick of the hand.

"I don't like to wear clothing in my private chambers." She wiggled her hips and let her breeches fall to the floor. She stepped out and sauntered over to the bed, where she slid her buttocks onto the comforter and leaned her head back, letting her silver hair spill behind her.

The Invocari watched but said nothing.

"I should also warn you that I like to pleasure myself," she said, as she sucked on her fingers and ran them across the lips of her cunt, "several times a day. And loudly." She let out a moan as she inserted her fingers.

Her jailor flinched. She imagined him blushing under that shroud, his manhood pressing against him, insistently aching to fuck her. She licked her lips and watched as his folded hands rubbed ever so slightly against his waist. *So it is possible to get a reaction out of you.*

She leaned back on the bed and imagined her first lover, Jeran. He wasn't an attractive man, but he was skilled with his hands. Jeran had taught her about her body and how to use it as a weapon—and for pleasure. He had taught her how to caress herself, how to arrange her body in the most pleasing configurations. Under his ministrations she had learned to maintain the pleasure of climax for hours.

And she had little else to do right now. She let her mind drift and felt the presence of sky and water all around her. The ephemeral building around her faded, replaced by the voluminous whirling of clouds and the steady plunge of the river below. She let her mind become one with the current, drifting out toward the ocean.

A loud series of raps came from the door. The Invocari jumped.

"Enter," Satryn called languidly as she sat up on the bed. *No, I won't need to make myself decent.*

The Invocari floated aside as a clanking locking mechanism ponderously slid in the heavy iron door. It opened, and she saw her mortified, judgmental daughter in a frumpy black smock that passed for Rivern fashion. "Mother!"

"My darling dear." Still she couldn't help feel a surge of pride. Jessa, her daughter, had survived her first assassination attempt. "Have you come to share my cell?"

"Nothing of the sort." Jessa angrily retrieved Satryn's blouse and threw it at her. "Please cover yourself. This is undignified...even for you."

Satryn tossed the blouse on the floor. "There is power in the naked form, Jessa. Even with your...modest endowments, you would be amazed at the effect it can have. Just ask our warder over there how he's enjoying himself."

"I am well and truly sorry for her behavior," Jessa told the Invocari. "Thrycean nobility consider modesty a sign of weakness. Mother, however, often confuses modesty with embarrassment."

Satryn laughed. Poor, dreary, little Jessa. What was she wearing? It was too big for her up top and cinched around the waist. It was matronly and morbidly plain. It had the countess's fingerprints all over it. "I seriously hope you're attending a funeral if you're going out in public dressed like that."

"Thank you for your fashion advice," Jessa said. "As it so happens, the untimely death of my fiancé has provided the perfect occasion for my attire."

"Poisoned wine, I hear." Satryn nodded sagely. "But I'm pleased to hear of how you handled yourself. Striking down your enemy in righteous anger is like feeling the hand of the divine caressing Creation." She brushed her fingers across the ugly green duvet. "Although...if you hadn't killed the assassin, they could have forced a confession from her and spared us this confusion. But one learns from her mistakes."

"You could also clear your name," Jessa said, gritting her teeth.

"Do they have any idea who was responsible?"

Jessa shook her fists. "They're saying it could be you! Why don't you just answer the questions in front of the Veritas Seal?"

"Because I'm a queen, and it's an insult to even be called to answer for this," Satryn said acidly. "And because they'll ask their questions in such a way that I might reveal something that isn't for them to know. The Invocari will simply have to complete their investigation with evidence and reasoned deduction. I'm content to wait here while they work to exonerate me."

"If you wanted Torin to call off the engagement, you could have simply introduced yourself. There likely isn't a man in the Free Cities who would agree to a match after meeting you."

"I'm growing weary of this discussion, dear."

"Did you kill Torin?" Jessa demanded.

"What do you think?" Satryn stroked her narrow chin and peered at Jessa with her silver eyes.

"I think you're capable of it, Mother," Jessa fumed. "But I cannot fathom your reasons. Your silence has killed the treaty and any chance of a peaceful resolution to our troubles at home. The Assembly doesn't trust that you even represent the empress."

Satryn's heart broke for the girl, although she didn't let it show. Jessa had grown up on land, with no connection to the sea. She believed life was about rules and righteousness rather than a vicious struggle for survival. She found comfort in having her life planned out and had no appreciation for the thrill of opportunity that chaos brought. *I have failed to raise you*, Satryn thought, *but we all have our role to play.*

"You must write to your aunt Nasara." Satryn flicked her wrist. "Let her know diplomacy has failed, and the Assembly won't support us…if they ever intended to. You did your part admirably, so there's no shame in admitting defeat."

"And what"—Jessa bristled at her insinuation—"shall I write to her?"

"Simply that while I'm indisposed with this legal matter, you need her aid to oversee the removal of Duke Rothburn. She should have a sizable force of Patrean marines in Amhaven within the month."

"If I we do that"—Jessa went on to finish the rest of the utterly predictable line of reasoning—"we'll be admitting Amhaven can't sustain its independence."

"But it can't, Jessa." Satryn exhaled loudly. "Duke Rothburn had only minimal support from his benefactors in the Assembly, and you were outmatched. You lack the Patreans to protect your supply lines, and your militia is untrained. It was a house of cards, built on your grandfather's legacy, but now the winds have shifted, and it can no longer stand.

"Better the crown return to the Dominance, where you'll at least get to sit on the throne as vassal without needing some Genatrovan noble to mount you for the approval of the Dukes."

Satryn hopped off the bed and began to pace. She threw her arms out to her sides, motioning to an invisible scene around her. "There is room to expand in an empire, my small-minded princess. There's even the slimmest of possibilities that you might one day sit atop the Coral Throne yourself if you put those wits of yours to good end. And then you can make the laws whatever you wish."

"I don't want the Coral Throne. Unlike you, I actually *want* to be a wife and mother."

"The Silverbrooks will ply you with kindness and pay lip service to your father's memory, but they aren't your kin." She played with a strand of Jessa's straw-blond hair. *So much like her father.* "They're admirably duplicitous, but they're cowards who hide behind their shame and call it honor."

"I have no interest in your games or the machinations of our twisted family." Jessa threw her hands in the air and marched out the door. "Rot in here for all I care."

Satryn called after her, "You may be a lowly pawn in this game, but you do get to choose whose pawn you are."

THE WAKE (JESSA)

My pulchritudinous sibling Sireen,

I have been well and am pleased to hear that your crabs remain a continued subject of discussion at court. And congratulations as well for getting Glasyr and Boromond to fight for your honor. It's quite the coup to make men fight for a prize… and even more impressive you managed to convince them such a prize exists.

And might I also say that I admire the persistence you've shown in regard to your swordsmanship. To claim that you could best Boromond bespeaks that you have come very far indeed. I look forward to seeing how much you've improved for myself.

Tell my dearest and eldest sibling Nasara that everything is well in hand, but there's another player in the game who seeks to crush this alliance. They may be useful toward our other ends, but their identity is concealed.

I grow fonder of you each moment we are apart,
Satryn

Torin's funeral service was held at the Lyceum, along with that of the former dean, Tertius, who'd been the latest victim of the harrowings. The room where the services were held had twelve alcoves with statues of old wizards. An inlaid metal circle dominated the center of the chamber. Two urns of ashes floated side by side.

I think Mother might actually be insane. She's always been erratic; she has no sense of proper boundaries at all. Perhaps she concocted this whole thing; there probably never was a treaty to begin with. Maybe her aunts sent her to Amhaven so her mental infirmity wouldn't reflect poorly on the imperial line back at court.

Jessa nodded and smiled—but not too much—as she spoke with Assemblyman Cameron and a floating golden sphere that called itself Magus Aurius. The assemblyman was poorly dressed, and the sphere was, well…intricate. She'd read about artifact mages, but actually speaking to one was disconcerting. She didn't know where to look when it—or rather *he*—spoke.

His voice was metallic, and Jessa suddenly realized she was being addressed directly. "…and of course Scholar Torin's death happening so close to the other deaths has been a devastating tragedy for the school. Three of our best and brightest gone in the span of a couple days."

"So much tragedy," Cameron agreed, stroking his grizzly beard. "Torin's betrothal would have offered real hope to the refugees. I'm holding a benefit gala for all three of them later this week. We would of course be honored if you could attend, Your Majesty. Your presence would make quite the statement of support."

Jessa quickly agreed. "Anything I can do to help the less fortunate. Where are the refugees from?"

Cameron paused. "Why…Amhaven, Your Majesty. They flee the civil unrest."

Another detail Mother didn't bother to mention. Jessa laughed nervously. "Of course. My apologies. This has been a trying day. How are my people?"

Cameron sighed. "They're getting by, Your Majesty, but just barely. We have temporary shelters in some unused warehouses, but they're filling up quickly. Most people came here with very little when they lost their homes, and there's sickness from the close quarters."

"I would like to visit them," Jessa said, "and I'll absolutely be in attendance for your gala in whatever capacity you need. You have our gratitude for the kindness you've shown our people in these troubled times."

"I'm sure that would bring them great happiness, Your Majesty," Cameron said with a smile, "but you should be aware that the Backwash isn't the…safest or most affluent district in Rivern. It's nothing increased patrols and new construction couldn't remedy, but my recommendations fall on deaf ears in the Assembly. You would be excused if you didn't make the journey down the falls and instead focused your relief efforts up here."

"Nonsense," Jessa said. "I'm the proxy for the queen regent, who's holding my eventual title, and I won't cower while my people suffer."

"Well said, Your Majesty. And if I might say…" Cameron flushed just a bit around the cheeks. "No, I've taken too much of your time. We'll have more opportunity to discuss the gala preparations."

"Thank you for speaking with me. You have my leave," Jessa said.

The sphere mage Aurius inclined himself slightly in imitation of a bow and also silently withdrew into the crowd.

Jessa sighed. The idea of her subjects stuffed into a warehouse haunted her. They were hardworking people who hadn't asked for any of this. She knew Duke Rothburn was to blame, but still her feelings toward Satryn burned the most of her vitriol. *How could she not inform me? I doubt she made any effort to aid them or even cared at all. No wonder the people hate her so much.*

"You look like you could use a drink." Countess Muriel came upon her, frantic and agitated. The old woman shoved a flute of wine into Jessa's hand and buzzed off to console another woman.

Muriel's eyes were so wide that Jessa feared they might pop out of her head. The Assembly had temporary legalized a foul-tasting elixir called dragonfire that kept one awake for all hours of the day and night as a way of eliding the rash of harrowings. As far as Jessa could tell, half the nobles in attendance were high.

She smelled the glass, and while the fragrance was pleasing, she couldn't stomach the thought of tasting it. Pictures of Torin gasping for breath in his fearful final moments rushed back to her. She delicately cast about for somewhere to put the glass down.

"I can take that." A meaty hand reached for it and pulled it from her fingers. She watched a Patrean in a black leather jerkin with tattooed arms slug the contents of the glass. He carried a broadsword across his back. He let out a belch.

"Excuse me, but that's very rude," Jessa said, appraising the well-used condition of his leather jacket and scuffed boots. "And this is a private event, soldier."

"Oh, how dreadfully contumelious of me," he said, mockingly placing his hand to his collarbone. "I'm the Sword of Saint Jeffrey, last templar of the Order of Penitent Martyrs, and I'm here conducting the holy business of the Hierophant herself. And who may I ask are you?"

Jessa cocked her head. "I'm not sure I've ever had to introduce myself before."

"Aw, fuck!" His face lit up. "You're that storm princess everyone's talking about, aren't you? Yeah, you're the one who took out Kiria with a bolt of thunder to the face." He tossed the glass aside and clapped his hands together.

Miraculously the glass didn't hit the ground but rather floated off. Jessa noticed a short bald man in white robes casting a peevish sideways glare.

She laughed nervously. People were definitely staring now, if they weren't already before. "Kiria? Is that the name of my assassin?" She whispered, "Tell me what you know right now, or I swear you'll meet her fate and worse."

"I'm not here on any business of that sort, love." He casually put his arm around her shoulder and flexed his bicep.

Jessa was speechless. Never would a Patrean so much as address her without permission, much less touch her. And was he…hitting on her?

He leaned in close to her ear. "Kiria was one of Cordovis's people. A real nasty piece of work, that one. I once saw her dig out a man's eye and turn it back on him so he could watch her cut up his face. Then she popped the fucker back in."

Jessa shrugged the Fodder's arm off her shoulder. She shook her head with disbelief. "You have to give this information to the authorities."

He waved his hand. "Everyone knows that, love. I'm frankly a bit surprised they haven't dismissed your mum's charges during evidentiary proceedings. But law's a funny business. While we're chatting, you didn't happen to see an old blind man about yay high in a moth-eaten robe, possibly carrying a shepherd's crook, have you?"

"Um…no, I haven't. Who is Cordovis? Why would he kill Torin?"

"I don't know his business, but the short answer is money. Either someone paid him to do it, or there's a payoff. Cordovis wouldn't shit in a glove unless those fingers could grab a ducat, you get me?"

"I get the gist of it, yes. Do you know anything else about him?"

"Look," he whispered, "I wouldn't worry your pretty noble head about it. I used to be a Stormlord myself a while back, and he's nothing you can't handle."

"I didn't think Fodders were capable of…being so imaginative. Please excuse me." Jessa turned and walked to the first person she could find, a portly bald man wearing five gold medallions.

"Lady Jessa," he spoke with a soft, effeminate voice, "I'm so sorry for your loss. Torin was my favorite pupil. I'm Dean Archibald Turnbull, and yes, I'm required by Rivern law to tell you I bear the Veritas Seal. So you'll accept my sincere apologies if, for the sake of your privacy, I don't ask any questions about how you're doing." He offered a smile.

"I'm not certain how I'm doing," Jessa confided, "or how I'm expected to be doing under the circumstances. I knew Torin very briefly, but he was…I would have been happy with the match."

"I must admit I was concerned for his safety," Turnbull said. "The war with the Dominance has raged off and on for centuries. There are closed-minded fanatics in Rivern who view your mere presence as an insult. People in this corner of the Protectorate tend to think with their fists."

"It may surprise you to hear that I harbor no great affection for the empire or my grandmother. And it's refreshing to say that to someone and know he'll believe me." Jessa grinned.

Turnbull raised his eyebrow. "Honesty is wonderful, isn't it?"

"You have no idea." Jessa sighed with relief.

"I think Torin would have considered himself fortunate." Turnbull smiled. "If there's ever anything you need, don't hesitate to ask. People may not equate the dean of the College of Seals with a position of citywide authority, but I also oversee the licenses for the Burners Guild, and I can easily cut off the city's hot water with the stroke of a pen."

Jessa took his hand in hers. "I'm grateful for your offer of friendship. I may call upon you."

Turnbull removed a square of silk from his pocket and dabbed his eye. "Come by and see me anytime, Lady."

Jessa grinned to herself as she left Turnbull's company. He seemed genuinely gentle and good-hearted. In fact everyone in Rivern had been nothing but kind and helpful. Her mother had warned her to mistrust the charity of strangers, but these people exuded a sense of friendliness and sincerity that seemed almost alien.

Jessa stopped short. A tearful woman under a black veil stood trembling in her path. Makeup ran from her eyes, and her mouth was twisted with grief. "I don't care what they say…*You murdered my son, you fucking imperial cunt!*" Torin's mother slapped Jessa across the face.

Jessa turned and pressed her hand against her stinging cheek as attendees at the wake swarmed the women. She felt hands guiding her away as others restrained Torin's mother. Shouting and panic ensued as Jessa's cousins rushed her out of the chamber.

THE HOUSE OF THE SEVEN SIGHS
(MADDOX)

For students seeking a value in arcane education, the Lyceum at Rivern has much to offer. While not as prestigious as Bamor College, it once was regarded nearly as highly. Its engineering program is still the most prominent in all Creation, and nearly all recent advances in automata can be credited in part to their faculty research. They also offer curricula in glyphology, blood magic, and alchemy.

It is unfortunately the only school in the Protectorate not to offer classes in necromancy, owing to the infamous indiscretions of Dean Pytheria. The scandal of her administration led to the formal revocation of their charter in that discipline, and fifty years later, the reputation has remained somewhat tarnished.

For nontraditional education the Twin Magisteriums of the Mirrored City offer a much more varied selection of arcane modalities. But for traditional mages uninterested in necromancy, the Rivern Lyceum offers comparable education to Bamor at a fraction of the cost.

—Nolan Harding's annual university ratings, 565 A.N.

The inscription probably was meant to say, the house of the seven signs, but the High Archean writing above the battered doorframe used some of the modern alphabet so signs became sighs. It was about what you'd expect from a condemned house in the Backwash: a weathered structure suspended above the rushing water by barnacle-encrusted footing made from young, tall oak.

A scarlet wax seal bound a piece of official parchment to the door, which had been kicked in then propped back in place. The inside was dark, with candles set on shclves to augment the illumination from the boarded-up windows. The floor was covered in ragged bedding and the detritus of squatters. A few shitty chairs were scattered around, along with a table in moderately good repair. A stack of books and a small makeshift alchemy station sat on one end of the table.

Riley motioned Maddox inside. He had recovered somewhat on the walk over. Enough to be properly disgusted by his surroundings. It was messy and foul, with a haze of smoke that smelled like dragonfire and other noxious substances. His incredibly keen sense of smell gave him pungent bursts of information, none of it good.

A girl with multicolored but naturally blond hair sat at the table, her hand splayed in front of her as she quickly and methodically jabbed an expensive-looking knife into the space between each finger. She looked up. Her vividly blue eyes were lined with deep black. "Who the fuck is this?"

Riley beamed. "This is Maddox!"

"Heard a lot about you," she said casually. Her voice was unusually high and pretty. In fact she was actually quite attractive for a girl. She didn't stop doing that thing with the knife, whatever you called it.

"This is Esme," Riley said, nudging him. "She's my girl. So hands off."

"How old is she?" Maddox asked. She couldn't have been more than sixteen.

"Older than I look," Esme sneered. "I've killed people."

Riley laughed. "She's feisty. Come on! The others are upstairs…"

Riley led Maddox up a set of rickety steps to the upper level. He glanced at Esme as he passed. Her eyes regarded him warily, with a glimmer of murderousness. He knew the routine and returned the glare. He'd been coming downriver since before she was born. She wasn't anything he couldn't handle. If it ever came to that.

Upstairs wasn't any better. The others were sitting on the floor in a circle around a smoldering hookah. In no particular order was an old lady who looked like she had one foot in the grave, a stout man with tremendous arms, a trembling skinny guy, a Fodder, and a black wolf with yellow eyes.

"This is Gran." Riley indicated the old woman. "We call her that 'cuz sometimes she thinks I'm her grandson."

The old woman gave a yellow smile, but her eyes were vacant. "I used to teach at the school." Wizards weren't immune to the ravages of dementia; it took their minds as well as their powers.

"That's Otix." Riley motioned to the large man. "He's an Archean. Doesn't speak much Thrycean."

"It's an honor to meet you," Maddox offered in Archean. It was a bit more formal than he'd intended, but wit and condescension were difficult to translate.

"Yeah, right," Otix replied.

"You can talk to him!" Riley said excitedly. "This is brilliant. We needed you here weeks ago. We've only been able to piece together a little of his story."

Maddox looked at Otix again. His neck was thicker than his head. "What's your story?" he asked in Archean.

"Came on a sky ship to load pickled fish, got fucked up in a bar, passed out, and missed the return trip. I've been stuck here ever since. There's no work for me, and I spent all my prisms on pleasure chemicals." His speech was easier to understand than Petra's dialect.

"Show him your thing, Otix," Riley said very slowly as he opened and closed his fist.

Otix sighed and held out his hand. After a moment a blue flame appeared in his palm. "I know a few tricks. Just stuff everyone knows." Maddox didn't see a seal on Otix, which meant he was using freeform magic. They didn't teach it at the Lyceum, because it was mostly useless.

"That's our alchemist, Falco." Riley grinned as he pointed at the emaciated guy with curly hair. "His thing will blow your mind."

Falco lifted his shirt, and Maddox barfed a little in his throat. Falco's nicely-toned-for-a-drug-addict abdomen featured a mouth-like orifice on the right side. Mutation was a common risk in working with alchemicals in an unsafe environment. Among some of Maddox's dad's friends, the disfigurations were sort of a badge of honor.

"That mouth can eat through anything." Riley explained before introducing the Fodder. "This is Crateus."

"Are you a magician as well?" Maddox asked. He'd never known a Patrean who wasn't a soldier, enforcer, or manual laborer. This one looked like a younger version of the one he'd sucked off in the alley behind the Flask. As a race they didn't possess magic but were more resilient to some forms of it.

"I'm trying to learn," Crateus said earnestly. "My mother was human, so I might have the gift." Patrean-human hybrids were always exact copies of the Patrean parent. There were no half Fodders.

"We accept everyone," Riley said proudly. "Not like the fucking Lyceum."

The wolf barked.

"Oh. That's Themis. Him and his brother Theril stay with us too."

"So this is your study group?" Maddox asked. "Half of them don't actually do any magic."

Riley sighed patiently. "Everyone has potential for something. It's not just scals or blood or necromancy or artifice. There's a ton of shit out there they don't teach or sanction. We may not be as good as the magi, but we want to be the best we can be."

"A little is more than nothing." Maddox sighed. It never had been an issue for him. He had completed a degree in alchemy to qualify for the College of Seals and earn the title of Scholar. He was on another level entirely, but he couldn't blame anyone for wanting knowledge. Still it was a sad collection of individuals.

Riley pointed to Maddox. "This is me oldest friend from the Lyceum, Maddox. He's a Master of the Seals and a Scholar of alchemy."

"Alchemy's *my* thing!" Falco said angrily.

"It's all yours." Maddox smiled. "I don't practice anymore."

"Just so we's clear." Falco nodded and took a pipe from the hookah. He lifted his shirt again and put the tip of the hookah into the gaping mouth on his stomach. He grimaced slightly and blew a plume of smoke out of his own mouth as the orifice in his belly suckled the pipe.

"I hope you all don't share that," Maddox said.

"The best part is coming up," Riley said. He sniffed, then rubbed his nose on his sleeve.

"My dead husband was an alchemist," Gran said to no one in particular.

"Come. I'll show you where you're sleeping." Riley grabbed Maddox's wrist and let him to a door.

Maddox had braced himself for anything but was rendered speechless when he entered the room. It was a great deal better in here. The walls and floor were decrepit but mostly hidden behind woven tapestries and lustrous carpeting. On one of the nightstands, a golden candelabra shaped like an eagle peered at him with glimmering ruby eyes. The bed, bedecked in red satin, was made of ornately carved, highly polished Maenmarth timber.

A second black wolf raised its head and snarled from the center of the soft red covers.

"Theril sleeps with us," Riley explained before addressing the wolf. "This is me best friend, Maddox. You try to bite him, and I'll take away your bedroom privileges."

The wolf rolled his eyes in a very human way and plopped his head down on the bed, nose turned to the side.

"Well"—Riley slapped Maddox's back—"I'll let you get settled in. Help yourself to anythin' you like. I've got to run some errands at the menagerie to pick up reagents and trade in a bit of dragonfire. Should be back before sundown. There's a bottle of wine in the drawer."

"You're leaving me alone with these people?" Maddox asked incredulously. Riley was an unsavory character but at least affable and, most important, familiar. To call this motley collection the dregs of "society" would have been an insult to the skeevy perverts, desperate addicts, and lascivious prostitutes of the Backwash.

"I'll look after him."

Maddox jumped. Esme was sitting on the bed next to the wolf, absently picking her fingernails with her shiny silver dagger. She posed herself sensually, as if she'd been there the whole time...but she hadn't been there a moment ago.

"Hands off me little lady." Riley winked and punched Maddox in the arm, rather harder than he should have, before trotting back downstairs and out the building.

"So," Esme said, "you and Riley go way back, huh?"

"I tolerated him," Maddox said, "which is more than most people did. How did you get in here without my seeing you?"

She cast a bored look over to the open window; there were no boards covering it, and a gentle breeze blew against red gauzy curtains. "I like to make an entrance. Didn't mean to startle you."

"You're not scary. You look like you're sixteen, and that knife would never make it anywhere near me. So cut the tough-girl shit."

"I'm sorry," she said suddenly choked with emotion. "It's just so hard, you know...I've been on my own since I was ten and it's just so hard to trust people. So hard to open up to anyone..." Her pale-blue eyes were wet with tears.

"Are you done?" Maddox said.

"I am now." She sighed, instantly regaining her playfully antagonistic composure. "I had a whole story about my father going off to war, a sick mother, and a baby brother I could barely afford to feed. So...was I overdoing it, or are you just a naturally callous bastard?"

"A bit of both. Any of that story true?"

"When I was young, I used to do a sad-orphan act to lure marks into an alley so my gang could jump them and take their shit. But I am an actual orphan," she admitted.

"Then it's all good." Maddox waved his hand and opened all the drawers in the room simultaneously. There were a couple of bottles of wine in one of the nightstands along with a pair of manacles, women's lingerie, and a cat-o'-nine-tails. Maddox drew the bottle to his hand and popped the cork from its wax.

The label on the bottle read, "House Lysenne Cuvée, 452 3E." An unreadable stylized autograph was scrawled on the bottle.

"This shit's almost a hundred years old," Maddox said, turning the bottle in his hand. "There's no way it's even close to drinkable." He sniffed the bottle and got promising notes of graphite, cassis, and earth.

"It was a banner year for the winemaker," Esme said casually.

Maddox shrugged and chugged. His sense of taste was nowhere near his sense of smell, but the wine wasn't half bad, which was remarkable because he detected no alchemical preservatives. A lot of shit happened with the flavor in his mouth. It probably *was* a banner year.

"So seriously you're, like, what? A nobleman's daughter who decided to go bad? Why the hell are you with Riley?"

Esme slid off the bed and snatched the bottle from his hand. "You don't know me, asshole. You don't know Riley either, but he thinks the fucking world of you. He's a special person to me, so let's be absolutely clear—if you fuck with him or talk bad about him again, I'll kill you so hard that your ghost has its own fucking ghost." She drank from the bottle and pushed it into Maddox's chest.

"Fair enough," Maddox said, taking another swig. The flavor had deepened even in the few moments they'd been talking. "I get that you don't want me here or whatever. I'm not staying."

"Right." Esme took the bottle and drank. "Because a charming guy like you doesn't need to spend time with a bunch of washed-up druggies."

Maddox snatched the bottle out of her hands and swished around what was left. "You said it, not me."

"You're as much a loser as any of us. Maybe more—at least we have friends," she said sweetly, leaning over the bed to scratch the wolf behind his ears. "Yes, we do, don't we, boy?"

Maddox walked out of the bedroom into the common area. The hedge wizards were getting high; a sickly sweet-smelling haze permeated the room.

Maddox sniffed the air. "Is that elder root?"

"My own concoction," Falco said. "Tincture with mandrake powder, essence of golden nightshade, and witch's tear. It works to expand the mind and facilitate the flow of theurgy by awakening the dreaming shaman mind."

Maddox parsed the formula in his head pretty quickly. It was basic euphorium you could buy off any crooked apothecary. The golden nightshade made no sense, unless you wanted to cure yourself of indigestion and sensory awareness at the same time.

He finished the bottle and tossed it into the corner with some other junk on the floor. He plopped down next to Gran, who was staring vacantly into space. "Remember when we used to go dancing, Charlie?" she said.

"Let me hit that," Maddox said, reaching for the pipe.

Falco's face beamed. "What's mine is yours, bro. In the House of the Seven Signs, we're all equal."

Maddox took the pipe and wiped it on his tunic. He placed the tip of the hookah to his mouth and tasted the smoke. It wasn't as pleasant as it smelled; the reagents hadn't been dried properly, so it was harsh.

Esme stood in the door to Riley's room and shouted, "Hey, asshole! You can't do that shit with alcohol. Do you have a death wish or something?"

"Maybe." He already felt himself going numb, the raw ache of his feelings melting into a monolithic sense of tranquility. "But it may not matter what I want."

He took another hit and blew out a massive plume of smoke.

He heard more voices, like buzzing, in the distance. Everything seemed hundreds of miles away. Someone was pulling the pipe out of his hand, and the world was tilting as he very slowly sank into the floor. He heard some yelling or commotion.

The crack of his head against the floor came like a softened thud; information disconnected from his body. The floor stretched on forever, and blotches of magnificent color sparkled all around him—motes of energy. The Guides! They were all around him—balls of luminous power floating in the room like a galaxy of spinning stars.

Maddox felt them gathering on his body, like butterflies alighting on a flower, as a golden light slid free from its mortal coil and danced amid the myriad lights.

WHEN KISSES CAN LIE
(HEATH AND SWORD)

Before the Reformation and Unification of the Orthodoxy, we teach that heathens practiced human sacrifice to the false god of death, Noha. This much is true, although the name of Noha often was different in every civilization. As an example, the modern Archeans still refer to him as Vitae.

It was from those casually accepted monstrosities that the way was paved for all manner of dark sorcery to corrupt the civilizations of the Second Era.

Our absolute mandate is to ensure that theurgy does not corrupt the natural order of life or death. Foremost against all Dark Magic, we must be ever vigilant of our own and certain that they adhere to the letter of Doctrine. And where heresy is found, or even suspected, it must be dispatched by any means at our disposal.
—preface to The Radiant Apocrypha: An Incunabula for Initiates to the Holy Order of the Inquisition

The Mage's Flask was fuller than usual that afternoon. Amhaven refugees who still had coin to spend nursed pints of cheap grog and nibbled at plates of cheese. Heath never had seen anyone eat anything at the Flask, and he didn't want to hazard how long that food had been sitting in Cassie's pantry.

He and Sword sat at a rickety table in the corner so they could see the door. A fresh stack of parchments from Loran was spread out in front of him. There had been at least eight more deaths that the Invocari knew of, most of them in the Backwash. The pattern Sword had mentioned seemed to apply less and less to these new cases. The Amhaven refugees didn't practice magic, and two of the deaths had occurred among their ranks.

There also was no shortage of gaunt old men wandering the docks, making Harbinger sightings difficult to corroborate. No one actually had spoken to Milk Eyes since he'd visited the Twin Shields.

Sword flipped through the pages of a book, his lips moving as his eyes trudged over the words.

"I suppose it's too much to hope you're reading something about the harrowings," Heath said offhandedly as he shuffled his papers around.

He shook his head. "It's called *When Kisses Can Lie*. A nuanced portrayal of a young immigrant girl's journey into womanhood during the siege of Karthanteum. You see, she's torn between fulfilling the expectations of her religious mother and establishing an identity for herself—"

"If I read what's on that page, is it going to be sex?" Heath asked.

Sword slammed the book shut. "Fuck off, mate. It's been two days of sitting in this shithole and no sign of the fucker. It's boring as hell, so sue me if I find refuge in a bit of titillating literature written for a discerning female audience."

"He'll show up," Heath said, pointing to an empty barstool. "Maddox is a creature of habit. And for whatever twisted reason, this is his bar."

Sword glanced at a raddled prostitute with a peg leg chatting up one of the refugees. "This place is like the elephants' graveyard for old drunks. There's probably a big pile of bones under this place where they go to pop off when it's their time. The fuck are we doing here, mate?"

"I told you, I want to warn Maddox," Heath patiently explained. "He used to be a friend, and I want to make sure he gets out of town before Daphne gets hold of him."

"That's right big of you mate, but no one's seen hide nor hair of him…or that dodgy drinking buddy of his. Um…what's his name?"

"Riley."

"Anyway," Sword said, "he's long gone. Probably offed himself, which seems a very reasonable course of action given our current dispiriting environs. But an equally reasonable conjecture is that he bolted."

"Read your book if you're not going to offer anything productive."

Sword scratched the back of his neck. "Look, I gotta take a leak. I'm going out back to relieve myself. If Maddox turns up, distract him. Show him your dick or something."

Sword headed for the back, stopped, snatched his book off the table, and continued on. "I may be a while."

Heath leaned his head back against the wall. Sword had been his loyal companion through several incarnations. Heath knew that Sword wore each personality like a mask, just as he wore their bodies. The last two Patreans had been military and acted like trained soldiers, even calling him "sir." This new body, however, was a different story altogether.

"It's a very good likeness," the Harbinger said, examining the parchment drawing of himself. He was sitting in Sword's spot, elbows perched nonchalantly on the table, as if he'd been there the entire time. The likeness was in fact quite good.

Heath startled briefly then composed himself. "The fuck?"

"I'm called the Harbinger," he said. "I know you've been searching for me, and I would have come sooner, but that artifact is always close to you. It's one of the only things in Creation that can harm one of my kind, and it has a fickle temperament."

Good to know. Heath smiled. "Sword? He's amazingly nonviolent for a ancient instrument of decapitation."

"Its brutality has been the subject of many epic poems, some of them in your own Doctrines."

Heath shrugged. "I think people tend to put more stock in myths and folktales than is truly warranted."

"An odd sentiment for a priest." The Harbinger produced an ivory flask from his sash and set it on the parchment.

"Former priest," Heath corrected. "And I have firsthand knowledge that most of what people believe is bullshit. What I do believe about *you* is that you're old, and you're powerful, and you know something about what's going on with the harrowings."

"Old by some measures and powerful in some respects." The Harbinger bobbed his head in agreement. "And a good deal more learned on these subjects than most. Though knowledge isn't what you seek. You seek understanding."

"I read up on you Travelers. Your people like to speak in riddles, so let me ask this plainly. How do we stop these Harrowers?"

The Harbinger sighed. "No one likes to speak in riddles, Priest. But sometimes a riddle is the only way to get at the truth without changing its meaning. The answer isn't always the words themselves but the experience of realization. In fairness I can see how such statements would be annoying to one as pragmatic as yourself. Have a drink."

Heath looked at the ivory flask on the table. It was finely crafted but otherwise nondescript. "No way in the hells am I drinking that."

"Suit yourself." The old man leaned back. "We can't stop the Harrowers. They're an inexorable force that can bend the very fabric of our universe to suit their whims…when they have whims. We exist only because they don't wish us dead."

"What do they want then?" Heath asked.

"Nothing."

Heath forced another smile. "You came to tell me *something*. So talk."

The Harbinger nodded with a hint of approval. "I've foreseen the inevitable because that's the source of my theurgy. I can't foresee the exact future. That gift is a burden none should carry, but I see any futures that will never happen."

"Your theurgy is making predictions that are wrong? That's not even a power. Half the fortune-tellers in Rivern have your gift."

"Ah," he replied with a twinkle in his milky eyes, "but they're right sometimes… They just don't know it. My predictions are always 'wrong,' as you say. From that certainty I can see the shadow of Fate. In no future do the towers of Rivern still stand in two months' time. Great death and darkness are coming to all."

Heath folded his hands together. "I don't believe in fate any more than I believe in invisible gods. People believe in fate because it absolves them of taking responsibility for fixing their problems."

"Let me give you a familiar example." The Harbinger smiled with yellow teeth. "A woman is born with a slight irregularity in the smallest building blocks of the stomach tissue. Over time it becomes more than an irregularity; it starts to grow out of control, and her body turns on itself to repel what it perceives as an invader. Eventually the illness causes her body to waste away. Eating is painful, and she spends every waking moment in agony."

Heath didn't like where this was going. Not one bit. "People get sick—it's not the Will of Ohan or fate. It's bad luck."

"The woman's youngest child is called from a life of crime to join the priesthood to save his mother, to learn the ways of the Light," the Harbinger continued, "but there's blood on his hands when he stands before the altar of the Father of All, and the elders lead him down a different path—a path of both darkness and Light, where he learns the god of life is also the god of death.

"And though your physicians don't yet understand this, the Light can't heal cancers because there is no injury, no infection, no toxin. It can restore a damaged body to health, but it can't restore health to a body that has turned on itself. In fact Light only feeds the illness. They call her death the Will of Ohan. And a young man loses faith in his god, believes in nothing, and turns to greed."

"You make me sound more complicated than I am," Heath said with a wry smile. "Things are simpler when you look at the facts. My mother died because we were too poor to afford treatment that *would* work. It's a sad statement about society; it doesn't prove anything about fate."

"Your life has been a straight line to this very moment, Heath. Every decision you've made about your luck could have had no other outcome than you and I sitting together in this place."

"Is that why you were in Reda?"

The Harbinger confessed, "I'm drawn to death by my wyrd. A Traveler's magic is more than his spells—it's the very essence of who he is. In a way our magic controls us more than we control it. I'm taken where I'm needed, where the dark shadow of Fate stretches across the river of time and the course is forever altered. I'm a collector and shepherd of memories of possibilities lost." He pushed the ivory flask toward Heath. "These memories are the children of Reda. All that's left of them, and the future that never came to pass."

Heath recoiled. "Why would I ever want that?"

"I'm returning your ghosts," he said, taking the sketch of himself and pocketing it. "In exchange for this memory of myself."

"Fuck you," Heath said. "You say the city is doomed, but you won't tell me how or why. I may not be able to stop it, but it's because you won't help me. That blood is on your hands."

"I don't follow this wyrd to make friends." He gave a grim smirk, tipped his head, and vanished.

"We're not finished!" Heath reached out into the empty space, hoping to catch something, but the air was empty. If the other patrons noticed the heated exchange, they didn't indicate it.

Teleportation was beyond any magic practiced in the Free Cities and probably Creation itself. That kind of power could move armies, open supply lines—a nation with that capability would rule the world.

Heath looked at the flask and fumed. He'd killed a lot of people, most deserving, and it never got under his skin. It was always about the job. Except when it wasn't. He picked up the flask with his silk handkerchief and slid it into one of his hidden pockets. Then he went out the back.

Sword was sitting on a barrel, the book folded in his lap as he stared forward into space. He looked over at Heath and wiped his bleary brown eyes. "What's going on? Did the prostitute drag that drunk bloke back to her aquatic troll cavern?"

Heath said, "What the hells are you doing back here? Are you…crying?"

"No." Sword sniffed unconvincingly.

"It's that book," Heath said, looking over his shoulder.

"I thought I was going to have a tug, but…" Sword sniffled. "He was the love of her life, Heath. And he's dead." Sword tossed the book to the ground and kicked it away. He folded his arms like a truculent child.

You do a really good job of making people forget you aren't human sometimes, Heath thought.

"You came out here to rub one out?" Heath's fingers felt for the launching mechanism on his hidden springblades.

"Human beings don't fully appreciate the myriad benefits, both physical and mental, of being able to do that to themselves at will."

Heath snapped, "The Harbinger just appeared and told me the city is doomed. But he cut out before telling me anything concrete. I could have used you in there."

Sword looked down like a scolded puppy. "Sorry."

"Apologies don't pay bounties. We have a job, so show some fucking professionalism," Heath spat.

Sword listened very quietly, nodding attentively, as Heath gave him a rundown on the conversation. Heath tried to keep to the facts, but part of his mind was stuck on everything he should have said. Possibilities that didn't exist. He showed Sword the flask but omitted the mention of his mother's illness.

"You've faced these guys before. Was he right about what he can predict?" Heath asked, then offered more gently, "I'd appreciate your wisdom."

Sword grimaced slightly and shook his head. "I don't know that a Sword that possesses people is the right authority on the existence of free will and self-determination."

"Other thoughts," Heath said, pacing and searching the air for ideas. "Were there any clues he might have left?"

"Well…" Sword began tentatively, "he did give you that flask. He probably was more concerned that I'd drink it than anything about my trying to kill him. Travelers can be bleeding superior assholes, but I got no particular bone of contention with this one."

"Why wouldn't he want you to drink it?" Heath inquired. "Is it poison?"

"Wouldn't work on us, most likely." Sword shifted slightly on the barrel, "Memories are like…food for us, you know? I can absorb a lifetime of experiences and remain the same person. Traveler theurgy always comes with some fucking life lesson. They get off on that shit."

"He wants to change me?" Heath asked skeptically.

"Good luck with that." Sword laughed a little.

Heath pulled the flask out of his pocket. "Fuck."

"Look, mate"—Sword reached out to put a hand on his arm—"this job is a lousy ten thousand ducats. We don't need the fucking coin anyway. We tell the client what happened, turn in the flask, and let the Invocari sort it out. We keep the advance and go on our merry way—preferably to a city that's not doomed."

"Sword, even in a stupid body, you're brilliant," Heath's face broke out in a wide grin as the realization hit him. "That's what the Harbinger wants. If nothing can be done to stop the destruction, why even talk to me? He wants me out of this city. He thinks I won't drink the flask because I'm afraid to face my ghosts. This is probably just water."

"I *seriously* doubt that, mate."

"He's not getting rid of me that easily. And if he thinks he knows what scares me, he's dead wrong."

Sword bit his knuckle. "Or he could be leveraging your pride against you."

"If it's poison, I'll heal." Heath opened the flask and drank. The liquid tasted like rain and ash and pine, not pleasant but interesting in a way that wasn't entirely horrible. He downed the flask and tossed in onto the boardwalk.

"It was just water." Heath kicked the flask across the boardwalk. It clattered between one of the planks and plunked into the river below. "So what's our next move?"

"Now you see the truth," Sword said in a little girl's voice, which made Heath's skin crawl.

He scrambled backward, but Sword merely sat there, staring at him with a vacant stare.

Fog closed in; color and sound drained from the world around him. The world was swallowed by mist, and Heath gazed across an endless gray nothingness. He turned and felt frantically for anything to anchor him, but he found only cold mist and the gentle kiss of rain as it gathered on his skin. He stumbled toward the bar, but his steps carried him past where the wall should be.

His fingers brushed against the rough bark of a tree.

He called on his Light, but to his horror, his hands no longer were his own. His flesh was ghostly pale—nearly translucent—and instead of Light, a ball of fire blazed in his palm. In his right hand, he clutched the Sword, drawn to his side and thirsting for battle.

The laughter of children echoed in the distance as fleeting shadows darted through the mist. He snarled and lashed at the fog with his flame, igniting trees and plants. The fire burned hot enough to disperse some of the mist, and he found himself up to his ankles in thick black mud.

He had dallied too long in the moors. He needed to get to Reda.

REFUGE (JESSA)

Armed with the power of the Thunderstone and the knowledge granted by the Deep Masters of the Abyss, the Storm Raiders brought their flotilla to the Shining Bay and descended upon the coast of Mazitar.

The Wavelord priests were potent in magic but weak in spirit and fell before the fury and ruthlessness of the Storm Raiders. The Raiders' Blood Sages burned their holy symbols of Kondole, the Thunder Whale, and raised the banners of Kultea, the Sea Terror. The Raiders' women took the Wavelord men as consorts...and when the women were ripe with bastards, they slaughtered the lot in offering to the many-limbed witch of the deepest oceans.

From these Sacred Bastards, the Storm Raiders begat the Stormlords, and the Wavelords vanished into obscurity. This may seem cruel...but it is the way of nature. The strong devour the weak. So it can be said that weakness is the source of strength.

The strong need the weak to survive, just as our pirate ancestors needed the bloodline of indolent island dwellers to secure our mastery of the elements. Never forget they are a part of us. Master them wisely.
—*Treatise on Orderly Governance,* a book by exiled monarch Dao-Chui

Jessa felt bad for thinking ill of her subjects, but they were dirty and malnourished. Their Thrycean was coarse and simple when they spoke. Most of them didn't believe she was actually their princess or, worse, mistook her for her mother. She tried to remind herself that these people had lost their homes and endured a harrowing ordeal, many of them losing loved ones.

Her father had told her the people of Amhaven were resilient and noble in their commitment to simple life. She, however, just saw poverty and privation and wondered how much her father had gotten out among the people he had spoken so highly of. It said something about the state of affairs back home when the crown of Amhaven was ripe for the taking and no one from Rivern was even interested.

But Jessa forced herself to smile and handed out blankets and food, which she had paid for by selling Satryn's jewelry. It was fitting because this whole situation had been her mother's doing in the first place. Some of the people were grateful, but most took their charity and scuttled off. Her mother's words floated into her mind: *These people have no influence. Why are you wasting your time with them? You need to find a wealthy lord who can sway the Assembly.*

Assemblyman Cameron had been very diligent in organizing the event. Jessa was positioned at the end of a pier, facing the refugee shelter. He had everyone form a line with checkpoints of made of up the city guard and Invocari, documenting names, and a seal mage to verify their status as refugees as opposed to beggars from the Backwash looking for a handout. The guards kept things moving swiftly and assisted those who were too enfeebled to keep pace.

As the line dwindled, Jessa noticed her supplies running low. It seemed, at the time, like a good idea to start handing out gold instead. With the countess graciously covering her living expenses, Jessa had little need for coin. Just a ducat to each person would do.

In this case her generosity was well rewarded with praise from an old woman with a stooped back, probably from a life of hauling kindling. Women collected bundles of fallen branches to use for the hearth; it was said that burning naturally fallen sticks would not offend the witches.

Cameron whispered, "It isn't wise to show so much coin, Your Majesty."

"It's just a ducat," Jessa protested, handing a coin to the next man in line.

The riot started shortly after she heard someone shout, "She's got gold!"

Across the long end of the pier, her subjects charged toward her, each of them pleading. Mothers held their children in one arm, their palms extended as they rushed past the guards. Young men pushed the elderly out of the way as they trampled forward. She watched two men break out into a fight as the crowd stampeded around them.

Assemblyman Cameron placed an arm in front of Jessa protectively. "You'll want to get clear. This is going to be extremely unpleasant."

Jessa looked back toward the edge of the pier. It was only five feet away, the currents of the river lapping reassuringly at the dock posts. "I'm perfectly fine where I am and more than capable of handling this situation."

"Suit yourself," he said, as he turned and hunched against a shipping crate. He took in a huge breath and closed his eyes, as if he were trying to make himself invisible.

"What are you doing?" Jessa almost said.

The chill came upon her as if she had plunged into freezing cold water. Normally cold wasn't an issue for a Stormlord, but this chill penetrated her flesh and made her bones ache. White mist rose from her mouth as her breath left her. When she tried to breathe in, she could find no air.

Across the pier she saw people falling to their knees, shivering, and clutching at their throats. The Patreans stood tall, bracing themselves with all their might, but even their faces were twisted with discomfort. Above them, three Invocari had risen a good twelve feet in the air, their hands outstretched.

Jessa continued to gasp for air, but she felt dizzy and tumbled to the planks of the pier. Desperately she dragged herself to the edge, trying to fill her lungs with lifegiving water before she suffocated. Then, just as she was about to pull herself over, it ended.

Warmth returned instantly to her body, though the chill remained. She heard a collective chorus of gasps from everyone on the pier. Out of the corner of her eye, she saw Cameron stand up and extend his hand to her. He pulled her up, and she stood unsteadily.

"The Invocari's craft is unsettling, especially the first time," Cameron observed. "If you hold your breath before, it helps. A little."

"I couldn't breathe…" Jessa exclaimed. She'd never been unable to breathe before. "Is that what it feels like to drown?"

"Most people would prefer to drown." Cameron threw his coat over his shoulder. "We should get out of here."

He looked up at the Invocari and forced a smile as he led Jessa down the pier. The Patreans cleared a path fairly easily. Most of the refugees scattered as soon as they caught their breath, but a few remained on the pier, not moving. Jessa's silver eyes widened as a woman desperately shook an older man whose body looked drained of life.

"Is that man dead?" she asked.

"It's possible, Your Majesty." Cameron said as he ushered her along. "The Invocari don't choose who they affect when they use their void magic for crowd control. A few seconds is all they need to disable a person, but for some folks, that's more than they have. It's not unusual for a heart to give out from terror either."

Jessa shuddered. Of course she knew the Invocari were the reason the Dominance hadn't captured the free cities, but to experience their power first-hand was another matter entirely.

She felt better as they made their way toward the falls. The cold mist from the waterfall invigorated her skin with a natural coolness that chased away the sense memory of the Invocari's power. "Apparently Mother was right. I lack the common touch." Jessa laughed grimly.

"Poverty and squalor turn decent folks into animals," Cameron said. "Say all you want about character and resolve, but it only gets you so far down here. Your people are at the bottom rung of a very tall ladder. I should have stopped you from passing out your gold. The ones who won't be robbed will spend it on drugs."

"This entire situation is utterly unacceptable," Jessa fumed.

He grumbled in assent, "I've been telling that to the Assembly for years. Maybe they'll listen to you."

"If it's my destiny to be a tool for the political ambitions of others, I'd feel most comfortable in your hands, Assemblyman Cameron." She offered a wan smile.

"Careful with your words, Majesty. I'm not known for my manners, and turns of phrase like that inspire my less-refined nature."

Jessa sniffed. "Sometimes I wish people would treat me with less consideration and greater honesty. Truthfully what do you think will happen to my people? The problem goes beyond meager handouts and bedding."

"Yes, it does. The problem is the entire structure of the city. With every new invention of the artificers, the city needs labor less and less. Do you know what a bath attendant is?"

"Of course," Jessa scoffed. "I am, however, surprised you'd even know of such a thing. At the Silverbrook estate, the hot water comes through pipes in the wall."

"And who cleans the bath?"

"One of Muriel's automatons."

"That used to be the job of two servants...three, giving allowance for an alternate," Cameron emphasized. "Those three jobs no longer exist, and three unlucky souls scrape by for survival in the Backwash, Majesty."

Jessa cocked her head. "But who would want to be a bath maid? It isn't pleasant work hauling those large vats of boiling water."

"It's a shit job, but it's a job. The people down here don't benefit from new innovations. What happens when the scholars discover how to make cheaper automatons to fill the roles of porters, fishermen...hells, even whores?"

"I hadn't considered this…" Jessa paused. "But surely there's a better solution."

Cameron chuckled. "If I could, I'd give everyone money who didn't have it. But that's why I'm not popular in the Assembly. There's no opportunity in Rivern. The more the city progresses, the less it needs its citizens. Less use it has for refugees. There's no refuge for them here in Rivern."

Jessa nodded. "Then what would you advise?"

"You won't like what I have to say. The ones who come here are too destitute to start over, even if they had homes to return to." Cameron sighed. "If I were in your shoes, I'd use my connections to the empress, reunite Amhaven with Thrycea."

"My people fought bitterly for their independence," Jessa recalled. "Thousands died under my grandfather's rebellion to throw off the yoke of imperial influence."

"And how many of those who sacrificed still live today?"

Jessa nodded stiffly and followed him back to the lifts to the Overlook.

As they walked back to Silverbrook Manor, Jessa said, "Perhaps I should abdicate my claim."

Cameron looked at her with curiosity and disbelief. "Your Majesty, it was a shit show down there, but it's hardly reason to give up. You made a good effort, and no one can fault you for that."

"People died. In front of me," Jessa protested. "And it's all because of a dispute over my claim. I can't allow this fighting in my own kingdom to continue and say it's for the good of my people when they clearly suffer. I can't defeat Rothburn, and he can't defeat me, so he attacks those who are defenseless. If one of us is to lead, then perhaps it's best that it be a duke with no ties to Thrycea."

Cameron paused as the first drop of rain fell on his hand. He looked to Jessa. "Have I said something to upset you, Your Majesty?"

Jessa looked up at the clouds as more rain splashed across her face. "This isn't my doing, but I'm certain to be blamed for it."

The rain fell harder.

Cameron raised a hand to shield his eyes. "Can you becalm this weather? It's some distance to your residence."

"Oddly we can only make storms. We have no dominion over what Kultea sends of her own volition," Jessa confided.

The rain descended in sheets, causing her to laugh. The roar of falling water echoed off the street and the Trident River. The few people in the street scrambled for cover as merchants hastily covered their wares with tarps. She had to yell over the rain, "I can't soothe the storm. We need to get inside."

She grabbed Cameron's hand and led him down the street. Her clothes were soaked, and the raindrops lashed her eyes, but she felt nothing. Cameron stumbled behind her, blinded and shivering from the ice-cold water that clung to his coat and shirt.

They raced down the street, Jessa focusing on pushing as much of the water away as possible. Deep puddles split before them as she navigated through the downpour. They raced down streets and alleys until they arrived, breathless, at the gates of the Silverbrook estate.

Still holding his hand, she waited with him in the storm as the automaton gate recognized her and retracted.

"I should take my leave, Your Majesty." Cameron offered a slight bow.

Jessa grabbed his hand again. "Nonsense. You're soaked. Come inside."

He didn't resist her as she tore open his shirt the moment they walked through the door. Cameron was a sturdy man with a firm chest—more rugged than handsome, but he exuded a raw flavor of masculinity. He pressed his mouth to hers, scraping her face with his rough stubble. He shrugged off his shirt and coat, revealing his ripped torso. His black hair was peppered with gray, and long thick scars ran across his right chest and abdomen.

"Your Majesty…I'm old enough to be your father," he started.

She covered his mouth. "My proper style of address is 'Your Grace,' and I find you incredibly appealing."

His kiss was hot and firm as his tongue explored her mouth. Jessa surrendered herself to the experience of his hands squeezing her breasts. The length of his hard cock pressed against her as he pushed her against the wall. His burly hand moved with practiced precision as he unfastened the back of her dress.

Impatiently she grabbed the collar and ripped herself free of her garment, letting the delicate fabric tear with a satisfying ripping of the seams. Encouraged by her efforts, Cameron joined in earnest, yanking and pulling at the garment till it fell ruined to the floor. He paused, in awe of her nakedness, with a look of unbridled animal lust gleaming in his eyes.

She set to work freeing his cock from his trousers. First she unfastened his belt and whipped it free. She kept it in one hand as she forced her other hand down the front of his pants. She felt his hardness twitch in her fingers as she ran them through his coarse pubic hair. She squeezed his girth and directed it upward so the head of his cock peered over the rim of his pants.

She took the leather and looped it around Cameron's neck and led him into the solarium. He followed her, allowing her to pull at him, his eyes fixed on her breasts. He forced his trousers down and stepped out of them as he followed. Jessa paused to let him kick off his boots and ran a finger up his muscular, hairy thigh.

His cock was rigid and already dripping with seed. He was hunched over and panting, ready to fuck her, waiting for her to pull him close.

Jessa tugged the belt, and Cameron fell on her. His lips were all over her neck; his hands slid up her buttocks and back. He lifted her and brought her down on his throbbing dick. Jessa moaned as he slid inside her. The belt slipped from her hand as she returned the embrace and kissed him passionately.

Gently he lowered her to the floor and lay back, letting her ride him. Jessa writhed, exploring sensations from the angles of his manhood inside her as he bucked beneath her. His hands massaged her breasts as their bodies found a rhythm and built toward climax.

Thunder crashed outside, and hard rain pelted the windows of the solarium. Out of the corner of her eye, Jessa noticed an automaton with a feather duster attending to a sculpture.

She arched her back and felt the power of Cameron's cock sliding into her wet cunt as she guided it to her spot. She smelled his musk and felt the slippery sheen of his sweat as she pressed her fingers on his heaving chest.

Jessa came hard, but Cameron didn't stop. With each thrust, her body shivered in ecstasy as thunder clapped outside. It was more than she could take, but she didn't want it to stop. She grabbed his nipples and pinched. She felt the electricity build in her own body and released it through her skin—a low, gentle shock that went straight into Cameron's aching balls and nipples.

"*Unf!*" he bellowed, as his back arched and his hips pumped against hers. His legs shook, and his eyes rolled back in his head from his explosive orgasm. Gasping and spent, Jessa rolled off his cock onto the floor beside him.

"That was amazing," he panted, "Your Grace."

"Yes," Jessa agreed. "Now I know why Mother always has made such a fuss about sex."

He laughed. "Don't tell me I'm your first."

"It's the first time I enjoyed it." She rolled over and laid her head on his chest. "My mother sent for a priest of Kultea to initiate me when I turned thirteen. That side of my family takes a dim view of virginity."

He ran his fingers through her hair. "That sounds horrible."

"Alicio," Jessa recalled. "He was fifteen and very kind. We discussed religion more than seduction. I could never…feel the flash of passion with him, but I learned to fake it so he wouldn't be punished. Everyone in the castle knew my mother's cries of passion, but I must have sounded absurd, parroting her. Mother had him killed anyway."

"Because he couldn't satisfy you?" Cameron's face darkened.

Jessa frowned. "No, she suspected him of being a spy for my aunt Sireen, so she accused him of heresy. She said he was a follower of Kondole rather than Kultea. He was from Mazitar, where such practices remain, and she was of high enough station that she could act as she saw fit."

Cameron grabbed her hand. "I'm sorry you had to endure that."

Jessa squeezed his hand in return. "I share this with you only to assure you that you haven't stolen my innocence, nor am I some delicate flower to be protected. I gave myself to you because I decided it."

"Your cousins won't approve of this," he mumbled, as he nuzzled the nape of her neck.

She craned her head against his and smiled. "I don't imagine *anyone* will approve of this."

BLOODLINES (SATRYN)

My twin,

I wish you could someday join me in the Abyss, at least to experience it for your-self. Seven miles beneath the ocean, you can truly realize the power of our Heritage.

Though my title is for all intents and purposes an exile, I reign over more sub-jects than our mother does. I don't think anyone realizes how much life and civiliza-tion is down here. None but the imperial line could survive the crushing weight of the sea, so I'm relieved of the tiresome, petty intrigues of court.

Yesterday I swam the Agnathan water singers' grotto, navigating by echoloca-tion—a sense I didn't even know I possessed! To perceive the world as a canvas of sound textures and liminal vibration is far beyond the limited scope of vision. Words don't do it justice.

I'm truly and finally happy in this strange realm. I'm not just their emperor but a God and the voice of Kultea. How I weep at the thought of a lowly Genatrovan placing his hands on your ivory skin, putting his common seed inside you.

Seek your vengeance as you must, but it is here where you belong—with me, dear sister. Let Nasara have her throne of brittle coral. Let Sireen parade around in her ridiculous garb like the tiresome strumpet she is. Even my lowliest estates surpass the Coral Palace in their majesty. The sky is empty, and the sea is limitless.

Yours always,
Maelcolm, emissary to the Abyssal depths

Satryn reclined on a sofa in the center of her cell, which now featured a sit-ting area for visitors. The Grand Invocus had been most accommodating in letting her entertain discussions with inquisitive scholars from the Lyceum.

Mistrust had given way to curiosity, and she had been filling her days by granting various audiences with curious visitors.

Magus Quirrus adjusted his spectacles as he peered into his copper dish. "I must say, Lady Satryn, I'm incredibly grateful for the opportunity to study a Stormlord's humor. Aside from the Patreans' complete lack of arcane aptitude, it's the only example of hereditary theurgical capability we've been able to discern."

Have you also looked at Jessa's blood? Probably not. The girl might as well be a Genatrovan but for her silver eyes.

She smiled. "In Thrycea our blood mages are priestesses of Kultea. It's equally curious for me to meet one who learned his trade outside the teachings of our faith. What was it exactly that drew you to blood magic?"

Quirrus blushed. "I…um…I was always fascinated by blood. Even as a boy. I know that sounds odd, and perhaps it is, but I always knew this was my calling. There's something sublime and mysterious about the humors."

He was a handsome man but for those stooped shoulders, which bespoke of his timidity. Beneath his crimson robes she appraised him as a decent specimen of manhood, especially considering his age. But if he was aware of his attractiveness at all, it didn't display in his nebbishy demeanor.

"I find blood quite fascinating as well," Satryn said, "and intimate. Blood is something we aren't supposed to see, like a bride beneath her veil. Yet when it appears, it commands our absolute attention."

"Oh, it does!" Quirrus said excitedly as he peered at her sample in his dish. "Yours tells me so much about who you are, where you came from, your capabilities. your possibilities. I am curious, though…who was your father?"

Satryn reached for her wine. The Grand Invocus turned out to have quite the interest in vinology and had sent her a bottle of an exceptional white eclu from the Lowlands to compare tasting notes when he came for her nightly interrogation, which quickly had devolved into little more than an excuse for them to debate politics. He made formidable arguments for a man not known for speaking.

"My father was a master electrician in Thelassus, responsible for collecting lighting from the Everstorm and powering the city's lights and telegraphs," Satryn mused. "I suppose he'd be the equivalent of your artifact mages or guild of engineers. He wasn't as prominent as the empress's other consorts, but when your mother is the empress, the father's status matters less than birth order."

"So the empress isn't married?" Quirrus asked.

Satryn understood his confusion. She explained, "Her husband, the imperial consort, is her cousin, Clavus. He's the most powerful member of a separate, distantly related bloodline. But that union is purely political. He isn't much older than I am.

"The offspring of the empress are born to different fathers, lesser consorts. This allows her to maintain a healthy line of succession and give favor to her political allies in the form of heirs. Nasara is the daughter of King Pentios of Veyal, and Sireen is the daughter of Viceroy Bu'ma ibn Atid al-Or. My twin brother and I are the only two in recent history to share both parents."

Quirrus leaned forward. "Fascinating. And why does such a practice exist? I imagine the union of two Stormlords would produce more powerful offspring."

"It does." Satryn finished her wine and poured two more glasses. She handed one to Quirrus, who hadn't finished his first. "However, I believe there's a Genatrovan saying that states, 'Branches that grow too close together bear odd fruit'...or something of the like. Pureblood Stormlords tend to be...*unpredictable*, to put it lightly."

"That's interesting, because your mother and father's humors share the same characteristics as yours, which leads me to conclude he was a Stormlord and very closely related to your mother."

Quirrus set his bowl down on the mahogany table. The inside of the copper dish was etched with finely detailed symbols and geometric patterns. While he was swishing it, some of her blood had collected in the grooves, forming a complex diagram. Satryn had seen similar implements used by the priestesses.

She peered into it, but of course the pattern didn't make any sense to her. "Your inexperience has led you to a false conclusion. Children of Stormlords tend to favor that side of the family, with very little from the consort. None of us much resemble our fathers. Except Jessa, who was so much like her father that I wouldn't have believed she was mine if I hadn't pushed her out of me. And I'm still uncertain whether she isn't a changeling." Satryn laughed.

"A changeling?" Quirrus's eyes lit up.

Satryn waved her hand dismissively. "Her great-grandfather, Raegur, was supposedly the son of the Witch Queen, according to local folklore. I had Jessa tested when she was born—the blood priestess found nothing, much to my disappointment."

Quirrus pondered the bowl. "Perhaps I should look into this matter. It seems your priestesses missed a fairly obvious family connection. They may have overlooked it with Jessa as well."

"No offense to your college, Magus, but blood magic in Thrycea is a far older and more established school of theurgy. As a child I had my blood read more times than I care to recall by the most senior of Kultean priestesses. And none of them brought my parentage into question."

"With respect, we practice the *science* of blood magic, not the religion." Quirrus finally was showing some backbone. "It can't be any more plain to even an utter novice that you were born from the union of two Stormlords. The only reasonable question is why anyone would go through the trouble to conceal it from you."

Satryn opened her mouth to reply, but the words died on her lips.

She breathed in sharply and set her glass down. "By Kultea's cold tits…"

Quirrus bit the side of his finger nervously, his conviction wilting. "I didn't mean to upset you. I was merely making an observation based on the empirical data. There are always factors that can't be accounted for…Even in blood magic, we find that sometimes predicted outcomes don't always match the anticipated results."

She wasn't paying any attention to him. *Uncle Nash always showed an unsettling interest in me. Was it him? It would explain the shark I got on my fifth birthday and the jewelry every year after.*

Who else in the family knows about this? Nasara most certainly…Why else would she go to such elaborate lengths to have me sent away while that little idiot Sireen parades around court?

And my brother…sent to be the emissary to the Abyss. I thought it was their intent to separate us, but…were they secretly afraid? Two purebloods in line for the Coral Throne, though I'm older by a scant few minutes.

"Lady Satryn, are you all right?" Quirrus asked cautiously.

She smiled, breaking from her reverie. "This has been a revelation, Magus Quirrus. Though it is somewhat…embarrassing to realize one is a product of incest in the company of a respectable gentleman like yourself, it has given me great clarity regarding my current situation. The blood priestesses of Thrycea could learn a thing or two from your intellectual rigor."

"Well, I certainly would be amenable to an exchange of knowledge. It seems wasteful that we should pursue the same discipline in parallel," he said enthusiastically, if also unsurely.

She leaned back on her sofa and glanced back to the Invocari who guarded her cell. They had replaced the last one with a rather sour-looking woman.

"Test Jessa," Satryn said. "Only Mother would have the authority to meddle in the results of the Red Liturgy. I ask you as a friend, out of concern for my daughter. But don't mention what we discussed. I don't want to upset her."

Quirrus nodded eagerly. "I will arrange it."

THE DEATH ROOM (MADDOX)

The reason Volkovians are masters of necromancy lies in our cultural heritage. We survive winters that bring armies to their knees. There is a saying: "If Volkovia is invaded, wait six months." During the entire month of Frostbane, we don't see the sun. It's natural that our thoughts turn to death, for it is around us always.

In Vicheryad our dead are always with us. The bones of our ancestors guard our city, clean our streets, and repair our roads. What need have the departed souls for their skeletons? Is a shoemaker buried with his hammer and shears? Any Volkovian gladly donates his flesh to the service of his family and province when he passes.

Yet necromancy is maligned at every turn by those who don't understand our way. People will wave their hands and say, "Oh, no! Look at Pytheria—she killed all those students for her own experiments." But meanwhile no one is claiming all seal mages are Achelon the Corruptor.

The continued sanctions against the Lyceum for opening a necromancy college are prejudicial and punitive. If every modality of theurgy were to be judged by its worst actors, then there would be no magic.

—letter from Ivan Zacharov, dean of necromancy at the Vicheryad Institution of Learning, to the Council of Deans

Maddox found himself staring at a closed door. He was standing in what looked like an abandoned pantry. The shelves were crammed with silver dishes, ornately carved jewelry boxes, statuettes, and loose gemstones. He heard a splash of water below the floor, so he knew he was in the Backwash, and he heard voices upstairs.

He turned his head slowly to survey the room. Falco stood slightly in front of him, facing the door. He was shirtless, and his wiry back hair made his flesh look ghostly pale. The mouth on his side was gaping open and moving slightly.

"You were right. That was fucking *incredible*!" Maddox said, slapping him on the shoulder. Falco turned his head slowly, his eyes missing. The sockets had been burned out, and fine black veins spidered out from the holes.

"Guides preserve…" Maddox stepped back, tripping on a rolled-up carpet and clashing into the shelves. A jewelry box tagged him on the shoulder and burst open, spilling strings of pearls that clattered on the floor. Grabbing his shoulder, Maddox reached for the door.

Falco's head tilted, and he emitted a gurgling, chittering noise from his throat as he sniffed at the air. *A fucking revenant.* Maddox hurled him against the opposite wall of the pantry and levitated an assortment of silver serving dishes to form a barrier. Falco thrashed at them with inhuman strength and dented the metal.

Maddox opened the door and slipped out backward as the revenant flailed against his prison. The door shut abruptly, and a chair slid under the handle, locking it in place. As Maddox was no longer able to see his plate barrier, it clanged to the floor. He heard a fervent pounding against the door that nearly took off the hinges, but it stopped abruptly.

Maddox stood in the dreary ruins of an abandoned kitchen, but the scene was familiar. He knew exactly where he was.

He felt something sharp and cold press against his throat. "Gran, if you can't control these things I'm going to fucking kill them." Esme's sultry voice was unmistakable.

"Hey! It's me," Maddox said, grabbing her arm. As he turned to face her, her expression grew slack with shock. Her weapon nearly fell to her side.

She smiled. "Holy fucking shit! You're really alive. Riley! Get down here!"

"Yeah. I'm immortal or something," Maddox explained offhandedly. "Look, I need to get some more of that shit Falco had. Like a lot more."

"Whoa there, champ!" Esme stepped back and patted his arm, still smiling playfully. "When you start chasing the dragon, you don't stop with the tail. You were fucking dead an hour ago."

"I figured as much—"

Maddox didn't get another word out before Riley tore into the kitchen and embraced him in a rib-crushing bear hug. It took the better part of five minutes for them to peel Riley off and calm his exuberant blubbering into something resembling coherent speech. The other lodge members watched quietly from the kitchen door.

"I were so messed up about it," Riley said, a catch in his throat. "Me best mate just offed himself not an hour after I got him home. I blamed meself for it. I weren't there for you when you needed me, you know? I were so fucking pissed at Falco for messing you up like that. You was in a fragile state of mind and not in a good way…"

Maddox sighed. "I was pretty sure I'd come back. It happened once when I was pushed off the observation tower, and even fucked-up seals are usually reliable. The drugs were just the cleanest way to test my theory."

"Should have asked me," Esme said sweetly. "There's lots of better ways to go."

"No." Maddox held up one finger. "When I was dying, I saw something. The Guides came to me and lifted my spirit out of my body. They wanted to show me something. Don't you realize? I can see the mysteries of the universe revealed at the exact crossroads between life and death…and I can come back from it."

"I fucking told you!" Riley slapped his knee and pumped his fist. "This guy is the greatest wizard in fucking Creation, he is."

"This should be entertaining," Esme said under her breath.

"Where can I get more drugs?" Maddox asked. "I'll also need alcohol and some equipment. Did Falco have a formula anywhere?"

"So you aren't mad at me?" Riley asked plaintively.

Maddox shook his head in irritation. "What? No. Why would I be?"

"Gran kinda did…her thing on you too," he admitted sheepishly.

Maddox looked at the frail old woman who waved back at him with bony fingers. "You turned me into a revenant? What? Why? To guard that shitty treasure pantry?" He paused, parsing the implication that he hadn't just come back from regular death but undeath as well. "Whatever. I don't give a shit about that."

"You make a good revenant," she said in her gravelly old voice. "So supple and easy to work with. Not like Falco—they're always so crunchy when they die afraid."

He had to hand it to Gran; she wasn't half-baked like the others—at least in the theurgy department. The idea of a doddering old wizard was somewhat of an oxymoron. Magic required sharp faculties and an ability to handle the physical strain of channeling energy. The fact that she could raise two revenants meant there might be much more behind those vacant eyes than she let on.

"And how did Falco die?" Maddox asked, suddenly concerned his formula might be lost. He could guess the ingredients, but it would take a few days of testing to get it exactly right.

"Falco…" Riley's shoulders sank. "I didn't…I were so pissed at him, you know? My last words weren't kind."

"Harrowers," Esme said. "Totally random freak event."

"Tertius died in his sleep after he killed me." Maddox started thinking out loud, "Maybe there's some kind of connection."

"Bastard deserved it," Riley said under his breath.

"There's no connection," Esme said, kicking her legs. "People have been dying all over the city lately. It's no biggie. You should do your thing—unlock the secrets of the universe."

"Yeah," Riley agreed. "We put up some more wards. Should be fine."

"I know it's a big risk," Maddox said, "but this could be the discovery of a lifetime. To actually commune with the Guides in their own realm. The theurgical power we could unlock could make us—"

"Gods?" Riley asked hopefully.

"Maybe. How soon can you get me some more of that shit and a case of firebrandy?"

The first order of business was creating a proper laboratory. As Maddox suspected and partly feared, Falco's notes on the formula were less than exact. He'd thrown a bunch of shit together and hoped for the best without much regard for proportion and timing. The recipe was almost laughably simple. Calling on the full might of the Seal of Ardiel, Maddox was able to tidy up the front area without having to touch any of the garbage on the floor.

For a pack of degenerates, the others were surprisingly efficient as they went about various tasks—all except for Esme, who sprawled cat like on an old bench and flung her dagger at the ceiling. Riley sent Otix and Crateus out shopping while he helped set up the lab—he didn't know much about alchemy. Gran puttered about, redrawing wards with a stylus that had been snapped in half and tied back together with string.

Maddox worked into the late hours of the evening, concocting the euphorium as best he could from Falco's recipe. He made some improvements of course—the quality of Falco's admixture was poor at best, suitable for turning a profit and making a large volume by taking shortcuts and using inferior reagents.

He concocted several drams of green crystal with the materials Crateus and Otix brought back. It was far more than he would need, given that a single hit had reacted so violently with the alcohol in his body last time.

The others were upstairs, whispering and talking. Esme's voice carried throughout the whole house; it was a lovely musical sound that belied the crude, brash content of her words. He packed the hookah and lit the fire. Next to him was a bottle of firebrandy freshly opened and already half empty. He wanted to be alone for this.

He took a hit of his euphorium. The fumes were cleaner and easier on the throat than during his first experience. As the vapor spilled from his mouth, it felt like silk brushing his lips. He allowed himself a small measure of pride about that, even though it was just basic alchemy that anyone could learn if he or she bothered to.

Within moments time slowed to a crawl, and the colors around him intensified to fluorescent hues he'd never seen before. Oranges and greens and purples emerged from the dull palette of the decrepit house, and instead of looking drab, it became a cheerful, happy place. The walls breathed around him as intricate patterns worked their way across everything, hinting at a subtler geometric order to things.

"I'm ready," Maddox said. His mouth moved laboriously to utter the words, "*Sephariel, Azzailement, Gesegon, Lothamasim, Ozetogomaglial, Zeziphier, Josanum, Solatar, Bozefama, Defarciamar, Zemait, Lemaio, Pheralon, Anuc, Philosophi, Gregoon, Letos. Anum…Anum…Anum…*"

His eyes shut, and suddenly he was standing on a vast bluff that overlooked a verdant valley surrounded by mountains. The sun was rising to the east, and rays of golden light washed across his face as the light pushed its way through the mountains. He was staring into the sun, but it wasn't the sun—it was a seal. No… it was *the* seal. It was massive and intricate.

He stared into the face of Creation and realized the seal was its true name.

The blinding light cleared, and he found himself back in his chair, completely sober. Riley leaned on one end of the table. Esme sat on the stairs, playing with her knife. Sunlight poured through the windows.

"It worked!" Maddox exclaimed. "I saw a seal—bigger than a city. Quick, I need a pen and parchment!"

"You okay, Maddy?" Riley asked with a touch of concern. "We was kinda surprised when we found you down here."

Maddox searched desperately around the table for Falco's formulary, but some things had been moved, and it took him precious seconds to find it. He pulled out his leather pouch with his tools and hesitated slightly when he grabbed the gold stylus Tertius had given him. He began to draw what he could remember of the Great Seal on one of the blank pages, careful to get it exactly as he saw it.

"That looks pretty interest—"

"Shh!" Maddox snapped. The memory already was fading, and he'd only seen the top third of the seal. Still he felt his rendering was fair; at least it was a start. "Don't move my journal."

He reached for the firebrandy and hammered it, letting the liquid spill over his mouth onto his clothes. He set the bottle down and waited for the alcohol to hit while he went to grab the small hookah. "I had a full rock in here."

"Otix," Riley said. "He really likes the stuff. And after he tried it, we figured it was safe, so we had a little celebration of sorts. It's a good thing Falco popped off when he did—I don't think he could call himself a proper alchemist after trying that shit."

Maddox checked the flask with the euphorium crystals. There were only two left. "This should have lasted months! What the fuck?"

"Everyone in this house pulls their weight, so if you want to stay here and send us on shopping trips, you need to provide something in return," Esme said.

Maddox cocked his head. "And what do *you* do exactly? I haven't seen you so much as lift a finger since I got here."

"I facilitate."

"Look, we'll get you more supplies," Riley said. "The boys'll be back any moment, and you can make up a bigger batch, right? We need to recover costs and all that."

Maddox already was getting tired of this. He didn't have time to sit around cooking up drugs for a bunch of junkies all day. His exploration was too important. "Gran," he said at last. "The recipe is in this ledger, with my notes. Anyone with half a brain can do alchemy—you don't need me to cook for you. Just have Gran do her reanimation thing after I pass away. With the proper direction, a revenant can make all the euphorium you need."

"I don't like this, Maddy." Riley clutched his body uneasily. "You've changed since you came back. Maybe it's time we slowed down and thought about this…"

"His body. His choice," Esme said.

Maddox packed the hookah and drew another hit. The alcohol was starting to hit him at the same time as the drugs, but he just felt calm and peaceful. He took another hit and another drink and waited for the visions to take hold of him.

This time he was in a library, but there were no walls, only mist curling between massive bookshelves. Pale, faceless figures wandered about. In place of a proper face, each one had a seal. He recognized Ardiel and Sephariel among them. There was another there—a figure with childlike proportions whose face was hidden. It ran from him, and he chased it through a vast, endless library until he cornered it against a shelf. It turned and showed him its face; it was an entirely new seal that he glimpsed for only a second.

Awake.

Maddox reached for his stylus and journal and sketched the seal from memory.

A pair of naked men were watching him. They were twins with ginger hair and yellow eyes. He didn't even pause to admire their bodies as he packed the hookah, only to find a rock already waiting for him. There was a fresh bottle of firebrandy and, he noted, a case of the stuff under his feet.

"Who the fuck are you?" he asked the twins as he gulped the brandy.

"Your roommates," the one on the left said. They were seated on a velvet sofa placed against the far wall. Another new addition.

"How's your leg?" the one on the right asked.

"It's…fine," Maddox said, warily feeling for any injury. "Why? Should it not be?"

The twins smiled at each other. "Nothing you should be worried about. We just want to make sure you're okay."

"I'm peachy. Thanks for asking. Now seriously who the fuck are you?" He gulped again, bringing the bottle down to half empty. He already was feeling the effects.

The twins smiled deviously and, in a single fluid motion, got off the couch and shifted into a pair of large black wolves with yellow eyes. The one on the right barked, and they trotted upstairs.

"Huh. Changelings. Don't see that every day." It was wild magic, the domain of witches and not on the Lyceum curriculum. Witches usually preferred the great forests like Maenmarth to cities, where their affinity for nature strengthened their theurgy. Sometimes their human offspring had their gifts, but it was rare.

Maddox took another hit.

The next vision seemed to last forever. He stood in a hedge maze that he realized was laid out like the Great Seal. He made his way as thoroughly as he could, committing the path to memory.

Awake.

Gran sat on the couch, knitting and humming to herself. On the floor the wolves Themis and Theril gnawed on a bloody bone that looked suspiciously human. Maddox recorded his vision and drank again. When the buzz hit, he took a hit of the smoke and drifted off.

Each time the visions offered only a glimpse before hurling him abruptly back to reality. Drink. Pipe. Smoke. Dream. Die. Awake. Draw. Repeat. Each day he awoke at exactly the same moment: the moment he bound his seal. To him, no time passed, but the passage of time was marked at each waking interval by some minor change.

Some member of the house would be watching him. A fresh bottle and a fresh rock would be ready. A new journal appeared when the old one was filled. He jotted down some notes on the formulation—to prolong the arrival of the drug's fatal onset, to give him more time in the world that he had come to believe was the true reality.

He wandered through a ruined city with square glass towers that reached to the heavens. He consulted sigil-faced prophets in a living library. He aided the White Duchess in her campaign against the Red King in an epic battle across realms and dimensions. He spent a summer as the pleasure slave to a handsome demon lord who used him until he was ragged. He learned dream magic from a six-finned fish that lived in a grotto of glowing fungi.

Eventually Maddox found himself in another house, his supplies still in their same positions. It was a fancy ballroom filled with old furniture covered in white sheets. He couldn't tell at first whether he was dreaming. Esme reclined on one of the covered couches as she flipped through one of his journals.

"Esme?"

"He speaks." She didn't look up from the book. "Don't you need to write down whatever you saw before it goes away?"

"I just learned dream magic," Maddox explained. "You can only know or learn it in dreams. Where are we?"

"The house was getting a little crowded, so we moved in here," she said.

"You didn't answer my question." He flicked his wrist, and the journal flew from her hands and placed itself on the table.

"The DiVarian estate. The widow DiVarian died from a harrowing, as did her heirs shortly after. It's slated for destruction, but I have a friend on the Assembly who says it's going to be months before anyone goes near this place. The whole city's in a total panic. It's beautiful here, really."

"When I've finished my research, I'll be able to stop the harrowings."

She laughed and sat up. "Research? Is that what you call this? Buddy, you have the most hard-core drug habit of anyone I've ever met in my entire existence."

"I see visions that can only be given on the precipice of death. I'm so close to unlocking secrets you couldn't possibly imagine."

"So close yet never actually there," she mused. "There are no great secrets that are revealed to us when we die. Sometimes it hurts, and sometimes you don't even notice, but when you go, there's nothing. Just darkness and oblivion.

Sometimes the fevered mind plays tricks. That's all it is. None of this shit is real, Maddox."

"How many times have you died?"

Esme smirked. "I've seen enough death to know it's not a sacred transition—it's just the machinery of the body failing to support itself. And I've done enough drugs to know what it's like to see a false epiphany conjured from the fabric of my own imagination. Yes, it's draped in meaning and significance and yet…what things do you really know that you can verify?"

"I know you're not what you say you are."

"Oh? What am I then?"

Maddox rubbed his chin and was surprised by the fullness of his beard. "I don't know…but you're way too intelligent to be a sixteen-year-old street orphan. And you're not nearly traumatized enough by the shit you say you've seen."

"You're fucking insane, dude." She tossed the dagger into the air and caught it in her hand. "But we need you to make fifty drams of the good stuff by tomorrow. So you can either get cracking on your own and do your little ritual with the pipe, or I can kill you so Gran can do her thing. Doesn't matter to me."

"In a minute." Maddox grabbed the bottle of firebrandy and chugged. "Where's Riley?"

"Do you care?"

He took another gulp of brandy. "Kind of. I mean, you're like this ruthless murderess, and I wake up in a strange place with just you watching me. Maybe you two had a fight, and you cut him open. Just saying."

"Fair enough." Esme sighed. "But he's busy. You have my word that when you wake up tomorrow, he'll be here. If he's not, then you'll have no problem walking out of here, I'm sure."

She tossed her dagger again, and it froze in midair, the point spinning toward her. She took a step back, but the hovering dagger kept its pace.

"Don't forget"—Maddox smiled—"that knife can't do shit to me."

Esme snatched her blade by the hilt and nodded. "Wouldn't dream of it."

Maddox fired up the hookah and sucked in as much vapor as he could stand. It wasn't as smooth as his original formula, but by the time he started coughing, he already was drifting off into the true reality.

REDA (HEATH AND SWORD)

THREE YEARS PREVIOUSLY...

The witch-hunter shook the rain from his cloak as he stalked into the White Trout Inn. The lightning from the storm outside cast him ominously in silhouette, a lanky shadow of a man with long curls of hair. The tables of drunken fishermen and farmers regarded him warily as he headed to the bar. He slammed his hands on the counter and peered at the bar owner. His teeth were rotten, and his gaunt face was cut by a long scar.

He looked the part.

"I'm looking for the priest," he growled.

"Upstairs. Second door on the right," the innkeeper stammered.

"Shitty weather," the hunter commented offhandedly.

"Y-yes. The queen's moods have been erratic as of late. But the farmers aren't complaining. We need the rain."

"Yeah." He didn't feel like finishing the conversation. The weather didn't read like brontomancy either. Weatherly was a good fifty miles from Reda, and Satryn, empress's brat or not, wouldn't have the juice to maintain a squall this far out.

He headed up the stairs to the rooms and pounded on the door. "Priest! Open up."

The door swung open, spilling warm light into the hallway. Heath leaned against the doorframe, bare from the waist up. His chocolate-colored chest was covered in old scars. He grinned. "Sword, we need to work on your manners. It's impolite to intrude on a gentleman's personal time."

"You need to get dressed," Sword snarled. "Unnatural theurgies are spilling out of the orphanage. You can rub one out when the job is done and this shit hole is behind us."

Heath walked over to a battered old wardrobe and pulled out his leather jerkin. "How many warlocks?"

"Half a dozen to thirteen," Sword said. "I watched the door for most of the day while you were doing Ohan's work in the selectman's office, thank you very much. No one in or out. Best entry point is a pantry door facing the shipyard. And partner, I don't like this weather."

"For your information, I was finessing the local authorities all day. This isn't going to play well for the constable any way it goes down, but I did let him negotiate me into parting with two thousand ducats to fund a new orphanage." Heath slipped on his jerkin. "So you think the storm's related, or is this just another item to add to the growing list of your new host body's dislikes?"

Sword grimaced and scratched his bony hand. "I wouldn't mention if it wasn't important." His current skin suit was prone to irritation and paranoia, which were actually some of its more charming traits. After the untimely death of Lord Dalrymple, the abbess had dug this asshole up out of the bowels of the Invocari prison—life imprisonment, with no hope for execution.

"Noted," Heath said, strapping on his springblades. "Did you happen to come up with a plan for once we get inside?"

"Kill everyone," Sword said.

Heath rolled his eyes. "I was thinking a little more tactically. Your body still looks like it's spent the last twenty years locked in a five-by-five cell. Are you able to fight?"

"Twenty one years, three months, two weeks, and five days…." Sword shut his eyes. "In a hellishly cold ice prison in the lightless bowels of the Invocari dungeons. Sometimes without food or water for days at a time. The only thing that kept me alive was the thought that I didn't deserve the mercy of death."

"Uh-huh." Heath crossed his arms. "Those were all horrible things…that happened to someone else."

"Didn't need to know about them." Sword stared him dead in the eye.

Heath leaned in, his expression softening. "I need to know I can rely on you. So can you get that scrambled head of yours together enough to pull this off?"

"Appreciate the concern"—Sword cracked a smile—"but the abbess ain't no fool. I'm deadly as ever." He extended his hand and flexed his fingers, willing a ball of fire into existence. The flames were mesmerizing as they danced, bending the air around them. The crackle of the blaze was like a song.

"I'll never get used to that." Heath flicked his eyes briefly down to Sword's flame.

"I know lots of magic," Sword replied cagily, "more than anyone's probably forgotten. Just don't like to use it. The whole point of being a sword is to cut, but this body's still too stiff. Try spending two decades in a cell too small to stand in." It was different having seals again; the binding schools of magic were most closely related to the one that had forged him.

"Spell-casting sword, assassin priest…a little different from our normal routine. But this could work." Heath rubbed his chin.

With great effort of will, Sword extinguished his hungry, beautiful flames. The world felt emptier without the presence of all-consuming fire.

Heath grabbed a length of rope out of his backpack and slung it over his shoulder. He secured one end to a metal grappling hook. "I'm thinking we come at this a different way. We don't know what we'll face once we're inside. So let's not go in."

"Burn it down?" Sword smiled gleefully. The house was old and weathered, the wood in need of treatment. The thatched roof would dance in a pageant of fire…if only it weren't wet from the storm. Maybe that was why he hated rainy weather. "Too wet."

"So we burn it from the inside," Heath suggested. "What's the best way to burn down a house?"

"Seriously?"

"Yes," Heath reiterated. "It's not classy, but we can't take on six or more warlocks, and I don't want to wait for the abbess to send backup and cut our bounty. The local clergy are true believers—they would have a crisis of faith over this."

Sword rubbed his bony hands together. "Start in the basement. That'll seal off the exit through the tunnels, if there is one. Some lamp oil on the support beams could bring the whole thing down on itself. The fire will work its way upward, so if we can have fuel there, the blaze will engulf the place fast. What about collateral damage?"

"The fire should stay contained if you actually know what you're talking about." Heath shrugged. "As far as I'm concerned, everyone in that house is a fair target. We have total absolution on this one in any event."

"Tonight?"

"There should be pine pitch at the shipyard. Barrels of it. We'll get it into the cellar first. Then I'll bring it up through the house as far as I can go without being spotted. I'll give the signal, and you start the blaze downstairs. A jump from a second-story window is a broken leg at worst—nothing I can't heal. I'll take out stragglers as they come. You can join me and help finish them off."

"The locals?"

"I explained the situation to the mayor and constable. The citizens can't know this was sanctioned by the Orthodoxy," Heath explained. "If we need a scape-goat, you take the fall as usual. I'll pretend to be a concerned senior officiate of the Orthodoxy ready to offer my healing services. You get a speedy execution, and I carry the blade back to Rivern."

"Every time I think Daphne can't find a worse body, she finds one."

"She won't." Heath smiled. "You're ugly even for you. And you're even more uncouth than usual. And frankly you scare me a little."

"You sure about this?" Sword asked, "It's an orphanage. Some people would have a problem with that."

"Why do you think I had you verify the accusation instead of just laying waste to the target the second we got to this miserable hamlet?" Heath said testily.

"In my day they had actual witch trials," Sword affirmed.

"What's the point of a trial if the verdict's always guilty?"

"When do we start?"

⊱✠⊰

Saint Lucian's orphanage was a simple two-story building on the outskirts of Reda.

In the days of the early church, before the Orsini Council, the real Saint Lucian was a healer of impressive talent known for his predilection for young boys, especially those who had no home. The Cantos remembered him as a pro-tector of lost youth. The council either had a very short memory or a keen sense of irony.

Sword had been tempted to take two barrels of pitch from the shipyard, but his body was still feeble, and Heath, naturally, refused to carry anything. Sword's Seal of Movement dragged one barrel along as they made their way through the driving rain to the orphanage.

Heath took only a few seconds to pick the lock on the back door. Sword tapped the doorframe with his blade to dispel the warding enchantments. He had been forged to cut through magic as well as flesh, and modern theurgies were weak at best. They broke like glass.

The door led to a darkened pantry and a set of stairs leading down to a cellar. There were no lights on the first floor. The sounds of children chanting echoed from upstairs, like simple rhymes of playground in a language long forgotten. Heath moved quietly as he found a stout metal pot and held it out in front of him.

Sword waved his hand, and the lid on the pitch barrel pried itself off and silently floated near a pile of firewood next to an iron stove. He willed a tendril of the viscous substance to collect in Heath's pot.

They shared a nod, and Sword went downstairs, the pitch barrel hovering in tow. In his early life, he had been joined with mages of incredible power, so the novelty of his host's seals gave him only the slightest bit of pleasure. He doubted his vessel could even pull off a basic Sarnite hex, but one made do with the tools one was given.

The cellar was completely dark, so he brought a small flame to his finger, no more than a candle. If the people who ran this place had any notion of fire safety, it didn't show. Laid out on shelves were a cornucopia of dry flammable materials: bedding, grain—hells, even lamp oil—to say nothing of the cobweb-encrusted shelves they rested on.

Sword swatted at his shoulder, and his fingers brushed against something small and foreign. He snatched it in his hand and brought it in front of him. A hairy spider crawled slowly across his palm.

Memories returned of his time in the lightless oubliettes in the deep earth. Things crawling over his shivering, naked body, through his hair. Centipedes, spiders…*Fucking spiders! What do spiders even have to eat so far underground?* The arachnid reared up, its legs retracting from the rising heat in Sword's palm.

The spider started fervently in each direction, desperate to escape the slowly growing heat. Sword smiled as smoke rose from its body. It flipped over in its final death throes, its tiny legs flailing up at the sky. Sword maintained the rippling heat at a low, even rate until the body was still and crispy.

He relished the taste as he popped the creature into his mouth and crunched it between his teeth. There was a trick to getting them to that perfect level of smoky flavor.

"Mmmmph!" a woman's muffled voice said.

Sword cast about the cellar until he found a sac of webbing he'd mistaken for a pile of sheets. It was roughly woman shaped—and a hefty woman at that. A single blue eye peered desperately from the strands of spider silk.

He pulled out his blade and ran it against the cocoon. It was tougher than silk should have been, but he could cut through the enchantment. Hands and limbs burst from the silk and frantically grabbed at the strands, shredding them now that the spell had been broken.

The woman looked to be middle-aged, with corn-silk-blond hair and a haunted expression. She blubbered, "Please, please, please…don't kill me! I have a grandson and a good-for-nothing husband and a lousy job, but I don't deserve to die here."

"Run," Sword said.

She picked herself off the ground, hands brushing furiously at the sticky webbing. "You're not one of them?"

Sword peered at her and raised his blade to her neck. "Are you?"

"No!" Her eyes were wet with tears.

Sword indicated the door with his head.

"Thank you."

"Wait."

She froze.

He reached out his hand and pulled a spider out of her hair with his seal. The thing floated helplessly above his palm. "Now you can go."

She laughed. She couldn't help it. The whole situation was probably too much, and Sword wasn't going to make it any better by eating another fried spider in front of her. But he wasn't used to eating regularly, and the first one had whetted his appetite.

"Get the fuck out of here," he scolded.

"Is it safe?" Suddenly overwhelmed with worry, she glanced up the stairs to the pantry.

"You're ten feet from the exit, you stupid…" Sword sighed and handed her his blade. "Look, just take this and leave it outside when you're clear of this place. I'll be able to find it. And if you have any mind to keep it…don't."

She took it in her hands and raised it in front of her. "Thank you," she whispered as she fled up the steps.

Sword cooked the spider, ate it, and went back to work. He willed the pitch barrel to the center of the room and, with his mind, brought forth long tentacles of sap to caress every flammable surface in sight.

Absently he brushed another spider off his shoulder and saw two more on his hand. They burned to ash instantly, but a carpet of swarming arachnids poured out from the ceiling and the cracks in the basement foundation. He felt a hot sting of agony as one bit his neck.

As if on cue, he heard Heath's muffled shouts from upstairs. It was a shrill string of panicked expletives consistent with one being covered in venomous spiders.

He sifted through the memories of his borrowed life. He thought back to those sunny spring days in the Lyceum courtyard, sketching with his fellow

Scholars. He wanted to be an engineer, to use his Seal of Fire to power the steam engines of Rivern's great industry. He remembered setting his first fire…and his last. It wasn't a lot as far as happy memories went.

He lit the blaze.

An effulgent conflagration blinded him as tendrils of flame raced over everything in sight. The heat scorched his skin. He was immune to the flames he emanated but not fire that burned its own fuel. That's why they had kept him naked, why they had fed him soggy slop, why they had imprisoned him in that cold dank cell.

The crackling fire ate mercilessly at the wood and fed gluttonously on the pitch as the licks of fire climbed higher and the scent of smoke filled the wavering air. The roar and crackle spread through the house. Spiders died in droves, emitting high-pitched, tormented screams as the blaze consumed their bodies. His own agony was an afterthought.

Sword cackled maniacally as he turned his fire on full blast, pulling at the weakened support of the building with his other seal. *Heath will be fine.* His skin crawled with raw anguish, but the paralytic in the spider venom provided a buffer that kept him from completely shutting down. He worked at the support beam until it broke, bringing tons of flaming timber and ash on top of him.

And the tortured soul finally would be delivered to the embrace of his life-long love.

⚊⊹ ⊹⚊

Sword watched the blaze from behind a barrel in the alley.

She smacked her forehead. "I told you to just leave it, you stupid…" As she sifted through the recent memories, it became apparent that she had recognized the monetary value of the blade and wanted to do the noble thing by returning it to the man who had saved her, even though every second she remained had terrified her half to death.

Sword stood and brushed her hair back, raised her blade in front of her, and walked toward the inferno. The screams were a mixture of human and inhuman. An upper-story window encrusted with swarming spiders slowly revealed the blaze within as the creatures died off one by one. But nothing came through the pantry except smoke and the hot ripple of air.

Absently she noted, from a memory that seemed almost too distant to recall, that the windows probably would blow out at any moment. The fire somehow was still accelerated by seal magic, which normally wasn't possible, but sometimes seals worked better than they were intended.

She headed toward the front. Broken glass from an exploding window sprayed into the alley, just missing her.

Heath lay in the muddy street, one leg angled painfully beneath his prone body. His hands were pressed against this chest, softly glowing, as dual pinpricks of Light sparkled across this skin like twinkling stars in a night sky, sealing shut hundreds of spider bites. He didn't look happy.

A flaming figure hurled itself from the window—a child in a night-robe flailing wildly. She struck the ground beside them with a thud, and the body disintegrated into a swarm of spiders. The fire clung to their carapaces as they curled, juddered, and burned to a crisp.

"It's not like you to land badly, love," Sword said cheekily as she stuck her hand in the rain.

Heath healed his shattered leg with the last flicker of his Light and dragged himself to his feet. "Sword?"

"Name's Catherine," she said. "To the locals anyway. Not Cathy or Cath or Katrina or Kate or Caitlin or Kitty or Kay…and most certainly not Sword if I'm to be your cover story about why you're out here, dressed in assassin's clothes in front of a burning home for abandoned children.

"Also…I'm forty eight, a proud grandmother, raising my deceased daughter's son, and please don't ask who the father is. I work as a knife sharpener because my lousy husband is too much of a drunk to keep a job, and he's too busy whoring around to notice that I was detained by an evil spider cult in the basement of an orphanage and to alert the proper authorities…who likely could have handled this whole thing without calling in a pair of witch-hunters, thank you very much."

Someone yelled, "Fire!" in the distance.

"Ah. That would be Henry," Catherine explained. "Bit of a busybody since he lost his leg. Spends most of his time looking out his window and most definitely saw the whole thing. Given that you're the only black man who'd set foot within a ten-mile radius of this backwater, it's a fair wager he'll have a good physical description when the guard comes running."

Heath shook his head. "I don't feel good about any of this."

"Nonsense, love," Sword reassured him. "I'm a pillar of this community and a regular fixture at church events. I'm a volunteer in the fire brigade even…Now if that's not ironic, I don't know what is, given my previous situation. We haven't had a fire in Reda in years."

Expressionless, Heath stared at the fire. "No. I don't feel good about what we do. You didn't see what I saw up there. Those children—they turned them into unholy things. And all I could think was that I can make triple the bounty fetching artifacts. This is bullshit."

"Been saying that for years," Sword said, "although I did just rescue myself, so…I may have a different perspective on the work we do."

"Daphne could have sent anyone." Heath's gaze didn't leave the fire. "This nest was a cakewalk. She sent me because she thinks I'm weak—that because I prefer to talk my way out of things, I won't make hard choices."

"She's grooming you to take her place, love," Sword said, admiring the blaze. "Bloodthirsty zealots are a dime a dozen these days. Give them a license to kill and they're happy, but the best soldiers don't always make the best generals… unless you're Patrean—then it's all the same."

"I don't want her position."

A crowd of villagers was gathering at one end of the road. Some carried buckets, others weapons. There was shouting. A few of the town guard came running to the front, including their portly Patrean constable.

"You know what the real tragedy is?" Sword mused. "Besides the obvious, of course, it's that most of those kids had parents living here, *in this very town*, who were too ashamed to raise bastards. Hell of a thing. Well, that's what Harrowers do, I suppose. They show us at our absolute worst. Hold up…Who's that?"

Sword peered at a figure standing against one of the buildings. She didn't recognize him, and she knew pretty much everyone in town. *Someone's father perhaps?* He was gaunt and ancient, leaning on a crooked staff like a shepherd might carry. An odd thing to see in a Lowland fishing village. And his eyes were so cloudy they were nearly white, yet they were somehow familiar.

Heath grunted. "You think he's a warlock?"

Sword shrugged. More people were spilling onto the street, huddled in their oiled cloaks against the rain as they jockeyed to see the source of the commotion.

"Halt!" the constable yelled to Heath and Sword, waving a blade. He was trotting quickly for a man of his impressive girth. Some of the village men behind him were literally carrying pitchforks, bless their little hearts.

"Evening, Barney." Sword sighed as she cracked her knuckles. It felt good to finally be the one doing all the talking.

TODAY...

"Evening, Barney," Heath muttered as Sword's memories disintegrated and he found himself lying on the docks.

Sword straddled him, smacking his cheek, his scarred Patrean face etched with worry. "Wake up, mate."

Heath rolled over and vomited hard against the boardwalk behind the Mage's Flask. He clutched his stomach and channeled his Light, but it did nothing to abate the nausea.

"The fuck did that shit do to you?" Sword gently rubbed Heath's back.

Heath caught his breath. "It showed me your memories back when you became Catherine. I know where we need to go."

MINAS CREAGORIA (MADDOX)

Don't get me wrong, diary—I love that Maddox is a part of our little family, but I'd be dishonest if I didn't say I wish he'd spend more time alive than dead. I know he's got important experiments, and we need him to make the drugs and whatnot. But I miss me old buddy always teasing me in the playful way he does it. Like a big brother to me, he is.

Well, I were right pissed to find out Themis and Theril was helping themselves to me best friend's leg meat. But I seen it for meself—every morning the seal lights up for a quick sec, and he's right as rain again. So no harm done, I figure, and the boys get to eat human flesh any time they fancy without someone turning up missing.

It got me thinking, though…the leg bone they cut off was still there, along with the foot. Figured we could get some more parts off him, you know? There's a brisk market for hearts and brains, and Gran doesn't need them to make her revvies. Besides we got Falco working the other alchemy station anyhow and no shortage of new bodies coming in to cover the work.

So then I had me another idea—could Gran make a revvie out of parts she stitched together patchwork-like if they was all from the same body? Her eyes lit up like fireworks, and she says to me, "Charlie, you're a genius! We're going to be published for this!" So I got my own personal Maddox to pal around with.

He don't talk or nothing, but he lets me boss him around and lugs heavy shit out of the houses. He's got the seals on his chest, but they're just tattoos near as I can figure. Every morning I sort of hope he'll wake up and say to me something cheeky, like, "Riley, you fucking idiot, what am I doing here?" or "I'm going to kill you for this, Riley." You know, like Maddox says all the time.

I miss the days when things was easy.

— page from Riley's journal

Maddox sat in the grass, scribbling a seal onto a piece of parchment. Birds chirped from their perches in the flowery trees that shaded the park. Dotted across the lawn were fabulous living topiaries that gamboled between the fountains and flower beds. A gentle trickle of water flowed from a fountain beside him. In the distance the sun was setting over the skyline of an ivory city. Spires and domes took on the yellow and orange hues of sunset. Floating towers circled above the city in a languid dance.

A woman sat on a nearby marble bench, watching. Her hair was golden and wavy. She bore traces of a smile and a patient expression as she studied him. She wore long white robes.

Maddox looked up from his seal. His hands were black with charcoal. "I'm dreaming again, aren't I?"

She nodded. "If you have to ask, the answer is usually yes."

He stood and wiped the charcoal on his brown britches. The ground around him was littered with drawings and designs of various sigils and emblems. He looked at them intently, trying to commit them to his memory.

The woman stood and walked toward him. Her hand rested on his shoulder. "The Grand Design can only be learned in parts. You've seen all you're going to on this voyage."

"I just need to remember more." Each time he was resurrected, the lore was purged from his mind, although he retained fragments and memories.

"I want to show you something," she said, pulling him gently.

He didn't want to go, but almost without transition, the scene shifted to a long walkway, bordered on either side by rows of flowery trees with boughs that formed an arch overhead.

"I need to learn that seal," Maddox insisted, but when he looked around, the drawings were nowhere to be found.

A young couple sat on a bench, feeding each other softly glowing red fruits out of a golden bowl. Everyone in the park looked youthful and healthy. They wore loose clothing or sometimes nothing at all, their perfect sculpted bodies bare to the balmy air.

She explained, "This is what Minas Creagoria used to look like."

"It's pretty," Maddox said, admiring the scenery. The path they walked was both a park and a street. Monolithic buildings with gentle edges and inviting arches flanked the edges of the wide thoroughfare.

They reached an intersection of treelined streets. A central fountain bubbled as helixes of water floated around the statue of a woman. She headed left, and Maddox followed her.

"What are you?" he asked.

"I don't understand your question."

Maddox rolled his eyes. "Look, every time I'm about to die, I have a dream. You're always here, telling me information I would have no way of knowing. Am I completely imagining you, or are you something else?"

"Both." She continued to walk. "But I think the answer you're looking for is why I'm here."

"Okay, that would be helpful information," Maddox acknowledged.

"You asked what I am, and that question is unanswerable. I am, have been, and will be many things. We've been called Guides, and our purpose in this instance is to teach and reveal truths, as we did for your kind when they arrived in this place. But we've been called other things as well."

"Which Guide are you? Sephariel?"

"If you like, but your names have no meaning to us," the Guide corrected. "When our actions please you, you call us gods, and when our actions displease you, we're named demons. Who's the person you see in front of you, the form of this woman who guides you?"

Maddox chuckled. "You look like my aunt Cara. About twenty years ago, when she first came to stay with us."

"Was she kind to you?"

"Sort of. I lived with her and my father till I was five. When dad came up from the distillery in our basement, drunk on whatever alchemical mixture he'd concocted that day, sometimes he'd hit me. She never stopped him, but after—"

The Guide was smiling at him, but her expression conveyed deep sadness and remorse.

"Afterward she'd comfort me. She'd say my dad loved me, but seeing me reminded him of my mother, and that was why he was always sad. She'd give me a potion to help with the pain, and when the time came, she got me an apprenticeship through Magus Tertius." He didn't know why he was telling her this, but the dream was taking its own course.

"Magus Tertius practically raised me," Maddox continued. "I never went back home. I'd see Dad sometimes on Alchemists' Row or Aunt Cara doing the shopping in the marketplace. We never exchanged more than a few words. She looked tired."

"That's why I'm here," the Guide said.

It made sense. Cara had been there at a time in his life when he felt afraid and abandoned.

"I'm sorry for what happened to you," she said, as tears formed in her eyes. "You didn't deserve any of it, and I should have protected you."

"Stop it," Maddox whispered. His eyes stung with sadness and the fresh pain of reopened wounds. He knew dream magic now; he knew how not to get pulled into the story.

"I'm not asking for forgiveness." A tear fell down her cheek. "I just want you to know that it wasn't your fault. I was afraid of your father, but I should have been afraid for you. Instead I lied to you. I betrayed your trust by telling you that man loved you."

"You're not her." Maddox grabbed her shoulders gently. "You want to make up for her mistakes? Then help me. Help me finish the Grand Design. At the very least, tell me what it does."

The Guide straightened her posture and returned to her poised demeanor. She regarded him quizzically.

She continued on the pathway. The scene shifted more rapidly through other parts of the city. They passed an open plaza arranged like a marketplace with tables of wares piled high, yet there seemed to be no merchants. People took what they wanted.

They followed another street. The trees were older and blotted out more of the sun.

"Once you start down that path, you can't stop," the Guide said, brushing her hands against the trunk of a great tree. "The Grand Design gives complete and accurate knowledge of all things to come. It sees all possible outcomes and what must be done to achieve them. Do you understand what that means?"

"Can I change the future that it reveals?" That was an important caveat. Of the thirteen evils Achelon the Corrupter had unleashed, the final one was hopelessness—knowing the inevitable. Even it was too dangerous for the mad king, so he contained it while the other twelve roamed across Creation.

"There would be nothing to stop you," she said after a time, "but you no longer would have your freedom to decide."

"I don't follow you."

"If I offered you a choice between a pleasant fragrance and an eternity of senseless torment, which would you choose?"

"Fragrance, obviously."

"Would you ever choose the other?"

"No."

"Now imagine I've placed each outcome behind a door—one green, one red. Which would you choose?"

"Neither," Maddox scoffed. "There's nothing worth an eternity of torment, especially if all I get out of it is a lousy whiff of something sweet."

"Even in the simple scenario, you made a decision outside the ones I offered. You exercised freedom. Now imagine if I told you the green door holds eternal torment, and you knew that to be absolutely certain. Which door would you choose?"

"I still might not choose either—you really need to come up with a better incentive."

"The fragrance comes from the bloom of the century orchid, at the very moment of its hundred-year blossoming. No living creature but you could ever appreciate its beauty."

Maddox looked at her. "Because it's instantly fatal. Yeah, okay, I might check that out."

"The Grand Design lets you see through the doors, and all the doors that follow. You'd never make a mistake or misjudge a situation. The right choice always would be apparent, so you'd always choose the best possible path. So is that a future you would want to change?"

"But if I made those decisions, I would be changing my future—but to something I wanted."

"You assume that what you want is the best possible outcome. If you were armed with the knowledge of all things to come, and with your illusions about the world shattered by the truth of clear perception, who's to say you would even still care about your desires? Perhaps you would wish to end mankind's suffering only to learn that the best choice for humanity is to allow suffering.

"You may see the only course of action is to continue bumbling through life in solitude and anonymity because the full and true account of things is disastrous knowledge. I can't say for certain. But we've tarried long enough. I wish to enlighten you further."

The Guide walked toward the side of one of the buildings, where Maddox saw a narrow alley filled with grass and wildflowers rather than pavement. Stepping-stones led to a stairwell to some kind of a cellar.

The stairwell was dark. Whereas the architecture of the city had seemed soft and inviting, the stone here felt oppressive. At the bottom was a massive iron door, scribed with green sigils of protection.

"You have to open it," the Guide said.

"A green door? It's not eternal torment, is it?" He smirked at her, but she remained impassive. The door flew open; the sounds of screams and sobs filled the stairwell.

When Maddox and the Guide walked in, they found a large square room with tunnels branching off each of the walls. In the center stood a tank of heavy crystal with motes of light swimming through a briny green liquid. Around the edges of the wall, cots were set up with women chained to them. They were naked and ghostly white, with large pregnant bellies.

A hairless man in white robes glided from cot to cot, serene and oblivious to the shrieks of pain and terror. One of the women cried out in pain as her body pressed against the cot. She looked ready to give birth. The other women babbled incoherently and sobbed.

"Is this some sort of slave pen?" Maddox asked.

"Worse than slaves. They never learned to speak," the Guide whispered in his ear. "They live their entire lives down here like animals."

"What the fuck, Cara?" Maddox recoiled in horror. "What is this place?"

"In the late Second Era, this is how your people used our gifts. They didn't need their slaves in any great numbers because theurgy provided for all their comfort. But they still needed living sentient beings to power their theurgy. Look there."

She pointed to the robed man as he bent over the woman about to give birth. He placed his hand on her head and another on her stomach. Golden Light flooded into her pregnant belly. Then, with practiced quickness, he reached his hand through the wall of her abdomen as if digging through a jar for cookies. The woman kicked and shouted, but after a moment, he yanked a screaming infant from her.

"Holy shit."

"Imagine the horror of this times a hundred. Times a thousand. Times a million. Times a billion. In every city, save for Archea."

The robed man waved his free hand, and the umbilical cord dissolved into particles of golden sunlight. He took the child toward the tank, and while it was still screaming, he cracked its neck. The infant's lifeless body exploded in a burst of luminance and coalesced into a pulsating speck of energy that flowed into the tank. It was brighter than the rest. Maddox noticed many more dim specks of light whirling through the liquid.

He couldn't speak.

"Would you put an end to this if you had the power?"

"Definitely."

"Would you punish the people responsible?"

"I mean, shit…this is totally fucked. Yes."

"And if you could feel their pain and their cruelty as if it were your own, would it drive you to utter madness to know this was all part of the Grand Design?"

"How?" Maddox demanded. "How is this shit even applicable to…aw fuck!"

He clenched his fists in anger as the scene around him dissolved. He was so close to learning something that he could taste it, but his body was failing, drawing him into the oblivion of death.

GROWING PAINS (JESSA)

All modalities of magic, Stormlord Heritage excepted, incorporate the concept of an initiation. For alchemists it's a grueling practicum, while glyphomancers must discover their True Name. Blood-magic initiation, whether practiced in Thrycea or abroad, is perhaps the most curious.

One can only hear the "blood song" once one has contracted the blood fever from another blood mage (or sage, as they're called in the Dominance). The disease causes debilitating pyrexia, which lasts three to seven days, during which there's delirium and a strong aversion to bright light of any kind.

Death is entirely possible but rare. Initiates are carefully screened for viability, and healers are retained to arrest the process should it progress to dangerous territory. Mages who survive the trial become immune to the symptoms of the illness but remain carriers for the rest of their lives. Once the body accepts the illness, it can't be healed, unless the humor is fully exsanguinated.

It's both an affliction and a source of power. For every use of their power, they must consume their own vital humors and replenish them from others. Patrean blood is especially nourishing—which leads me to wonder whether that wasn't the original intent of the mages who created them.
—Initiation: Principles and Practice in Comparative Modalities, research notes of Dean Tertius of the Rivern Lyceum

Jessa fidgeted nervously as Magus Quirrus drew out his tools: a copper dish and a long needle attached to a vial. He was a mousy man with an unusually strong jaw and delicate hands. Cameron sat next to her in the Silverbrook observatory, holding her hand. Although their affair was now something of an open secret, everyone seemed to welcome the scandal. The rowdy assemblyman fucking an imperial daughter played into everyone's hatred of the Dominance without impugning the good reputation of anyone they actually cared about.

Muriel was quietly livid over the affair but said little. Jessa realized she'd probably worn out her welcome at the Silverbrooks' after her mother had been detained on suspicion of murdering her fiancé. The fact that Satryn refused on every occasion to testify in her own defense only made matters worse.

"As much as I enjoy giving my blood to strangers, might I inquire as to your interest, Magus Quirrus?" Jessa asked.

"Your mother found some anomalies in her humor that the Kultean priests may have concealed from her. As a favor she asked me to reexamine your blood to ensure there are no additional anomalies."

"Will this exonerate her?"

"I'm afraid not, Lady Jessa."

"Then by all means proceed." Jessa offered her arm to the blood mage and looked at Cameron. He squeezed her hand as the needle plunged into her skin and kissed her softly on the neck. "Mother thinks I'm a changeling because I don't share her predilection for pointless cruelty."

"Perhaps you are." Cameron winked and stroked her cheek.

"Nonsense," Jessa said. "I would have transformed before I was eighteen. Believe me, I would have liked nothing better growing up than to have turned into an owl and flown off to Maenmarth to reunite with my great-great-grandmother's people."

"Here we go." Quirrus squirted the blood into the copper basin and observed it. He didn't, to Jessa's mild surprise, taste any of it. The process went on for a good while longer than it would have with the Kultean priests. She wondered whether the Rivern blood mages actually consumed blood to nourish themselves at all.

"I'm glad you came to Rivern instead," Cameron said, smiling.

"Oh, this is…interesting." Quirrus furrowed his brow and looked at Jessa. "Perhaps we should discuss this privately?"

Jessa shook her head. "Anything you have to say, you can say in front of Cameron. We already know I'm a Stormlord. There can't possibly be anything more damning in my blood than that."

"Perhaps we could speak with the queen. This is of some concern to her as well."

Jessa scowled. "Magus Quirrus, you surely aren't an idiot. Please tell me Satryn hasn't convinced you to be her spy. It would likely end as badly for you as it did with Torin."

"No one believes she has anything to do with it," Quirrus assured her.

"She's done worse, with less provocation," Jessa retorted. "Make no mistake—if you know something that's damaging to her, your life is in danger. Tell me what you see."

"You're pregnant," he said, flinching at his own words. "The humor indicates that this happened recently. It's too early to determine the sex, but the father is—"

Cameron leaned forward. "By Ohan."

Jessa placed her hands against her belly. "That's impossible."

"Th-the blood does not lie," Quirrus said hastily. "I'll keep this discreet of course. And I can recommend an alchemist if you want to take care of it early. It's a fairly common remedy for noblewomen, at least in the Free Cities."

"As it is in Amhaven," Jessa said sharply. "Thank you."

It took Quirrus a moment to realize he was being dismissed, but he couldn't be gone fast enough as he gathered his bowl and implements and scrambled toward the door.

"I didn't think I could even have children," Cameron said, disbelieving.

She took a moment to let it all sink in. Her first thoughts were of her mother's reaction. She would be apoplectic. Dark clouds would loom over the Invocari tower for weeks. But after that thought faded, the enormity of it hit her. Being unwed and having consorts was fine in the Dominance, but the people of Amhaven frowned deeply on such behavior. Her child's claim would be even less accepted than hers.

And the father was an assemblyman in Rivern. She doubted the empress would be too happy about that as well. Jessa's thin prospects of marriage in Rivern would be ruined for sure. The countess would have her banished back to Amhaven, where she would wait out her days in Weatherly until her forces fell or she called on her aunt Nasara. There was no good solution to her situation before, but now things looked absolutely bleak.

Cameron placed his hand on hers. "It's okay. It happens from time to time. The potion might make you a little sick for a day, two at most, but after that it'll be like this never happened. We just need to be more careful in the future."

Jessa nodded slowly. "Of course. You're right, although I'll require a stronger remedy. Stormlord bodies are more resilient to toxins, even at early ages. My mother always travels with some."

"You don't have to be scared. No one will know about it."

Jessa looked at him. "What if I want to keep it?"

Cameron's eyes widened. But he gathered himself and took her hands into his. "I would love it every day it was alive. But Jessa, these are precarious times for you and for this city. The timing is just—"

"I know." She nodded again. "I'll take Mother's potion tonight. It shouldn't enfeeble me too badly, and I'll be able to carry on just as I have. Without a home or prospects or a kingdom…" The sky outside grew overcast, but she held back her tears.

"There's a place for you here," Cameron insisted, "and maybe after some time, when all this dust settles, when we've really gotten to know each other, we can try again."

"That's just it," Jessa said. "There isn't a place for me here. My presence is tolerated because the countess thinks she can marry me off to a politically convenient ally and ship me back to Amhaven."

They both started at the sound of a latch coming from behind one of the wooden panels. A soft mechanical sound accompanied the panel as it recessed slightly and slid back. The countess stood behind the wall, looking uncomfortable in the darkened passage behind it. "Well, I can't listen to any of this anymore."

She mustered her dignity and stepped out. "I apologize for my sudden appearance, and I know how untoward it must seem to discover me snooping behind the walls of my own solarium like a scullery maid, but your comments beg me to address them immediately, and I don't think you'd give me the opportunity to answer them by stating them to me directly.

"Jessa, dear." Countess Muriel walked over and took a seat on the other side of her. "I can only imagine what horrors you have endured at the hands of Lady Satryn and her kin, but the Silverbrooks aren't the imperial family. You're as much our blood as you are theirs. If you choose to stay with us, I'll be fully supportive in that endeavor.

"It might make things easier." Muriel tried to say it delicately. "The crown of Amhaven isn't widely coveted here, and Duke Rothburn has extensive relationships with many of the assemblymen. But there is a consensus among some of us that a line of Stormlords could be welcome in Rivern."

"Muriel"—Jessa smiled—"I don't know what to say."

Cameron squeezed her hand. "I'll talk to my allies in the Assembly as well. It's not many, as you know, but you can count on our votes."

Muriel sighed wearily. "I'm sure you have every good intention with your offer, but I think it best if you stayed out of this, Mr.—oh, I do apologize—is Cameron your first name or last? We've never had the pleasure of directly addressing each other, it seems."

"How unfortunate for us both," he answered. "I was an orphan, so my family name is unknown to me, but I doubt in any event that you would have heard of it."

Jessa interrupted, "Why does he have to stay out of it? Cameron is a member of the Assembly. It's shortsighted to turn down any aid at this point. Not that I've made any decision yet, though you've offered me the first real possibility in this situation."

The countess shared a knowing look with Cameron.

He met her stare and looked to Jessa. "There are some people in the Assembly who don't like that voice has been given to the common men and women of Rivern. For my part, I haven't always been cordial to them. Frankly I've told many of them, including your cousins, to fuck off. I'd hoped we could put past differences aside."

"Some may see an association as a political liability," the countess added delicately. "Fortunately we have a good foundation of support. The rest we will need to buy, but there are plenty of seats up for sale, with the elections coming soon. We'll need to act quickly."

Jessa pressed her temples. Give up her claim and stay in Rivern or keep her claim and live under the rule of her mother's family. Under imperial rule, Amhaven would be at war with its eastern neighbor and its largest provider of income. The only question that remained was how badly she wanted to be queen.

She glanced at Cameron. He was one of the most compassionate and principled men she'd ever met, even more so than her father. Father talked a lot about the common people, but he never really understood them.

"Amhaven is my home," Jessa said, "but I don't wish my people to suffer if they don't want me as their ruler. If I were to marry and be coronated as queen, I would have less authority than I would as acting regent."

"Excellent." Muriel patted her on the hand. "Now we're going to have to deal with this scandal. It goes without saying that you must terminate your pregnancy, but if we're to pursue this, you also must terminate your relationship with Mr. Cameron."

Jessa shook her head. "That's out of the question. Without my title, I'll be a queen no more. Why does it matter with whom I share my company?"

Cameron grimly studied the floor. "Rivern dethroned its king when it became a democracy, but the lords still carry their useless titles."

"I know I'm an old snob, and my values are traditional," Muriel said, smiling, "but it will be precisely those people's opinions we need to sway. Your dalliance is amusing because you're young and foreign, but if people think your intentions with Mr. Cameron are serious, then they won't welcome you into society. The last eligible suitor in our family met an untimely end—Ohan rest his soul—and your betrothal is an opportunity."

"To own a Stormlord bloodline," Jessa said. "After everything, that's all I'll ever be reduced to, it seems."

"They just need to believe it's possible," Muriel encouraged her. "After the votes are cast, you can marry whomever you choose. And if after time passes, you still feel a fondness for Mr. Cameron, you can resume your…friendship. But for now there's no harm in at least entertaining other options."

Cameron grumbled, "She means options with more money and proper last names."

"This isn't just about my own prejudice," the countess quipped. "Jessa is a queen, accustomed to a life of luxury and privilege. One that will be all but gone if she doesn't find some other source of income. Unless you want her to end up like another Genevieve Gardner."

Cameron looked as if he'd been slapped. "That's hardly—"

"Fair?" The countess arched her gray eyebrow. "Is it fair that you still have your seat on the Assembly and your business interests while poor Miss Gardner's life is in ruins for running off with you? I heard she was working in a candle shop of all things. Life isn't about fairness, Mr. Cameron; it's about reputation."

"What happened?" Jessa asked.

Muriel said nothing.

Cameron sighed, "Her fucking twat of a father disowned her because of our love."

"And you abandoned her?" Jessa asked.

"We drifted apart," Cameron said. "The candle shop was always her dream, and I made sure she was provided for."

"I will not have to sell candles." Jessa frowned. "I don't care about the money, and I suspect someone with my skills will always have a means to earn coin. I hear the Lowlands have had a particularly dry season, and there's no shortage of pipes that need to be welded," she quipped.

"You'll need a lot of money, Jessa," Muriel said solemnly. "You'll need protection from your family, and the services of the Invocari don't come cheaply. I wish your circumstances allowed for more freedom, but there you have it. I can't stop you, but I won't risk my own reputation to support you in this."

"She's right," Cameron said in a low, strained voice. He didn't look up at her. She could tell by the stoop in his shoulders that his fire was gone. Whatever had transpired between him and Miss Gardner had dredged up a dark cloud of guilt.

"It's disturbing that you both agree I can't protect myself," Jessa said, anger building inside her. "Mother may not have nurtured me or been particularly kind to me, but she did teach me to defend myself. It was my lightning that protected me while your Invocari stood by. I am not Lord Renax. The only people capable of challenging my power are in Thelassus. There's little they can do to me from there, and I—"

Jessa felt a stabbing pain in her stomach. Pain radiated throughout her body, and she collapsed screaming to the floor. It was like a nest of angry hornets had hatched within her stomach. The agony came relentlessly.

Cameron rushed to help her, but Jessa kicked him back. "Stay away from me! *Get out!*" she shrieked.

Cameron scrambled back. Muriel bit her knuckle and clutched her other hand to her chest. "Do you want me to fetch the healer, dear?"

A thunderous crash filled the room, shaking the floor and furniture. Clocks and curios went flying. The sofa tipped backward, spilling Muriel out on the floor behind her. Her thin legs kicked from the ruffles of her long dress. Cameron was hurled back into an antique end table.

Jessa scratched at the hardwood floor with her nails, as arcs of electricity danced across her skin. The pain ended as quickly as it started, as if it were never there at all.

Cameron rushed to the countess, assisting her off the floor. She looked ashen and disheveled, but she didn't appear to be hurt.

Jessa stood, her eyes glowing with the cool blue flicker of electrical current. "Someone in my family just passed me their Heritage. Someone close to me. Very close."

"You should check on your mother," Muriel offered, trying not to sound pleased.

LEGACY (SATRYN)

My oldest and dearest sibling Nasara,

My time among the people of the Protectorate has been enlightening to say the least. I daresay a part of me will miss these people when I return to Thelassus to take my rightful place.

Jessa is serving her purpose masterfully, disarming the Assembly. She plays the part of the hapless pawn better than the Queen of Lies herself. Sometimes she's so convincing I almost don't think she could be my blood.

Speaking of which…I wouldn't wait for Jessa to request your aid. Rothburn's insolence is an insult to our family that can't be allowed to stand, but she risks credibility if she addresses it herself. Claim it for your son Nerrax to keep suspicion off my daughter. She must continue to play her part as victim in our family infighting.

Pay my respects to Uncle Nash,
Satryn

Satryn surveyed the smoldering ruins of her chambers with evident satisfaction. The center of the bed was a smoking crater, and black scorch marks marred the glowing wards that covered the walls. She picked up one of the chairs and set it on its legs only to see it collapse on a broken leg. "And I was just starting to get settled in. I'll need all new furnishings."

The metal door clanked open, and Satryn regarded it defiantly.

"Mother." Jessa stood in the door wearing a sleeveless white dress that didn't look half bad on her. The plunging neckline drew the eye toward her cleavage. *Is she fucking someone?*

"So you do care," Satryn cooed. "I was beginning to think you'd never come to visit. But family tragedy has a way of drawing us closer, doesn't it?"

"What the hells happened?" Jessa lifted the hem of her dress off the floor and marched over to her mother.

"How would I know? I've been detained." Satryn laughed musically.

"And I was enjoying that immensely."

Satryn backhanded her; it was mostly reflex at this point. Jessa caught her wrist in midair and squeezed. Her silver eyes flared. "You'll never lay a hand on me again, Satryn."

Satryn giggled and nodded approvingly. The girl's reflexes had vastly improved. "Very well, Jessa. I respect your defiance, and I'll look past your disrespect." She yanked her hand free of her daughter's grip and caressed her wrist.

Jessa regarded her flatly. "The empress still sits on the Coral Throne. The Protectorate spies confirmed this hours ago. So if you're still alive, who was it? Because I destroyed a priceless collection of clocks during the death throes. There was a *burst*. Those only happen for direct ancestors."

"Probably an uncle," Satryn said dismissively. "The imperial death rattles are always dramatic affairs. You've always been unusually sensitive to them. When your great-uncle Caritas passed, you were just a baby, but I swear you cried for a week."

"Look at this place!" Jessa put her hands on her hips. "Did you also demolish your chambers at Weatherly Castle? Because Father never told that part of the story. Nor do I remember feeling Great-Aunt Aluria's death so keenly."

Satryn threw her hands in the air. "I don't know what to tell you. I have no idea who it was, and I don't know why you trashed Muriel's precious clocks. Perhaps you secretly desired a reprieve from the incessant ticking."

"Perhaps we should consult with a blood sage then. Magus Quirrus said he found anomalies in your blood, minutes before I felt the passing of a direct relation. Imagine my surprise to learn both you and the empress are still drawing breath."

Satryn stroked her cheek, but Jessa flinched. "Are you disappointed it wasn't me?"

"If I wanted you dead, you'd be food for the sharks, Mother."

Satryn rolled her eyes. "What could you do to me? Poison my wine? No, you wouldn't even get your hands that dirty."

"I wouldn't have to. I'd simply wait till you passed out from your drink and bash in your skull with the heaviest thing I could find." Jessa folded her arms.

"It's a miracle you've managed to survive this long, considering how careless you are."

"You're exceptionally moody today," Satryn said. "Tell me, do you feel the roil of the Everstorm growing within your chest?"

"That must be it," Jessa said. "It certainly isn't the frustration of your lies, or the unceremonious discovery that I'm the likely product of inbreeding, or the loss of my home, or the maddening politics of this Assembly, or the child that's growing inside me. No, my mood is certainly the result of theurgy. What other thing could it *possibly* be?"

"You do manage to surprise me sometimes." Satryn's eyes flicked across her daughter's belly. "That certainly would explain your death rattle. The child bears your power, as you now bear mine. You feel the transition of power for the both of you."

"The father is an assemblyman," Jessa said. "We're in love."

"Good for you." Satryn tapped her arm playfully. "I think motherhood would suit you. Or at least give you an appreciation of the sacrifices I've had to make."

Jessa blinked.

"Oh, honestly, Jessa." Satryn sighed. "Did you think I would be angry? It matters not who the father is. Your child is a Stormlord, for Kultea's sake. The father could be the bastard of a deckhand's bastard, and his pedigree would be worth more than all the breeding of the castrated Genatrovan nobility. I couldn't be happier that you finally get to experience the unremitting hell of ingratitude and disappointment that parenthood brings."

Jessa turned away sullenly. "I don't intend to keep the child."

"Then don't!" Satryn exclaimed. "You really are exhausting sometimes."

Jessa headed toward the door. "You managed to teach me that, at least."

"Wait."

Jessa stopped.

"Let me see your blade. You may provide some challenge for me now," Satryn suggested. She reached out her hand and summoned the lightning to her fingertips. The electricity arced and within seconds solidified into a crackling scimitar of lightning.

She gave the Invocari warden a look to let him know this was just a game. "We're too close in power to hurt each other, and the room is already demolished."

The Invocari guard nodded silently.

Jessa turned and held out her hand. At first the electricity was rough and crude—a shapeless, forking mass of blue light in the shape of a blade. But to her amazement, the energy condensed into a rapier, complete with cup hilt. It was delicate but elegantly constructed.

Satryn put one hand behind her back then held out her own blade.

Jess laughed despite herself. "It's so easy to maintain." She quickly flicked the sparkling rapier back and forth as her shadow danced behind her. She raised her blade and approached Satryn, her off hand resting against the small of her back.

Satryn executed a series of slow, easy strikes, letting Jessa parry. The sparks flew from their blades like dazzling confetti. "You know, when I was pregnant with you, I swore I'd never be like my mother."

Jessa lunged, testing Satryn's parry. "You mean bitchy and cavillous?"

Satryn twirled her scimitar. "I barely knew her. I was raised by priests and an older sister who despised my very existence. The empress had no time for the folly of children."

"So she never came into your room in the middle of the night, drunk and raving about her sexual exploits? I pity you." Jessa lunged again, this time harder. Her attacks were quick and angry but also clumsy and easily parried. She executed a flurry of strikes as Satryn effortlessly deflected them and stepped out of the way. *She's better than Sireen at least.*

"Mothers are supposed to feel connected to their offspring. I know this." Satryn spun and slashed at Jessa as she twirled forward, bringing her blade high and low in alternating cadence.

Jessa staggered back at first but managed to parry some of the blows as she caught on to the rhythm of Satryn's attack. "Do you? Because you've said on multiple occasions that attachment makes us weak."

"Attachment to weaker things, yes." Satryn pressed harder, raining blows with greater quickness. "But I didn't close myself off. I simply never had that feeling to give you. I wanted to feel it, Jessa. I really did. But even as you were growing inside me, all I could think about was how I was expected to treasure this helpless little parasite. How could I put your needs before my own happiness when no one ever had shown me that courtesy?"

"Then why even give birth to me?" Jessa slashed viciously with her rapier, cutting through Satryn's scimitar and forcing her mother to take a delicate step backward while she reconstituted her blade.

Satryn crouched. "It was expected of me, and you pleased your father. He and I had a complicated relationship."

Jessa pointed her rapier at Satryn's heart. "Did you kill him?"

"He was a feckless ruler and an insufferable idealist, but I would have respected him enough to give him a king's death rather than watch him waste away like he did."

Satryn charged and raised her blade in an uppercut strike. Jessa caught the edge of the strike on the handguard of her conjured rapier and thrust it down. It withstood the blow and stopped her momentum.

"Everyone will betray you eventually, Jessa," Satryn said. "Siblings betray you, parents abandon you, husbands die, friends leave, and children end up hating you. Even the goddess herself will turn a deaf ear in your darkest moments. You have only yourself in this world."

Jessa banished her weapons. Her eyes were wet with tears. "I wish you'd just tell me what you're playing at. I don't know what to do, Mother. Please, for once in your life, can you just—"

Satryn gave a wan smile. "Do whatever the fuck you want, dear. You're an elemental *goddess* among men now, and it's high time you started acting like it instead of waiting for others to decide your fate. Just set a course and don't falter. You can't fail unless you abandon your conviction."

"Fine." Jessa wiped her eyes. "I'm becoming a citizen of Rivern and disavowing my imperial ties. I'm abdicating the crown to Rothburn to spare my people the bloodshed of an extended war. And…I'm having this child."

"You're your own woman now," Satryn mused. "I won't gainsay your choices, for they're your own, and it's your right to make them. We're equals…of a sort anyway, and I can't ask more of you."

Jessa looked confused for a moment. "What in the five hells are you plotting?"

"I'm looking out for our family." Satryn beamed. "I'm going to be a grandmother after all. Ugh. That makes me sound so much older than I am. I'm not ready for high-collared frocks and comfortable shoes. But I do have some ideas for names."

"You're a disgraceful ruler and an awful mother," Jessa sneered.

"Mayhaps," Satryn conceded, "but you're *lost*, Jessa. Your contempt for me is the closest thing you've ever had in the way of a personality. I wonder how virtuous you'd be if weren't the one thing you could do to irritate me."

"As you're fond of reminding me." Jessa narrowed her eyes. "But if you really wanted to make me doubt myself, you'd give your approval. I can't think of a worse recommendation than to be respected in your eyes."

"You've never had much of an imagination either."

Jessa blinked. "We're done speaking. As acting regent, I dissolve your position and privileges. You're no longer the sovereign ruler of Amhaven and no longer subject to the protections entitled under Protectorate law."

"That's hardly legal." Satryn shrugged. "Besides I'm still the daughter of the empress and hold many titles in the Dominance, none of which you can revoke. But best of luck with that squalid forest that passes for a nation."

"A nation that defeated the Dominance."

"With the aid of the witches, which you no longer have."

Jessa spun on her heel and made for the exit to the warding chamber. "Goodbye, Satryn. I'll make sure the Assembly replaces the furniture with something more suited to a lengthy incarceration."

"Let me know if you decide to keep your child," Satryn called after her. "I think you should call him Noah."

THE DOLMEN (HEATH AND SWORD)

My brethren and I are a handful of beings who can say we walked the ancient streets of Sarn. (Aside from the Travelers, who are never forthcoming with anything, we may be the only ones left.) Given that they're a generally taciturn lot, and not known for their intellectual curiosity, it falls to me to relate my experiences in hopes of enlightening modern scholars who wish to plumb the great mysteries of the Second Era.

Now it is true that theurgy was abundant in those times; in fact it was over-abundant in many cases, which caused no end of problems. It wasn't simply that after the wizards eliminated hunger, aging, disease, and ugliness there was no need for industry. The theurgies became self-aware and self-sustaining to the point that there was no need to even study wizardry.

The Aeromancer Guilds, once a highly sought-after posting in the mid-Second Era, faded to near obscurity by the end. Who needed to spend decades learning how to raise another floating city when cities already were floating? Who indeed needed to master the calculation of teleportation magic when portal engines were abundant throughout Creation?

Magic was instead put toward different applications—there was no curren-cy, but some approximation of wealth and status was devised to approximate an economy. In Archea and Maceria, it was called "merit," and in Sarn it was called "liberty" (or a loose translation that included both the freedom from obligation and the freedom to perform certain actions without legal consequences).

The Long Night saw an end to those long-standing theurgies and the loss of the few who remained capable of understanding them. It is for the reason of their overdependence that these nations fell so quickly (though they did not fall completely).

The modern Archeans, while preserving traditions, have no doubt lost much of their founders' arts. It's doubtful they know how to lower their impractical city to earth, even if they were so inclined.
—preface to Quill's *The Fall of Nations*, Volume 1

Heath paused from digging mud out of the heel of his boot. He'd never been fond of leaving the city, and the boggy terrain and undergrowth of the marsh had set him in a foul mood. The Harbinger's flask had given him Sword's memories, and those memories pointed to the dolmen near Reda. It was hard to look at his friend the same way, knowing what it felt like to become other people. Going from a crazed, tortured fire mage to Catherine had been a jarring juxtaposition. Sword's current, and mostly carefree, Fodder body seemed even more alien.

"I had a family once," Sword said offhandedly. "Started out with me and a barmaid I knocked up coming back from a war I can't remember. Raised the kids, passed myself down to the oldest son. I kept it going for three generations before the Bloodfangs sacked our village. Then I was a Bloodfang."

"Wait," Heath said. "Your own son?"

"Would have taken 'em all if I could have, but only one host at a time."

"But when you take people, they stop being themselves. Their lives as individuals effectively end."

Sword shrugged. "And when you die, you stop being a person altogether. What's your point?"

"I don't know," Heath said. "Why would someone even create you?"

"People had a lot of free time in the old days."

"But you never talk about the old days," Heath chided. "Look, I understand keeping secrets. And I certainly understand lying about the past. I've never asked you, but I need to know—what are you?"

"I don't want your stupid soul…if there even is such a thing," Sword said indignantly. "My invented purpose wasn't to enslave humanity. I was meant to preserve the memories and battle prowess of the House Crigenesta's champions. They weren't blade thralls; they were rightful owners. I was never built to be like this."

He continued, "The Sarnians had fucked-up rules about ownership—that's why they put curses on everything. I'm not some insidious monster trying to fuck your head into thinking I'm your friend. I'm a fucking theft deterrent. No one in his right mind would steal the sword of House Crigenesta or the Arrow of House Dulcorda, because they'd find themselves bound to the service of the house."

"Let me get this straight." Heath stopped him right there. "There's an *arrow* like you?"

"Right pompous prick he is too," Sword said. "There's a whole arsenal like me."

"How does that even work? Don't you have to be within a hundred feet of your host or else they die? And if you shoot you at someone…" Heath was still thinking about the arrow.

"I never said the Suzerains were practical. Besides the hundred-foot bond was only to make sure the weapon couldn't be forcibly removed to get out of the Geas. If you weren't the rightful owner, the only way out was to return to the house and have them release you. Only there's no one left to do that."

"Can't say I'm too sad to hear there aren't any more left," Heath said. "As an occasional thief, I'm glad that practice fell into obscurity."

"I was proud to serve House Crigenesta. Couldn't feel any other way about it, even if I wanted to, but they were an all right sort…for their time anyway. Probably wouldn't be too popular in the Protectorate, but they had a sense of humor."

"So how did you get free? Was it during the Long Night?"

"Centuries before." Sword sighed. "Factional power struggle. The houses were slaughtered along with the champions. The Suzerains killed the last survivors and just made new Great Houses. We were made by the Artifex, so destroying us would've been like burning an art gallery. So they did like they'd done with all their most dangerous artifacts—put us on display in the forum. In Sarn it's not like treasures were locked up or kept out of sight, you know? You put them out in the open as a show of strength and dared anyone to steal them."

"Why would anyone pick you up then?" Heath asked. "The permanent bond to the sword and loss of free will seems like a pretty serious downside."

"If you had the stones to beat the curse, the thing was yours. People got cocky and greedy, and over the centuries, they got stupid. Some kid, not even fifteen, picked me up on a dare because he didn't know his history, and his 'friends' wanted to have a laugh. The Sarn I awoke to was a shit hole. The new Great Houses were just families of inbred warlocks living off the legacy of theurgy left to them by the old. So I told the Suzerains and the houses where they could stuff my pointy end, and I left."

Heath mused, "I know what it's like to see an institution you're a part of betray every principle that made it worth believing in."

"That orphanage thing was right fucked, mate."

"Yeah."

"So…"

"We should get moving."

The dolmen sat in the center of a circle of barren stony earth. Four eroded stone pillars supported a circular rock with a hole in the center. Dead trees, covered in hanging moss and vines, surrounded the circle like bleak sentinels between the soggy marsh and the tainted ground. Even in the bright midday sun, the place felt sinister to Heath.

These dolmens were the source of pact magic, where dark bargains were struck and sacrifices made. They were often in remote locations, though they sometimes moved. This one had been here as far back as the histories went. Whatever Dark Magic flowed through them made them impervious to any attempts to destroy them.

Heath and Sword approached cautiously and took separate paths around the perimeter, examining the ground for tracks or any signs of recent use. They saw wax drippings on some of the rocks, but none of it looked recent, or it was impossible to tell.

"It's rained here," Heath said offhandedly. "Ashes would be our best bet, but it'll be hard to find anything we can use."

Sword sighed and unsheathed his blade. "I was afraid of that. Time for the backup plan?"

Heath sighed as well and opened his backpack. "I don't like this. But I brought the materials to do the lesser invocation from the Grimoire of Hecuba. Maybe the spirits of this place will tell us something. But we'll need to wait till nightfall."

"Let me try something first…" Sword swaggered over to the pillars of the dolmen and shouted, "Oi! It's me—Sword of fucking Saint Jeffrey! We need to talk to you!" He swung his blade and hacked into the stone repeatedly. The metal rang through the quiet empty clearing as it struck the pillars.

"Sword," Heath said with a laugh, "you think that's going to work? It's broad daylight."

"It don't matter, mate," Sword said, wiping his brow. "These things were called Memento Mori back in the old days, before the Corruption. It was a place you could chat with the dead, or their echoes anyway. Didn't take a fancy ritual to work."

"I doubt most people tried to cut it down, but subtlety was never your thing." A stout woman stepped out from behind one of the pillars. She was nearly fifty and handsome for a woman, with a mane of blond hair she kept back in a ponytail. She wore chain mail and a yellow tabard. Strapped to her back was a bastard sword set with heartstone.

Sword stared at her, mouth agape.

"It's strange to be lookin' at yourself, isn't it love?" She smiled warmly.

"Catherine…" Heath whispered.

"It's a pleasure to really meet you, Heath." She walked out from the shade of the dolmen and stared up toward the sun, enjoying the warmth. "We weren't properly introduced. By the time I found you, I'd been carrying the sword. Wasn't quite myself."

"You're not Catherine," Heath said flatly.

"I feel like her, though. I'm a truer representation than *that thing* ever was." She indicated Sword with a thumb over her shoulder. "Catherine was just a jumble of dead memories rattling around in that heartstone of his."

"This is really awkward." Sword rubbed the back of his thick neck.

"I need information," Heath stated flatly.

She laughed. "Right to business then, is it, love? I might have a mind to help you, but then I might also want to see your bloody scrotums on a plate. I had a life—a grandson. His mum passed, and he had no one to look after him. You had some grand adventures with my body, but it's not like I have a ancient Geas telling me what to do anymore."

"It wasn't meant to happen to you, and I'm truly sorry," Heath started to explain. "Give me his name, and I'll make sure money gets sent to look after his expenses."

"But it did happen," She let out a disappointed sigh. "And I don't want your money. Honestly, love, you've made more money than a person can spend in five lifetimes, yet you're still working these jobs like your next meal depended on it. It's not worth getting yourself killed over, and that's exactly what's going to happen. You're not an immortal construct who can just swap bodies any time he feels like it."

"Fuck, mate," Sword growled. "She's a manifestation of corruption trying to get in your head. Shameless is what it is, dragging her up with her sob story. I sent money after the boy from my share. It's sorted, not that it matters to her."

She shrugged. "Aye, you did. And that money went right to my ex-husband, so on behalf of the whores of Reda, thank you. But listen to me prattle on. You lot are the last people I expected to see in one of these places. So has life outside the strictures of the Orthodoxy treated you so badly that it's come to making pacts in haunted moors?"

"Harrowers." Heath looked to the ground. "There's been a rash of killings in Rivern. Victims dead in their sleep, eyes burned out. We think it might be a warlock who made a pact, but there's no pattern to it. I need a name."

"I don't suppose if I told you your name was Heath, you'd offer up your soul?" She chuckled a bit. "Sorry. Pact humor. No, the name you want is Lord Evan Landry."

"It can't be that easy." Heath regarded her from the corner of his eye.

Catherine looked at the ground and coyly brushed the stone with the tip of her boot. "The Harrowers must be in a generous mood. Maybe it's your good looks. Could also be all those orphans you burned to death. Says a lot about the kind of person you are that the maddened echoes of corruption admire you, doesn't it?"

"Could also be the fact that the last time one of these fuckers walked the earth it was me that lopped its smirking head off its shoulders." Sword raised his blade and admired its pristine edge. "And it's me they answered when I came round with my steel."

"I just relay the information as it comes to me," Catherine said, "but if I might add my own commentary, it does seem that one would be well advised to be wary of a gift offered so readily. I might even wager it was some kind of trick."

"Is it?" Heath asked.

"Of course it is, love." Catherine threw her hands up in exasperation. "I shouldn't have to tell you this. Coming to a dolmen and asking for anything is a death sentence we've seen played out time and again. No matter how harmless it seems, it always comes with a price. Do not under any circumstances follow up on this information unless you want to die."

"Now I'm intrigued," Sword said.

"That's all I know." Catherine slumped her shoulders. "Or at least all the powers that govern this blighted place are willing to share anyway. A name is good… for them. Most days they can't tell any two of us apart, let alone the difference between past and future."

"A description or location would be more helpful. What do they want for that?" Heath asked.

"Heath…" She looked at him coldly. "This is low, even for you."

"I'm trying to help people," Heath said defensively.

"If you're counting yourself as a person," Catherine said, smiling.

"I'm different now."

"A little late for those nine orphans and the two women looking after them." Catherine cracked her knuckles and looked at the sky. "I mean this in the nicest way possible, but you're a murderous, selfish, piece of shit, love. Always have been. Oh, except maybe for that brief instant you stopped running with Cordovis and joined the church to save your ailing mum. That was a real stand-up moment for you until they recognized you for a heartless killer and inducted you into an order of assassins."

Heath balled his fists. "What happened in Reda was unfortunate, but I realized—"

"You'd rather murder for profit than ideals. Yeah, I was there, remember?" Catherine snorted. "And don't begin to pretend you ever gave a damn about the cause. I could count on one hand the number of times I saw you pray. It came down to coin, pure and simple. I don't even think you have a soul to bargain with."

"Allow me, mate." Sword placed his hand on Heath's shoulder and addressed the shade of his former body. "First let me just say, as one arcane construct masquerading as a person to another, you're doing a great job with Catherine… the cadence and judicious use of biographical information really humanize the character. But using a dead woman's skin to make moral judgments on a bloke—that's shameless.

"Second, it was you lot who raised up that cult of demonic spider orphans in Reda. So if anyone here has blood on their hands, it's you. Plain and simple, that orphanage would still be standing if someone hadn't got the brilliant notion to pay a visit to a dolmen. And for what, exactly?"

"I couldn't begin to tell you. I'm just the messenger," she began.

"I wasn't finished." Sword twirled his blade. "I'm older than the Harrowers by a couple of centuries and have some insight into human nature. People don't need the shades of dead loved ones to remind them that they're terrible. People have to be assholes. It's a basic fact of survival that people sometimes have occasion to kill each other, just as much as they need to keep each other alive and indebted.

"A bloke who kills another bloke in an alley for a sack of coins is evil. A soldier who kills on the battlefield for the same stipend is good. Moral codes are a fucking snarl of inconsistencies—and they're supposed to be. If everyone was a fucking saint, people would have died of starvation. There's really only one moral prerogative: survival."

Catherine folded her arms. "Are you quite finished, love? Because it sounds like you're trying to use a moral argument to convince the Harrowers to abandon their eternal hatred for humankind. And if that's the case, I can save you some time."

"I'm saying the Harrowers' whole fucking thing is stupid. And they know it's stupid. And they know that I know that they know…" Sword paused then continued. "Anyway just fucking tell us who Evan Landry is so we can go kill the stupid blokc."

Catherine looked at Heath imploringly. "Don't ask me to do this. Our relationship is complicated, but despite your numerous flaws, I do give a shit about you. I shouldn't, but I do, so there it is. The voices in this place are screaming for your blood. I suppose one benefit of having my mind shoved into that sword is that I know how to deal with that kind of magic, but if you ask me again, I'll have to tell you."

Heath smiled. "I can handle it."

"Maddox knows who Evan Landry is," she said after a moment's hesitation. "He's your safest path. But if you go back to Rivern, there'll be nothing but death ahead for you. There's more going on than you realize, and Landry's just the beginning."

Heath nodded. "I wish things had worked out differently for you, but I also have to say I was proud to know you." He bowed slightly.

She forced a grin. "Me too."

"Wait…" Her expression suddenly soured with worry. She raised her hand cautiously as she strained to hear something. "Ohan damn it."

"What?" Heath asked.

"They want to make an offer," she said warily. "To me."

"It's bullshit," Sword said. "They're masters of this kind of chicanery."

"It's a good one." Catherine laughed to herself. "They say they can bring me back if I can convince you to do something. And I have to say I have a mind to do it. I wouldn't ask if I didn't believe it was the right thing to do. It's a chance to genuinely atone for something. But I'm terrified you're going to say no."

"It was lovely seeing you again." Sword grabbed Heath's arm and started to lead him toward the edge of the clearing, but Heath didn't budge.

Catherine clasped her hands. "Kill him. Kill the poor Fodder and release him from the sword's Geas. Then leave the blade here. Their magic can draw it into the stone so no one will ever touch the cursed thing again. Do that, and I'll walk out of here with you, as much the person I was as the echo can muster."

Heath said, "There has to be some other way. Something else they want."

"She's playing on your guilt, mate," Sword said. "They don't want me at your side because they know you need me."

"If you take your money, you can leave Rivern," Catherine pleaded. "Avoid all of this and start over somewhere else. We both can. You just need to let go of the Sword. It's always been there by your side, to give you a pat on the back and a gentle nod of encouragement with every bloody transgression. It's manipulated people for centuries."

Sword rolled his eyes. "Okay. I think you're being a little unfair, and just for the record, the parties you represent are clearly no strangers to emotional manipulation."

"I don't feel good about this, Sword," Heath said quietly.

Sword tensed. Those words were usually followed by some radical, unpredictable behavior.

"He's sick," Catherine stated. "The same affliction that killed his mother is ravaging his body as well. He can't heal that kind of sickness on his own, but the Harrowers can temporarily grant him the power to fix it. If you really cared about Heath, you'd do this for him at least."

Sword turned to Heath. "I fucking knew something was wrong with you."

"It's how my grandmother died," he said. "And I'm around the age my mother started getting sick."

"Fuck!"

Catherine eyes were wet with tears. "I feel bad for doing this, love. Really I do. But I want to have a life—the one I should have had, simple and shitty as it was some days. And you…you deserve a chance to make up for all the wrong you've done. Leave the sword here. End the cycle of misery. Give us both a chance."

Sword frowned. "I can't tell you what to do, mate. I may not be flesh and blood, but I'm a person, and whatever happens to me if you leave me here won't be pleasant. And we can find a way to heal you. Cancerous afflictions were treatable like colds in Sarn, and there are tomes waiting to be rediscovered."

Heath rubbed his temples. "There has to be a solution. The Harrowers want the blade, and they're driving a hard bargain. If we understood why Sword was so important, we could unravel their intentions."

"They don't give a fuck what you decide," Catherine said. "No matter what you do, you'll have to live with that choice for the rest of your life, regretting it each day and always wondering. There's no middle path to negotiate. This anguish is what they live for, love. Yours, mine, or his, they've already won."

Heath inhaled deeply. "Then I won't give them anguish." He walked slowly toward the stones. "I didn't believe. I didn't join the Inquisition out of any sense of purpose. I didn't leave it out of any sense of purpose. I wasn't your enemy. I honestly didn't care one way or the other. Hells, your pacts were a source of income."

He rested his hand on the stone and shut his eyes. "But you made a mistake, and that mistake has made you an enemy. Because now I do see the light. I do see the reason for this crusade against darkness. Before it was just about the payday, and I still beat your warlocks every single time. But now I'm going to do something I've never done before. I'm going to care.

"First I'm going to beat this illness. Then I'm going to give Catherine her life back. And after that—Ohan help me—I'll dedicate my life to ending the Harrowers forever. I'll become abbot of the Inquisition, and I'll turn the Order into a holy army, if that's what it takes. This I swear."

When he looked up, Catherine's shade was gone. Sword stood in the clearing, his sword arm dangling by his side.

"Heath, mate…" Sword gently sheathed his blade. "We don't even know if what that thing said is true."

"They don't lie," Heath said, "but they do bend the truth. My mother died because we were too poor to pay for treatment without charity. I may not be able to heal my disease, but money isn't a concern. I'm more focused on Evan Landry right now."

"Right," Sword said. "No idea who the bloke is. There was only one Landry left living in Rivern, and he was one of the first to bite it."

"That we know of," Heath added. "If you had the power to kill anyone without it ever being traced back to you, what would you do? Assume you're someone who doesn't have connections in professional circles."

"I'd get even with whoever pissed me off," Sword said, "but there's no way the killer knew all his victims. Some were refugees from Amhaven. They didn't have time to make any enemies."

"So why kill them?"

"Maybe he just likes fucking with people."

"The city is practically under siege," Heath said. "Trade has been halted; the government is in virtual exile. People are too afraid to sleep at night. Who benefits from that?"

"Thrycea," Sword said. "I bet it's those bleedin' Stormlords!"

"One of them is in the Invocari tower because she refuses to testify before the Veritas."

"So we check out Landry or the Storm bitch?"

"Let's get the fuck out of these woods and back to civilization. Evan Landry has a lot to answer for."

ACHELON (MADDOX)

I cannot say how long it has been since the Long Night descended. Time seems to waver and melt into a long, infinite nightmare. Wild ravings come from the streets below as people fall to the haunting call of delirium. The archwizards, who should protect us, have all drifted into madness and seek to drown the world in shadow mischief.

Twisted creatures prowl the corners of my vision, segmented shivering shades, creeping over the dark places in our home. My beloved wife cradles our son in a bubble of protective magic. It's all she can do to maintain it, and she's far stronger than I.

The orgy of violence and sex calls to me and makes my blood run hot. I'm no archwizard, but I'm puissant enough to feel the infection of madness creep through my mind. The world is disintegrating in front of me, and I don't know how much longer I can hold on.

The world is ending, and the Long Night is upon us, from which we may never awaken. For who would ever want to awaken from the fever of the Harrowers? How I hunger for them to consume me forever and always.

It was Achelon who brought this ruin upon us. And it was Achelon who showed us the truth.

I see the truth because I have too many eyes.

—fragment of an old journal, an account of the Long Night

Maddox awoke from his slumber of death with a start, his newly awakened heart pounding. The visions had shown him some fucked-up shit, and he wasn't even sure they were factually accurate scenarios—they tended to be symbolic. But seeing that chamber and his aunt Cara gave him pause as he went to light the next hit of euphorium.

That was no reason to avoid the firebrandy, though. For him the waking world had become the dream, a recurring event where truth and certainty faded from his mind. He'd been going at it for only a few hours by his waking sense of time, but maybe it was time to take a break and see what the hell Riley and the other losers were up to.

Maddox nearly leapt out of his chair when he looked over.

At another workstation, ten feet over, there was another, quite deceased, version of himself going through the motions of cooking up drugs. The reagents were different. He guessed the revenant was making dragonfire or some watered-down derivative. The thing paid him no mind.

Maddox noticed stitches around the wrists and neck, along with canine bite marks on the arms. His undead double wore a long robe to preserve his modesty. "Holy mother of all…" He glanced back to two more tables, where Falco and Crateus were busy at work. Falco looked rather decayed, but Crateus looked fresh. He wore a pair of tinted safety goggles that made him look like a green-eyed bug.

"Oh, hey, Maddox." Crateus waved. "I didn't see you there. How are the visions coming along?"

"What the five hells is happening? Where's Riley?"

"Mr. Riley's very busy," Crateus said. "He wishes he could visit with you, but he asked me to look in on you. I'm trying my hand at alchemy. I figure if a rotter can do it, so can a Fodder, right?" He laughed cheerfully at his joke.

Crateus poured a blue liquid from a glass tube into a wide-bottomed flask, swirled it, then poured it back into the test tube. He repeated this a couple of times.

"Riley," Maddox said more insistently, "where can I find him?"

"He's out gathering disciples." Crateus said, "but if you want to wait for him, you can join us for dinner. I don't think I've ever seen you eat. Or shit."

Maddox drank more firebrandy. "Riley…has disciples?"

"Yup. 'Bout fifteen." Intently concentrating on his task, Crateus continued to transfer the liquid between the flasks.

"There aren't fifteen people in Creation dumber than fucking Riley," Maddox said angrily. "Except maybe you. What the hell are you doing?"

"Practicing," Crateus said a little nervously. "I want to master the motions so that when I'm ready to mix solutions, my body will be trained. It's hard to get it from the big one to the small one without a funnel."

Maddox snatched a funnel off the table and held it up. "That's why we use funnels. And this is why your people don't understand magic. I'll ask you one more time before I get really angry. Where can I find Riley and his disciples?"

"Dunno," Crateus said. "It's him and Esme that do all that. Me, Gran, and the brothers just keep a watch on the house while they're out. I remember Esme saying something about handing out food at the docks. I figure maybe they're paying a visit to the refugees. There's a lot of hungry people in the city, and food is getting expensive on account of all the trade drying up."

"Really? There's a food shortage?" Maddox said sarcastically.

"On account of all the harrowings that have been happening. No merchant will spend more than an hour in the city, if even that, and they're charging double prices."

"I don't give a shit about a fucking food shortage! Why is there a revenant over there who looks exactly like me? Why are we in a grand ballroom cooking up drugs, and where the hell can I find Riley?"

"There was an…accident with your leg. But it grew back! And so Gran and Riley came up with this experiment—"

Maddox waved his hand. "I've heard enough. Just destroy it, okay?" He had to admit it was kind of ingenious. If anyone in the house knew magic, it was probably Gran. That kind of skill would have made her a magus. A female magus from an era when that sort of thing practically had been outlawed.

"I can't destroy it. Riley would get real mad if I did. He calls him Deaddox."

Maddox forced a laugh. "Of course he does. Where the hells are we?"

"Landry estate. Riley moved us in here because he liked it better."

"Why's there a drug lab in the ballroom?" Maddox took a chug of firebrandy and wiped his mouth.

"It does seem odd," Crateus said thoughtfully. "He said no one was buying silver and jewels anymore with traders being afraid to enter the city and all, but Cordovis would pay good money for drugs."

"Riley's full of shit. We're squatting illegally in a dead man's house," Maddox said flatly. "And since when did he become a criminal mastermind? Cordovis has assemblymen in his pocket and pretty much runs every shop on Beaker Street. What the hells is going on?"

"We're moving up in the world. And it's all thanks to you."

"I never woke up." Maddox threw his hands in the air. "That's the only explanation for any of this. This is all part of the Guides' journey. I've seen wonders and horrors that have inured me to strangeness. This little shit show is so far beneath my notice that I…don't even notice it."

Crateus smiled. "I can't wait to see what you've seen. Once we all get your seal, we're going with you."

Maddox tipped the bottle back and let it empty into his mouth. He threw it against the dusty parquet floor and said, "I'm becoming a transcendent being. Tell Riley he can go fuck himself. He knows where to find me."

"Anything else I should say?"

Maddox staggered back over to his workstation and plopped down in the chair. He gave a solemn nod to Deaddox before sparking up his hookah and letting the euphorium hit. It fell on him like a ton of bricks.

"Oh, thank the Guides I'm back," Maddox said, finding himself laid out on a cool white marble floor. The circular room was luxuriously appointed. Intricately carved archways led out to a balcony that overlooked a pink-and-gold sky filled with ornate white clouds.

"Greetings," a man's voice called from across the room. Maddox saw a man in loose white robes seated in a white marble throne. He was in his midfifties, with silver hair, but his body was muscular and trim, lending him an almost mythological appearance. He was clean-shaven and imperious in his manner.

"I don't entertain visitors, so I had to invoke this space rather quickly. If I had more time, I would have come up with something more regal."

"This is fine by me," Maddox said, glancing around. The place was stunning, filled with plush sitting areas and beautiful artwork. A bed the size of a small room, draped in ornately folded silk, dominated one end of the chamber. There were no stairs in or out and no privy.

"You misunderstand. This is far too humble for one of my stature. It doesn't convey nearly a fraction of the awe that you should feel in my presence. But you're hardly worth the effort of re-creating it for my own vanity." He paused. "Know that you stand in the presence of the creator of this universe, Architect."

He said that last word as if it were almost physically painful for him.

"You're *the* Creator?"

"Of *this* universe," he said. "I can't take credit for the one you call home. Surely you know who I am. You have come to my realm."

"I just end up in random places," Maddox said. "You know, visions."

"Ah, yes, I see that now." He sighed. "I've finished reading your soul, Maddox of Rivern, and I know everything that has brought you to this place. The Grand Design—abandon it; abandon your search. Choose a life of humble service to others, and you may yet find some meaning in your immortality. That's the best I can offer you."

"First, let me say," Maddox began very politely, "fuck off. Second, let me also say that I have no clue who you are. And finally I can't die in a vision, and I can't die in real life either, so...the whole angry-god thing isn't working."

"First," he replied, "though I'm omnipotent in this plane of existence, I'm also omnipresent, so the one request I'm unable to fulfill is to 'fuck off.' Congratulations on finding my weakness. Second, you do know my name, even if you don't recognize me. And finally, while I can't harm you, if you decline my hospitality, I can make your stay here very unpleasant, so I would advise you show the proper respect."

"Who are you?"

"You knew me as Achelon, the Great Desecrator."

"Fuck—" Maddox stopped himself. "I was just in Minas Creagoria and—"

"I know."

"And I saw—"

"I know."

"And you probably know what I'm going to say before—"

"Yes."

"You attained the Seal of the Grand Design, didn't you?"

"Yes, but you're also very predictable." He shifted in his throne and toyed with his robe, briefly revealing the mark of the Grand Design over his heart. "Seal magic thankfully doesn't work in this universe. I've replaced mysticism and sacred geometries with a more logical system in my own version of Creation."

"So what will happen if I attain it?" Maddox peered at Achelon's chest, studying the edges of the symbol. The man had rock-hard pectorals dusted with fine silver-and-black chest hair. For an ancient-mass-murderer-turned-god, he wasn't unattractive. In a totally evil way.

"What do you think will happen, Architect?" Achelon said peevishly, covering his chest. "You'll become a monster."

"Nah." Maddox smiled. "We've already had one of those. It didn't work out so well."

"If a man's virtue could be measured in drink, you would sully the saints." Achelon leaned back in his seat. "But you're no saint, and your principal failing is pride. You need to feel superior to those around you. You want their adoration but settle for hatred because you tell yourself it's envy."

"I'm not perfect, but you set a pretty low bar," Maddox scoffed. "I've been to your city, and I know the dirty secrets hidden from sight. I may not like humanity as a whole, but I'd never allow people to be bred like cattle in a underground dungeon so I could harvest their infants to power my machinery."

"I found it abhorrent as well. But even as King Achelon of Minas Creagoria, I was beholden to the interests of others. Not only of my supporters on the Hidden Council but also those of my people. Do you think the lords of Sarn or Maceria would follow suit if I shuttered the mills? Or would they use the power of their own harvests to bring us to heel? It's human nature to exploit. Selective empathy is how humanity survived before we became a detriment to our own survival.

"The only way to change a man's nature is to control him absolutely and utterly." Achelon grimaced. "That was the best possible world the Grand Design showed me—all of humanity happily enslaved under my benevolent rule. Robbed of choice and freedom and set upon an efficient path of maximized virtue. A world of slaves or a world devoid of life—those are the only answers to suffering."

Maddox pondered the thought: every man, woman, and child in Creation singing his praises, fervently believing in his truth, and living in accord with his mandates. Although glory and recognition were recurrent themes in his daydreams, he found the idea of absolute control unsettling. "But you didn't... Sephariel said—"

"Even though I attained the seal, I denied it...and made a different choice." Achelon put forth his arm and slid back the sleeve of his robe. On his forearm was a plain black circle filled with what looked like ancient numbers: 6-62606957. The ink wasn't merely black; it was like peering into a gateway into an absolute void. Maddox looked away. That wasn't something he wanted to remember.

"You knew what would happen when you brought the Guides here."

"Of course not. They exist outside the Grand Design." Achelon shrugged. "They were the only thing I couldn't predict. The only way to deny the seal is to invite uncertainty."

"Nice job," Maddox declared. "You're the most hated warlock ever. Seriously. Not one of the histories has a single good thing to say about you. And the people who do praise you are fucking lunatics who make Harrower pacts."

"How will your legacy read, Maddox of Rivern?" Achelon sighed, waving his hand. "You gained your power by repeatedly inducing your own death through the willful overconsumption of deadly contraindicated intoxicants. I don't envy the poet charged with writing your epic."

Maddox smiled broadly. "I think the whole rising-from-the-dead thing gives me a lot more fruitful material to work with. It worked with Ohan's Luminaries."

"And you have no idea why or how that particular trick works and even less of a clue what it means." He shook his head.

"Then why don't you fucking enlighten me, oh, great one?"

Surprisingly Achelon answered the fucking question. "You were born with the ability to store and channel large quantities of raw theurgy, much like men who are endowed with exceptional memory or a penchant for music. Only one or two individuals in a generation of all living men are born with your gift. None have ever been fortunate enough to enroll in the study of magic until you. Without your gift you'd be unremarkable—a bitter, drunken shell of a man with tenure in the alchemy college who drowns his sorrows every night and spends his coin on whores."

"At least, in your worst-case scenario, I have money to drink, and I'm getting laid. If you want to offend me, you need to try harder." Still what Achelon said pissed him off.

"I'm merely illustrating a point, if you'll allow me." Achelon considered his next words. "The Principia Arcana contains the laws of magic, does it not?"

Maddox looked at him blankly and folded his arms. The question didn't dignify a response.

Achelon rolled his eyes. "A student is never too advanced to engage in a disciplined inquiry, but clearly you're impatient, so I'll summarize thusly: there are no laws of magic. None whatsoever. Magic is power in its purest form, able to act without limit. The Principia is merely a set of guidelines to keep inexperienced mages from killing themselves. The true limits of theurgy are whatever you can get away with."

"Like coming back from the dead."

Achelon shook his head. "That's a perfect demonstration of the kind of contortions someone with your ability can inflict on the cosmic order. You see that this is dangerous, yes?"

"In the wrong hands"—Maddox nodded—"surely."

The Desecrator continued breezily, "If you could choose anyone in the world aside from yourself to have that kind of potential, who would it be? Perhaps the associate you name Riley. He seems a friendly sort, not given to spite."

"Fuck no!" Maddox said. He thought for a long uncomfortable minute about the people he knew: his abusive father, his feckless aunt, his emulous mentor, the shifty band of scoundrels. "I don't know who I'd choose. People are all pretty much dicks, at least the ones I know."

"They are most often, if I understand your vernacular…untrustworthy, yes? So imagine for a moment that the gift is handed out randomly, with no greater cause than an accident of breeding. There's no 'Grand Design' in nature, just simple probability that one day a person with the right gift will discover the wrong Lore."

Maddox opened his mouth to challenge the Desecrator. The world was lucky to have him instead of Riley or, Guides forbid, Esme. But if he had to take a completely candid look at himself, there were probably one or two better candidates out there. At last he said, "The Guides…they chose me."

Achelon laughed. "You mean the Lights? The Guides are beings beyond understanding—you couldn't witness one with your limited senses except in dreams. The Lights are a manifestation of your own power. Your people really misinterpreted the Principia."

"Fuck you!" Maddox kicked over an end table, sending a bowl of fruit clanging against the floor, disgorging apples in all directions. He regained his composure. "Okay. We're all fucking idiots. Someone—not naming names here—destroyed every record of the old magic and left us to scrabble in the ruins of the Second Era to piece together some semblance of discipline from thirteen barely intact drawings. So I find it highly inappropriate for you to find humor in that."

Achelon flinched, and for a moment, Maddox saw something like pain and remorse in those impossibly blue eyes. "Know that if I hadn't done what I had, your people—or some eugenically cultivated version of them—would still be in those tunnels."

Maddox shuddered; the horror of the incubation chamber flashed through his mind, only this time he was the infant ripped from the belly of his mother and consigned to the soul engine.

He looked around. The edges of the world were growing fuzzy. Bits of stone were slowly breaking away from the floor and pillars, drifting off into trails of wispy dust. His physical body was shutting down. He felt the vibrations of his heart pumping frantically as it struggled to cling to life. *Keep it down, asshole. We've done this dozens of times now.*

"It seems our time together has ended," Achelon said without emotion. "The way here won't be open to you again until you're ready to face me as an equal. You've seen the Grand Design and the Seal without Name. Only use them if…"

Maddox tried to hold on, but the vision was falling apart. *I spent the whole time arguing with this fuck when I could have been getting answers.* He tumbled toward the floor, his astral representation falling back into his flesh. He braced for darkness.

"Surprise!"

Maddox nearly fell backward out of his chair. He was sitting in a restaurant with red wallpaper and an elaborate chandelier that glittered with crystal shards that seemed to glow within. At a large table in the center were the members of the House of the Seven Signs. Around them a crew of liveried servers stood with pitchers and serviettes, watching expectantly. The rest of the lavishly appointed dining room was empty.

"'E's awake!" Riley cheered beside him and slapped him hard across the back. He sported a slick hairstyle with freshly shorn sides, giving an angular configuration to his face that was almost handsome. He wore a lord's coat, complete with ruffled collar.

The entire crew was present. To his right sat Esme, spinning her dagger on its point into the fine mahogany table. She wore a sleeveless dress and a diamond tiara, looking every bit the highborn daughter, save for her dark eye makeup.

Even Gran was dressed in something other than her filthy robes; someone had thrown a pearl necklace on her. Otix, who looked so emaciated he could have been a revenant, wore a black-and-gold dinner jacket and scratched at his skin. Themis, in wolf form, lapped at a dish of wine, while his brother Theril, in human form, completely naked from the waist up, sipped a glass of bubbly. Crateus was diligently practicing pouring wine from one glass to another.

"Happy birthday," Riley said. "Crateus told me you was missin' your old pal, and I'm sorry I were out of pocket last time you came round, but old Riley never forgets a friend or a birthday."

"What day is it?" Maddox asked.

"Fourth of Ember, 565 in case you forgot the year."

"It's not my birthday," Maddox said hesitantly.

Riley shook his head. "You told me it were! You was at the Flask last year, and I asked you for some ducats, and you says, 'Fuck off. It's me fuckin' birthday, and I need to be alone.' Exact words."

It hadn't been his birthday, but he probably would have said anything to make Riley go away. The fucker remembered.

"Huh. Maybe I'm just confused. It's been a rough morning. Where the fuck are we?"

"The Turley," Esme said, her sweet voice dripping with sarcasm. "It's the oldest restaurant in Rivern. Goes back over four hundred years, if you count the original location, which burned down."

Maddox knew the Turley, but he'd never been inside. It was a private facility that offered tables by invitation only, a place for the old aristocracy to feel exclusive. The walls were covered in stuffy oil portraits of the old monarchy. He felt suddenly embarrassed about his dirty tunic and rough breeches.

Maddox grinned back at Esme. "Hey, kid, I think places like this provide you with silverware."

She feigned a pout and put her knife away. "I would never cut food with Lucky."

"When I use to come here," Gran said, "I sat over there, and they had a fireplace place next to a long table where you could make any kind of salad."

"Wow, Gran," Riley said. "You really got around in your old days."

"I was so sad when this place burned down," she said wistfully.

Maddox turned to Riley. "So what the fuck is up? With all this shit? Why are we sitting by ourselves in the most prestigious restaurant in Rivern? What the hells is going on with the revenants and the drugs and the disciples and the mansions and your clothes and the fucking diamond tiaras and fucking all of it?" He took a deep breath.

"Had to be done, though. They were catching on," Gran whispered to no one in particular.

Maddox held up a finger to the old woman. "I'll get with you in a minute."

Riley slid his arm around Maddox's shoulder. "We got us a legitimate operation, licensed and everything. The city needs all hands on deck making dragonfire since they legalized it, and Mr. Cordovis has taken us under his protection. He owns this place, and I told him I wanted your birthday to be special, so he were like 'Here, have it,' so we can celebrate as a family. You're one of us now."

"Wait...Cordovis? That man puts more people in the river than the Thrycean flu."

"We got us an agreement, and he knows better than to come for any one of us. Besides what you got to be scared of, eh?" Riley punched his arm. "The old man don't do nobody who don't need to be done in the first place. He's the one who offed that twat Torin Silverbrook on the riverboat."

"Torin's...dead?" Maddox felt nothing when he said it, but it was a tangible nothingness. A placeholder for emotions happening far beneath the surface.

"I'd have done him meself, the fucking asshole." Riley spat on the antique Turisian rug beneath them. "But yeah, he died same day your old magus kicked the bucket. Cordovis wanted to keep him from marrying that Storm princess, but it were all a misunderstanding about a peace treaty or some such."

Esme snapped her fingers at one of the waitstaff. "Excuse me. Can you give our friend some wine, perhaps a fortified cippriatto from Barstea? Nothing from 543—that was a terrible vintage. Not that he would know, but it is his birthday."

Theril looked at Esme. "How's a street rat like you know to order wine like a lady and such?"

She set her elbow on the table. "I was a high-class prostitute till I hit puberty."

"That shit's not funny," Maddox said coolly.

Esme laughed innocently. "We all deal with tragedy in our own little fucked-up ways. I like to make jokes and…be alive all the time. It's not for everybody."

One of the waitstaff appeared with a bottle of dark liquid and a glass balanced on a silver tray. She was dark skinned enough to pass for Bamoran, but she probably was Turisian if she was serving Rivern nobility. A single trickle of sweat ran down the side of her face as she gently lowered the tray to the table. Her eyes looked straight ahead, terrified.

At the last moment, her hand slipped, and the glass tumbled off the tray along with the bottle.

Maddox caught both midair before they hit the table, but the wine splashed out on his rank old tunic. Liquid was next to impossible to handle by seal, but he saved a sip in the glass. "I'll pour," he said, willing the bottle to refill the glass.

"I should have poured," Crateus whispered to the wolf next to him.

The waitress had gone pale. "I'm so sorry. I'm so sorry…"

Riley touched her arm gently. "Hey, it's all good. You didn't get any on me coat and people make mistakes, and you can't get mad for things people can't help. Now run along and see where we're coming on that thing." He winked at her. The second his hand came off her arm, she marched to the kitchen. The other servers stood perfectly still, barely disguising their terror. .

"What are these people scared of, Riley?" Maddox demanded. The glass slid into his hand, and he took a swallow. It was like drinking liquid walnuts and cinnamon, like someone had distilled his grandmother's house into a cloyingly sweet beverage.

"What's anyone scared of, Maddy? Fear is the enemy of us all."

"Fucking shit." Maddox rubbed his temples.

"Houses," Esme said. "We wait for people to die in their sleep. Then, after the body is cleared out and the remaining family members flee, we go in and loot whatever valuables we can move on the street. We use that money to buy reagents for dragonfire and other drugs. We take bodies from the river and turn them into revenants so they can cook the shit. We've made a fucking killing, and now we're the toughest crew on the streets. People who piss us off have a habit of turning up dead."

Riley shrugged. "City's falling apart anyway. The whole fucking place. It's free money."

Maddox scooted back from the table. "I can't be a part of this."

"Sit the fuck down!" Esme grabbed his arm and pointed her dagger at him. She smiled sweetly. "Riley went through a lot of trouble to give you this party, and all of us have better shit to be doing, so have a seat, drink your bottle, and eat some cake with your family."

Maddox flung his wrist slightly, and Lucky the dagger flew out of Esme's hand and thunked into the ceiling. After the fact he noticed it was actually embedded into a mural, which was probably priceless. Still he wasn't about to be coerced by a teenage girl. "Don't ever point that fucking thing at me again, or I'll stick it in your face, got it?"

She licked her lips.

"She's fucking nuts!" Maddox turned to Riley.

He shrugged. "It's hard for her to share my affections, but I love you both. Still Esme's my girl, and that means I have to do the right thing here." Riley stood and faced Maddox. The waitstaff had vanished. The others at the table were watching intently, except for Gran.

"Riley," Maddox said evenly, "I just want to walk out of here and never, ever see another one of you sorry fucks again."

Riley scowled for a second but went back to his usual obsequious contrition. "You're just overwhelmed. This is a lot to take on, and you're saying stuff you don't mean. That's just your way, like pointin' daggers is Esme's way. You've got the gentlest heart of anyone I know, Maddy, and you're not cut out for this sort of life. This weren't just a birthday party—it were a going-away as well."

Riley fished something out of his pocket. It was a long metal key on a festively colored silk ribbon with a little card on it that read "Maadaux" in horribly scripted Archean. Riley held it in the air between them then gently let it go. It hovered there for a few moments before Maddox took it.

Riley's eyes were moist. "It's yours. It's your own alchemy shop so's you can continue your studies in peace. Anything you ever need, you just ask. The boys'll be by to check on you daily, and if you want to get in touch, let me know. The city belongs to us now, and you was a part of that."

"Thank you, Riley. That's very kind," Maddox said robotically.

"Don't thank me. It were your dad's shop and all." Riley patted his arm. "The cantankerous old fuck finally passed in his sleep, if you catch my drift. It were just a simple matter to give the mages a blood sample and prove relation. Got the title moved to your name a day or two after he died, but I wanted it to be a surprise. Fucking good riddance to the old fuck, I say."

"Yeah, sure, Riley. Whatever you say."

Maddox pocketed the key. There was nothing left to feel—no regret, no satisfaction. Months of the bullshit he'd been willfully turning a blind eye toward had come crashing down on him in the space of a few minutes. He had faced down Achelon in his own godly exile and not flinched once. But now the gnawing feeling of emptiness consumed him. And there was no escape from it.

"How's 'bout we swing by tomorrow, around breakfast?" Theril said. "You be up by then or…uh…napping?"

"Such a waste, all those people…" Gran sighed.

Riley grabbed Maddox and kissed his cheek. "Just because we're under different roofs don't mean we're not still close. I love you like a brother. You're welcome."

"I need to go home."

"I need drugs," Otix said in broken Thrycean.

REUNION (JESSA)

The system of government in the Protectorate of the Free Cities is a bit confusing for one acquainted with a traditional system of peerage.

There is no king, but there are nobility who are addressed according to local custom. However, it would be wrong to assume that a count holds any real responsibilities. There are, for instance, a profusion of beggar princes in Bamor who inherit their title because the son of a prince is always a prince, and there is no king to name an heir apparent.

This isn't to say the titles are always honorifics. Old families with wealth and resources are well represented in the democratically elected Assembly. Wealth, as it does in every nation, secures influence even if it doesn't translate to a seat on the Assembly.

The Assembly writes laws, collects taxes, and allocates funds for its local municipality according to the vote of its majority. However, a plethora of independent chartered organizations work within the official sanction of laws according to the guidelines given by the Assembly. This includes at minimum the Patrean military, the Lyceum, trade guilds, and the Orthodoxy.

To give an example of how confusing this can be, the city of Rivern's security is enforced by four separate groups, with different functions. The Patreans and Invocari coordinate to enforce the law and defend the city. The Orthodoxy and the Lyceum work, often at odds, to manage rogue magical elements.

—Suang Xiau, *Comparative Governments*

The streets were eerily quiet in the light of day. The latest round of harrowings was said to be the most yet, and people whispered that even daylight couldn't protect them from the visitations. Screaming faces with black holes for eyes had been painted on the doors of some of the houses Jessa passed. Someone was marking the sites where people had died. One home had five faces painted on the door.

The Upstream Locks District was a neighborhood of modest homes, built with adjoining walls so that they huddled together on the narrow, vacant streets. Behind the cheerfully painted facades, dark curtains hung across the windows like burial shrouds.

Jessa found number fifteen easily. She wore a long cloak to conceal her identity, but it was unnecessary. The street was abandoned. Carefully she knocked three times, as Cameron's mysterious letter had instructed. The door swung open ominously, and Jessa stepped into the cool, dark interior of the house.

Cameron's place was small and narrow. A set of stairs greeted her at the foyer, and a living area sat off to the side. The walls were minimally adorned with a couple of swords and a scattering of small, unremarkable landscape paintings. "Hello?"

"Hello, Jessa." Cameron emerged through a doorway, bare chested and tipsy from drink. He was tying his trousers. She clearly saw the outline of his erection. He gave her a cold look and put his finger to his mouth before she could say anything. Something about the way he did it made her pause.

Jessa felt a visceral stab of anger when she saw the thin hands of another woman reach out of the darkness and run themselves across his chest. Then a face peered around the side. "Jessarayne! It has been absolutely ages!"

It took a moment for the pieces to fall together. The woman was older but incredibly striking. Lustrous hair like coils of metallic silver spilled over her shoulders and breasts. She wore a bright-blue leather bustier and a chain-mail skirt studded with sapphires. Her eyes were lined with black kohl that curved into wicked points at the corners. Her irises matched the silver in her hair.

Jessa gasped. "Aunt Sireen?"

Sireen squealed in excitement and nearly tossed Cameron to the floor as she ran to Jessa, her arms extended in a warm embrace. For a shorter woman, Sireen's embrace was surprisingly strong. Jessa remained motionless as she allowed her aunt to lift her into the air, twirl her, and set her down.

"Let me get a look at you!" Sireen said breathlessly, running her eyes over every inch of her niece. She smiled warmly as she ran her hand through Jessa's pale golden hair. "You're so magnificent. And as tall as your mother. I remember when I could hold you in my arms. Oh, I just wanted to eat you up." She giggled. "Not literally."

"It's probably for the best. I imagine children would be fatty," Jessa said.

Sireen let out a musical peal of laughter. "Cameron, you bottom-feeder. You didn't tell me she had such wit!" She glanced back at Cameron and slapped his arm.

Jessa's eyes met Cameron's, and he shook his head gravely with a look that said, *I haven't told her anything.*

Sireen grabbed Jessa's hand and yanked her down to a sofa. "You must have so many questions for me. And we have much catching up to do. But first I want to hear all about your adventures in Rivern. How are the suitors? Are they handsome at least?"

"Torin was cute," Jessa said matter-of-factly, "before someone, possibly my own mother, murdered him."

"That's terrible"—Sireen pouted innocently—"but your mother had nothing to do with it. She can be petty and vindictive, with the emphasis on 'petty,' but Cameron tells me it was local politics."

"Cordovis," Cameron said. "He's a smuggler who, among other things, was responsible for shipping weapons and supplies from Rothburn's allies into Amhaven. He also served as a proxy for the Patreans, supplying him with troops."

Jessa glared at him, but he didn't react. *Were you going to mention this to me at some point?* she wondered.

"Cameron has been faithful to the Dominance for years." Sireen explained. "He's proven extremely resourceful in getting us information we need."

"Of course, you're a spy." Jessa buried her head in her hands. "The Stormlords really pull all the strings, huh? Why would an assemblyman take interest in me if not to report my every movement back to the empire? What with my mother indisposed with her apparently baseless arrest. How could I have been so foolish?"

"Now look, Jessa—" Cameron started.

"You disgust me," she said angrily. Without thinking she added, "And to think I was considering carrying your child."

Sireen started to laugh then quickly covered her mouth. She motioned for a pause in the conversation while she mastered herself and finally said, "You have fine taste in men, Jessa. He fucks like an animal and is as devoted to the empire as any of the empress's consorts. He would lay down his life for you. Your instincts were right to trust him."

Cameron added, "The Dominance isn't as bad as your mother makes it out to be. You've seen the Backwash—the beggars, the whores, the undesirables. Is that really the kind of justice you expect from a government supposedly run by the people? I spent half my life arguing common sense to an Assembly that can't even wipe its own ass without holding a referendum on what to wipe it with.

Their empress is strict, but she gets things done. People don't go hungry; they don't get tossed aside. Anyone who wants a job has work."

"I suppose slavery is a profession," Jessa said sarcastically.

"Mandatory term-limited labor contracts don't constitute slavery." Sireen chuckled congenially. "In any event, political discussions are so dreadfully boring. So tell me—am I a great-aunt or what?"

Jessa tossed her blond hair back and cast a withering glance at Cameron. "For the time being. And provided I can ever escape the machinations of my family."

Sireen smiled sadly. "Your mother is a troubled woman. It couldn't have been easy growing up with her as the only example of our kind. I begged her on endless occasions to let you come stay with me in the summers at Mazitar Beach. The pink sand is the most beautiful in the entire archipelago, and at night the sea glows like a starry sky. But she was always so afraid I would turn you against her."

Jessa deadpanned, "Would you not?"

"To be perfectly honest"—Sireen shrugged nonchalantly—"I think your mother did a fine job of that on her own. I just wish she hadn't soured you on the rest of your family with her instability."

Jessa smiled. "So you prefer to manipulate through kindness rather than bravado. Is that the gist of your strategy?"

Sireen put her arm around Jessa. "I believe being a good person and getting what you want aren't mutually exclusive. Yes, I'm forced to play the games of court because it's expected, but my targets are always deserving of their comeuppance."

"So who are you here to kill, dearest aunt?" Jessa asked as she slid away. "And what's my role in this endeavor?"

"You'll help us reclaim this city. Rivern will bend to the Red Army, and the Dominance will gain a foothold on the continent of Genatrova. The empire will expand to cover half of Creation." Sireen said.

"And should I decide, for whatever reason, that I have no interest in doing so?"

Sireen tipped her head back. "Nasara and I are your family, Jessa. Though you don't know me, the connection of our blood is a stronger bond than you realize. Cameron is the father of your child, and he fights for a society he can be proud of. Even your mother, flawed as she is, needs your help."

"You left out the part where you threaten my life if I don't agree to what you next propose," Jessa said.

"I would never," Sireen gasped. "No, but you can't escape who you are. The people of Rivern will turn on you before any reprisal by the Coral Throne. You can swear everything before their Veritas Seal, and they'll still mistrust you as an outsider. The empress needs only whisper from across the ocean to implicate you, if your enemies in the Assembly don't do it first."

"There are whispers already," Cameron avowed, "that you've threatened Muriel's family and bewitched me to secure our allegiance. The countess has fallen from favor, and some even accuse her of treason, for no other purpose than to eliminate her assemblymen as rivals. Ask her why she has to make a case to keep you in Rivern when the Assembly was ready to let her negotiate a peace treaty with the Dominance. Her star is fading."

"Tell me, Cameron, exactly how many members of the imperial family have you fucked?" Jessa spat.

"They'll take our child," Cameron said, angrily looming over her, his arms resting on the back of the couch to either side of her shoulders. "It's true they want a line of Stormlords in the Protectorate, but they only need the baby, not the mother. Think about it. Why would they keep you around if there was even a sliver of a chance you held even the slightest loyalty to Thrycea?"

"Then I'll get rid of it," Jessa said. "I'll drink the black potion until I'm as barren as the Zarabi waste. For I couldn't wish a worse fate for a child than to be born into this madness."

"Tell me," Sireen said. "What have Cam or I told you that rings untrue? You may not trust your instincts, but I believe in your heart you know."

Jessa sighed. "You two obviously need me for something, and I'm poor at playing intrigue. Just explain to me what you want."

Exposing the conspiracy might backfire on me, she thought, *but I should at least learn what it is.*

Sireen looked disappointed. "Not all of us follow Alessandria's teachings. I want to help you, Jessarayne, but I need to know what you desire."

"I want guarantees," Jessa stated calmly. "The Silverbrook family will not come to undue harm. Muriel and her family have left the estate in light of the recent harrowing. I would see it restored to them when they return to the city. They have offered me hospitality and suffered for it. I would see them remunerated for their troubles, and the enemies who conspired against them in the Assembly will be given the full measure of Thrycean justice."

"Done," Sireen said. "Surely there's more your aunt can do for you."

She's better at manipulation than Mother. I need to tread carefully.

"Amhaven." Jessa folded her hands. "Rothburn's supporters will be stripped of their resources to replenish the treasury. The refugees will be repatriated and compensated for their travails in coin first, then in blood should coin not suffice."

"A very noble gesture," Sireen replied, "and there will be abundant plunder to restore Amhaven. Even now Nasara brings her armies against the usurper."

Jessa stiffened. "Nasara's actions without my express consent constitute an invasion!"

"It's essential to the plan. We need the army close to Rivern but without arousing suspicion. In this regard Rothburn has been useful to us," Sireen explained.

"The insurrection was a ploy. Rothburn works for you." Jessa recoiled in disgust.

"Let's just say...the financiers of the uprising aren't solely confined to the Assembly."

Jessa fumed, "People have lost their homes...dear aunt."

"All too true." Sireen pouted. "Nasara is the architect of this plan, and I was privy to it far too late to protest. Which makes it all the more imperative we end this charade as quickly as possible and focus on our true objective."

Jessa chuckled. "Unbelievable."

"Amhaven will be yours again—truly yours, without the need for a husband to legitimize your claim. Stormlords have always known that women make better leaders. You'll be the undisputed queen of Amhaven, but surely there's something you want for yourself."

You mean "What matters enough to me that I can use it as leverage?" I have to be very careful about this. "Cameron," Jessa said at last.

He gulped in surprise but nervously eyed Sireen.

Sireen brushed it off. "A fine choice for a consort. He's yours, with my warmest regards. If he'd been forthcoming about your little liaison, I never would have laid a finger on him. I'm certain his secrecy was motivated by a desire to protect you."

"I can't be given away like a Patrean bodyguard, Sireen," Cameron protested, "but if Jessa will still have me, I would be honored to be her consort exclusively."

Jessa shuddered at the creepiness the conversation was veering toward, but she needed to stay the course. "My honor has been offended, dear aunt, and I'm sorry he's made you an unwitting party to it. I took Cameron into my confidence, offered my body, and considered carrying his child. There's one thing I can't abide, and it's dishonesty. This betrayal can't go unanswered."

"Jessa!" Cameron glowered. "Listen to yourself. You sound like—"

"Silence," Sireen said, lowering her voice. "My niece hasn't finished speaking."

"In Thrycea I would be justified in killing him, would I not?"

"Sireen..." he said through clenched teeth.

Sireen smiled and gently placed a hand on Jessa's shoulder. "By the blood law, you have the right. And in your situation, I might have the same temptation, but what truly defines a Stormlord isn't her temper but her *mastery* of anger. Cameron has been nothing but loyal to the cause and, recent transgressions aside, has worked tirelessly on your behalf while your mother has been imprisoned. Please consider that while making your decision."

So do you need him alive for your plans, or is he dear to you?

Jessa's stern expression broke into laughter. "Then it's good I have no intention of claiming blood vengeance. Honestly the look on his face was priceless."

Sireen sighed. "That's more the kind of cruelty I expect from your mother, Jessa." She glanced at Cameron, who was breathing a huge sigh of relief.

Jessa said more seriously, "I want nothing from you, dear aunt, save clemency for those who would fight against your uprising and fairness for the people of Rivern."

"You can't imagine my relief to see that even after all those long years of living with Satryn, you're nothing like her." Sireen let out a long sigh. "That does bring us to the reason we asked you here."

Finally.

"One more thing…I want Satryn gone from my life," Jessa demanded. "She's never to speak to me or meet any of my children. She's to be banished from Amhaven, Rivern, and any other place I may call home. That's my final condition before I agree to anything."

Sireen leaned back on the couch, letting her arm drape over the armrest as her fingers absently traced at some tatty embroidery. "Satryn's task will be the most dangerous of any of ours. There's a very good chance she won't survive the weeks to come."

"She created this situation," Jessa said. "I don't care if she is my mother. I won't put myself in any danger to protect her from the consequences of her own designs."

"It pains me to hear you speak so hatefully toward my sister. She wasn't always the woman she is today. She used to light up Thelassus with her smile and carefree wit, but after Maelcolm left, she grew darker. I never put any credence into the scurrilous rumors that the two of them were romantically involved, but he gave her stability and helped her think outside herself."

Sireen leaned her head against the sofa and picked at a loose thread. "She isn't well, and she hasn't treated you well. You're a kind person, Jessa, even though you pretend for my sake to be made of ice. I know you can't let her suffer, even though she has abused you."

Jessa scowled. "In this matter I'm colder than ice."

Sireen looked at her, a sparkle of tears in her silver eyes. "If your mother perishes in her endeavor, you may one day, years from now, find yourself regretting that decision. However, you must remember your anger in this moment vividly and know that justice was satisfied."

Huh? "I thought you said Satryn needed my help."

"Desperately. She grows in power, and she's unstable." Sireen plucked the thread out of the couch and examined it. "She'll become something far more dangerous than she is today. If she survives, she'll be a threat to you, Amhaven, Rivern, and your own family. She won't let you go from her life, and I may not be able to stop her."

Sireen motioned to Cameron, and he retrieved a bundle of cloth from inside the flue of his fireplace.

"This isn't revenge," Sireen continued. "It's mercy for a suffering woman who'll never know any love in her heart." She took the bundle from Cameron and unwrapped it. The thing inside appeared crude and jagged—a fang carved from dull-gray rock and porous to the touch. Flashes of electricity danced across its surface.

Jessa gasped. "The Thunderstone."

"One of five actually," Sireen corrected her. "The Thrycean translation for this one's name is something like 'Hungry Mother's Tooth Eating Her Eggs.' It sounds much more terrifying in the coelacanth pronunciation, but it's difficult to make the sounds outside of water. I assume you know what this does?"

Jessa nodded. "It can kill an emperor."

"Or any other Stormlord," Sireen said. "When our ancestors made their blood bargain with the coelacanth for mastery of the upper oceans, they provided us these tools to effect the transfer of power from individuals too dangerous or unworthy to wield their gifts. It nullifies their power, and one scratch can do it, so be careful around it." Sireen handed it to her. "You should be the one to do it."

"Kill my mother?"

Sireen closed her eyes and looked away. "My sister is already lost. When the time is right—and you'll know it—you must offer her mercy."

Jessa fondled the stone and laughed. Her laughter bubbled up from somewhere deep inside her, nervous and uncontrollable. She couldn't look at Sireen or Cameron without cackling uncontrollably. Their carefully orchestrated expressions of worry and false sympathy inspired hilarity. Tears formed at the corner of her eyes.

"My whole life I've tried to be the dutiful daughter, the noble princess…whatever," Jessa chuckled to herself. "Satryn was right. Everyone will disappoint you, and in the end, you have only yourself to look out for."

"Jessarayne," Sireen said gently. "It's not that simple."

"Don't try to play to my sympathies," Jessa said. "If killing Satryn is the price, then I'm more than willing to pay."

LANDRY MANOR
(HEATH AND SWORD)

L andry Manor occupied a large plot of land behind a tall stone wall. Cypress trees provided privacy from the neighboring estates and the street. The once-manicured lawn had started to grow wild. Heath pulled himself over the wall and slid down behind some bushes. Sword made his way over as well and retrieved the grappling hook.

In its heyday the manor grounds were patrolled by a regimen of private Patrean security guards and a few Invocari who served as personal protection for assemblymen. But the grounds were empty and neglected. Whomever the home belonged to now hadn't bothered to claim it. A pair of bored-looking Fodders from the city detail stood in front of the iron gate, chatting casually.

Heath absently imagined how he'd use the terrain and positioning of the to-piary to make his way to the house, evading patrols, dogs, and vantage points. It would have been fun. Instead he walked to the front door and waited for Sword to break the protection ward.

The foyer had a distinctive zigzag pattern of black-and-white tiles—a play on the traditional checkerboard that made his eyes bounce. Twin marble staircases curved from an upper balcony, one for the lord and one for the lady to make their grand entrances. Portraits of old dead Landry lords graced the walls, ideal-ized depictions of men in armor or jackets draped with chains and ribbons of their various offices.

"You know," Sword commented, "if you wanted to do some good old-fash-ioned thieving, this is a perfect time to do it, with all these lords off at their country estates."

"See something you like?" Heath joked. The grand foyer was bare of anything that looked especially valuable. Or at least anything valuable and portable. The chandelier featured four golden eagles rendered in flight, their wings dripping with strands of crystal. It was easily worth a million ducats, but buyers for that kind of art would be rarer than the piece itself.

"You could buy this place for a song, I reckon." Sword tapped his blade against the banister of one of the twin staircases. "With a bit of fixing up, it could be quite homey—I prefer parquet to marble."

"That would raise the inevitable questions of how I acquired my money," Heath said with a smile.

"I'd wager this lot stole their fortune too, just it's been so long no one remembers." Sword scratched his head. "So what are we looking for...aside from any journals titled, *The Evil Plots of Lord Evan Landry?*"

"A portrait..." Heath's eyes scanned the names on the pictures in the foyer. No Evanses. "Barring that a family tree or an entry in the registry."

Sword indicated one of two doors that led out of the foyer. "Office then. In most of these places, the office is on the first floor, close to the entrance, so as to limit the traffic of the occasional lowborn riffraff who might happen into the family's business."

Heath and Sword stepped through the double doors into a library. Books were spilled and scattered over the floor. A display case had been broken open and tipped on its side, the outlines of its contents—a dagger and some coins— still visible on the green-felted mounting. One of the paintings had been slashed, and the upholstery on the sitting couches had been torn open.

"Careful, mate." Sword grabbed Heath's shoulder and indicated a spot on the floor. "That's a pile of shit right there."

Heath glanced down and saw Sword meant that literally. Could have been dog crap or human. "Looks like it's been here a couple days. This place has been tossed pretty good. Think it was vandals?"

Sword started working through the wreckage, turning over books with the tip of his blade. He tapped a bottle. "Maybe. Whoever did it was getting drunk on the job. That's Archean brandy—probably worth more than Lord Landry's coin collection."

"It's personal," Heath said, examining the slashed portrait. Lord Willifer Landry, had been shredded, his eye sockets colored black. "Someone didn't like the reigning lord of the house."

"Disowned, most likely," Sword said. "I know that hurt from personal experience. Remember when I used to be Lord Dalrymple?"

Heath chuckled. "That was…an interesting period. It never ceases to amaze me how many different ways you can find to be an annoying pain in the ass. It's been the one thread of consistency through all your personas."

"Pshhh," Sword scoffed. "I know your secret, mate. You could've given us up at that dolmen, but you didn't because you looooove us."

"I couldn't kill you if I wanted to." Heath made his way over a pile of torn-up books. "You're a deadly fighter in a body that's twice as strong and fast as mine, and you know all my moves."

"Aw," Sword said. "That's sweet of you to say, but I know you have a contingency up your sleeve. You've probably thought long and hard about what it would take if it came down to it."

Heath didn't respond. He had several contingencies in fact. One needed to plan for any eventuality, and he had learned long ago not to place his trust in others.

He stepped toward a pair of sliding doors at the end of the library. The lock had been broken open, presumably with a chipped marble bust that lay facedown on the floor. He pushed the door open and stepped into the dark study.

Ransacked, like the library. The mahogany desk was broken into splinters, and everything in sight was demolished. Bookshelves had been emptied and smashed, their tomes scattered on the floor. A stern portrait of one of the Landry founders dominated the wall behind the bookcase, the regal gray-haired figure surrounded by crude drawings of penises ejaculating onto his face.

"More shit in here. Looks like dog crap," Heath called out. There were papers everywhere. It would take days to look through all of them. "Fuck."

Sword came through and went directly to the painting. He felt under the heavy gilded frame until he found something, and the portrait swung free from the wall, revealing an unopened safe. "Obviously whoever ransacked this place didn't grow up in a wealthy family. I mean, the hidden safe is practically a cliché. You want to crack this? These fingers are a little fat for delicate work."

"Wards?" Heath asked.

"Oh, right." Sword tapped the end of his blade to the safe. The air rippled slightly as the binding magic dissipated.

Heath examined the locking mechanism and whistled. "The dial is decorative…the actual lock is an automaton. Fully capable of identifying authorized family members, probably rigged with some kind of deterrent. We need tools, possibly acid."

"Do I have to do everything?" Sword held up his blade, aiming the heartstone jewel in his pommel at the dial. The red gem pulsed with inner light a few times, and the safe clicked open.

Heath glanced at Sword. "Mind explaining how you did that?"

"Heartstone resonates at short range," Sword said casually. "The piece in the automaton is just a sliver looking for a password. I emptied every word in my lexicon of three thousand languages and dialects until I found the right one. Might have just overloaded it."

Heath opened the vault, and soft bluish-purple light poured through the cracks. He smiled as he pulled the door open and gazed upon three radiant Archean shards. "Jackpot," he said, reaching in the vault and removing a leather folio of parchments. "Grab the other stuff while I go through this."

"Shit." Sword hefted one of the glowing shards of Archean prismite. "We're fucking rich, mate. Could buy us a castle with this."

"Here," Heath said, flipping through a folio. "Last will and testament of Willifer. It names successors, beneficiaries…Wait. Here it is—a trust for an E. R. Landry to cover the expenses of education at the Lyceum. And a stipulation that he never would inherit the title or land."

"A bastard then."

"Looks like." Heath tossed the folio to the floor. "Who do we know at the Lyceum?"

Sword looked at him. "Maddox?"

Heath sighed. "Who *else*?"

"No, mate…" Sword pointed toward the library at a lean figure shuffling listlessly through the debris. The shoulders were slumped, and his arms swayed at his sides. "Fucking drunk as usual to boot."

Heath marched out to the library. He spread his arms wide and offered his dazzling smile. "Maddox! Buddy, what are you doing—"

The thing that looked at him had Maddox's face, but the croaking noise that came from its mouth wasn't human. The skin was pale, and the eyes were milky with the pall of death. His neck looked slashed and tied back together with thick black stitches. The revenant lunged for him.

Heath's blades were already drawn and readied, but revenants were fast when they needed to be. The thing slammed into him and knocked him backward as hands scratched and pulled at his clothes. Maddox shook and snapped at him like a ferocious animal.

They crashed to the floor, Heath's head exploding with pain as it came down on something hard and sharp. The edges of books and shattered glass poked into his back as the monster on top of him went for his neck like a lover in the throes of passion.

The wet feeling of blood crept over on Heath's neck as the revenant gnawed his flesh. Somewhere in the back of his mind, he knew he'd bleed out in a matter of minutes, but the pain was washed away by the rush of battle. He jammed his blades into Maddox's rib cage. The abraveum sliced through skin into organs, but the revenant didn't even flinch.

Sword charged out of the study, his blade in midswing as he leapt toward Maddox and kicked him in the ribs. Revenants were made stronger by necromancy but not heavier. Sword's blow sent the creature a good couple of feet into the air, with Heath's bloody flesh still in its mouth.

Heath scrambled back, desperately pressing his hands against the wound. Light poured from his fingers, its radiance easing his pain even as it drew more of his strength.

The revenant lunged at Sword again, but he calmly kicked it, square in the head, back to the ground. Sword let out a roar and speared Maddox through his mouth, pinning him to the floor. The revenant bit at the steel, his limbs flopping and eyes darting frantically.

"Now that's just sad, mate." Sword knelt next to Maddox. "Good news is that it looks like he's already been decapitated and stitched together."

"He caught me by surprise." Heath pulled himself off the floor as he massaged his neck. His fingers traced the edges where his skin had regrown softer and smoother.

Sword brushed off his hands. "You want to do any last rites or whatnot? He was sort of a friend...I suppose."

Heath laughed incredulously. "That fucking sick, manipulative, evil...bitch!"

Sword shrugged. "He was a bit of a twat, but that's kind of harsh for a send-off, mate."

"I'm talking about Daphne," Heath growled. "She wanted me to kill him because he's some kind of immortal warlock. But look at that shit. Does that look immortal to you? She's fucking with me, Sword. She wanted to see if she could make me follow orders again."

"You could...you know, take care of her. It is a rule that the leaders of the Inquisition are all horrible bastards, but they span the multitudinous diversity of ways that people can be horrible bastards."

Heath had thought of killing her after what had happened in Reda. Sending him to kill children was a test of loyalty. Sending him to kill someone he knew— that was personal.

And unnecessary. "Let's see where the current takes us," Heath said. "There's no use dropping him in the river if there's a price on his head someone's willing to pay. But now we have another problem: someone killed him before we did."

"What luck, right? Three shards, and we've bought our way back into the abbess's good graces practically guilt free. And you go in there bawling like a baby about how hard it was and how you feel nothing but emptiness, et cetera, and she thinks she's got one over on us. Classic."

Sword grabbed Maddox's hair, which had grown tangled and greasy, pressed his boot on his shoulder, and yanked. The blade pinning the head popped out of the floor, accompanied by a sickening ripping noise as the leather stitches tore from the neck. Sword stumbled backward and let the head slide off the blade onto the floor. The revenant's body lay still.

"Someone killed my friend," Heath said, surprising himself by his use of the word. "This will need to be answered for."

Sword cocked his bushy eyebrow. "Will it really, though? I mean, he can't have mattered that much to you."

Heath nodded. "No. Our courtship was a mistake. He was rude, arrogant, clingy, and half the time so drunk he could barely get it up. The world isn't greatly diminished by the absence of his Light, but...mutilation? Reanimation? I knew him. He was a person, a better one than either of us, if you consider it objectively, and he never in his life did anything to deserve this."

"It's your vendetta. I just like killing things," Sword acknowledged. "You think Evan Landry's responsible?"

"There's a connection for sure," Heath said. "It just doesn't add up yet. But why would he kill Maddox? And why leave his revenant in Landry Manor? Why loot the place for trinkets and not hit the safe?"

They both spun around at the sound of crunching glass.

A short, lithe figure in a black cloak crept along the wall, holding a bundle of fabric. The gentle pulsing glow of Archean prismite showed through the cloth. The thief bolted for the door.

Sword lunged at full speed, aiming to tackle, and probably crush, their unexpected visitor. Sword was Patrean and strong as fuck—when one of those guys ran at you, there wasn't much to do but get out of the way or brace for injury.

The thief changed direction and sprinted toward the wall, gaining footholds in the emptied bookshelves. The cloak fell back, revealing a woman with a mane of long multicolored hair. By the time Sword got to her, however, she was gone, and he went crashing into the wall.

She somersaulted off the wall and landed into a crouching roll across the floor a good ten feet away from Sword. Heath was moving to intercept. Their eyes locked for an instant. She was maybe seventeen. She flashed a grin then darted toward the door to the foyer.

Heath ducked and unleashed a springblade into the wall, creating a tripwire of abraveum filament at calf level. She cleared it with a flashy midair tuck and roll.

He extended his other hand and let out a flare of brilliant light. Illumination flooded the room, glaring and bright. He let his other springblade loose, lodging it in the wall in front of her. She didn't see it, and it nearly took off her head. She caught the wire at chest level and fell back, shrieking in pain. The shards tumbled to the floor, still glowing softly.

Sword was on top of her, a meaty hand pressed against her neck. "Stay the fuck down, bitch!"

"Please don't kill me...I work for Daphne," she sobbed softly.

Sword lifted her off the ground and slammed her against the wall. "The fuck you do!"

"Sword..." Heath retracted his blades until they clucked back into his arm braces. "She's just a kid. Lay off a little."

Sword didn't lay off. "Give me one reason I shouldn't gut this cunt right now."

It was somewhat of a cliché in interrogations for one party to be aggressive while the other seemed reasonable. And Sword usually followed Heath's lead. But it already had started. Best to go with it. Heath smiled. "Nice moves. I'm Heath, and this is my associate. Whom do I have the pleasure of addressing? Madame Landry perhaps?" He turned to Sword and added, "At least give her enough air to answer questions."

Sword let her down but kept his left hand digging into her shoulder. The wince on her face suggested he wasn't being gentle with her. Her shirt and chest were slashed from her having hit his abraveum filament earlier, but it was a surface wound. It would sting for a few days, but it would heal.

She pleaded, "I was just looking for food..."

"Let me provide an alternate explanation, if I may." Sword slammed her against the wall again. "You're mixed up in this. You overheard my mate and me having a collegial discussion about internal matters. Then you set your little revenant pet to distract us while you made off with the shards."

"Fuck it," she sneered, dropping the pathetic façade. "Just kill me. I already would have done it myself if I had the guts."

Heath rubbed his temples. "How about you just answer our questions? I don't like torture. In general I don't like to get my hands dirty. But I just lost a piece of my neck to a revenant, and I just want to go home and take a nice, long, relaxing bath. So let's start with your name."

"Esme."

"Now," Heath said, "as a duly appointed agent of the Inquisition, you were given a pass phrase to identify your rank within the Order. What is it?"

"Clever." She smirked. "There isn't a passphrase. You can find the black coin in my left pocket. Your friend can dig it out."

Sword reached into her trousers pocket and pulled out a folded square of parchment and a black disk bearing the seal of Ohan. He tossed the coin to Heath and unfolded the parchment. It was stuffed with green crystal shards.

Heath caught the coin. It was legit. She still could have come by it through dishonest means, but if she had called bullshit on the pass phrase, she knew enough about the Inquisition to pass. She was thin, a little too thin, but pretty enough to stand out. And if she were a street rat, she'd be prime Inquisition recruitment material.

Sword dipped his finger into the green crystals, held it to his nose, and sniffed. He shook his head and tipped back a bit. "Fuck! That's some good shit."

"You mind, asshole?" Esme said. "That's gotta last me all week."

"What was your assignment?"

Esme blew a few stray strands of hair out of her face. "I was infiltrating hedge-wizard circles, looking for evidence of warlocks or pact magic and reporting it back to the church. Daphne wanted me to stay close to this guy…He's nothing big, but he's well connected. My job was to stay close, observe, and report."

"How did she contact you?"

"I only met her once." She frowned. "My last pimp liked to get his girls hooked on dragonfire so he could…" She shook her head. "One of her agents said she could cure my addiction if I worked for her; in the meantime she hooked me up. That was two fucking years ago, so I figured this whole offer was bullshit, but it beat the brothels. Besides hedge wizards aren't so bad. When I saw the shards, I saw an opportunity—one of those will pay for an education at the Lyceum."

Sword added. "Very convenient."

"I know who you are, Heath," Esme said. "You're already rich. I didn't think it would hurt to make off with the shards."

Heath calmly asked, "Why were you here?"

"It's a big empty house full of shit. There's a lot of them since all the high and mighty bailed and left us to the Harrowers. And the Inquisition hasn't exactly been paying me."

"You ever heard of Evan Landry?" he asked.

"Who?"

Sword threw her against the wall again. "He asked you a fucking question!"

"Sword!" Heath said emphatically.

He looked at Heath almost in surprise. His eyes glittered with bloodlust. "Oh, for Ohan's sake…what particular part of this fabricated bullshit are you buying? She's a fucking warlock, and for all we know she *is* Evan Landry. These nobles name girls after anything these days. She tried to fuck us, and she deserves to get fucked."

Heath looked at her. She was scared but masking it with an attitude of defiance. He searched her eyes; she was hard to read.

He waved his hand. "Let her go."

"The fuck I will!" Sword said. "She's going to die tonight, mate."

"What the hells is your problem?"

"Gut feeling," Sword said. "Besides, if she does work for Daphne, which I don't believe for a second, then she also overheard our little conversation about offing the bitch. And if she was being truthful with us with a minimal amount of coercion, how's she going to keep that information from a ruthless psychopath with a Veritas Seal?"

Sword had a point. The story didn't add up. Even so, Heath reiterated, "Let her go now."

"You fucking idiot!" Sword shouted, and punched his hand into the bookshelf behind her.

Esme ducked under his arm and darted toward the door. Sword lunged after her, but she stopped, crouched, and reached her arms back, grabbing his waist and tossing him over her head. With his force and momentum suddenly turned against him, Sword smashed into the floor. Esme furled her cape back, grinned slightly at Heath, then bolted out to the foyer.

"The fuck!" Sword gathered a book from the floor, ripped it in half, and chucked the pieces across the room. "You let her get away!"

"The fuck happened to you?" Heath challenged. "That was unprofessional. When I tell you to stand down, you do it."

"You're a child!" Sword puffed out his chest and stood in Heath's way. "I'm ancient, and I've been fighting for centuries. This body here was crafted as the perfect weapon. I'm stronger and faster than anything on two legs. A little girl shouldn't have been able to dodge me. It's impossible."

"Easy now." Heath smiled and leaned into Sword's ear, whispering, "I have her blood on my springblades. We can find her any time."

"You fucking brilliant fucker, you!" He threw his hands around Heath and squeezed.

Heath continued, "We pretend this never happened, bring Maddox's head to Daphne, and see what she knows. There's a fair bit of my blood here, so we need to burn the room. You still remember how to set fires?"

"Psssh." Sword waved his hand. "Burning a library isn't pyromancy. You want to get food after this?"

Heath surveyed the wreckage, the forgotten shards on the carpet, Maddox's corpse. "I could eat."

THE SHOPPE (MADDOX)

I've sat through 183 sermons in twenty-five temples of Ohan and listened to forty-two priests' homilies on the life of Saint Juliette. She's unique among the saints in that her exploits are well preserved in both the Cantos and the dry military logs of the Patreans.

Saint Juliette was, by general account, a farmer who, in defiance of Thrycean authority, led a brief and ineffective revolt in Fishers Bay, a former settlement in Gorin. The Patrean records objectively tabulate the slaughter of the recalcitrant villagers (127) in a ledger against Patrean casualties (three) to arrive at an invoice for the counterinsurgency.

We've never been given reason to doubt Patrean accounting practices when it comes to death gratuities. Saint Juliette was killed and her head presented to the presiding legate of Thrycea, who proffered a bounty of thirty and thirty crowns for her bones, which were lashed to the prow of the Dragon Wind.

No serious student of history can lend any credence to the story of Saint Juliette's miraculous ascension into Radiance as described in the Cantos, while her bones are on display in Thelassus. It isn't unexpected for the public to believe what they're told, but priests receive a comparable education to most learned scholars, including those of history.

Yet never once in all 183 sermons did I hear a single telltale reverberation of deceit, even from men who were well acquainted with the evidence. The Veritas Seal isn't infallible. While it is sometimes accurate in detecting lies, it is far less so in detecting truth. Particularly in matters of faith. A mage's own sound judgment is always the final arbiter.

—Magus Archibald Turnbull, *Veritas: Certainty vs. Complacency*

The windows to Badlands' Philters were boarded shut. The door had been painted with a chalky white face with hollow eyes and a mouth frozen in a scream. A parchment with a wax seal hung from the doorway: writ of foreclosure. Maddox pulled his ragged cloak tightly around himself and turned down one of the shop's alleys.

Most of Beaker Street was asleep during the day, save for some strung-out-looking shop boys carrying crates of dragonfire to the day laborers who would bring it up to the city. Aside from a mangy, partially mutated stray cat, the alley was clear, although a soupy runnel of opalescent slime had coalesced along the footpath.

Maddox picked his way across it as best he could in boots that were a size too large for him. Whatever had happened to his boots during his time in the Seven Signs was better left out of mind. The back entrance to the shop was locked and boarded, with a similar writ posted on the planks.

He popped his hand in a largely unnecessary arcane gesture, and the boards neatly pulled themselves free of the doorframe, floating freely in the alley. The hard part would be remembering where they went back in. Maddox shrugged and let the planks tumble into the disgusting alchemical runoff. He wouldn't be here long enough for anyone to report it anyway.

Someone of reasonable skill had warded the lock on the door against tampering. The mechanisms resisted his telekinesis. Maddox started to dismantle the door plank by plank before he remembered Riley had given him a key. It worked.

The back of the shop was where the ovens and bulk alchemical solutions were kept. The oven was new; one of Magus Aurius's students had pioneered a new form of convection that was all the rage. The oven wasn't one of those, but it was a later model, probably a secondhand unit from the Lyceum.

Maddox searched for the ingredients he needed to make more euphorium. It was a fairly simple recipe, and Dad's system of organizing hadn't changed much, but the back had been picked clean of any substance that could even remotely be used to get high. He went to the front to check for more reagents.

A woman in white church robes sat, legs crossed delicately, in a shabby chair that had been placed in the center of the room. She had dark skin and a mildly amused expression; her hands thumbed idly through a copy of the Doctrines.

"The fuck are you doing here?"

"I'm Abbess Daphne, anointed hierarch of the Order of Penitent Martyrs." She stood up, removed a long silk glove, and offered her hand. "It's a pleasure to finally make your acquaintance."

"Fucking Inquisition." Maddox shook his hands in exasperation. "You've had an unlicensed *magus* necromancer raising revenants and slinging drugs right under your nose for the last month. And you decide to show up here of all places? You people are fucking useless bureaucrats."

"We only know things if people bring them to our attention, but your concerns are duly noted," she said casually. "I'd be more than happy to take your statement and have it handled through the official channels. However, we've been just a bit busy trying to liaise with a rogue Traveler, identify the cause of these Harrower killings, and of course verify some disturbing claims that a mage from the university has violated one of the cardinal laws of the natural order and risen from the dead as one of the living."

Maddox laughed. "If you came here to kill me, you're shit out of luck."

"I admit I was skeptical," Daphne said. "There are probably a hundred thousand people in Creation with a longer-than-average lifespan—more and more wizards are putting their souls in artifacts every day. Of those who keep their flesh, perhaps five hundred are truly ageless. But every single one of them can be killed. It might not be easy, but once they die, the only way they get up again is with the aid of necromancy."

"Funny you should mention that."

"Funny indeed. I have something of yours."

The abbess sat back in her chair and pulled a thick leather bag from beneath it. She slid the bag toward him.

Maddox kept one hand trained toward her. The gesture was unnecessary for taking her out, but he felt it was a useful reminder that he could at any moment turn this room into a cloud of burning acidic death. He bent down and flipped open the backpack. A large glass jar rested inside. Carefully he slid it out.

"That's my head," he stated flatly, examining his dead visage sloshing around in a amber liquid. Strands of his brown hair floated in the viscous preservative as the head lolled around inside. Dead milky-brown eyes stared back at him. No matter which way he turned the jar, the head gazed directly at him, like the needle of a compass. "You tracked me with blood magic."

"The head was cut off a revenant by one of my votaries. The tracking spell works only when you're alive, which apparently isn't that frequent these days. It's undeniable evidence. Blood magic can't work on the dead, and necromancy can't reanimate the living, yet there you are."

Maddox dropped the jar to the floor beside him, not taking his eyes off her. The jar thunked but didn't break as it rolled over the uneven slats of the floor. The head's eyes remained fixed on Maddox as the glass spun around it.

"You've returned Deaddox," he said. "Was there anything else?"

"Deaddox? We called it Headdox." She shrugged. "I have a bit of a problem. Obviously my Inquisition mandate is clear, but I'm in a bit of a quandary about what to do with you. You aren't like most heretics. In fact we know through eye-witness accounts that you obtained this ability through an accident of glyphomancy, not some dolmen or pact ritual. It doesn't mean you aren't dangerous, but…you seem like someone who can be persuaded."

"You aren't seriously trying to convert me." Maddox laughed. "I haven't prayed to your bullshit god since I was five."

"See?" Daphne smiled. "I knew you were reasonable. Most people believe that nonsense their entire lives. Oh? You thought I'd be offended by your off-color remarks and casual sacrilege? I know the Doctrines are a sham. They were cobbled together inside of a month from faiths of every part of Creation by the Orsini Council in 32. Any student of history can put that together. Faith is just a lie that serves a higher purpose."

"Don't you need faith to have a higher purpose?" Maddox asked. "I mean, at least to dedicate your life to enforcing the repressive whims of the Orthodoxy?"

She nodded, acceding his point. "There are a large number of unbelievers in the Orthodoxy. We don't minister to the laity, but we believe maintaining a system of shared values, no matter how arbitrary, is essential to a strong social order and an effective society. People need an incentive to follow rules, especially when it comes at the cost of their own personal desires."

"So you found me."

"I think your curse is the worst possible fate I could imagine," Daphne said. "Immortality. How terrifying it must be. The world changes faster than we do. It's not just seeing the people you know grow old and die but knowing that the ones who replace them have less and less in common with you with each passing generation. Could you imagine if one of the original revolutionaries were alive to see Rivern today? Female landowners, no slave trade, the descendants of the hated nobility sitting on the Assembly—they'd be horrified.

"Imagine what the world will be like in a hundred years. The Hierocracy and College of Seals are seeing a year-after-year decline in admissions as alchemical remedies and feats of mechanical engineering make theurgy overpriced and obsolete for the everyday person. Imagine it in a thousand years…I'd be surprised if the Protectorate remains united that long. And in ten thousand years? You'd be onto the eighth age of history, if anyone could even remember how many came before.

"You'd be utterly and completely alien to future generations. Even more alone than you are now."

Maddox shrugged. "That's one theory. No one's ever carried a seal for more than three hundred years, so we don't know if they're actually permanent or just effectively permanent. Regardless, that's not high on my list of concerns right now."

"Mr. Baeland"—her expression remained deadly serious as she spoke quickly and incisively—"you have the key to absolute immortality indelibly inscribed on your left pectoral in gold. How long before someone figures out that your body bears the ultimate prize and decides they want it for themselves? People will cut and poke and prod and torture you until you either give up a secret you don't possess or are rendered a maddened shell of the man you once were. Because no matter how many times you die and come back healthy, you'll bear the scars of whatever trauma you experience…forever."

Maddox didn't answer. The folks of the House of Seven Signs were a ragtag bunch of hedge mages and euphorium addicts with barely an ounce of sense among them. Still he had been cut apart and eaten with impunity when they realized he couldn't truly die. *They still have my notebooks*, he suddenly remembered.

She added, "Count yourself lucky that senile necromancer let you walk away and didn't peel your skin off every day just to watch it grow back."

"How'd you know she was senile?"

The abbess pursed her lips.

Maddox rolled his eyes. "Ugh. Cut the bullshit. I get it. You're a scary Inquisition lady who's probably murdered a fuckload of people for checking the wrong entries in the card catalog. But since you can't kill me permanently, I assume you have another plan that requires my cooperation."

Daphne began, "I think the reason people inscribe Hamartia is because their temperament is ill suited to the magic they're trying to bind."

"You're a glyphomancy expert as well? I'm impressed."

"The Veritas Seal." Daphne postulated. "It lets you know the truth, which is ostensibly useful; I have one myself, by the way. But consider someone who doesn't want to know the truth. Our ability to deceive ourselves isn't a flaw in our design; it's a survival mechanism. The truth is scary, and what happens to someone when he learns that what people really mean by their words can literally break him? He may just sabotage his seal to give himself what he *really* wants: trust, assurance…even faith."

"Interesting theory," Maddox said. He was being honest.

"So the Seal of Sephariel," Daphne continued, "grants extended life. But I proffer that people who seek to attain it do so because they fear death more than they love life. So when it comes time to alter their relation to the inevitable, the seal grants them their strongest attachment, regardless of whether it's love or fear. So the people who want longevity the most are, ironically, the least likely to succeed at attaining it." Daphne leaned forward in her chair. "But what happens to someone who doesn't fear death as much as they hate the prospect of living?"

Maddox stepped backward.

"By many accounts you were the most brilliant student to pass through the halls of the Lyceum in decades. There wasn't a single subject you couldn't seem to master with seemingly little to no effort. That's quite different from the testimony of your peers and faculty, who describe a bitter, hotheaded, alcoholic pervert. It's not the portrait of a person who's happy with his life."

Maddox said, "I wanted to be *respected*, not dead."

"You have *my* respect, Mr. Baeland, and I don't typically make home visits." Daphne sighed. "But respect doesn't fix a broken man. If anything it gives him even more opportunity to disappoint."

"Just tell me what you want." *Church people and their fucking words.* Maddox felt exhausted, and more than anything, he wanted to puff on euphorium and drink until the shitty world around him fell away and his grand adventure began again.

"Eventually I want to kill you," Daphne said. "I want to do it efficiently and humanely, using the full resources of the Inquisition. We have the largest collection of Lore on the forbidden theurgy in Creation. We have beings serving our order who are thousands of years old, committed to the sacred task of protecting Creation. I'd even be willing to bet that the Archeans don't know as much as we do. I can help you mercifully end your existence and give you a purpose while you still breathe."

He looked at her. "What kind of purpose?"

She smiled. "You could be a white knight, a holy crusader rooting out Dark Magic and researching the forbidden secrets of the lost civilizations. You're a scholar of tremendous ability. You could use your ability to save the lives of others…and maybe, just maybe, find something of value in your own."

Maddox sighed and looked around the empty shop. He had spent every day of his life for the past twenty years trying to avoid ending up here, and Riley—stupid fucking Riley—had sent him back. Turning into his asshole father was the least of his concerns, however; Achelon had basically handed him the knowledge to destroy Creation by showing him the seal.

"Fine. You've persuaded me. Just get me the fuck out of here."

Daphne stood and placed her hand on his back. "I can't promise this will be easy, but you have the full support of the church behind you. The first step is to get you somewhere safe, where you can change clothes and get some rest, and we can learn exactly what's going on."

"I could use a drink first," Maddox said. The last drink he'd had was that burnt-walnut-tasting shit Esme had ordered.

She hooked her arm through his and led him out the back doorway. "As I understand, the Invocari recently have renovated their warding chamber with a full selection of spirits. And you can tell me everything on the way."

So he told her everything.

ROOMIES (SATRYN)

I touched the Dark Star for the first time and came away changed.

It's a strange and wondrous thing to behold, completely black and weightless yet massive. A stillness surrounds it, as if it draws in all light and sound. Nothing echoes in its chamber.

I brought my fingers within an inch of the surface before my will gave out, and I struggled away from it. I'd never felt such sheer panic—of what I can't even say— as my body flung itself away.

The warders were ready to catch me as I fell backward, grabbing my hand and pushing me back as I fought with all my might to stop them. I kicked and I flailed and I bit at them, but they performed their duty with focus and precision.

It didn't feel like anything as they pressed my hand to it. There was no sense of temperature or texture, as if my hand simply had been stopped at the edge of the world, beyond which nothing more existed.

The fear died inside me. Not simply my dread for the task at hand but all my fears. The unsettling emptiness settled me, and the rest of the world seemed cluttered and chaotic. Even in the emptiness of air, I felt the gnash of currents and the bustle of particles.

—Serra's entry in *The Book of Initiations*

"Absolutely not!" Satryn huffed at the pair of Invocari wardens who hovered in front of her.

An apologetic clerk in a black satin tunic wrung a piece of parchment in his bony white hands. "It's only for a few days, Lady Satryn. I don't understand why you would want to remain here—"

"I don't have to explain myself to sniveling toads like yourself. Give me that paper!" she demanded. She didn't wait for him to hand it over.

Satryn paced like a caged tiger as she ran her fingers over the script. "You wish me to swear to abide by the terms of your house arrest? In my mother's own embassy? Are you mad?"

"The Thrycean embassy is currently vacant, and it would give you more privacy." the clerk offered helpfully. "It even has a pool you could use."

"This is a ploy by my enemies to lure me into the open." She crumpled the paper. "Until I'm completely exonerated of these charges in the eyes of the Assembly, I'll remain here. You'll have to find some other place to put your prisoner."

He sighed heavily. "That's not possible. The prisoner must be kept here."

"That isn't my concern." Satryn tossed the paper at his chest. "If the Orthodoxy can't afford to build its own warding prison, perhaps it's time to impose a tithe."

"It's not a matter of cost, Lady. The warding chamber is powered by the Dark Star directly below. We simply couldn't build another one of comparable strength, and it was never really intended for long-term residence. If you prefer the tower, we have other rooms in the dungeons."

She regarded him icily.

"So...the embassy really is your best option," he said. "You'll have a full security detail. More, I imagine."

"No." Satryn walked over to her fainting couch and plopped down on the tufted leather. She crossed her legs and arms. "I'm satisfied with the current arrangement, and you'll simply have to convey that to the Grand Invocus."

The clerk nodded. "I suppose I should be pleased that you've enjoyed your time with us, but if you don't leave, we'll be forced to...put you with the other prisoner."

"Then I'll kill him, and the blood will be on your hands."

"Fine, Lady." He glowered as he waved his hands in the air. "I'm not authorized to remove you, but..." He opened the inner door to the chamber and stepped out while the locking mechanism performed its dance, sealing her inside and allowing him to storm off into the tower.

Satryn savored her small victory as she pored through the addendum to volume fifty-eight of the Rivern common law. Her counsel had delivered it to her earlier that morning, and she didn't want to appear too eager to read it. The Assembly had been busy passing legislation and sanctions against Thrycean trading partners. It seemed Nasara's assault had them rattled. She flipped to the coded letter her spy had slipped in and, seeing Sireen's name, chucked the papers aside.

Her mood was further ruined when she heard the airlock mechanisms kick in. The other prisoner was a scruffy young man, in clothes too big for him and a brown Scholar's cloak. He shuffled his feet awkwardly as he waited for the door to slide open. Satryn was unimpressed to say the least. But if the Invocari were half as terrified of him as they were of her, then she'd have to at least see if he was useful.

"Nice place," he said, looking around at the battered secondhand furnishings the Invocari had scrounged from the Thrycean embassy. It probably did seem nice to a commoner, but there had been two Tempests on the Coral Throne since the furniture was built, and Keltax's dynasty (*may their shame be eternal*) wasn't famed for its taste.

"Who are you?" Satryn said in her commanding voice.

"Maddox." He nodded toward her. "Who are you?"

Satryn rolled her eyes. "You're addressing the Lady Satryn Shyford, duchess of the Bleak Atoll, admiral of the Tiburon Armada, storm priestess of the Western Gale, daughter of Her Majesty Iridissa, and queen regent of Amhaven."

"Amhaven?" He cocked his eyebrow. "Really? You were kind of on a roll till you got to that one."

He had a point. "I hold the title for my daughter. One of the many unrewarded sacrifices I make."

A smile played at the corner of his lips. "How did you end up in here? Are you a wizard?"

"I'm a Stormlord," she stated. "Surely they teach you Scholars about us in your school...or have you not advanced that far in your studies?"

"The eyes." He gestured at her face then looked around the room, inspecting the walls. "Elemental magic's not really the same thing as theurgy, though. I mean, sure, these wards can keep you from electrifying anyone outside the chamber, but resonance is a whole other—"

She cut him off. "Why are you here?"

He sat on a chair opposite her, bold as brass. "I heard there was alcohol."

She laughed and waved toward a small cabinet. "It's all shit, but help yourself to anything on the bottom shelf."

He glanced over at the cabinet, and the door swung open. A bottle pulled itself free and hovered next to him. He looked around for glasses.

"There's no one to wash crystal in here, and Thryceans drink from the bottle," she said, feigning boredom.

Maddox uncorked a bottle and took a pull from it. It was a mediocre Thrycean rum from Mazatar, the only thing still coming through the trade blockades from the archipelago. His face scrunched as he swallowed. "Yech. I can't believe you're from Amhaven. Not that I'm disappointed, but I thought the queen there would be some fat troll on a donkey."

"An apt description of the last three to hold the dubious honor." Satryn reached for the bottle, and Maddox floated it over to her. "So now that you've had your first taste of fine Thrycean rum, you can tell me why you went to such great lengths to raid my liquor cabinet."

He kicked off one of his boots. "I accidentally made myself immortal, and the Orthodoxy decided I'm a danger to all Creation. So they're keeping me here until they can figure out a way to unbind my seal. Lucky you."

"You've mastered *death*, and you wish to give it up?" She sounded almost offended by the notion. "If any of what you say is truth, you're an idiot."

"Too smart for my own good." He kicked off his other boot.

"Imagine the power you could possess." Satryn found her thoughts reeling at the prospect. "In the hands of someone with ambition, you'd be unstoppable. I can see why they would fear you, but why would you submit to imprisonment?"

"Because life is pretty much shit," Maddox said. "I have no money, no friends, no job. My seal makes me a fucking outcast, and I don't want to spend the rest of eternity alone. The last people I lived with used my dead body for dog food."

"That is well and truly the most pathetic thing I've ever heard," Satryn said.

"Fuck you."

"You will insult a Stormlord to her face," she said, "and yet you're perfectly willing to accept imprisonment for a crime you haven't committed. This city has fucked you over for having power, and you're willing to let them take it from you because they won't accept you? If they don't respect you, you must make them. Respect isn't given easily or willingly."

"I want people to respect me, not fear me."

"Therein lies your problem," Satryn said. "People are fearful and mediocre. For all their lip service to success, they despise greatness and work tirelessly to drag their betters into the mire so they can feed off their potential. You can't see yourself as their equal when you are not."

"I met Achelon," Maddox said. "He was kind of a dick, and I don't really want to follow in his example."

"So you're both immortal and insane. Splendid..." Her voice trailed off. Whatever his ridiculous story, this young man was clearly unbalanced.

Maddox smirked. "So seriously why the fuck are you living in the Invocari tower like it's some kind of hotel? This place isn't known for its hospitality."

"I'm a political prisoner of the Assembly members who supported my usurper Rothburn. My station affords me certain considerations...until they decide what's to be done with me." Once she had drunk some rum, she continued, "They claim I arranged the murder of my daughter's fiancé, Torin Silverbrook."

Maddox's eyes lit up. "Did you?"

"You knew him." It dawned on her. "He must have been a friend of yours at the Lyceum. As for my involvement in his murder, it scarcely matters. The Assembly has any number of other reasons to keep me here."

"Not a friend." Maddox drank more rum. "He was kind of a dick too."

They stared at each other and the bottle between them. The silence was long and uncomfortable. Her drinking companion was common as dirt, possibly insane, and badly needed to attend to the wretched condition of his toenails.

They reached for the bottle at the same time. Satryn gestured toward the cabinet. "This might be easier if you grab me my own bottle out of there."

⇒⊹⇐

Satryn teetered on the sofa, bracing one hand against the armrest as she waved an imaginary saber in front of her. "Enemies to the starboard! Bring her round and arm the ballistae!"

The sofa scooted across the floor, bearing its broadside to a coffee table. Maddox stood majestically on the bed, directing the battle wearing only a burned naval jacket and a pair of Satryn's frilly long underwear, which she had coaxed him into trying on after his second bottle. He was red cheeked and blind drunk but doing his best to reenact the naval battle at the Bleak Atoll.

She was wasted as well and, strangely, having the time of her life. A trunk of clothing rammed her portside, and she toppled off the couch onto the floor, laughing and gasping for breath. She struggled to stand up and found herself lifted to her feet by an unseen force. She wobbled unsteadily.

"You're gonna have to kill me," Maddox said. "'S'fine. I'll be back good as new but...no hangover."

"That's quite a gift you got there, *rear* admiral." Satryn snickered as she stumbled toward the bed. Sure, he was wiry, but he had a nice cock from what she could see through the sheer fabric of her undergarments. She contemplated just putting it in her mouth and seeing what would happen.

The sound of the airlock broke her train of thought, however, and she wheeled around, suddenly furious at the intrusion.

Jessa. So prim and perfect in her Rivern sundress, as if she'd just left a cocktail party on the dart lawn. Her disapproving scowl was like a wet blanket of darkness smothering all life and fun from the universe. Jessa waited patiently for the door to open then stepped through, gazing in confusion at the disarray of the furnishings.

"You're drunk." Not a hello or even a clipped intonation of the word *mother*. Just a cold accusation.

"The fuck do you want?" Satryn slurred.

Something about Jessa's eyes was different. There was a coldness there, deeper than the usual resentment. Satryn saw a glimmer of murder in them that made her skin crawl. "Nasara has launched a campaign to retake Rivern, even though I gave her no express permission. My warmasters in Weatherly have pledged themselves to her aid despite the fact that their contract is with me. And yet here you are drunk in an Invocari prison with…"

"Maddox," he said from atop the bed, suppressing a belch.

"I made him my rear admiral," Satryn explained. "It was a field commission. We'll get him a proper uniform once we've sunk Felchior's fleet and returned to port in Thelassus." She motioned to the scrambled collection of furniture.

Jessa balled her fists. "Is this the reason you refused the Assembly's offer to take up residence in the Thrycean embassy? You've embarrassed your only allies with your erratic behavior. They'll be powerless to offer you any protection."

"The embassy is even more of a joke than the Protectorate embassy in Thelassus," Satryn scoffed, "and *that* has been turned into a fucking whorehouse. Besides you wanted to see me rot in here. It seems I can't please you no matter what I do."

"Fuck, yes. Catfight!" Maddox shouted, as he flopped backward onto the bed.

"You have to forgive him," Satryn casually commented. "He sucks cock. Our living arrangement is temporary."

Jessa rolled her eyes; she really had mastered that facial expression. It was a common way for people to convey exasperation, but with Jessa it carried an even more deeply wearied nuance—as if her eyes were going through the motions of something that no longer held any expressive meaning. And then her sigh. "What do I have to do to get you out of this city?"

"You could take my place as hostage while Nasara liberates Amhaven," Satryn offered. "They really only need one of us here. You can keep Maddox company. He's a little rough around the edges"

"Who is he really?" Jessa asked.

"A drunk faggot who broke one of the thousands of laws of either the Assembly or Lyceum or Orthodoxy or Invocari. I've been here for months and still don't know who actually runs this city," Satryn said. "Now do you want something, or can I take a nap now?"

"I want you to petition the empress for amnesty and return to Thelassus. Your presence here is no longer necessary, and frankly you've overstayed your welcome. Muriel has rescinded your sponsorship at my request and—"

"Listen to you. You even sound like an assemblyman."

"I mean it," Jessa said. "I want you gone from this city, or so help me Ohan, I'll tell them *everything.*" She let that last word hang in the air and fill the room like a gentle roll of thunder.

Satryn peered at her daughter. There was something more to her tone than her usual insolence. Jessa's eyes appeared hard and cold. *I warned Sireen not to involve her in our plans. The girl is too foolish and sanctimonious to be trusted.*

"Do it." Satryn waved her hand. "Tell them whatever you think you know. They won't send me back to Thelassus. They'll torture me for information until I break or until I'm dead. But if you want someone dead—and I speak from experience—it's far more satisfying to do the thing yourself than to rely on intermediaries."

"I can't deal with your insanity right now."

Satryn repeated in a mockingly nasal accent, "I *can't deal* with you right now. You're even starting to talk like them."

Jessa put her hands on her hips, "And what of it, Mother?"

"You're in line to be the fucking—-"

Satryn's senses exploded.

The jolt through her body made her shudder. Jessa did the same where she stood. Both women locked eyes, grimacing through the pain as their Heritage flowed into them. Satryn gritted her teeth and held the lightning inside her body. Jessa struggled to do the same. And after a moment, it was over.

The fog of inebriation lifted. Satryn collected herself. She felt her power growing slightly inside her, and the color drained from her face. There were only three people in the bloodline she could have felt. With the empress she would have felt the burst as she had with her father. It was wishful thinking to believe Nasara, the walking definition of meticulous caution, had fallen to Rothburn's motley army of Fodders.

"Maelcolm," she whispered, a tear falling from her eye. The transfer must have been more painful than she'd first imagined.

"Uncle Maelcolm—are you sure?" Jessa reached out gently to comfort her mother.

Satryn flinched. She could stomach, even somewhat respect, being black-mailed by her own flesh and blood; betrayal was a family tradition. But she'd be damned a thousand times over if she accepted Jessa's pity.

"Mother..."

Satryn yelled, "*Get the fuck out!*"

Jessa didn't linger and didn't look back.

Satryn waited, completely still, until her daughter exited the airlock. Then she grabbed the nearest chair she could find and hurled it against the glass wall of her cage. The warding runes flared briefly as the chair bounced off the boundary of her arcane prison. She pulled at her hair and wailed in frustration, her voice echoing strangely in the sealed room. The Invocari outside watched with total detachment.

How her sisters had managed to reach Maelcolm in the Abyss she couldn't begin to fathom. No one but a few ever returned from that lightless depth, and those few who did spend time among the coelacanth were so drastically changed by the experience they were hardly recognizable. Maelcolm was lost to her twenty years ago, but his passing stirred dark currents of rage.

Satryn curled up next to Maddox and ran her fingers through his hair as he tried to sleep. He needed a trim.

Maddox murmured, "If the wards were foolproof, you two wouldn't have felt the transfer—"

Satryn gently shushed him by placing her hand over his mouth. "Enough about the damnable wards."

Her emotions were raw from the loss of her brother and threatened to cloud her mind. Maelcolm always had been her inner strength, as she had been his outer. He was miles beneath the surface of the ocean, but the weight of his death pressed on her from all sides. They had been born two halves of one soul, and now she carried the burden of both. If she let her sentiment make her careless now, all her scheming would have been for nothing.

"It's nothing personal, seal mage...but I was here first." She sighed as she unloaded all her electricity into his body.

Death happened quickly, but his body continued to dance to her lightning. He flailed and twitched but eventually went rigid as the smell of smoke and burning flesh rose from his corpse. The skin on his face where she touched him turned black.

She braced herself for the sound of the airlock opening, the inevitable chill as the Invocari leached the air and warmth from the chamber. They might try to kill her, rather than put her down, but it was a calculated risk.

Instead there was silence.

She flung Maddox's smoldering body to the floor and whipped around to gaze at her captors. A dozen or so were positioned around the cell, watching. The faces of the hovering, shrouded figures were devoid of expression, their hands folded.

She looked down at Maddox. "Fuck."

THE SWORD OF SAINT JEFFREY
(HEATH AND SWORD)

Item 415: It is a longsword constructed out of a single piece of Archean alloy, and the simple design is clearly inspired by the Meritisan School, which places it at late Second Era. The weight is minimal, and the edges show no signs of sharpening or wear. The core jewel is heartstone, which suggests it can house some intelligence, but any attempts to communicate can be done only in emotive tones, which are distinctly uncooperative.

The Hierocracy says it is a holy relic, but I find this claim dubious. There are no markings on the blade, religious, arcane, or otherwise.

I believe this sword may be an ancient precursor to our own study, if not one of the first true artifacts. Just as the first magi inserted consciousness into clumsy humanoid forms, the creators of the sword may have lacked the utilitarian sensibilities of modern artifice. Inside 415, I believe, is a human soul stripped of memory, retaining only the characteristics its creators wished to preserve.

Item 415 is a marvel, but why not give it the power of mobility? Why rely on meat that is prone to pain and fatigue to fulfill its design?. A circular (or optimally a spherical) design, for instance, would allow maximum lethality in all directions. Without self-propulsion it is at an extreme tactical disadvantage against aerial assault.

As with most Dark Magic to emerge from those lost eras, the blade's original purpose may never be known.

—notes of Magus Aurius in the Repository Manifest

Sword slammed Maddox's head on a stack of important-looking parchments. If it perturbed Daphne at all, she gave no outward indication. Heath had learned his trade in deception at her feet, so there really was no telling, but the thought gave Sword some sense of satisfaction.

The abbess folded her hands. "What is this?"

"The head of Maddox Baeland, Your Worship. Recovered from the body of a revenant. Please enjoy." Sword bowed and offered an exaggerated flourish of his hand as he stepped backward from the desk.

"It is his head." Daphne picked it up delicately and stared into its eyes. "But I'm afraid that particular commission already has been filled. And as for his severed head, I'm already well supplied with that particular item."

"What?" Heath asked.

"His head," Daphne stated. "I have one already. I don't really see the need for two. However, if I should ever require more, I have an unlimited supply. You see, I found him myself and have him sequestered in the Invocari tower for study."

"This doesn't add up," Heath said. "How is he even still alive?"

"Immortality," Daphne said.

"I'm immortal," Sword said. "You don't see my heads rolling around."

"You wanted out. I don't have to share any information with you," Daphne explained. She tossed the head aside and let it roll across the hard stone floor of her office. It bounced against the wall and rolled around, finally settling on its side.

Sword looked to Heath, whose face was an ocean of serene tranquility. He was masking his emotions, making it impossible for Daphne to read his intent. Heath shrugged. "I'm at a loss, Daphne. I didn't think you had the stomach for fieldwork anymore."

Daphne flashed a tight grin. "I'd wondered the same about you. It seems we were both wrong about that. Was it difficult, watching Sword cut the head off your…friend?"

Sword interjected, "He cried like a fucking baby, if that makes you happy. Where's our payment?"

Daphne chuckled. "You know, when I recruited Heath for the Inquisition, the first question he asked was, 'What does it pay?' Most people do it for the cause, or the safety of Creation, or some shred of deeply held personal conviction regarding the work we do. But not Heath. He wanted money. That's how I knew he'd be willing to do anything. But you, Sword, this isn't like you."

"Nobody ever asked me if I wanted this work," Sword spat. He didn't need money, but Heath was the first Inquisitor to actually treat him like a person.

"Money is simpler," Heath responded, "but this isn't the first time someone beat us to the punch. Comes with the profession. I just wanted to let you know that I still value our friendship. Honestly it wasn't even that dangerous. Maddox had been turned into a revenant by the time we found him. I'd feel guilty accepting payment in any event."

Daphne cocked an eyebrow. "What do you want?"

"I think you're holding out on better opportunities," Heath said. "Sword and I have come across some information while working a separate inquiry on behalf of our mutual acquaintances in the tower. I think we should combine our investigations into the harrowings. We could help each other."

"Go on…"

Heath folded his arms. "We're your best agents. Why aren't we working this?"

Sword crossed his arms as well. "Yeah. I'm the only one with the theurgy to kill one of those Harrowers if it comes through."

"While I appreciate your enthusiasm, the Inquisition has had five hundred years to prepare for another incursion," Daphne said. "You're not the only tools at our disposal."

Sword glared at her and pounded his chest. "I am the Sword of Saint Jeffrey. I brought down Vilos of Bamor single-handedly. I lived through the Occultation and witnessed firsthand the fragmentation of reality and the manifestation of Fear. I know more about the Harrowers than any sentient thing in Creation."

"So what tools are you using, Daphne?" Heath chimed in.

"If you know something, tell me." She folded her hands and perched her chin.

Sword glanced at Heath. *She's hiding something.*

Heath shrugged nonchalantly. "Evan Landry. Heard of him?"

Daphne took out a quill and ink and wrote something on a parchment. "No, but I can check the records. What's the connection?"

Heath and Sword shared a glance.

"Not a clue. I was hoping you'd tell us," Heath said.

"Anything else you'd like to share?" Daphne asked pointedly. "A name by itself isn't much to go on. Where did you hear it?"

Heath shook his head. "What do you think, Sword? Should we tell her the truth?"

Sword smirked. He knew where Heath was going with this, so he dropped the name and lied. "Esme told us."

Daphne froze, just for a split second. "Who?"

"We know she was working for you," Heath continued. "She said she was looking into a circle of hedge wizards. Oddly she was in Landry Manor, where we found Maddox's head attached to a revenant."

"*Very* odd," Sword concurred.

She addressed Sword. "Did you two fight?"

"Something about her made me want to," Sword admitted. "Heath is a bit of a softie, though. It's what we love about him."

"Evan Landry," Daphne drawled. "I hate to disappoint you, but there probably isn't anyone that goes by that name in Rivern. Landry is an old name. Esme likely gave that to you to send you on a wild-goose chase. The girl has talent, but she's a compulsive liar."

"You called it, Sword." Heath sighed and slumped his shoulders.

"Told you, mate." He puffed out his broad chest.

"I'm very sorry to have wasted your time," Heath apologized. "You know where to find us if you want us in on this investigation. I do have one more favor to ask before we take your leave."

"Anything." Daphne smiled.

Heath said, "I want to see Maddox."

"What?" Sword did a double take.

Daphne leaned back in her chair. "I'm not sure that's wise. Besides it's out of my hands. The warding chamber is also occupied by another resident…an imperial. There are political complications, and adding you to the visitor list would be next to impossible without approval from the Assembly. Do you *have* a compelling reason?"

"No," Heath lied. "I just feel bad about how things ended between us. I acted uncharitably."

"I'll see what I can arrange." Daphne made another note on her parchment. "Now if that's all, I have some urgent business to attend to. I'll send for you if I need anything further."

Heath bowed and took his leave, with Sword trailing behind. Neither said a word to each other as they made their way through the temple, vestibule, and out onto the street. They took zigzagging paths through the city, carefully watching to see whether they were being followed. They were. A few green Inquisition spies but none of their heavy hitters.

It took a half hour to ditch their tail, and they ended up near the Lyceum at the Silver Stave, a bar that catered to students. The interior of the tavern was cheery, with dark wood paneling, and pennants representing the various colleges hung from the walls. The Artifact College's banner hung prominently over the open dining area.

The bar was doing some business, but Heath and Sword secured a booth without hassle. The place was covered in a hazy green mist of dragonfire as patrons smoked it out of long glass pipes and chatted maniacally. Most of the students were artificers. Automatons wandered the floor, relentlessly refilling glasses, filling pipes, and wiping down tables.

It was noisy enough to have a private conversation.

Sword broke the silence. "The fuck was that?" He motioned for one of the automatons carrying a tray of drinks and pipes.

"The Daphne I know wouldn't have let us walk out of that office without our spilling everything we know. Especially if it involved even the slightest whiff of pact magic. She knows something."

"Do you think Maddox is really still alive?" Heath asked.

"The dead can't rise," Sword said flatly. "Not with the magic you lot have today, and even back in the old times, it was hard as fuck. That's one of the principal limitations of magic. Dead is dead."

"She has at least two severed heads," Heath reiterated. "And apparently a living specimen in the tower. Can heads be regrown?"

"No." Sword waved his hands. "That's ridiculous. The only way that could happen would be if there were multiple copies of him, so he's either a simulacrum or—"

The serving automaton came by their table, and Sword threw some coins on the tray and helped himself to a pipe and a glass. He took another glass and put it in front of Heath.

Heath drummed his fingers impatiently as Sword put the pipe in his mouth and fired up a small alchemical burner on the table.

Sword exhaled a plume of green vapor and coughed. "Chronomancy. Reversing time to the exact point of death...but mate, he'd need to have a greater seal, and that Lore was buried deep and forbidden before the Occultation. Chronomancy doesn't exist anymore."

Heath waved the smoke out of his face. "Maddox is still a seal mage. He could have drawn a greater seal."

"If he was an archwizard maybe." Sword rolled his eyes. "Could be anything. I'd know for sure if I actually saw him or checked his body for seals."

"The body we burned along with the library..." Heath said dismally.

"Fuck."

Heath sipped his drink. "We need to talk to him. Daphne's not doing anything to stop this, which means she's probably in on it. Catherine—the echo of her—said Maddox would know who Evan Landry is or lead us to him. That's the key."

"Wouldn't be the first time an Inquisitor went rogue." Sword's skin started to buzz with energy. "All that Dark Magic is awfully tempting. And it's not like we haven't used a bit of the forbidden arts ourselves to fight the good fight."

"Harrowings are a good way to drop bodies in the river without drawing suspicion," Heath said. "The city's been turning to religion a lot more since this started. Daphne also got a more cooperative dean of the Lyceum out of the unfortunate demise of Maddox's mentor. And if Maddox really can't be killed, he might be the only person who can survive an attack and name the perpetrator."

Sword rubbed his neck. "Do you think Loran can get us into the tower?"

"We don't know he's Invocari…officially anyway," Heath said. "I don't want to kick that hornets' nest by naming one of their secret police. Plus if Maddox is in the tower, it means they've got a channel of communication open with Daphne somewhere higher up. She has a lot of influence there."

"We could tell them what the Harbinger said about the city being destroyed… and the fact that Daphne doesn't seem to be doing fuck at all about it," Sword suggested. He was really just spit-balling ideas at this point. The tower was one of the most secure places in city and possibly Creation itself. And since Invocari could float, there weren't any secret escape routes through the tunnels.

"That's hearsay at this point," he said. "Even if we swore in front of the Veritas, there's no proof the Harbinger wasn't lying. And if they question her, she'll just stonewall. We need actual proof she's concealing information."

Sword took another hit off the pipe. "You want to take her down."

"We need to get on the visitor list first." Heath smiled. His eyes twinkled with a glimmer of a scheme falling into place.

"You have a way in, you cheeky bastard."

"Not exactly, but there may be another way onto that list," Heath explained. "The imperial's daughter is still a free woman, right?"

Sword grinned, and they shared a toast.

THE DARK STAR (MADDOX)

Maddox awoke, strapped to a sturdy wooden chair, in a dark chamber lit by a single shaft of light. He and Daphne were illuminated, but he made out shadowy forms moving in the darkness. He blinked against the brightness of the light.

"The fuck?" Maddox looked at his bonds: solid bands of starmetal clasped by a locking mechanism.

"Your fellow inmate killed you," Daphne said, making notes in her ledger. She reached for his wrist and checked for a pulse.

"Uh…where am I?"

"Shh. I need to sense your health."

"I'm fine," Maddox said irritably. "Why am I bound in an Inquisition torture chair?"

"If it were a torture chair, you'd be much less comfortable." She smiled. "The bindings are just a standard precaution. The last time my agents encountered your body, they had to cut the head off a revenant."

"Yeah…that was Gran's work."

Daphne referred to her notes. "Yes. The old woman? Do you know anything else about her?"

"She's fucking nuts. Can you pretty please let me out of this chair now?"

"Does the name Pytheria sound familiar at all?"

"Of course. She was dean of the Lyceum a hundred years ago and…" His jaw went slack. "No fucking way. They burned her alive."

Daphne made another notation and shrugged. "That's the official story anyway. The Lyceum doesn't have a long history of honesty and cooperation with the

209

Orthodoxy. Especially in those days, they preferred to handle matters internally. It would be fine if security at the Asylum were on par with the Invocari, but—"

"Fuck," Maddox said.

Daphne turned to another page in her book. "It isn't our main concern. We found notebooks of yours that detailed some rather unbelievable events. What do you have to say about those?"

Maddox looked down at his restraints then up at Daphne. "Are you interrogating me? Is this an interrogation? Because you told me you'd take care of me. I was going to be your white knight."

Daphne patted his knee. "If this were an interrogation, you would know. First I would cut out your eyes—just a precaution to keep you from using seal magic. Keep in mind I can grow them back anytime I want to with Ohan's Light. Then I would remove fingernails, burn your chest—standard things before I moved to more inventive techniques.

"In fact I could do any number of awful, painful things to you and wipe them away, only to do them again and again and again until you're broken and begging for the release of death. Again we're just having a conversation, and you've been completely honest with me at every point, so I see no need for that to change. Now what's really in those notebooks?"

Maddox sighed. "Drawings of my dreams. Seal partials. But it's not finished—those idiots won't get anything out of it. Even if Gran is Dean Emeritus Pytheria, there isn't enough theurgy among them to finish the seal, let alone bind it."

"It's incomplete," Daphne said to herself as she made more notes. "How close were you to finishing the...you called it the Grand Design?"

"Let me out of this fucking chair," Maddox said.

"How close?"

"I didn't get a chance to get it on paper. There's no fucking way they'll be able to fill in the blanks. Trust me on this. It doesn't follow the standard geometries. If you could even say they existed."

Daphne made another note. "You know the seal?"

"Yeah, but it's too powerful to ever use. I spoke to Achelon. Only a fucking idiot would attain that mess. You say you have the Veritas? I'll never, ever inscribe the Seal of the Grand Design. Now...let me out of this chair before I rip it apart."

"Thank you for your candor." Daphne made the last notation in her book.

"Luther"—Daphne indicated the chair—"release our guest."

Luther stepped out of the shadows. He was young, short, but well built enough that his athletic definition was clearly visible beneath his silk shirt and blue satin vest. He smiled broadly as he stepped toward Maddox and undid the restraints on his arms.

Luther had lips that begged to be kissed. *If you want to get secrets out of me, put me in a room alone with him for two hours*, Maddox thought.

"He thinks I'm attractive." Luther said, mildly amused.

"Don't let it go to your head, Luther."

Luther smiled. "I could leave you in this chair and have my way with your body."

"What the fuck is this?" Maddox asked, suddenly nervous.

"I'm a Binder," Luther explained. "Don't worry—if you knew what sort of filth went through everyone's mind, you'd have no reason to feel embarrassed. It's just noise to us really."

"Get the fuck away from me!" Maddox pushed hard with his seal, causing the air in front of him to ripple with force. But Luther didn't move.

"I'm not really here," Luther said. "Neither is she. This place isn't even real. It's a construct. You have some experience with those, from what I understand."

"This is a dream?"

"It's my dream," Luther explained. "I don't really look like this. But…I know what you like."

"Get on with it," Daphne said, as she rose from her chair then vanished into darkness.

If this was a dream, Maddox had power here. He summoned his strength and willed the chair away. He now stood eye to eye with Luther. "This kind of theurgy is unsanctioned. It's fucking illegal! How are you working for the Inquisition?"

"We'll use any tool at our disposal," Luther said.

Maddox sneered. "I grew up around wizards who could tell whether I was lying. It's not mind reading, but it's damn close. So I'm not intimidated that you know all my dark little secrets. I'm not hiding anything from you or her."

"I know"—he frowned—"but I'm here to make sure your secrets stay buried. What you know is too dangerous for anyone ever to attain. Achelon nearly destroyed the world once, and there's no guarantee that you won't one day decide to draw that seal. We can't kill you, so the only thing we can do is make it so you can't ever use that knowledge."

"A quelling." Maddox gasped. He'd read about them in the old texts: the removal of all emotion. It was a punishment reserved for the most dangerous, for whom death was too merciful.

"Now this might hurt a little…" Luther cautioned.

Maddox's vision exploded into a kaleidoscope of red agony. His fury and rage poured from his skin, burning like fire and twisting into sharp, angular lines that lashed indiscriminately at the endless void around him. And he felt it dissipate in the darkness. His strongest feelings burned so hot they threatened to consume him.

He cried out with a howl of rage, but the sound was growing weaker. The flames that filled his vision were getting smaller. A lifetime of stored resentment toward his father, the world, himself—all that drove him seemed weaker and less significant.

He was getting colder even as the fire still burned around him. The layer beneath anger was fear, and he dreaded it before he even felt it. He was never safe, never protected—he had no one he could trust. Every time he trusted, he was betrayed. Even now.

And the rage burned hotter than before.

His thoughts were a single speck in a turbulent red sea of unfolding emotion. He needed to find clarity. He needed to find an escape.

Maddox tumbled hard onto white marble flagstones, gasping for breath.

He sucked in the cool evening air and stared into a starry sky above. In the distance he heard the roar of a cheering crowd. The moon loomed huge and full. He made out the twinkling lights on its surface with his naked eye. This close the lights almost looked like cities.

He was standing on top of a circular tower. A woman was draped over the parapet, staring wistfully into the sky as the wind brushed back her long black hair. She held a bottle of Archean brandy. He saw telescopes and astronomical instruments like they had at the observation tower at the Lyceum, but this place was larger and infinitely higher.

The woman turned and smiled; her eyes were thin and almond shaped. "Hey, there. You come up to watch the game? It's Maceria versus Archea."

Maddox struggled to his feet. His body ached. He made his way to the edge of the tower. Below was a city bathed in light. Domes and spires glowed with pulsing geometric patterns. Across a lake he saw a vast arena, lit up like daylight, where thousands of people were sitting in bleachers. Above the arena, massive semitransparent images of men in armor charging across a field telegraphed the events on the field. A scoreboard displayed large Archean numerals: fifteen to twenty-two.

"Where am I?"

"This is Archea," the woman said, "but I have no idea where *you* are."

"Another vision?" Maddox said, peering down over the edge of the tower. It was at least a thousand feet in the air. Beyond the edge of the city, he saw nothing but sky and stars.

She nodded sagely. "Makes sense."

"But I didn't take any drugs..."

"Why would you need to?" The woman cocked her head at him. "You have no idea what you are, do you?"

"Achelon called me an Architect," Maddox said.

"Which is what exactly?"

"Dunno. A powerful wizard who shapes the fates of nations?" he said casually. "Something too dangerous to exist."

She extended her hand and pointed at the sky. "You see that little star next to the Eye of Ohan? The white one they call the Tear?"

"Uh-huh."

"We think it was our home...or at least our neighborhood. We called it Lakinea, and it's made of billions of suns and trillions planets, but they're so far away that it just looks like another point of light."

"A star?" Maddox chuckled. "It's not the most ridiculous thing I've heard."

"We're not completely sure if it really is home, but it's plausible at least...and it's academic. There's nothing there to go back to."

"You're one of the First Mages," Maddox said.

"*Ding ding ding*! They called me the Stargazer. It was my job to map out where we were in the universe."

"I have so many questions," Maddox said, "about everything."

"Better make it fast. I don't think this vision will persist much longer." She looked down at the arena below. A fanfare of trumpets and horns erupted as the crowd let loose an ecstatic howl. The score changed: nineteen to twenty-two.

"What am I? What is an Architect?" Maddox asked.

"It's whatever you want it to be," she said. "Architects make the rules. In this whole wonky paradigm the Guides created for us, the Architects have the most direct line through dreaming. They help decide what is and isn't possible. Not just for people or nations but reality itself."

"The laws of fucking magic?"

"Those laws preserve some sense of normalcy in this crazy, broken universe—the guarantee that one moment follows another. The persistence of things you observe still being there when you look away. The certainty that all matter and substance won't blow away in a puff of smoke. It can get seriously crazy."

"The story of my life," Maddox moaned. "Every time I find out I can do something cool, it turns out to suck or be fucking useless."

"Not many people can say they save the world every day in their sleep," she offered.

"It's not really that great a place." He sighed. "I'm kind of over it to be honest."

"Sorry you feel that way." She rubbed the back of her neck. "Not really a convenient thing to realize a few months into immortality."

"Can a seal be unbound?"

"Yes," she said. "Some of my people know how. The Harbinger, the Storyteller, and the Keeper—they all have the ability to erase what was written. But it won't matter."

"Why?" Maddox asked.

The Stargazer looked up at the sky. "The stars are going dim. The little ones have been winking out of existence the whole time we've been talking. A few at first, but the rate is increasing exponentially. Whoever's in your mind is following you here, erasing them."

"The telepath at the tower. I need to fight him. What can I do?" Maddox asked.

"You're powerful but not experienced. Maybe this is for the best. You won't miss your gift when it's gone. You'll just exist. The quelling is quite peaceful actually. You'll have your mind, but you'll have no motivation to use it. You won't be bored or angry or restless."

"No!" Maddox shouted at the heavens. He saw the stars winking out of existence. "Please tell me how to fight this!"

"You just said you're over it!" the Stargazer exclaimed. "Make up your fucking mind! You didn't have to let Tertius shove you off the tower. You didn't have to surrender to the Inquisition. Do you even know why you want to live, what you want, or who you want to be? The only way to stop a quelling is to know the answers to those questions."

"I…" He stared up into the vacant black sky. "…don't know."

"Think harder."

He looked at her with sad green eyes. "I don't want to be me anymore."

"The first lesson of being an Architect"—she laughed a little—"is to be very careful what you wish for in dreams."

And darkness swallowed him.

Maddox blinked awake. He was restrained in a chair. Daphne and an older, fatter version of Luther were seated across from him. Luther's clothes were rags, he noted.

"It's done, Abbess," Luther said, his voice sounding grave and exhausted.

Daphne rose from her seat and brushed her hand through Maddox's chestnut hair. He didn't move, although it felt nice. He stared ahead as she removed a small dagger and thrust it through the top of his hand. His body reacted with a shudder at the new sensation, but that was the extent of it. The pain was just a different flavor of experience, a mechanism to force his body to preserve itself.

There was nothing more inherent in pain to the flesh than seeing a displeasing color through the eye. In fact it was only memory that connected the word to the feeling of a knife digging into the flesh of his hand. Pain and hurt were something deeper than mere physical sensation.

"How are you feeling?" Daphne asked him.

Maddox understood her words. His mind offered a memory of something he'd likely tell her. *How the fuck do you think I feel, you crazy bitch?* But it wasn't his thought, and there was no reason to offer a response.

"He is quelled," Luther said. "He understands who he was, but he doesn't have the emotion to drive him toward any action. He may speak again, but it's unlikely."

"Good." Daphne smiled. "You've done very well, Luther."

He looked up at her hopefully. "Does this mean you'll let me see my family?"

She slashed his throat with her blade, spattering thick gouts of blood over her pristine white robes. The man who had torn Maddox's mind apart grasped feebly at his throat as he bled out through his neck and fell to the floor. Maddox stared at his bulging brown eyes as he choked and gasped for life.

I'm sorry. I'm so sorry.

Those weren't his thoughts. He felt no sorrow or satisfaction, even though he understood the situation clearly. Daphne obviously had some immunity to Luther's power. She never would have been in the same room with him otherwise. And if the knowledge in Maddox's mind were that dangerous, she would have been a fool to let Luther live.

Daphne wiped her blade on her robe and tossed it to the floor next to Luther's body. "I know you can't appreciate this, but I went to great expense to help you. Now you won't hurt anyone, and you won't ever have to hurt again."

Her face was a mask of sympathy. A furrowed brow, sad intent gaze, down-turn at the corners of her lips. Maddox knew what it meant but no longer saw it as anything other than a contraction of facial muscles in a performance of some social ritual. Lines to be read—a woman who seemed so in control, acting out a play with herself as the audience and not even aware why she was doing it.

"Just one more thing remains," Daphne said. "Your body will heal itself of any damage, but I need to be certain that your mind will remain as is."

And then she slit his throat.

THE BLACK POTION (JESSA)

The Spirit folk of Maenmarth are a reclusive, mysterious people, and it's widely debated that they may comprise several distinct races. Witches are, as far as we can determine, the ruling faction among the Spirit folk, but their biomantic relation to the more common changelings has thus far been elusive. The second-most-recent witch to claim governance of the forests was Illyara the Witch Queen, who was deposed by Briala the Silver shortly after Josur's rebellion in Amhaven.

While we have studied no specimens of witch blood, I recently procured a sample from one of the Witch Queen's putative descendants, a Stormlord princess named Jessa. Her humor is quite remarkable in many respects; though the Stormlord essence is overwhelmingly dominant, there are unusual aspects not shared by her mother, who is pure-blooded. (Another interesting anomaly.)

Her humor shares a similarity with the humors of changelings, having the occasional characteristics of animals. The humans of the Maenmarth call people with such stock but no outward manifestations "quicklings"; they're abundantly common in Amhaven and the border nations. (The term apparently is used among Spirit folk to describe children born with "quicker" human life-spans.)

Rarely the trait will become active in a particular individual, even after multiple generations. While we have recorded no demonstrations of the witches' power (e.g., glamour, precognition) in such cases, they do possess the ability to assume the forms of certain animals, typically mammals.

Jessa's blood provides the first well-documented link between the mysterious witches and changelings, as her pedigree is well documented, and her ancestors, aside from Illyara, were all born outside Amhaven, where quicklings' blood is uncommon. This case provides enlightening insight into the workings of another form of possibly hereditary theurgy.

—Magus Quirrus's first draft of "Observations on the Phylogeny of the Elemental Subspecies"

"What?" Jessa swirled the brandy in her glass as she met the gaze of her advisors. She felt good and drunk from the brandy and slightly buzzed from the dragonfire. Her council sat around the long table in the Silverbrooks' formal dining room, which had been converted to a war room. The entire room was twice the size of the Amhaven embassy.

"Perhaps Cameron should be present for this," Lord Fincher offered. He was a timid slug of diplomat from Amhaven.

Warmaster Sarnia or Genata—Jessa couldn't tell the Fodders apart at this point—offered, "If Nasara is bringing her army into Amhaven, then what's the purpose of surrendering to Rothburn?"

"This is a betrayal of your supporters," Duke Clayborne insisted.

Jessa felt a stab of sadness for the old man. The Claybornes had suffered the worst assaults from Rothburn's forces. The frail white-bearded man, who'd been her father's mentor, was practically a refugee himself.

"Even under the inept leadership of Rothburn, our people will be better off," Jessa slurred, "but as the fates would have it…it makes no difference. Rothburn works for Nasara, and this whole stupid, fucking war has nothing to do with Amhaven. So whatever it takes to stop people from killing each other should be our top priority."

Lord Fincher interjected, "Your Grace, perhaps we could pick this up tomorrow when you're more…"

"Lucid," one of the Patrean warmasters said.

Jessa took a swig from her glass. "Look…Rothburn, Nasara—it doesn't matter. The Dominance *will* annex Amhaven, and I *will* be appointed queen. In the interim no one else needs to die to dispute a claim that nobody fucking wants."

The council grew silent.

"I realize you're under pressure, Your Grace," Duke Clayborne said, "but it's imperative that Josur's heirs sit on the throne in Weatherly castle. I swore an oath to your grandfather—"

Jessa rubbed her temples, "Who is dead. Along with your son and your grandson…whom I could have wed, had he not died."

"That is…uncalled for, Your Grace."

"Uncalled for?" Jessa hurled her glass against the wall. "This entire campaign is uncalled for! This war is bullshit. I've done everything you've advised me to do, and it's only caused more suffering while lining the pockets of the Patrean warmasters."

Sarnia protested, "We've held Weatherly with minimal resources."

Jessa scowled. "I could hold Weatherly myself. I could walk into Rothburn's camps and rain lightning and thunder upon them until your Fodder brethren are nothing more than ash. Arrows and steel are nothing before the power of the elements."

Genata countered, "Patreans have defeated Stormlord magic on multiple occasions."

Lord Fincher offered, "Perhaps we could pick this discussion up tomorrow."

Jessa walked over to the liquor cabinet and poured herself a fresh glass of brandy. "No. I've signed the declaration of surrender. If you wish to carry out this war behind my back, I no longer have the will to stop you. But my decision is made. Now please leave me."

She didn't turn as she heard the scoot of chairs and the hasty shuffle of boots toward the doors.

When the dining hall was silent, Jessa drew a small vial of black liquid from a fold in her dress. Grinning, she poured it into her glass of brandy and swirled it. The taste was foul, but she knew that once her unborn child was dead, she would have nothing more left to lose.

Jessa writhed in agony. Her body was slick with sweat although she shivered intensely. It was one of the few times she could remember wanting to be dry. The black potion had worked its way through her veins, wracking her with nausea. A sheet half covered her lower body. She had abandoned trying to make herself comfortable, and in her tossing, the bedding had wound itself between her legs.

She wondered whether the potion was supposed to feel this awful or whether her mother spitefully had schemed to poison her. Delirious with fever, she chuckled at the idea. The memories that flashed through her mind were happy ones. Satryn had been an erratic parental figure at best, but there had been times when her father was still alive when she and her mother had been close. It hadn't always been awful. That didn't start until she grew older and became something her mother couldn't control.

In the winters Satryn would disguise Jessa in a heavy cloak that hid her silver eyes and take her into the village on adventures. They'd go to the cider house and buy a copper's worth of hot apple cider and sit at their usual table in the back, where sawdust covered the floor and the air was heavy with smoke. They'd giggle and listen to the local gossip and maybe meet with a snitch or two.

They'd spend the hot summer days swimming at their remote lakeside chalet in Maenmarth, even though her mother complained about the taste of freshwater. They chased each other under the cool water and devoured raw trout with their teeth. *Would I have done the same things with my own child?* Jessa wondered.

Satryn's callow disregard for Weatherly's traditions and her disdain for her exile became a wedge between them. Over time the outings were replaced with distant glances, the laughter with disapproving sighs.

She couldn't kill her mother, no matter how terrible things were between them. She could get her out of Rivern, before her plan could come to fruition. She could sign the document of concession, yielding the throne of Amhaven to Rothburn or Nasara; it didn't matter as long as there was peace. But she wasn't the one to bring it.

And lastly she could spare her unborn child the torture of her legacy. Let the Shyford line and all its misery die with her. If the black potion killed her as well, then she didn't begrudge the ending. If the poison didn't kill her, the imperial family's retribution surely would seal her fate. She did all she could. Save Rivern, stop the war in Amhaven, end the family line before another child found himself a pawn in the twisted struggles between the empires.

Jessa leaned over the bed and wretched into one of the bedpans. The parquet floor was spattered with puke, but nothing could be done about it until the cleaning automaton made its rounds, which was usually on the hour. The machines were designed to maintain a full household. With just Jessa their routines bordered on obsessive.

She shuddered miserably and dragged the sheet over her body. Vomiting had made her feel better, and sleep started to feel possible. Jessa shut her eyes and prayed to Ohan and Kultea for a measure of oblivion to see her through the nausea.

She barely had drifted off before the sound of voices jerked her from a sweet second of slumber. Loud crashing came from the floor below. Jessa bolted up in bed and reached for her night-robe. She was wracked with illness and unsteady on her feet as she made her way to the hall.

Steadying herself against the doorframe, she flung the door open and stumbled into the hall. She froze. Standing there were a pair of black wolves with yellow eyes. Behind them were two men and a woman who looked to be in even worse shape than she was. Their eyes were empty sockets, their flesh pale. They carried sacks over their shoulders.

She brushed her hair back. "I'm afraid you've caught me at a bad time."

The wolves snarled as they stalked closer, their eyes hungry.

"I don't know if you're really here or whether this is another product of delirium, but in either event, I know you can understand me…changelings."

The wolves stopped, confused for a moment. Wolves were rare in Amhaven and practically unheard of in the Free Cities. But they clearly weren't ordinary wolves, though how Jessa recognized them she couldn't entirely place. She just knew.

"State your business." She curled her fingers to summon her lightning. Anemic crackles of electricity danced over her hand. The poison in her body had weakened her abilities to almost nothing, but she was relying on reputation.

"They don't talk much," a young feminine voice came from behind, causing her to spin and nearly fall over.

A girl a few years younger than her, with wild multicolored hair, stood in the hall behind her, a long stiletto in her hand, which she was using to peel an apple. "Hi. I'm Esme. I'll be your burglar this evening, but I want you to think of me as your friend."

"My friend?" Jessa scoffed.

She sighed and took another step toward Jessa. "I live with a bunch of dudes, which is fine, but…they all just want to talk about magic and pussy and make fart jokes. I miss having girlfriends, you know? You seem like one of those really nice, proper girls who has, like, a million best friends. Am I right?"

"I am a Stormlord, not a ladies' maid." The rush of adrenaline gathered in her like a thunderhead. "Get out. I won't warn you again."

Faster than she could react, Esme flicked her dagger into Jessa's stomach. The pain exploded through her gut like fire as she collapsed to the floor. She let out a blast of lightning at her assailant, but the shot went wild, and the girl had stepped away from her spot. Jessa couldn't see where she was.

She'd never been stabbed before; it put a lot of her other pain in perspective. Out of instinct her hands clutched the wound, but she was too hurt and shocked to move or touch the knife. All she could think about was her child, the one she'd chosen to abandon. She sobbed as she curled into herself.

"I have to admit"—Esme was crouching next to her, bent over so she could whisper in Jessa's ear—"I was kind of expecting a fight. I was going to kill you regardless, but it's not personal. You should have left with the rest of the Silverbrooks."

Jessa was in too much pain to reply. Revenants shambled up the stairs; she lost count, but there were at least ten filing into the various rooms. The hallways were raucous as things were broken, moved, and riffled through.

"Have two of the ghouls toss her room," Esme said to the wolves. "I'm going to make my new friend comfortable."

Esme sat back against the wall. "I know what you're doing. You're going to play helpless and weak, and then, when I go to pull that knife out of your gut, you're going to unleash your electric blast."

"Just take what you want and go..." Jessa rasped.

"I timed this perfectly." Esme continued blithely carrying on the conversation with herself. "You see, depending on exactly where you stab the abdomen, you can control whether someone bleeds out in minutes or hours, or even just nonfatally injure them. Your injury is fatal, and you should be done by the time we're finished here."

Jessa closed her eyes. It was hopeless to fight.

A loud crash resounded from downstairs along with a chorus of guttural rasps. Jessa forced her eyes open. She heard the swing of steel followed by the thunk of bodies hitting the tile in the foyer.

And then a man very loudly sang off-key:

Ohhh, I'd rather be a sword than a cutting board,
'cause cutting boards are boring.
And I'd rather be a sword than a pillowcase,
'cause I hate to hear guys snoring.

Esme grabbed the dagger from Jessa's abdomen and ripped it out. Her expression was twisted into an inhuman mask of rage. She growled, "Sword..."

I'd rather be a sword than a chamber pot,
'cause that is just disgusting.
And I'd rather be a sword than a big codpiece,
'cause those take readjusting.
With a heave and a ho
and a thrust and a blow,
all the heads will roll,
and the bell will toll.
I'm a big-ass fucking swooooord.

Another voice responded, "How many verses are there to this battle shanty?"

"Nine hundred seventy-two," the other man's voice replied cheekily.

Cresting the stairs at the end of the hallway, a big Patrean with a gleaming bastard sword swung his blade in wide carefree arcs, chopping the heads off revenants the second they got into reach. Each time the blade sliced clean through the neck.

The Vorpal Blade of Arix. The sight of it made Jessa smile.

Behind him a dark-skinned priest strolled, arms folded behind his back. He wore white robes and medallions of office. They stopped when they saw Esme. The wolves gathered to either side of her, preparing to pounce.

"Well, well, well, if it isn't our old friend Esme," the swordsman said. "I should have fucking known. She's holding the accursed letter opener of House Setahari. I knew there was a reason I hated her."

"You mean…she's like you?" the priest asked. "You didn't mention this before."

"I didn't see the knife. It's easy to hide a few inches of metal." He looked back at Esme. "Step away from the princess."

She cooed, "You have maybe a few minutes before she bleeds out. It's a good thing the church teaches their killers how to heal. In fact let's make it interesting. Heath—that's your name, isn't it?"

The priest nodded, stepping forward with his hands raised. "You want money? Running smash-and-grab jobs on abandoned houses for trinkets is amateur. So what is it you're really after?"

Esme stepped back. "Themis, Theril, take what you can and meet back at the place. Give them the priest's name."

The wolves darted off to Jessa's room. Heath flicked his wrist, and long silver blades shot out of his sleeves, stabbing one wolf in the neck but missing the other. Jessa heard a crash come from her room then the breaking of glass.

Heath brought his hands up and drew back his blades.

Esme somersaulted back down the hallway another ten feet. "You can help her or help your buddy Sword. Your choice."

"Cover me!" Heath ran to crouch next to Jessa and pressed his hand on her wound. Immediately golden Light spread from his fingers, and the pain receded. The Light glowed with greater intensity as he focused his energy.

Sword charged Esme, his blade aimed to skewer her. She jumped to the side and took a stab at his kidney, but almost as if he had predicted it, he twisted himself out of the way and elbowed her in the face.

Sweat formed on Heath's brow as he channeled his Light. "What the hell did they do to you? This feels like poison."

Esme staggered back and readied her stance, tossing her blade from one hand to the other. Sword raised his blade and brought it around in a wide slash aimed at her neck. She flung the dagger in the air and bent herself backward so the blow missed her. She caught the dagger in her hand as a few pieces of multi-colored hair fluttered to the ground.

"You were always so slow and clumsy," Esme told Sword with a smile.

"At least my house could afford the metal to make a real weapon," he chided.

"You're really disparaging the honor of my *house*?" She laughed. "I was never bonded to Setahari like you were to Crigenesta. Who do you think leaked those secret letters that financially ruined my house in the first place?"

"You destroyed Sarn, you fucking psychopath!"

Esme shrugged. "Little old me. Not bad for a letter opener. I guess it's true what they say—the pen is mightier than the sword."

He brought down a furious strike, and she ducked out of the way.

She tried to take the opening, but Sword was ready before she could reach. They repeated the pattern. Esme was more dexterous, but he was a Patrean and incredibly fast for his size. They were almost too perfectly matched. Each knew how to exploit the other's weakness but also seemed to know what the other would do.

Jessa started to feel better as the Light spread through her body. She felt the flicker of power awaken in her blood. "You should go help him," she whispered.

"He'll be fine," Heath reassured her. "Something in your body is resisting the Light, reacting to something in your blood, thickening it somehow. If I don't finish now, it'll just worsen again when I'm at full strength."

Esme sneered, "You fight like a blind gorilla with a stick trying to hit a butterfly."

"Do you need a breather?" Sword feigned concern. "All that gymnastics looks awfully tiring…" He executed a flurry of slashes, weaving the sword in wide arcs with a single hand. Esme tumbled farther down the hallway and came up with her dagger drawn above her head, with her weight resting on her back leg.

"Don't get too attached to that body. There's a reason they're called Fodders."

Esme launched herself from the ball of her foot into the air, letting herself spin feet over head toward Sword. This time he stepped out of the way and readied himself for an attack as she hit the opposite wall of the hallway and launched herself at him.

And then she flickered and vanished from sight.

Jessa gasped as she saw Esme reappear behind Sword, still retaining her momentum, and drive her blade into his kidney. His brown eyes widened with realization as his chiseled jaw went slack and his arms fell limply to his side.

Esme twisted the knife as she pulled Sword's head close to her ear and whispered something in a language Jessa didn't understand. She flickered and vanished again, reappearing on his other side as she slashed his neck.

He sank to his knees as she flickered again and cut the other side of his neck. "Better luck next time."

Jessa could take no more. She flung her hand and sent a blast of lightning toward Esme. The girl stepped to the side with inhuman quickness. But Jessa no longer felt the stupor of the poison. There was a reason they called them lightning reflexes.

Jessa threw out her other hand and tagged Esme in the shoulder with a secondary bolt of electricity. In fact she was just showing off at that point. Lightning, when not channeled, could go anywhere and often went everywhere.

Esme flew backward and flickered away. But Jessa had seen the agony on her face. Her secondary bolt wasn't as powerful as the first, but a lightning strike always left a reminder. She turned to Heath and shoved him off her. "Help your friend! I'll be fine. If she reappears, she'll be outmatched."

"Sword's dead." Heath kept his hands on her abdomen for a while longer while the Light faded. "There. Finished."

"Did any of what they were saying to each other make sense to you?" Jessa tightened her night-robe and stood. "Who is she, and by what sorcery is she able to displace herself?"

"It looked like Asherai shadow technique," Heath said. "Never seen it before…just know it from reputation. I do know that she works for a very powerful woman in the Orthodoxy who has access to a lot of forbidden arcana. This doesn't look like something she'd sanction…but for now we can't trust anyone. I need your help."

"I owe you my life," Jessa said. "And it's my own stupidity that weakened me and led to the death of your friend. It's a debt I fear I can never repay."

She walked toward Sword's body. "He was so brave defending me. I know Patreans don't have families, but I'll gladly pay his death gratuity and whatever stipend is required for you to replace him with another of equal quality."

"I need to see your mother," Heath said.

Jessa tensed. "You're one of her agents?"

"Hells no." He chuckled. "A friend of mine is being held in her cell. You're the only one who can get access whenever you want. If you vouch for me as your spiritual advisor, then you can get me in."

"Maddox?" Jessa asked. "The drunken…homosexual?"

"I couldn't think of a better way to describe him." Heath smiled. "He has information I need."

Jessa sighed as she knelt by the fallen swordsman. "I was rather hoping your favors would involve charity work, but I can arrange an audience. May I ask if this has anything to do with these intruders?"

"I don't know, but it very likely will. Either way Esme's not my concern."

"Then I'll do whatever it takes," Jessa avowed. She looked at the bastard sword on the floor. It featured a large red jewel in the hilt, and the design was unmistakable. "May I also ask how a Patrean soldier came to possess the Vorpal Sword of Arix?"

Heath stood next to her. "You recognize the blade?"

"It's a bastard sword with a thousand-carat gemstone set into the hilt and another of half that size in the pommel. There's no other sword in Creation like it...nor would any sensible jeweler or blacksmith craft such a thing. It belonged to my third great-grandfather and apparently drove him mad. It was stolen by his squire more than a century ago."

Heath looked at the blade. "Then perhaps it should return to its rightful owner."

"I should hardly need such a thing, but it is marvelously crafted." She bent down to grab the hilt.

Heath's hand snatched her wrist firmly. They exchanged glances, hers puzzled and his conflicted.

He smiled. "You don't want to touch it."

"But you just said..."

Heath shook his head. "It's cursed. Whoever touches it loses his or her will to the sword. It's the same type of magic that possessed that poor girl he was fighting. It did likely make your ancestor crazy...but it's also my friend. It's just his nature. He can't *not* possess people. I just need to find him a better home—and your child will need a mother."

"My child?" Jessa gasped. "Could you sense that?"

"It's why I needed to work so long to heal you," Heath said. "The poison was concentrating on your baby, and his Light was fading. If I delayed a second longer, you would have lived, but he could have miscarried."

"He?" Jessa asked.

"Congratulations," Heath said. "It's a boy."

Jessa hugged him. "Thank you."

He gently returned the embrace.

"We can't stick around," Heath cautioned. "I need to find something to pick up the sword so my skin doesn't touch the hilt. And you need to get dressed. When the wolf jumped out the window, he would have set off the alarms from the warding glyphs. Invocari will be here soon with the city militia. We can't trust them, so you'll need to lie convincingly about what happened. I would tell them—"

"I don't like deception." Jessa shook her head. "There are secret passages throughout this place. Grab the sword. I'll dress, and we'll escape through the tunnels under the manor. That'll put us out in the steam tunnels. From there we can make our way to the tower."

He grinned and shook his head slowly. "All right. Let's go."

Jessa bolted toward her bedroom. Her mattress had been flipped over and torn open. And the Thunderstone was missing from the nightstand.

THE STEAM TUNNELS (HEATH)

Heath and Jessa made their way down the old servants' corridors into the steam tunnels. The name was apt, as the air was hot and moist. These tunnels were arched, with greenish ceramic tile covering the stonework. There were ledges on either side of the passage, and deep aqueducts of river water flowed through the center. Brass pipes ran along the walls and ceiling, rattling and giving off periodic hisses of steam.

There were no lights, so Heath conjured some from his hand to guide them. He carried Sword on his back, hidden under his robes. Jessa followed with evident interest. She wore a leather hunting jacket and long riding dress. She arranged her hair in a braid as she walked on the surface of the water as if it were made of glass.

The tunnels were part of a utility network that provided compressed steam to power Rivern's mechanical marvels—everything from pressure plates to elevators and sewing assemblies. Hot and cold running water also came from here for the families and institutions that could afford the luxury.

A side tunnel ahead flickered with the amber light of a fire, and waves of heat radiated through the passage. Two bored seal mages sat on either side of a card table, taking turns hurling fire at the burner. They glanced at Heath and Jessa as they passed but didn't get up.

The tunnels were dark and uninviting, but they weren't off limits to citizens.

"Do you know where we're going?" Jessa asked.

Heath nodded. "There's an outlet that will put us on the side of the Overlook, facing the Clockmakers' District. There's a bridge we can cross a few blocks down if we can't flag a gondola."

Jessa frowned. "I have your friend's song stuck in my head."

He flashed a smile. "I'm truly sorry. There are limits to what afflictions the Will of Ohan allows."

"Will you find him another body?" she asked quietly.

Heath furrowed his brow. Speaking to Catherine and reliving Sword's recollection of Reda made him waver in his conviction. He could round up another Patrean pretty easily, but he knew enough of them to know that despite their identical appearance they were unique individuals.

He also was dying. He could feel the cancer in his body beginning to grow. He might have missed it entirely if it weren't for Catherine's warning. Blood mages and alchemists had treatments, but they weren't guarantees. What would it be like to take the blade himself and share his final days with his only true friend?

"Mother is quite fond of swordplay," Jessa offered hesitantly. "And jewels. And family heirlooms."

Heath narrowed his eyes and searched her face for any hint of irony or deception. He spoke very gently. "The bonding is irreversible, Jessa. Would you really do that to your own mother?"

"Is it…" She searched for words. "She's acting out some grand scheme, and I'm at a loss as to how to neutralize her. I don't wish her dead, but while she draws breath, even in a magically warded chamber, she's a danger, and her schemes threaten me and my son. If she were to become an ally…Oh, it's evil to consider such a thing."

Her idea was brilliant, but he needed to tread carefully. "The sword also takes on a lot of its wielder's personality and sometimes acts in line with what its wielder wants. It's almost like it becomes a new person. It's unpredictable."

"My aunts want her dead," Jessa said finally. "If my mother doesn't change her course, she's destined for destruction. She's her own woman, but her choices and her life affect more than just herself."

They continued down the tunnels.

"Losing my mother was the hardest thing I had to face." Heath went for the sympathy play. "It made me stop believing in…everything. She could be a strict woman, and we fought like hell when I ran with the dock gangs. But she loved me. I never once doubted that she wanted what was best for me, and she would have laid down her life to protect me."

Jessa placed her hand against her belly. "She sounds wonderful."

They came to an opening. The water spilled into the riverway, and the tunnel opened to a pair of flagstone landings with steps that led to the upper roads and causeways. The entire length of the river was contained in manmade walls five to fifteen feet in height. At this level Jessa could see massive waterwheels in the Clockmakers' District.

"What happens when it rains?" she asked. "It seems the city would flood."

"The whole river and waterfalls are controlled by dams and locks," Heath told her. "They have boat tours that explain it. Maybe after this is over, we can take one."

Jessa smiled, and for the first time, she seemed playful. "I would much enjoy that."

PARLOUR ROOM INTRIGUE (SATRYN)

Tyragorn: Isn't deception your claim to fame? Why should I believe a word you say?

Alessandria: Oh, no! You're, mistaken sir. You're thinking of the Queen of Lies.

Tyragorn: Is that not the person-creature to whom I address now with my eloquent mouth-words?

Alessandria: While your mellifluous voice could be the bastard child of a poet and a mighty stag, I must protest that you are mistaken as to my identity.

Tyragorn: But you conform to the very description of her.

Alessandria: Your perception is powerful indeed, but it is the Queen of Lies who uses my description to perpetuate her awful mischief, my burly lord of lords.

Tyragorn: Impossible!

Alessandria: Exactly possible, my stallion-lord. You see, I am the Queen of Flies. Our names are so much similar in pronunciation that people often mistake us. [pause for laughter]

Tyragorn: I have heard of no such thing

Alessandria: Just so. I am from the kingdom of Carcass, you see, and my brother is the duke of Maggots. My country is a dead cow the size of a continent.

Tyragorn: I am both disgusted…and inflamed with desire.

Alessandria: I am but an innocent virgin queen from a poor nation in need of your assistance…and affection. Lay with me and tell me your secrets.

Tyragorn: At once!

—*The Queen of Flies*, a ribald satirical play based on the biographies of Alessandria, the Queen of Lies

Maddox sat mutely on the sofa in Satryn's cell. He was upright, but his gaze appeared empty and distant. Across from Satryn, Abbess Daphne sat cross-legged in her shapeless white robes, her gloved hands folded primly on her knee. She'd heard that the Orthodoxy employed spies and secret police even as they preached the endless mercy of their invented deity.

"Come on now, dear, drink." Satryn placed a bottle to Maddox's gaping mouth. "This is very expensive."

His throat swallowed reflexively as she poured several hundred crowns' worth of Volkovian brandy down his gullet. Some dribbled down his chin. She set the bottle aside and wiped his mouth with a silk handkerchief.

Satryn tsked. "Well, I do need to give you credit, Abbess. He's completely broken, and you accomplished it in a single day. I don't suppose you're looking for employment. In the Dominance we have a relaxed code of dress for our torturers, and many of them enjoy the convenience of working in their homes."

Daphne uncrossed her leg, her face a mask of false civility. "I'll consider it if you embrace the Father of All as the master of your destiny. I'd leave you with some literature, but I didn't bring any."

"I like the ones with graphic depictions of the torture in the five hells," Satryn confided. "I'm not sure if it's a Genatrovan thing, but the pornography they provide here tends toward the stale side."

"Why am I here?" Daphne said. "I don't mean my motivations or any philosophical discussion. I know why I'm here. I'm here because you wanted to speak to me, and *you're* here. What I want to know is the reasons *you* are *here*. Because I can't think of a single one. You didn't order the hit. I know Cordovis killed Torin Silverbrook. I have records, testimony, and even an absentee writ of confession from the man himself. But then…you commit another murder of your cellmate… or assault—the courts don't know what to call it. Care to explain that one to me? Why am I *here*?"

Satryn sighed. "Yes, yes. I was quite mad with grief over my brother's passing, and it's becoming difficult to control my abilities. I fear it has made me a danger to myself and those around me. It's why I was so happy to receive your visitation, Abbess."

Daphne grinned and nodded. "And why I was so surprised to receive your invitation. Especially considering that you're a priestess of Kultea, born into a holy office of your faith. You have no reason whatsoever to speak to me or even have any idea who I am. Why am I here?"

Satryn smiled. "Our faiths have many similar commandments. The religion of your false god was copied, sometimes from whole cloth, from the basic tenets of the true elemental faiths. For instance we see free thought as an intrinsic quality of every person's potential for godhood. Thus we fiercely prohibit any theurgy that seeks to tamper with the minds of those unwilling. Just as it says in your scriptures."

"An interesting example." Daphne reached for her brandy glass and studied it. "Because if you think you have some kind of leverage—"

"If I didn't think you a woman of good faith, for instance, I might assume you enacted the practice of quelling on this vulnerable young man here. Now we're quite familiar with it in the Dominance, but it requires a certain *kind* of mage to perform it." Although Satryn was enjoying herself, the abbess betrayed no emotion whatsoever.

"Do you like it here?" Daphne motioned to the cell around her.

Satryn leaned in and confided, "It's not Thelassus, but believe it or not, I much prefer my present accommodations to my castle at Weatherly."

"If you murdered a man in cold blood, in broad daylight, and in front of a hundred witnesses, the penalty would be public censure and a ransom back to the Coral Throne." Daphne sipped her drink. "It's inconsistencies like this that make me interested in you. I'm not a person you want interested in your affairs. So why am I here?"

"You want reasons?" Satryn refilled her glass. "First, it is my legal right to remain silent as to my guilt or innocence. Second, the people of Rivern are beset by a plague of harrowings and ready to turn to any explanation for their misfortune. While I'm neutralized here, I'm not a suspect in these matters. Third, this place is secure. Members of the imperial family are being murdered. It's common practice to sequester oneself in precarious situations such as this. If Stormlords fear anything, it's the Invocari. And if you believe my daughter, I'm also quite insane, so what's to tell my motivation?"

Daphne set down her drink. "I don't want reasons. I want the truth."

"Your city is in a panic from the epidemic of harrowings," Satryn said. "The Rivern Assembly rules as a government in exile from the hinter provinces, if you can still call their deadlocked parliament a system of government. Trade is diminished, I'm sure. Nothing can get through Amhaven while Rothburn's insurrection wages, and no one from the other Free Cities will spend a night within ten miles of the city wall. There's a flood of hungry refugees, ripe for revolt, and an exodus of leadership. Aside from your Patrean mercenaries, who are bound only by coin, it is the Invocari and Orthodoxy that have the authority to hold any order in this city."

Daphne said, "I don't want facts. I want the truth."

Satryn leaned back and rubbed Maddox's hair. "You're an impressive woman in a society that doesn't see women as the full equal of men. You're of dark skin in a city where the skin of the nobility is pale. You're ruthless and ambitious, yet you come from a faith that preaches modesty and humility. You're *here* because I believe you'll be worthy."

"*What?*" Daphne exclaimed.

"I have a proposal," Satryn drawled. "Rivern will need leadership if it is to rebuild. I think you're the obvious choice, Daphne Stern of Bamor. I've done my research, and you're underutilized in your current function as Inquisitor. I would name you seneschal of Rivern. Take a moment to laugh incredulously and ask me again why you're here."

"You're out of your goddamned mind," Daphne accused. "You're locked in the most secure cell in all Creation. Your prison lies in the heart of the most well-guarded city in the Protectorate. Your jailers are the Invocari, who have served decisive military defeat to your Stormlord ancestors for five hundred years."

"I'm a guardian of Creation and of the Protectorate," she continued. "Not because I want power or adulation but because justice and equality are principles worth preserving, at any cost. Ohan may be a false god, but Creation needs him. People need mercy and humility."

Satryn shrugged. "I normally find sex with women boring, but I must admit, your passion has me aroused. I can give you leeway in how things are run."

"You're disgusting," Daphne spat. "I see a bored, pampered, paranoid, *coward* who's been deposed from the ass end of nowhere, disowned by her family, and left clinging desperately to any last shred of influence she possesses."

Satryn cocked her head. "It's odd you would dismiss me so readily. I mean, since I came to Rivern, almost to the day, there has been that horrendous rash of harrowings. And here I sit, as you say, in the center of an inescapable web, brazenly offering you dominion over my own jailers. Would that not lead you to wonder whether I am the cause?"

"Are you?" Daphne raised an eyebrow.

"No, but I should be your prime suspect," Satryn admitted. "Surely you would at least have your mind reader scour my thoughts. Instead you've ignored me. I would be offended, but then why would you bother interrogating me when you already know I don't have such knowledge?"

"Stormlords can't learn other theurgies," Daphne said, "and you're locked in here."

"Who says it's a Stormlord?" Satryn smiled. "As the well-connected daughter of an enemy monarch, could I not bring my own loyalists into the city? My own sister was within your walls not a fortnight ago."

"If you're here to confess, I'm here to listen," Daphne said.

"And be your scapegoat?" Satryn rubbed her chin. "You're obviously new to politics, so I'll explain this. I believe it is you, personally, who has unleashed this plague of harrowings on your own city to consolidate power, eliminate rivals, remove perceived threats to your mission, and frighten unruly refugees into moving on to other locales. I admire your work, and I want you on my side."

"You're insane," Daphne stated simply.

Satryn leaned forward. "That's merely an act. You have skill with subterfuge, but I'm better at this than you are."

Daphne leaned in as well. "I have a counteroffer. Work for me, and I won't testify in front of the Veritas Seal that you made a full confession to me claiming full responsibility for the harrowings. The Invocari will disintegrate you."

"Darling," Satryn preened, "I'd love to hear what plans you have for the daughter of the empress, but...we have visitors."

Daphne looked back to the airlock door. Jessa, wearing very rugged country attire, and a dark-skinned priest entered the room. They stood perplexed for a moment and exchanged whispers.

"Heath," Daphne said.

"Jessa, darling!" Satryn clapped excitedly. "This is like one of those parlor-room mysteries where all the characters gather in the drawing room as the brave inspector names the murderer! Oh, but who will play Inspector Margulies?"

Heath cocked his head then said with a twinkle in his eye, "But Countess... you said you only laid out three forks for Lord Uppington since he does not eat shellfish."

Satryn clenched her fists in mock outrage. "Damn you, Inspector Margulies!"

Oh, but this is going to be fun.

PARLOR-ROOM MYSTERY (JESSA)

Heath whispered to Jessa, "We can't use the sword here. Daphne will recognize it. We need to get her alone. Just follow my lead, whatever I say."

Jessa didn't like improvising. She listened as Heath and her mother traded quotes from a book she was unfamiliar with while she struggled to come up with a plan. He had a very disarming manner, playing into Satryn's jokes rather than refuting her nonsense. Mother warmed to him quickly.

"I must deal with her," Jessa said.

"Deal with me?" Satryn clasped her hands together in delight. "How do *you* propose to deal with *me*? Are you going to bore me to death?"

"By turning you over to the authorities," she said. "I'll give my testimony under the Veritas Seal that you and Sireen recruited Thrycean loyalists in the Assembly with the intention of doing great harm to this city. They'll never let you succeed."

"You really don't know how to do a parlor-room mystery. You have to build to the accusation, darling." Satryn pouted. "If you just say it, then you ruin the suspense."

Heath went over to Maddox and waved his hand in front of his vacant green eyes. "What the hells is wrong with him?"

"He's been quelled," Daphne said, "for his and everyone's protection. He'll remain here until we can build a prison from which he'll never escape. That prison will be shot through an Invocari gravity well into the blackest void of the firmament."

"He was much more entertaining before. Here, you can have Maddox's drink—he's not drinking." Satryn handed Heath a glass, which he took.

"You're very gracious, my lady."

"And you're very handsome," Satryn replied. "Tell me, what is a genial man like yourself doing with my plain, surly daughter?"

"Yes, Heath," Daphne crossed her leg. "I was wondering the same thing."

Jessa spoke up. "He came to me when I—"

Heath cut her off. "I needed to talk to Maddox to complete a contract, and she was the easiest way in. And she was exceptionally trusting. I told her a sob story about my mother, and she brought me directly here."

He looked at her and sneered slightly. It was as if his whole demeanor had changed without warning.

Jessa's face went hot with fury, but she restrained herself. "You're disgusting!" she huffed.

"She has no stomach for intrigue, does she?" Heath smiled to Satryn. "Is she really your daughter?"

Satryn stiffened slightly. "Careful, priest. She's still heir to the Coral Throne. I like you a very little, but you will not curry my favor by speaking above your station. That's a privilege I reserve exclusively."

"Apologies," Heath said. "I merely meant to say that you're too youthful to have a daughter so mature."

Satryn beamed. "Oh! Forgive my presumption. Now…shall we get down to business? I'll answer any and all questions from this point onward with complete candor and explain every aspect of my secret plan to conquer Rivern for the Dominance."

Jessa felt uneasy. Satryn was gloating. Her mother was fond of gloating, but she never did it presumptively. She racked her brain before blurting, "Torin? Did you have anything to do with his murder?"

"No, because that wedding never would have happened," Satryn said. "Next question?"

Daphne piped up, "Then why not exonerate yourself?"

"So I can learn the location of the Dark Star within the Invocari tower," Satryn explained. "I need to know where it is so I can destroy the source of power that protects the city. That was the original reason, but I decided my agenda would be better served if I stayed close to it until the appointed time."

"Oh, just fucking spit it out," Jessa demanded. "Your games are tiresome."

"You're looking in all the wrong places, daughter. The wheels of this endeavor have been turning everywhere but Rivern."

Perplexed, Jessa looked at the floor. Then her eyes widened with realization. "No."

Satryn ran her fingers through her silver hair. "Nash was my father. I was born of the union of two Stormlords. Quirrus was good enough to enlighten me to this fact, though I suspect a part of me always knew. Nasara may be my older sister and next in line by tradition, but my blood is purer. With Maelcolm's sacrifice, the power of another pureblood flows to me. I'll be more puissant than Iridissa herself."

"Mother…this is madness."

She sighed. "No. I've played the madwoman and the fool for years, but it was always just that—a calculated diversion. Perhaps it came more naturally to me because of my parents' blood, and there were times when the role consumed me, demanded more from me than I thought I could bear."

Jessa stood abruptly. "Are you saying my entire shitty childhood was theater? If those words carry a grain of truth, you're worse than mad, Mother. You're evil, pure and true."

"I needed to set you against me," Satryn explained. "Sireen and Nasara would use you to assassinate me, but I know in your heart you'd never do such a thing. And now we can be friends again."

"I wouldn't be so certain…" Jessa's eyes were hot with tears, and her voice shook with rage.

"Well, unless you're hiding Sireen's Thunderstone up your ass, I don't think a single one of you is capable of stopping me."

Heath slid behind her and let the blades from his wrist pop into place. He stuck them against Satryn's throat. "Don't move an inch. These blades are abraveum, so you can't shock me. And if you do, any movement of my body will slit your artery. You'll bleed out in minutes."

"Listen to me, Jessa," Satryn said, remaining perfectly still. "The empress has been sick for years; her mind comes and goes. The barnacle-encrusted sea hag you met on your tenth birthday had no idea what was happening. They drug her daily and sit her on that throne, restrained by manacles made to resemble bracelets of woven gold so she doesn't take her own life, as her honor would demand. Nasara has run her empire, keeping her alive until the perfect moment."

"Fuck," Jessa whispered.

"And as of this morning, Nasara granted her final mercy. Stand by my side, not as my resentful daughter, but as an elemental titan born to inherit Creation. Your childhood is nothing more than a footnote in the history you will create. I'm doing this for you, Jessa."

"Do it, Heath," Daphne ordered. "There's nothing to be gained from keeping her alive."

Satryn was quick. She grabbed Heath's wrist and flicked the mechanism on his springblades to retract the blades back into their hidden bracers. She slid aside and spun as she stood. She punched him in the neck with a clap of electricity, knocking him back.

Jessa's reflexes kicked in a second later. Her mother's motions were brisk, but Jessa reacted while the priest stood stunned. Time seemed to slow. Unfortunately Satryn was immune to her power; Jessa needed an edge.

Heath was still falling backward as Jessa charged for him. Satryn paused for a fraction of a second to consider her daughter then spun on Daphne. The abbess barely had gotten out of her seat when Satryn kicked her in the face. From his seat on the sofa, Maddox watched without any reaction.

Jessa kept running. If she could get to the Sword, she'd be able to stop her mother. She had some immunity to her mother's power, and the masterful skill the blade imparted could defeat her. Satryn was good with a sword, but without the protection of steel, she couldn't stand up to an onslaught like Jessa had witnessed at the Silverbrook estate.

It didn't matter that Jessa would lose herself. The prospect of her mother with the power of a fully realized pureblood tempest was motivation enough. It was her freedom or the lives of half a million people.

Daphne's body exploded in a flash of golden light as radiant plate mail formed over her body in response to Satryn's attack. The priestess grabbed Satryn's leg and flung her across the room with inhuman strength.

Jessa reached Heath and ripped at his robe, trying to find the blade's hilt. He grabbed her hand. "No."

She shook her head. "I have to. I'm the only one who can stop her."

Heath shook off the effect of Satryn's shock as golden light washed over his body. "No, there's a better option."

Daphne and Satryn were fighting. The priestess was clad in translucent armor made of sunlight, and Satryn struck her repeatedly with her Storm blade.

"I'm guided by conviction," Daphne avowed, as she punched at the Stormlord. "Something you'll never understand."

Satryn fell back, but her expression was calm, as if she were appraising a jewel.

Heath got up from the floor and pulled the scabbard off his back.

"Lady Satryn," Heath said, holding the blade aloft, safely ensconced in its leather scabbard, careful not to touch the hilt, "please, I have a tribute for your benevolence from your supporters within the city. It's a long-lost relic of your ancestors."

Daphne's luminous armor flickered as Satryn struck it repeatedly. And Satryn wasn't even trying. She was incredibly quick, yet she seemed almost bored.

Satryn glanced at the sword. "I'll pass."

"Backup plan." Heath set the Sword in Maddox's lap and tried to gently nudge the hilt under the mage's hands. "Just grab it," he said through gritted teeth, as he wedged the hilt under Maddox's delicate fingers. "Please…"

And then, in the span of a second, the fingers closed. Maddox blinked. "Ohhhhh, hells no," he groaned. "You've got to be fucking kidding me."

He bolted up and waved his hand. The sofa flew across the room, twisting in midair to miss Daphne, and slammed Satryn against the concave glass wall of the cell. He twirled the Sword in one hand and jammed it against the glass next to him. The blade glowed with white light as he pushed it through.

Maddox said, "She's toying with you. We can't kill her. She's already taken the mantle of Tempest."

"I would have sensed it if the empress passed," Jessa said.

"You looked pretty out of it at the manor." Maddox shoved the Sword through the glass. The glowing sigils flickered. "Besides, the lightning burst only happens with violent deaths of immediate family. Do you have a Thunderstone?"

"I had one at the manor, but I was—"

"I was there." Maddox grunted as he dragged the edge of the blade through the glass. He stepped back and stretched out his hand. The Sword moved along the arc of his hand, carving a circle through the glass. "We need to find Esme."

"So you're the swordsman who saved my life?" Jessa asked.

Maddox grumbled, "Him and a few hundred other people, including your great-great-great grandfather, Arix. So listen to me when I say that none of you have seen the power of an Archtempest…and let me work."

Jessa glanced over her shoulder. Satryn blasted the sofa that pinned her into wooden splinters and cotton. Daphne, still clad in her solar armor, fell on her with twin blades that sprang from the sleeves of her robes. She was holding her off but just barely.

The sword cut a perfect circle out of the glass. The glowing wards died. The circle of glass blasted backward into a million shards. Two Invocari hovered next to the wall, waving their hands and summoning their void magic.

"Good," Maddox told them. "You keep her busy. It's a long story, but Loran will vouch for me. And by Loran…I mean your fucking boss, the Grand Invocus."

The Invocari looked at each other.

"This blade is a starmetal alloy," Maddox grunted impatiently. "Plus it was designed to reflect magic, so don't even think about using that creeper sorcery on us. Princess, Heath—come on!"

A crash of thunder exploded behind Jessa, shaking the tower. Satryn glowed. Her body was transparent, and her eyes shone like cold moons. She stood gracefully, arms outstretched, as Daphne slashed her with her blades. But the metal passed through her; Satryn had become pure energy.

"*That's* why we need to get the fuck out of here." Maddox waved his hand and lifted Jessa through the hole in the glass. Heath was already on the other side.

"I know of a weapon that can slay her, but we must have your leave to find it," Jessa explained to the Invocari.

"Go," one of them said. "And Princess?"

"Yes?"

"I'm sorry I wasn't able to save your fiancé."

"Thank you." She placed a hand on her heart.

Maddox grabbed Jessa's arm and dragged her around the edge of the circular cell toward the elevator. "Cordovis did you a favor. Torin was a fucking tool."

"What did he ever do to you to earn such harsh words?" Jessa was stunned anyone could speak ill of the boy.

Maddox paused and blinked. "I have absolutely no idea. Give me an hour to process this guy's memories, and I'll get back to you. There's a lot to unpack in here, and it's a bit of a headfuck."

Heath took the lead. "We need to get to Esme's blood specimen from my house so we can track her. Hopefully the Invocari can deal with your mother."

"You can't suffocate living electricity," Maddox said sourly. "They're all dead."

As if on cue, a pair of thunderclaps reported through the circular chamber as blinding light illuminated behind them.

They made their way to the elevator shaft, but the lift was gone. Invocari floated up like vengeful spirits from the darkness and floated past. They had opened the airlock. Jessa saw that Daphne was still standing, but she wasn't looking hale or healthy. The light that sustained her armor flickered and waned as Satryn poured lightning into her.

"What about Daphne?" Jessa insisted. "We should at least make sure she gets out."

Heath placed a hand on her shoulder. "She can get out whenever she wants. She's buying us time. We need to use it."

Maddox scowled irritably and raised his hands. The metal cage of the lift came screaming up the shaft. Sparks flew from the sides of the cage as its tracks screeched in protest. The box slammed to a stop, and the gate flew off, ripped from its hinges by an invisible force. It slammed into the glass cage behind them.

"That's kind of cool," Maddox said, admiring his handiwork.

Heath and Jessa jumped inside, and Maddox joined them. He scowled at a control box with levers and buttons, and the lift plunged downward. Normally it was a slow process to get to and from Satryn's prison, but this time the cage was in nearly a freefall. It slammed to a stop, making Jessa stagger.

"Come on," Maddox said. "We need to move."

Heath rubbed his chin. "Are you okay, Sword?"

"Do you care?" Maddox snapped. "You never ask how I'm feeling unless you want something, and I am *done* being your fucking doormat. All you ever do is use people, Heath. You use them up until there's nothing left, and then you toss them aside like garbage. I won't be managed anymore!"

"Sword," Heath said calmly, "there was nothing we could have done differently in that situation."

"Stop it!" Maddox shouted as he made his way out of the tower with Heath and Jessa trailing behind.

Jessa wanted to interrupt, but the tension didn't lend itself to her opinion. And she didn't have anything useful to offer. She wondered what would have happened if Heath had given the Sword to her.

Maddox spun and loomed in Heath's path. His words were cold and sharp. "You could have taken the blade yourself. You didn't. I devoted my life to you, and you'd rather die than make me a part of it. I see you for what you are now. You're a coward."

"I wouldn't be me anymore," Heath explained. "I wouldn't be your friend."

"And I wouldn't be me anymore either," Maddox said. "We'd be something new together. You have to give up some part of yourself sometime, Heath, or you're going to have a long, lonely life."

"Maddox...or Sword," Jessa interjected, "I'm grateful for your assistance, but we need to find the Thunderstone. Mother is powerful enough to cause a great deal of damage to the city, and it's only a matter of time before she floods the canals. For the sake of the city, I ask you put your feelings aside. For now."

He rubbed his eyes with the palm of his hand. "Ugh. Just give me a second to process this. Every gestalt is different, and this one is intense."

He stormed off.

Jessa and Heath looked at each other. Heath shrugged, and they followed Sword.

INTEGRITY (SWORD)

It the great lie we tell ourselves to think of ourselves as single individuals. We are each a thousand warring factions fighting for control of a single narrative and rewriting history with each victory.
-The Storyteller, Traveler Proverbs

The problem was that Sword despised Maddox, probably more than anyone in recent memory. Maddox knew Sword as Catherine. He didn't much care for her either. In fact the two of them only barely tolerated each other when he and Heath were an item, something Sword, when it was Catherine, actively had told Heath to stop.

His brain felt as if it had been dipped in lemon juice, rolled over broken glass, and drop-kicked into a bucket of fire ants. His heart ached. His mind flashed back over his memories, reexperiencing events from Maddox's perspective. He didn't want Maddox's memories. He didn't want to feel the hurt of his best friend turning a cold shoulder to him.

Maddox was cocky and boorish. He wasn't even that good-looking. Sword tried to imagine what Heath saw in him besides wild sexual chemistry. Sword felt the heat of arousal as he recalled being bound into submission and fucked senseless. The hot sting of shame followed shortly after.

Sword felt betrayed that Heath had been so intimate with another person, especially someone as unworthy as Maddox. But the anger went worse than betrayal; it was...jealousy. Heath never had touched Sword, never even flirted. Catherine was a proud and beautiful lady, but she was older, and Heath was un-interested anyway. But he was smitten with Maddox.

And he felt a ping, a common point of understanding. He looked at his new reflection in the edge of his blade and saw a kindred spirit. Someone who also had struggled for the affection of someone who had remained forever out of reach. And then the gestalt fell into place, like pieces of a broken glass rising from the floor and fusing into something fragile but intricate.

"Okay," Sword said. "Assimilation complete or whatever. We're all good in here. Sorry about earlier."

"It's only been a few seconds," Heath said. They were still walking toward the exit to the Invocari tower. The Invocari had taken up positions in the stairs. They rasped orders in their creepy metallic voices for them to evacuate.

"You know how the people who piss you off the most turn out to be exactly the same as you? It's kind of like that," Sword said. "Give me a week, and I can probably remaster a new school of theurgy from my memories."

"Think of it as an upgrade," Heath said.

Thick gray clouds roiled above. The sky had a strange greenish pallor like it was going to throw up. The wind carried the scent of petrichor, which Maddox's nose detected very strongly. But beneath the fresh smell was a murky, salty undertone like the rotting carcass of a great sea creature washed ashore.

"I'm also immortal, so this was a hasty improvisation with permanent consequences," Sword added, "for me. And us. The feelings are difficult to control. This psyche was systematically eviscerated. As much as I'm using Maddox's infrastructure, he's coopting my emotive responses to repair the damage."

"Would it be helpful to sing your battle shanty?" Jessa offered. "I find it comforting to return to the familiar. Plus it's been stuck in my head, and I need a distraction."

Sword chuckled. "It's beneath my current vocal talents."

Heath rolled his eyes. "Maddox does have good pipes. You don't want to encourage him, or he'll be serenading on top of the bar."

"Explains why he got along so well with Mother," Jessa quipped.

"It was an interesting relationship," Sword admitted.

"So what happened between the two of you?" Jessa asked Heath. "You obviously have a history. I don't mean to pry too deeply if the subject is sensitive, but Mother did make known Maddox's proclivities."

"We had a thing. Maddox was a clingy alcoholic with a short temper," Heath admitted. "There was a lot of passion, but it…affected my judgment. Made me unfocused. With the life Sword and I lead, that can get you killed."

"The father of my unborn child revealed himself to be a spy for the Coral Throne," Jessa said. "I understand the need to be vigilant in matters of the heart."

They approached Heath's house.

"You live here?" Jessa asked, looking at the three-story property on the intersection of two canals. It had a small lawn with well-tended rosebushes and a skinny apple tree.

"It's modest compared to what you're used to, I'm sure," Heath said.

They stepped into the foyer, and Sword remembered it through Maddox's blurry, drunken memories. It was like reading the runny ink from a book that had been soaked in bourbon. Plus every person saw things differently. Maddox needed glasses, probably as a result of his reading practice with inscription.

"You've done well for yourself, Heath." Jessa marveled at the tile mosaic in the entryway. "I know assemblymen who can't claim such well-appointed accommodations."

The walls were adorned with artifacts and souvenirs from Heath's adventures. There were tons of weapons (falchions, flails, and more exotic implements of death) and paintings of far-off places. Sword remembered most of them fondly.

"That's high praise from royalty." Heath bowed. "I'll just be a minute upstairs. Sword, get her anything she needs."

He retreated up the stairs.

"So do I call you Sword or Maddox? Maybe Sworddox?" Jessa asked.

"We're not doing that. Sword's good. It's kind of stupid, but you know, it keeps things straight in my head."

"Sword"—Jessa turned to him—"I never got to properly thank you for the sacrifice you made to protect my life."

"It's nothing," Sword said, making his way to the dining room. "For me it's like ripping a favorite pair of trousers. A little upsetting but easily replaced."

"I almost took you myself," Jessa declared suddenly. "Would you consider me the equivalent of trousers? And forgive my naïveté in these mundane matters, but can't trousers be mended?"

"Sorry. That sounded anthrophobic. Some deaths *have* upset me; others were a huge relief. The big guy was somewhere in between. Do you prefer red or white?"

Sword waved his hand in front of the wine cabinet and withdrew a bottle from it. The cork separated itself from the neck of the bottle as it reached his hand. He drank, savoring the flavor and aroma of the newly opened bottle. Maddox's olfactory senses were phenomenal. Sword could equate every note of fragrance to a property of the soil or a step in the aging process.

Jessa folded her arms. "How can you drink at a time like this?"

Sword peered at her. "How can you *not*? You just found out Satryn raised you to be a pawn in her scheme to topple the Protectorate. I think that qualifies."

"Esme defeated you handily last time." Jessa was starting to sound a little whiny, "If you impair your reflexes, you'll stand even less of a chance."

Sword chuckled deviously to himself. "Yeah. This is going to be a fun fight."

Jessa shook her head. "I wish I shared your confidence. Perhaps if we show our strength, Esme will simply hand over the Thunderstone without bloodshed."

"Sure," he said without any hint of seriousness. He called up the stairs, "Hey, Heath! I just remembered something. I know who Evan Landry is. We don't need the blood."

There was no response.

"Did you hear me, Heath?" Sword's face darkened with concern. "Hey, buddy, you okay up there?"

They waited for a moment then went up the staircase with Sword in the lead and Jessa following. He charged to the armory and saw Heath collapsed on the floor, with the vial of blood in hand. He had hit his head on the sharpening wheel in the center of the room. Sword leaned in and grabbed his face. Heath's eyes were closed and fluttering back and forth. He smelled the faint whiff of char and sulfur. Wisps of it were coming off his eyelids.

"Harrowers," Sword said. "It's a psychic attack."

"What can we do?"

"Get me a stylus. It looks like a pencil with a gem on the end of it. There's one in the display case at the end of the hall. There's a poisoned needle in the handle, so just smash the glass. Hurry."

To her credit Jessa already was making her way down the hall as he was speaking. The sound of thunder and exploding glass echoed down the hall, and Jessa ran back with the stylus in hand. She tossed it to him, and he caught it midair.

The facts and theories of Maddox's mind clicked together with memories of old magic. What he was attempting was the height of foolishness. A seal mage required familiarity with his instrument. This stylus was completely foreign to his hand; it required practice. Performing glyphomancy on the fly without the protection of a binding circle—well, that was just idiotic.

Sword started to inscribe the seal on the floor. Between Maddox's muscle memory and the superior coordination that came from Sword's intelligence, it was simple to create the initial circle. His arm moved with mechanical precision.

He knew the seal he wanted—Amnayleth, the Seal of Mystery. It was impossible to know what it did unless you had obtained one (or shared a body with someone who had it), and the seal's magic preserved its mystery in a variety of unexpected ways. Fortunately it couldn't erase the pyromaniac witch-hunter's memory of having it. It gave you amazing, vivid dreams.

The dreams were of a secret realm filled with wonder and awe, a bountiful treasure of sensory delights to reward the endlessly curious. You could be inspired by your explorations, but you never could directly talk about them with anyone.

In ancient times seal magic was considered a basic art. There were seals for every possible purpose: to season food with thoughts, to lose weight, to restore lost hair, or even to have a larger penis. Good mysterious dreams were pretty low on the list of sought-after theurgy…until Achelon had released the Nightmares. The Seal of Mystery was the only known protection from the harrowings.

Motes of aethersprites gathered in the workshop. A few small ones. Sword whispered the words of the incantation: "*Anulia zanile sintur abradaste, Amnayleth.*"

With hot white light, the sparks of light flew to his design and the dark lines of the inscription. He slammed his hand on the inscription and placed it on his stomach, transferring the bound magic to his body. Then he placed his hands on either side of Heath's head and shut his eyes.

Without the binding ritual and with the feeble amount of power he'd gathered, he already felt the magic of the seal start to decay.

Heath opened his eyes and let out a bloodcurdling howl. Sword fell backward in surprise. It was the kind of scream you heard in the shadowed oubliettes of the Inquisition's prison. His eyes were hollow and charred.

Heath slapped one hand to his head and covered his ruined eye sockets. Light blasted from his hands, warm and steady. "The fuck happened?"

Sword stood. "You're one of the only men in Creation to survive an attack from a Harrower."

Heath pulled his hands away. His eyes were back, but they looked cloudy and half formed. He was a decent lay healer, but restoring lost body parts took a lot more Light than he could channel. He looked at Sword. "How?"

Sword grinned. "I used the seal of mystery to give you good dreams and drive off the Harrower. You're going to forget I ever told you that in a few seconds. The seal keeps its secrets." Some magicians went mad trying to find ways to talk about it.

Heath stood. "Fair enough. How could a Harrower have attacked me? I was awake."

"There's no reason it can't happen," Sword said. "The Harrowers are a dark aspect of the Guides, the beings that made magic possible for the First Mages. They can do whatever the fuck they want. They just normally don't give a shit about anything unless they're possessing or interacting with somebody."

"I'm confused. Does this have anything to do with my mother?" Jessa inquired gently.

"It has to do with Esme, the current Razor of Setahari," Sword said. "After we fought at Silverbrook Manor, she must have given Heath's name to Evan Landry."

"Who's Evan Landry?" Jessa asked.

He looked at Heath and smiled. It felt strange to do that. Maddox didn't smile, like ever. "You're going to fucking love this because it's so completely absurd. Hold on to your chamber pots because you're going to lose your shit when I tell you."

"Might we hurry this along?" Jessa insisted. "The thunderheads are gathering about the city."

"The only way into or out of that cell is an elevator, which I may have irreversibly damaged. We can spare five minutes." Sword held a finger toward her then turned back to Heath. "Remember that sketchy dude from the Mage's Flask who was always hanging around me? He was my old friend from school. He goes by Riley, but his birth name is Evan Landry because, get this, he's Lord Landry's illegitimate bastard."

Heath picked up on it right away. "And he goes by Riley because he hates his birth parents enough to have them harrowed and trash their library without checking the safe."

"Since the harrowings started, he's using his power to clean out rich people's houses because he's stupid...but, like, a genius of stupidity. Stupid people have bad ideas, but his bad ideas are so terrible they're like an art form. He's a maestro of incompetence."

"My mother would say that makes him a valuable tool," Jessa offered.

"Yes!" Sword clapped his hands. "But not for your mom, and Guides forbid those two ever meet. The Razor of Setahari is manipulating him. It loves chaos and destruction in the same way a teenage girl loves unicorns."

"You shouldn't joke. Unicorns are hateful menaces of Maenmarth." Jessa shuddered.

"Find the girl, find the Thunderstone, and stop Evan Landry," Heath said. "Not a bad day's work. Jessa, are you up for this? We could really use your help."

"I am."

"I keep a wide assortment of reinforced chain mail and leather armor in that trunk over there. I never know what Sword's going to need on short notice. Take whatever you want from the armory, and we'll head out."

"I'm ready now," Jessa stated. "Stormlords don't play with steel."

"Me too," Sword said. "Wizards don't need to fuck with armor. Besides I'm immortal."

The sound of thunder shook the house. A few throwing knives clattered off the wall. The three of them shared an uneasy glance and hurried down the steps.

THE MAELSTROM (HEATH)

The path ahead of us seems uncertain because we are always looking backward as we stumble toward destiny. The road ahead is no less certain than the one behind us.
-The Harbinger, Traveler Proverbs

His new eyes stung as the rain lashed. His vision was passable, but he'd have to cut them out and heal them again properly. The memory of the nightmare faded from his thoughts, like a dream he couldn't recall. He remembered an unending hungry abyss of fear, and even the attempt at recollection made him shudder.

Jessa walked in front; she wasn't bothered by the rain at all. Sword levitated a stone bench from Heath's garden in front of them to block the worst of the rain, but the wind made the rain's direction unpredictable. The torrential downpour soaked them either way. At least it was during Whitemoon, when the rains were cool but not frigid.

He had to stay shoulder to shoulder with Sword as they walked. It brought up a host of confusing memories and feelings. He had liked Maddox's wiry body and eager disposition, but he had found himself more attached than he'd intended, and it had been difficult to see the guy destroy himself. There wasn't room for love in Heath's life.

"You want a drink?" Sword asked cheerily. It was unsettling to see him carefree and smiling, holding a half-empty bottle of wine in the middle of a crisis of apocalyptic proportions. The Harbinger had said the towers would fall. Heath wouldn't let that happen if he could, but Rivern was more than its two towers.

"You don't have to adopt all of Maddox's traits."

Sword took a swig. "I used to hate the guy. But we have a lot in common. We don't mince words, and we're hedonists, albeit for different motivations. Plus since he had his personality sucked out by Luther, I kind of feel morally obligated to keep the party going. I like to be a good guest and accommodate my hosts."

"Luther…How was he…?" Heath had convinced Luther he would be a valuable asset to the Inquisition on one of his first jobs. Daphne had imprisoned the man in a lightless dungeon and threatened his family to ensure his cooperation. She had used Heath to lie to a man who could read thoughts.

"She killed him," Sword said, offering him the bottle. "My head is chock-full of the worst kinds of magical secrets, and she couldn't risk him knowing them too."

"Damn."

Sword put his arm around Heath's shoulders and squeezed. It felt…natural.

"Sword," Heath said, "you're wasted."

"We're good together, Heath."

"No, we weren't. You would come to my home blind drunk and sobbing at obscene hours of the night. Catherine was right—"

"No, I mean you and me, the Sword, are amazing together. We've been with each other through thick and thin. Fuck, we argue like an old married couple. And this body still has feelings for you. I know it couldn't work with Maddox, but he wasn't a part of this life. I'm your fucking partner *and* the guy you used to fuck. I—"

"Jessa, are you okay?" Heath asked, clearly looking to change the subject

"Capital." Jessa glanced back. He couldn't tell, but in the flicker of lightning, she might have been smirking. She continued walking.

"I love you," Sword whispered in his ear. "I'm in love with you. Maybe I always have been…but I've never had the psyche to express that through any of my bodies. Guides…this is kind of a headfuck."

"We have a job to do," Heath stated. His body struggled with its desire. His best friend's mind now resided in his hot crazy ex. Was that a dream come true or the beginning of another nightmare?

Heath blinked against the rain again. A lone figure stood on the roof of one of the mansions, his robes billowing wildly in the wind. *Probably just an Invocari.* Although Heath's vision was blurry, he caught something in a flash of lightning that sent chills down his spine and stopped him in his tracks. He pointed at the shepherd's crook in the man's hand.

"Fuck," Sword whispered.

Jessa stopped and glanced up. "What is it?"

"The Harbinger," Heath said, "and he's looking at the towers."

"You want to talk to him?" Sword asked. "Hold on. I'll get his attention."

"Maddox, don't."

"Who is he?"

"Someone very old and very dangerous." Heath grabbed Sword's arm, but it did nothing to stop the stone bench from flying toward the Harbinger's head. It missed by a good couple of feet, but the man's head snapped in their direction. Even in the darkness of the storm, his white eyes shone like slivery lamps.

Silence fell on the empty street. Around them the rain slowed until the shimmering droplets quavered in the air, inching along slowly toward earth. The bench Sword had hurled at the man rotated in a lazy, tumbling arc over the house where the Harbinger perched.

Heath shoved Sword. "What the fuck?"

"I wasn't trying to hit him," Sword said. "He knows that."

"We meet again," the Harbinger called warmly to Heath.

He appeared in front of them, leaning on his crook. "Don't fear. I've altered the flow of time around us to give us opportunity to speak so we won't miss our respective appointments."

"Please," Jessa implored. "You're clearly powerful, and we're in need of aid. My mother plans something awful for this city and its people. They're good and innocent of any crime that would merit this retribution. Simply name what you want, and I'll grant it willingly."

He raised an eyebrow. "Would you offer your life to save these people?"

"Jessa," Heath whispered, "don't bargain with him."

She raised her chin and said, "Yes. I'm but one person, and if it's to be my life or the lives of thousands, there can be no question."

"I was merely curious whether her selflessness was sincere, priest." The Harbinger shook his head. "The power of the Stormlords is locked by the most ancient of theurgies to any who don't carry the blood. My wyrd doesn't allow me to alter the course of events in any matter."

"If you do nothing, you're complicit in my mother's evil," Jessa declared.

"It is evil only from your eyes," he replied. "The world is rife with injustice and suffering. For one creature to nourish itself, another must give its life unwillingly. For one kingdom to flourish, another must languish. For one to be elevated, others must be oppressed. The solution isn't to change nature but to find balance in the greater pattern of history."

"Bullshit," Sword said. "You can stop this. I'm a fucking Architect—I know how magic works."

"Then stop it," the Harbinger challenged.

Heath nearly lost his stomach as his vision scrambled. When he recovered himself, they stood atop a tall tower. From the shape of it and the skyline, he judged they were on top of the Lyceum's observation tower. He lurched forward and recovered his balance. Sword fell on his ass. Jessa swayed for an instant but kept her footing.

"Do you remember this place, Architect?" The Harbinger motioned to the surroundings with his crook. The rain remained slowed in freefall, but it somehow became more transparent, almost invisible. The two towers—that of the Invocari and the Assembly—spanned the waterfall of the massive Trident River tributaries.

"It rings a bell," Sword said, picking himself up off the stone. "You want to throw me off the roof? Because that doesn't work so well."

"I'm one of a handful of beings in this cosmos who can permanently kill the mortal flesh you inhabit, Valor of Crigenesta," the Harbinger mentioned casually. "That isn't my reason for bringing you here. You're here to bear witness to the fall of the towers."

Jessa protested, "This is madness. If you can bring us here, you can bring us to the Thunderstone, and you can take us to my mother. You have the power to prevent this."

"It already has happened." The Harbinger sighed. "It happened as you walked toward your destination, minutes before you discovered me. The crash of thunder and pounding of rain prevented you from hearing it. Behold."

They watched the Invocari tower as the rapids of the waterfall surged past the dams. The water didn't fall over the cliff. Instead it turned upward as if falling toward the sky. The streams of white water reached toward the stars, misty at first but liquid as they grew closer together.

"No!" Jessa exclaimed.

"This is the past," the Harbinger said. "Only an Architect, not bound by wyrd or Geas, could alter what has been written. Everyone has the potential to change the course of history; a very few are given the opportunity; and vanishingly fewer have the resolve to go through with it."

The streams of water rising from the river waved like dancers in a line making sinuous motions with their bodies. The streams braided together, becoming pulsing blobs of water congealing into thrashing tentacles several stories tall.

"Mother's summoning Kultea," Jessa whispered. "I don't understand how. She's too far inland."

Heath knew of Kultea. She was the kraken sea goddess of the Dominance. The figurehead of a religion where priests were blood mages rather than healers. The Dominance used their menacing goddess to frighten their laity into submission. Kultea didn't offer redemption for the weak, only survival through placating her. He had thought it a different but equally effective way to enforce religion—Ohan was the carrot and Kultea the stick.

Surely as if he bore the Veritas Seal himself, Heath knew everything he saw to be true. He saw it with such clarity it was beyond vision. He thought only absently of his impaired eyes as he witnessed the events unfold.

Jessa grabbed his hand and held it firmly for comfort. He found himself returning the gesture. She needed an anchor; he needed it more.

"Kultea is real," Heath whispered. In all his years of training after his mother's death, he never had entertained the notion that such beings existed outside of the institutionalized superstitions of the various faiths.

Jessa turned to him. "Of course she is. They all are."

The tentacles gracefully lashed toward the towers, wrapping themselves around the stone like pythons encircling their prey. Even though the towers were at least a mile away, he heard the crack and groan of the stone as the watery appendages squeezed against it.

Flocks of Invocari floated around the tower, waving their arms and freezing chunks of the tentacles; the ice fell away, and water rushed in to replace it faster than they could freeze it.

"You proved your point." Sword turned away and drank from his bottle. "I can't stop this."

The tentacle lashed and struck the side of the Invocari tower, breaking through the stone. Then it pulled out a black sphere that absorbed all light around it. With a flexing motion, the tentacle crushed the stone and exploded into a cloud of black-and-purple dust. In that instant hordes of wraithlike Invocari tumbled from the sky, screaming and flailing toward the earth.

The tentacles around the Assembly tower tightened, and with a twist, the structure ripped apart, chunks falling to the Overlook and the Ambassadors' District below. The crown of the tower plummeted into the Backwash. Seconds later the Invocari tower broke apart, raining its stone across the city.

In one of Kultea's tendrils, Heath saw a spark of light—a willowy figure posed majestically and suspended within the water. *Satryn.* The tentacle lowered her gently into Oiler's Park, near the Grand Menagerie.

The Harbinger said, "I can't alter the past, but I can hasten the future. I'll give you ten minutes you wouldn't have had…"

With a sickening blurriness of vision, Heath found himself on a cobblestone street. Sword fell again, and his wine bottle shattered on the ground. Jessa seemed unfazed by the transition. "We must find the Thunderstone," she said. "If my mother has the power to call Kultea this far away from the depths of the Abyss, it's our only hope of defeating her."

"You may have to be the person who does it, Jessa," Heath said.

"Nah," Sword protested. "'S'cool. I can TK that shit right into her. Hey, look— we're here!"

The DiVarian estate stood at the end of Willow's Witness Wynd. Lightning flashes all around them illuminated the decrepit estate and overgrown lawn. The DiVarians were a fallen house, their last member claimed by the harrowings. Heath had considered buying the place and renovating it, but it was a giant architectural monstrosity with sagging gables and peeling paint. Half of it was still unfinished, nearly a decade after construction had started. One half of the rusted front gate hung by a single hinge.

The trio marched up the cobblestone path toward the front door. Side by side they mounted the steps to the porch, and Sword blasted the double-door entrance, creating an explosion of splinters and sparks from the shattered warding glyphs.

"Let's destroy these assholes," he slurred, a gleam of murder in his eye.

A horde of revenants charged from the foyer, their dead fingernails reaching forward hungrily as they rasped in unison. Sword waved his arms, and the parquet floorboards erupted with the force of explosive traps. Jessa blasted them with lightning, laying down an easy staccato of suppressive fire. Her powers were instinctive, and she seemed surprised at her own capabilities.

Heath tossed off his water-soaked priestly robes as his companions made short work of the small army. He cleaned his fingernails as Sword brought a gaudy gold fainting couch low under the revenants, scooping them up and spinning them off in all directions.

"Wheee!" Sword exclaimed.

Jessa flung electricity at the revenants. "This is oddly gratifying."

"Just let me know if either of you needs healing." Heath smirked despite himself. They might have failed to anticipate the extent of Satryn's power, but on the field, they made a fucking good team.

They strode through the destroyed double doors. Jessa paused over a dead body. "The embroidery on this one's clothing…She was from Amhaven. They used my people to create this macabre army." Her face went pale with rage.

"Maddox?"

Heath saw Riley storm out of a pair of double doors at the end of the hallway. Riley wore a white fur coat with no shirt underneath. He carried a walking stick adorned with the Landry eagle.

Esme walked by his side, nonchalantly twirling her knife and a blue chunk of pointy rock in her hands. Behind him stood a big man, a black wolf, and an ancient lady with a confused expression. Heath counted his blessings that the walking stick wasn't another of Sword's siblings. The eagle was clearly modern in design.

Esme sneered, "I thought you were in prison, Maddox."

Riley looked at her in surprise. "You said he were vacationing in Barstea."

"Your evil girlfriend lied to you, Riley," Sword said, whipping out his blade. "I can cut my way out of anything. Except kitchen duty. I tried to mince carrots for a stew once and ended up turning the butcher's block into kindling. But that's why they make smaller blades."

Esme narrowed her eyes. "You should measure a blade in blood, not inches."

Heath stepped forward. "I know we have our differences. You killed my guy. I killed one of your guys. You tried to kill me. We can settle that later. The city is falling around us. The queen regent of Amhaven, Satryn Shyford, has destroyed the Dark Star and manifested an avatar of Kultea in the Trident waterfall. There's no money in any of this if the Dominance claims Rivern. Give us the Thunderstone, and we'll fix this mess. We can settle our grievances later."

"They've used the bodies of my subjects for their foul necromancy," Jessa protested. "These crimes must be answered."

"Well"—Riley looked a little embarrassed—"we had this deal with the shelters. You see, we'd trade the silver we lifted from houses to the refugees in exchange for their dead. They was just droppin' 'em in the river, love. Figured we could do a little quid pro quo exchange of goods for charity. You need to think small to think big. That's right, innit?"

"Not all these deaths were natural," Heath accused, indicating a slain revenant behind him. "Some of their eyes are burned out."

"Well...I didn't have complete control over it," Riley admitted sheepishly.

"An ancient monument known for brokering dark bargains gives you a power you can't control? That's a shocking revelation," Sword muttered.

"But still kind of unexpected, right?" Esme retorted.

"This plan has your fingerprints all over it." Sword glared at Esme. "It was your idea to bust old lady Pytheria here out of the asylum and convince Riley to make a pact with the dark powers in the dolmen. Then you used the harrowings to destabilize the government and frighten people while convincing Riley it was for…?"

"For the school." Riley's eyes lit up. "There's going to be a new college, better than the one we got now, and right here where we're standing is going to be a giant statue of you, Maddox—Architect of the Grand Design. They've got you with a beard and staff, and your cloak is billowing behind you dramatically. This is all for that, mate." His hands motioned wildly as he described the scene.

"I used to teach at the school," Pytheria said wistfully. "I miss my old office."

"I'll prove it to you!" Riley's eyes went wide with excitement as he threw off his fur coat and spun around. Over his back was a large intricate seal. There were rings within rings, like nested sundials. He craned his head so he could talk to them over his shoulder. "I did it, Maddox. I attained the Seal of the Grand Design."

"Guides preserve us," Sword gasped.

THE GRAND DESIGN (SWORD)

True art is not the mindless puppet of its creator, no more than a child is the exten-
sion of her family's aspirations. God may have forged us for His own reasons, but
our true purpose is ours alone to choose.
-The Artifex, Traveler's Proverbs

Sword remembered everything in his hosts' memories as they remembered the events. Most people only recall 2 percent of the events in their lives and use their imagination to fill in the blanks. Sword looked at the unedited version. Some people were dutiful and objective when narrating the course of their lives. Maddox was what you might call an "unreliable narrator."

How much of what he saw in his visions was real or fabricated was impossible to determine. Sword cross-referenced every memory he could locate for any information about the Grand Design. Maddox believed it was real, but there was little to no evidence from the ancient scholars that such a thing really existed.

"What the hells is that?" Heath asked, pointing to Riley's seal.

"It lets him see the future." Sword blinked out of his recollection. "Which obviously doesn't work…because he'd have known you were my friend. He'd have known we were coming, and he'd certainly know Esme is being controlled by the malignant intelligence in that dagger."

"She's not so bad once you get to understand her, mate. She's a misfit, like us." Riley pleaded.

She elbowed him playfully.

Sword whispered, "If that seal is bound correctly, nothing can change the future he sees. He can see every move and countermove before it happens."

"Not like that, mate. I can only see one day five hundred years in the future. The world's an unrecognizable place, but you're still in it, and by proxy so am I, even if only because my school helped you make the greatest discovery in glyphology to ever happen."

"How long ago did you have this vision?" Jessa asked pointedly.

"A few weeks." His shoulders slumped a little, and he turned back to face them.

"And when was the last time you…purchased a body from the refugee wharfs? Was it more recent than that?"

"Um…I…yeah."

Jessa stepped forward. "Then if this seal reveals what will happen, will not those events come to pass regardless of which actions you take? So you didn't need to claim bodies. You could have offered your ill-gotten spoils to the refugees and allowed their bodies to be cremated or properly buried."

Riley looked at Esme. "I dunno…that sounds kind of right, don't it?"

"Destiny assumes people work toward it," Esme stated.

"If the seal works as intended," Sword said slowly, using small words, "the thing it showed will happen because it's inevitable. If the seal was incorrectly transcribed, then whatever it shows you may or may not happen, but you'll be dead by then, Riley. So it doesn't really matter."

Riley frowned. "I were never as smart as you was, Maddox. You was something special and everyone knew you'd be great. I were a fucking bastard put through school by a guilty arsehole of a father I only ever met once. I were never gonna amount to nothing more than a wharf rat nohow. What did I have to lose by saying some words at a big pile of rocks in the forest, yeah?"

"You killed a lot of people." Sword added for emphasis, "For very meager gains. Did you kill Tertius too?"

"Fuck him," Riley spat, "He tried to kill you, he did. If anyone ever tried to hurt you I'd do the same. Just like I did your dad. Maddox, I'd—"

Esme stabbed her dagger into Riley's throat.

Riley clutched at his neck as he fell to his knees. His pained expression stared into Sword's eyes. Blood spurted all over Esme's face as she watched him fall. For good measure she punctured his kidney and threw him to the floor. Otix, Pytheria, and Themis backed away nervously. The Patrean Crateus pulled a vial of some substance out of his bandolier.

"What?" Esme laughed. "This was getting way too sentimental."

Heath's square jaw dropped.

Jessa blinked but recovered herself more quickly. She lashed a bolt of lightning toward Esme, who flickered out of sight. Her attack was straightforward, and she telegraphed her moves with her body language. The Razor had adjusted to Jessa's speed.

Jessa screamed surprise and grabbed her arm. Blood flowed between her fingers. Esme stood next to her, holding the Thunderstone. Its edge was drenched in the crimson of Jessa's blood. Esme tossed the stone on the floor. "I don't need it anymore anyway."

Jessa's spine stiffened, and she punched Esme in the face. She stumbled backward, and Jessa fired a torrent of electricity that knocked the girl backward against the wall.

"I was going to do that," Sword protested. "I had the whole fight planned out. We were going to trade blows. I was going to let her cut me—you know, for dramatic effect. Then, when it looked like she was going to beat me again, I was going to rally my telekinetic powers in an unexpected way. You know, make it a fair fight, but then let her stab me again. And then I was going to unleash my *coup de grace* by breaking her neck."

Jessa lowered her hands, shutting off the stream of electricity. Esme's charred corpse fell to the floor, still clutching her pristine silver dagger. She glanced back at Sword. "My apologies. Were you saying something?"

Heath ran to her side. "Your arm. Let me see it."

"It's just a scratch," Jessa fumed. "*Literally* a scratch. The Thunderstone is a fake, probably glamoured sodalite."

Sword looked at the rock on the floor. It had broken into several pieces. "Well, shit."

Pytheria knelt over Riley's body. "Evan, you need to wake up. It's a beautiful day, and I won't have you spending all day in bed." Her bony hands pressed against his chest. Sword would have wanted to chop off her head, but the Maddox part of him was fascinated. If a senile old woman could still perform necromancy, how hard could it be?

"Please tell me you know where the real Thunderstone is," Heath said to Jessa. "If not, we've wasted our time here."

Jessa sighed. "My aunt Sireen obviously gave me a fake Thunderstone. She evidently has a peculiar sense of humor, but attempting to understand the rationale for her subterfuge will only squander more of our precious time."

"We need to flee this city before Satryn destroys it completely," Sword told Heath.

"You can't give up so easily," Jessa said. "I've seen both of you smile in the face of death. There must be another way to defeat her. Her life should be forfeit for her actions."

Heath placed his hands on her shoulders. "Jessa, I'm the best assassin in the Free Cities, but I can't kill someone who can't be stabbed. And I can't heal someone to death."

Sword retrieved the chintzy Razor of Setahari from the floor and levitated it in midair. Its sharp edges gleamed. "We need to find somewhere to put this. And find my notebooks. If Satryn doesn't smash this dilapidated eyesore, and someone else finds it, that would make this disaster look small."

Crateus stepped forward, head bowed toward Maddox. "You want me to fetch them? I mean, with Riley dead, you're the dean. It's in the bylaws."

As if on cue, Riley's still-warm corpse gurgled a raspy sound of assent through his destroyed throat as Pytheria's magic reanimated him.

"Don't look at me. I was better at teaching." The disgraced necromancer who had tarnished the Lyceum's reputation for half a century shrugged.

"Of course," Sword said to himself, "Riley saw it in his vision. There's going to be a statue of me right here. Founder of a fucking school for magical rejects. This was my true destiny the whole time. Some mages get Archea—I get this. Yes, Initiate Crateus, fetch my notebooks."

The Fodder trotted off, his bandolier of potions clinking. The black wolf and Otix retreated with him.

"I fail to see how mere notebooks could be more important," Jessa said. "This very moment my mother rips this city apart."

"Your mother was right—you *are* strident sometimes." Sword didn't mean to say that out loud, but he was kind of an ass. He winced uncomfortably. "Sorry. It sounded funnier in my head."

If her eyes could shoot daggers they would have; he saw a visible effort to restrain herself from shooting lightning. "My apologies. You saved my life, and I ask more than is my right," Jessa said. "You should go while you can. Nasara's army will sweep in from the east, and Mother will hand the city to the Red Army. I can't protect you from her."

"We can't leave," Heath muttered. "I swore I would stop this."

"We did!" Sword exclaimed. "The harrowings are done. It was my fucked-up sibling and stupid Riley who were the cause. They had *nothing* to do with the towers or the Harbinger's antivision of the future. Even Riley didn't see this coming."

Heath protested, "We save our fucking city. I'm dying anyway, and I don't want to spend my remaining years being a coward."

Sword grabbed his shoulders. "I'm immortal. Let me do this."

Jessa shook her head. "We do this together."

"Fine." Sword sighed. "Gran?"

"Yes, Charlie?" she said brightly.

"I need to borrow your undead army."

MOTHER KNOWS NOTHING (JESSA)

The world was crumbling around her, and despite the horror that her mother had unleashed, the chaos and uncertainty excited her. Politics were unpredictable, full of compromise and inaction. How grand it felt to swagger in and smite according to what her heart knew to be justice. It wasn't negotiation or trade agreements—it was thunder that flowed through her veins.

More than anything she felt elation that Sword was going to join the fight. "Again I can't thank you enough for all you've done."

Sword blushed a bit. "I mean, what's the worst she can do to me? She killed me once already. And then you had to go upstage my epic fight with Esme. I have a visceral need to show off."

Jessa went to throw her arms around him then froze when she saw the Razor of Setahari floating over Sword's hand. It was intricate, almost too thin to be any good in a fight, but she knew better. "We must get rid of that before we face my mother."

"Agreed," Heath said. "If there's even a chance the Razor can get control of Satryn…"

"I'm not leaving it with Gran," Sword stated. "Besides, Satryn wouldn't pick up a dagger and I'm the only person who can carry the thing without getting my brain hijacked. Again, that is."

"I'm coming with you two," said Heath.

"It's too dangerous," Jessa urged. "You're generous to offer, but my conscience couldn't bear to see you slain after what you've done to protect me. Mother won't kill me while I bear the heir to her bloodline, and Sword is doubly immortal."

"You're squishy, Heath," Sword said. "You've used up most of your Light, and you can't talk your way out of a fight with Satryn. You're smooth, but I think the Queen of Lies could take notes from her."

"I said I'm coming with you two," Heath reiterated. His words possessed an authority that left them silent.

The Patrean boy returned alone, carrying a stack of black moleskin notebooks with a blue sharkskin notebook on top. "Here's the notebooks and the copies, Dean Maddox, as requested, sir. The blue one's Riley's visions after he attained your seal."

Jessa snatched it off the pile and flipped it open, moving before anyone could stop her. She told herself it might contain valuable information, but secretly she was intensely curious what a true account of the future might look like.

She flipped through pages, astounded by the colorful artistry. In a public square, people in strange clothes (including women in trousers) chased after pigeons, the birds transforming into wineglasses in their hands. The next illustration showed a woman laughing as she held a strange sculpture against her ear and mouth.

The book slammed shut and flew from her hand, back to the pile.

Sword looked at her gravely. "You don't want to know. Knowledge of what will happen can ruin your life. Imagine knowing a future you can't change and how that would make you feel, being helpless to stop it."

Jessa nodded. It wasn't a pleasant idea either way; she didn't like the idea that the future was already set in stone.

"If we could have truly seen the future for what it was, we could have stopped this months ago," Heath argued.

"You say that like it's so easy," Sword countered. "If you could see the future, you'd see beyond this disaster to all possible disasters. You may realize that by averting one catastrophe you'll cause another and another and another. I don't know what's worse to believe—that life is random and meaningless or that it was deliberately designed to be shitty."

Jessa grabbed Riley's notebook off the pile. "If this is a true account of things to come, it might be our only weapon against my mother. Riley said the banners of the city will fly blue. The imperial colors are red. If we can convince my mother of the book's veracity, we can undermine her resolve."

"That's five hundred years in the future," Heath said. "Even if it's true, why would she give a shit?"

"Five hundred years is nothing to an imperial dynasty. Mother's plan was in the works for generations," Jessa said. "Iridissa bedded her own brother in secret while Thoras still sat on the Coral Throne. He wasn't a stupid man; blood mages would have been consulted. They knew my mother and uncle were pureblood. They wanted a tempest of vast power who was expendable enough to send into the heart of enemy territory."

"The Tempest's power would have been frightening even in the old Sarn empire," Sword said. "There's not much modern magic outside Archea that could stand against it."

"Sireen still has the Thunderstone," Jessa realized suddenly. "Nasara never would let my mother cling to power. They intend to kill her once Rivern falls. My role was to be a decoy assassin. The real one remains."

"Your family is fucked up," Sword said.

"You're certain Sireen is still in Rivern?" Heath asked.

"If she is, I know where she'd be." Jessa rubbed her temples. "I can feel the drumming of electricity; it's faint but present. It's how she's been communicating with Mother—through quiet rumblings in the clouds."

They left the manor in a hurry. Crateus and Pytheria headed out with the remaining revenants and made for Oiler's Park, where they could regroup. Jessa, Sword, and Heath headed toward Cameron's house.

The streets were empty, and water roiled in the canals. The squall lashed at them from all sides as the winds whipped through the buildings.

Sword turned to the house and ripped off balconies, siding, and shutters. The mass of splintered timber hurtled toward them, and Jessa reflexively flinched. At the last second the boards froze in midair and arranged themselves into an orderly makeshift semisphere.

Jessa looked at the cloud of floating barriers that shielded them from the worst of the storm as they orbited around the three of them. Doors, shutters, and planks of wood whirled through the air, fending off rain and, in one case, lightning. It was like walking in the eye of a tornado of detritus.

Sword glibly explained, "Part of the magic of the Sword is spatial awareness—gauging velocity and predicting the movements and positions of my opponents. Visualizing the field of battle in three dimensions and placing yourself accordingly is the key to victory. It's the same thing with telekinesis; adding my considerable power, there's probably all kinds of new applications. I could write a paper on it."

Jessa looked at Heath. "He seems…"

"Full of himself?" Heath finished for her. "He could get that from either personality."

"You know what power I *really* wish I had?" Sword said. "That teleportation thing Esme pulled. The Asherai monks train for thirteen years to learn those techniques."

"So how did she do it?" Heath asked.

Sword shrugged. "Probably knew it from a previous host. And don't ask me how she got an Asherai monk to pick up a dagger, because they don't need weapons. They have these tattoos that—"

Heath stopped in his tracks. "You can use magic from *other* bodies?"

"If they have the capability," Sword admitted, "but I'm a fucking sword. Magic ruins everything fun and honest. It's comes down to who can bend the rules the best. Then you have stupid shit where everybody is learning the bubble spell. There's no honor in it."

"The bubble spell?" Heath asked.

Sword shook his head. "I've said too much. Some lost secrets need to stay buried."

"So how would the ancient wizards have dealt with a Tempest?" Jessa asked.

Sword said, "Probability manipulation, ripple effects, precognition, synchronicity. It's just events coming together so that shit like this never happens. Rothburn coincidentally chokes on a chicken bone, and you're married to some bucktoothed Amhaven noble while your mother drinks herself to death in Weatherly Castle. Works amazingly well when you're the only one doing it."

Jessa stammered, "Then why...the...fuck...are we going after a rock when you wield the magic of the ancients?"

"Because this mind is shattered, and I need at least some of it working to maintain my own thought process. The strain would rip my brain into confetti— possibly literally, with the streamers bursting out the top of my skull." Sword wiggled his fingers in imitation of his description.

"But could you do it?" Heath asked.

"Would you ask me to?" Sword searched his eyes.

"No," Jessa said firmly. "One borrowed life is still a life. I can't consent to that kind of sacrifice. Kultea may be set against us, but we must remain faithful that Ohan watches over us. Our paths didn't cross by coincidence."

"They kind of did, though..." Heath said.

"Yet each of us has something the others lack," Jessa smiled. "Sword and Maddox needed each other to become whole. Heath, you want to become a better person. And I need to swallow my pride and become a worse person if I'm to face my mother. The four of us have struggled alone with our demons, and when we're united, there's nothing that can't be done. This is fate."

"Fate isn't always a good thing," Sword said.

⇥ ⇤

"This is Cameron's house," Jessa said, staring at the door.

"He lives modestly," Heath commented as his eyes scanned the house.

"I should go in first," Jessa suggested.

The door to the house popped open slightly. She heard the snap of a mechanism, possibly a deadbolt, as Sword ripped it out of the frame.

The inside of the house was warm. Jessa heard the crackle of fire and the soft notes of a violin as it played a subdued refrain. Many voices were coming from the living area, which had been set up like a war room.

"Full recognition of our hereditary titles would go a long way toward securing support for the nobility here and in the other Free Cities." Jessa recognized the woman as Dame Woodhouse, an elegant but snobbish woman who wore too much jewelry.

Her aunt Sireen sat in a high regal chair, her legs curled beneath her. Cameron stood to her right, dressed in the finery of a Thrycean admiral. Across from them she recognized Dean Archibald Turnbull and a red-haired man with a large mustache, whom she'd never seen before. His face looked bloodied. An older Patrean stood off to the side; his insignia designated him as a warmaster. A violinist played in the corner.

Cameron was the first to notice them. "Jessa! I went by the estate earlier. By Ohan, I was so worried about you…"

The violinist stopped playing and set her instrument to her side.

"Your concern is noted," Jessa snapped. "I just stopped by to let you know I have everything well in hand. I have the Thunderstone, and I'm going to use it on Mother. Do either of you have any advice or opinion on the matter before I go off to do this very dangerous task you've assigned me?"

Sireen smiled softly. "You don't have to go through with it. Stay here where it's safe. You can help with the arrangements for the surrender and reconstruction of the city. We have representatives from every institution present, save the Orthodoxy. We want to make the transition fair."

Jessa feigned consideration. "No, I prefer to kill Mother and let the people of this city decide how they wish to be governed."

She marched over to the table and looked at the parchments. She slammed her dripping-wet hands on a battle map, smudging some of the ink. She turned to Turnbull. "You were a party to this?"

The bald man winced. "Not a willing participant, Your Majesty. Loran and I were brought here to discuss terms for a surrender. With the Invocari stripped of their power, there's no hope for the city to stand against a Tempest. It seems we'll be joining the Dominance."

"Sireen has offered very generous terms of surrender," Cameron interjected. "The Lyceum will grow in its scope of studies and faculty."

Turnbull couldn't look Jessa in the eye. She wanted to comfort him somehow.

"Jessa," Cameron urged, "perhaps we should discuss this in private."

"No," she insisted. "In fact I prefer Dean Turnbull remain present. He possesses a Veritas Seal, so he'll be able to tell me whether what you're saying is true. Sireen may be too good of a liar, but Dean Turnbull can certainly vouch for your words."

Sireen waved her hand. "Cameron doesn't know the Thunderstone is a forgery, Jessa. Only I and one other person know of the true stone's location."

"Where is it?" Heath and Jessa said at the same time.

"Thelassus," Sireen answered. "In the Sunken Palace."

Jessa felt sick to her stomach. "You're lying."

"You couldn't go through with killing Satryn," Sireen explained. "Even if you were a match for my sister in battle, you don't have the heart for it. Satryn expects a betrayal, so I gave her one. Her true comeuppance is in motion, as I promised you, but it comes from an angle she doesn't expect."

Sword looked across the table and pointed at some wine flutes. "Is that bubbly? I need a drink."

Turnbull made a disgusted sound as Sword picked up the untouched glass from in front of him.

Jessa fumed. "You risk my life with your schemes, Aunt, and the life of my unborn son. You vastly underestimate what I'm willing to do to protect those dear to me."

"I know my sister's truest heart, and Satryn never would kill you," Sireen said. "In fact she would respect you for making the attempt on her life."

Heath addressed Turnbull. "So there's no Thunderstone here."

"Sadly, no." He shrugged. "At least everyone's being honest."

"We could still try without the rock," Sword suggested. "I mean, I've killed gods before. She can't be worse than Vilos. Hells, all we have to do is get her drunk."

Turnbull looked at him in shock.

"We should hear your aunt out," Heath said gravely. "She's doling out favors. I can represent the Orthodoxy as acting head of the Inquisition. What do you have for us?"

Loran sighed mournfully. "Heath…this is your city."

Jessa opened her mouth to protest but held her tongue. Heath was playing a game, and it was one she badly needed to learn. She would follow his lead, perhaps make it seem like she could be convinced in order to get more information. She wrung her hands at the thought of the drowning and destruction her mother was wreaking on Rivern's inhabitants.

"His name is Heath Gisasos, no connection to the Bamoran house. He's their best assassin," Cameron whispered to Sireen.

"Thanks." Heath smiled. "I voted for you in the last election. About a hundred and fifty times."

"Fair elections indeed. Utter nonsense," Dame Woodhouse scoffed.

"What do you want?" Sireen bubbled. "I've promised to restore the nobility to power for Dame Woodhouse, and she gladly accepted. To the Lyceum I've offered a new charter that will restore necromantic education and provide revenue through imperial scholarships. To the Invocari I've offered aid in reassembling the Dark Star and increasing their recruitment pipelines. And to Warmaster Jasyn, I've agreed to a wage increase for the troops and a tripling of new contracts over the next six months."

"What of the Assembly?" Jessa asked. "They represent the people. What do you offer them?"

"Darling," Dame Woodhouse cooed, "I speak for my assemblyman husband when I say the Assembly is two-thirds born of noble rank. We'll govern this city as fairly and ably as we always have."

Cameron glowered but said nothing.

"If you wish to return to the old ways, you'll address me as 'Your Majesty.'" Jessa quipped. "You'll be vassals to the Coral Throne, and you'll never rise above your meager stations. There are much bigger fish than sharks that swim the waters of the Sunken Palace. It's something to which you should give great consideration."

"Sorry, Your Majesty." Dame Woodhouse nearly choked on her words. Her face was bright red.

Sireen cleared her throat. "Let's not quibble. These are hard times, and all of us are unable to alter the events that have been set in motion. Still, transitions represent opportunity. The Dominance needs visionaries and new ideas. I'm very interested to hear how the Orthodoxy sees itself in this new age."

"Quick interjection," Sword said. "I have my own college of magic, recently acquired. It's more of an unstructured curriculum catering to magically gifted students with special needs. I'd like your blood oath that the derelict DiVarian estate will be the site of the new college and a statue of me will be erected in the center."

"Something needs to be done with the place. It's an eyesore," Dame Woodhouse said under her breath. Jessa was really starting to hate her.

"Why not?" Sireen said. "It sounds wonderful."

"You? A dean?" Turnbull looked appalled.

"I learned the Grand Design from Achelon himself, and I'm probably the most powerful mage in all Creation." Sword winked. "But I do respect your accomplishments. Was there any hint of deception when Sireen agreed to my request?"

Turnbull regarded him warily. "I haven't heard *anything* that has rung untrue…even when it should."

"Good enough," Sword chirped. "Is there any more of this bubbly stuff? It's really good."

Heath grabbed Jessa and took her aside, pressing his lips against her ear. "I need to know how you want to play this."

"I thought you had a plan," Jessa whispered back.

"I thought the Thunderstone was here. Can you defeat your mother with Sireen's help?"

"Satryn will always be stronger than anyone beneath her."

"If your mother dies, do you become empress?"

"I…don't know. Nasara should be Tempest, but Satryn is pureblood, which disturbs the rules of primogeniture. It will be one of us."

"You need to figure that out. Every move she makes hinges on that. All of this is just a distraction."

Jessa nodded. She had been raised in the shadow of the Coral Throne. Her mother constantly threatened that she may one day sit atop it. And now those empty-sounding words were coming to fruition.

She turned to Sireen. "Will the Orthodoxy have a place here, or will Rivern bow to Kultea?"

Sireen sighed, as if the question offended her. "The law can't dictate the heart. People can worship whichever god they like. You know that I allow heretic cults of Kondole to more or less practice openly in Mazitar. That faith is as much a part of our history as Kultea is."

No one from the Protectorate blinked, but it was a bold statement that could have meant death if uttered in the wrong company.

Jessa peered at her skeptically. "Kultea's tendrils lash this city. Are you certain you wish to utter the name of the Father Whale?"

"There's so much for you to learn. Come with me to Mazitar," Sireen pleaded. "Let your son be born amid beauty, where it is always summer. You can be far from the intrigues of court, protected from your mother until the time is right to deal with her."

"And what happens then?" Jessa asked. "Who sits on the Coral Throne after her, after you've had months to seduce me with your flowery words and promises of religious enlightenment?"

"I'm not your enemy, Jessa," Sireen insisted. "Cameron and I are your family. We want you to be happy and protected. I can teach you how to navigate the intrigues of court without losing your compassion. And, if and when the time comes, make you a great empress."

Sword sighed. "I guess I'll have to find more bubbly myself. Call for me if anything interesting happens."

"There should be some in the pantry," Dame Woodhouse whispered. "Fetch some for me as well."

"Ten million ducats," Heath stated. All eyes except Sword's fixed on him.

Sireen placed her hand against her chest. "That's quite a request, Abbot. I'd need time to consider granting such a large endowment."

"I wasn't asking you," Heath stated. "I was naming my price to Jessa. Ten million ducats, and we kill your mother tonight."

"It's too soon," Sireen cautioned as she stood.

"You have no authority over my decisions," Jessa said. "My mother's concentrated blood makes us of the same generation, and her status as Tempest makes me tied in the line of succession with Nasara. Either way you and your supporters draw breath at my mercy."

"Jessa…" Cameron said. "I swore my life to you."

"Fuck you," Jessa spat. "How many sides of this intrigue are you playing? Does Nasara also consider you a confidant? Tell me once and honestly if you ever loved me."

Turnbull giggled. "Now it's getting good."

"She's got you by the balls," Sword called from the kitchen. The sound of a popped cork shortly followed.

Cameron glanced furtively back and forth. "I enjoyed our time together…"

"You enjoyed fucking me!" Jessa shouted. The room rattled with the vibration of thunder.

He stiffened and met her gaze. "I care for you and our son, but I never loved you as anything more than a friend, Jessa. I did my duty as a faithful servant of the Coral Throne. I'll do anything you ask of me, but my heart belongs to another."

"Who?" Turnbull asked.

Jessa sighed. "It doesn't matter. I'm satisfied, and we have more pressing business. Heath, I accept your proposal. Kill my mother, and ten million ducats will be yours, along with the title of Imperial Viceroy over lands and nations to be determined."

Sword came out of the kitchen, bottle in hand. "I'm going to be doing most of the work here…"

"Ten million apiece," Jessa said. "The same offer stands for any who would join me." She turned and addressed Turnbull and Loran. "You're both released from these negotiations. You'll be given everything that has been promised should events favor us, in addition to any restitutions for damages incurred by the Thrycean Dominance. You're under no obligation to accept what Sireen has offered."

Loran nodded. "I wouldn't accept her terms in any instance, but I'll remember this."

Sireen grinned. "I misjudged you, Jessa, and I rarely do that. Your mother misjudges you more. Use that. I'll see the members of this council to safety and await you at the Red Army encampment."

"See that they are safe," Jessa said. "But I'm warning you: I'm not some porcelain doll for you to put on the throne and use to further your own agenda. Although Satryn failed me in so many ways, she schooled me well in intrigue—better than she suspects. Don't make me use those skills, and we'll know only love between us."

Sireen placed her hand on her heart. "You're free to deny my guidance, but I expect great things from you, niece."

Dame Woodhouse interjected, "The aristocracy would feel much more comfortable with Her Majesty than Satryn. Princess Jessa has made an earnest effort to understand our city and represents a softer image of the Dominance." She turned to Sword. "Could you pour me some wine, Viceroy?"

Sword waved his hand, and a tendril of bubbly snaked out of the bottle and congealed into a floating sphere. It formed a somewhat small avian shape, and its wings began to flutter like a hummingbird while the body remained still, with effervescent bubbles floating through it. It dive-bombed into Dame Woodhouse's glass, filling it perfectly to the bell.

"Amazing! How in the hells did you accomplish that?" Turnbull exclaimed.

"It's easy when your second brain can do persistent calculations of fluid dynamics," Sword explained. "I'm just that fucking amazing."

Turnbull shook his head. "Who *are* you?"

"I'm still working on that," Sword said, then paused. Finally he said, "Turnbull, as much as it pains me to put these words together in a sentence, we could use your help."

"Given your skill, I would be a liability," he admitted, then turned to the princess. "Jessa, I wish you every success. Torin would have been lucky to marry you. May I ask whether your child is his?"

"I wish he had been," Jessa said, ignoring Cameron's tortured gaze. "I knew very little of Torin, but he was kind and honest. It's a legacy that deserves to be remembered."

"That means more to me than you know."

"Okay, sore subject," Sword grunted. "Can we go now? I'm bored."

"You need a plan," Loran said gruffly. The Grand Invocus was beaten and powerless, but there was a glimmer of hope in his eyes.

Sword chugged some bubbly and slammed the bottle down. "Yeah, I got a plan."

UPRISING (SATRYN)

If there is a god looking down on us, he might see the world as we see the stars in the sky. Unchanging lights flickering in a tranquil void. What we see as global chaos is just a twinkle from the heavens.
-The Stargazer, Traveler Proverbs

Satryn had spent so many months in captivity that it made her giddy to be beneath the open sky. The cold rain pounding her naked skin felt like a re-union with nature. Night had fallen, but the darkening clouds blotted out the stars. The presence of her goddess flowed through her as she stood in the center of Oiler's Park. All around her lightning fell, hammering her foes as they strug-gled to launch assaults from behind crudely assembled barricades.

Kultea's tentacles swam through the water and brought the fury of elemental might to buildings and houses. She was in ten places at once, her body one with the water that was once Rivern's lifeblood. Now it was hers to command, and she was aware of the entire city. As troops scrambled, she shattered causeways. As the mages left the Lyceum, she swatted them into paste with tendrils of water.

She lashed and destroyed gleefully. For a city so proud of its engineers, how easily their silly contraptions shattered. Without the Invocari to freeze the water, Rivern was revealed for what it was—a glorified collection of mud hovels for Genatrovan peasants thinking themselves the equals of the gods.

The power intoxicated her. Satryn's own mother, who hadn't left the Sunken Palace in decades, never really saw what her Heritage was capable of. Had a Tempest been willing to leave the safety of Thelassus, he or she would be unbeat-able. Satryn wasn't just empress; she was a warrior.

Rivern had defied the Dominance for half a millennium because the Thrycean tyrants were weak and paranoid. Had any of them possessed the stones to truly wield their power, the empire would cover Genatrova. Rivern would be an example to all.

Satryn smiled as she felt a familiar presence approach from one of the canals. With a mere thought, she lessened the torrential downpour around her to a pounding rain. She gazed across the flooded park to see Jessa marching toward her with the priest and Maddox in tow.

She awaited them eagerly. The priest was no threat and Maddox was harmless. Her daughter, however, was inches from the Coral Trone. There was a Stormord proverb that every step toward power were ten steps from trust.

"Mother," Jessa said, "had I known your plans, I could have prevented this vulgar display of power. I had everything well in hand."

Satryn laughed. "You had nothing in hand, darling. You were flotsam in the shifting tide of the Assembly's whims."

"Yet I managed to get them out of the city." Jessa raised her voice over the rain. There was a hardness to her gaze. "Oh, come on, Mother. Who do you think framed you for the murder of Torin Silverbrook? You were supposed to remain in prison, but as usual you've disrupted my plans."

Satryn sneered, "You're pretending, Jessa."

"No." Jessa raised her chin defiantly. "*You* are pretending. I wanted you out of the way because you lack subtlety. While you were hatching your plan for brute force within the confines of your luxuriously appointed prison, I was going about the work of actually destroying the Assembly's authority."

Satryn rolled her eyes. "Jessa, I'm not for one second buying this charade."

"Then it is the will of Kultea that the harrowings happened when we came to this city?" Jessa challenged. "Why don't you ask her yourself?"

Satryn paused. It was an audacious lie, but she had no ready answer. The harrowings were random. Yet they had weakened the city, and Jessa had not accused her of them. Kultea's presence didn't respond to the question.

"It was me," Jessa stated. "I recruited a warlock to spread panic and disorder with his ability to create Nightmares. I started with the Landry house—Rothburn's principal allies in the Assembly—but I quickly discovered the nobles could be frightened, leaving their estates unguarded for me to steal their secrets and make it look like burglary."

"You would never kill for political advantage," Satryn chided. "You were always too much like your father."

Jessa stifled a laugh. "I killed Father."

Satryn's silver eyes went wide. "What did you say?"

"I killed King Josur Shyford," Jessa said, glowering. "I crept into his room in the dark of night, where he lay wasting from his illness. He was pathetic, as if someone had crumpled his portrait and tossed it onto his sickbed. It was a mercy to take his red velvet pillow and place it over his face. If he were a Stormlord, he would have been granted a dignified reprieve. Since you couldn't bring yourself to do it, I had to."

"You're lying," Satryn challenged.

"Not about Father." Jessa smirked. "Do you really think I'm so naïve and innocent? You killed that little girl a long time ago with your vitriol, and ever since I've been learning everything you can teach me."

"Oh, really?"

"The more I defied you, the more you taught me," Jessa stated. "Had I been your ally, you would have spared me the hardest lessons: 'You can have no one close to you. You can trust nothing anyone says. The only way to be free is to have power over those around you.' I drank in every word, Mother."

"You're better at deception than I thought," Satryn admitted. "Still this nonsense isn't fooling me. Nor are you distracting me from neutralizing the threats that crawl from the crevices of this city to challenge me."

"You mean those drowned bodies you've swallowed in the canal?" Jessa challenged. She raised her hand and tossed three thunderbolts to the sky.

Satryn laughed with elation as waterlogged corpses crawled from the canals. "Revenants? Jessa, that's amazing!"

"I wanted to rule Rivern through the Assembly," Jessa sneered. "With the nobility fleeing to their country estates, we could have called another election, one that favored Cameron and his coalition. The city could have fallen to the Dominance without so much as a whisper. Instead you ravage it with your weather mischief."

"You should have told me." Satryn wiped a tear from her eye. She walked toward her and embraced her daughter tightly.

Jessa stiffened.

She whispered in Jessa's ear, "Nice try, you ungrateful cunt. You will not usurp me."

Satryn grabbed her daughter's hair, snapping her head back. She kneed Jessa in the stomach then tossed her body aside as she spun to kick her in the face. Jessa fell to the ground.

"I don't care about my legacy," Satryn declared. "The empire can fold...as long it stands while I live."

The priest looked at Maddox. "Do it."

Satryn hurled a bolt of lightning into the mage's chest. She'd find out what this was all about tomorrow, but the idea of his disloyalty displeased her. His body tumbled backward from the force of her blast.

Satryn smiled. "Now what was it you wanted him to do?"

INSURGENCY (HEATH)

The source of all needless suffering... is time. Childhood haunts us and death threatens us. The only refuge is in the present, the last place anyone thinks to look.
-The Libertine, Traveler Proverbs

Heath let his springblades free as he tumbled to the side. A lightning bolt struck the ground inches from where he was standing. The thunder was deafening, and the force of the sound threw him back. He landed hard on his shoulder and rolled as quickly as he could beneath a park bench as another bolt slammed into the ground.

Satryn called, "Oh, bravo! You're quite fast."

Heath glanced at Jessa, who was picking herself up from the ground. Sword was splayed out in the grass, his chest still smoking. Breathing heavily, he tumbled out from cover and darted behind a topiary.

Their plan was in shambles. Jessa was supposed to stab Satryn with the Razor of Setahari when they embraced. Sword insisted the Geas wouldn't take hold if the hilt were properly insulated with glyph-inscribed silk. It had to be Jessa—not even Sword's reflexes were quick enough.

The bench Heath had been under exploded in a cloud of broken stone and lightning. He remained completely still. Satryn could sense motion even through the pounding rain, and he didn't want to reveal his location. Jessa wasn't looking good, and Sword was even worse, his chest charred and smoking. It had been a long time since Heath had been on his own.

Another crash of thunder resounded as Satryn electrified a revenant that rushed toward her. Pytheria and Crateus were fulfilling their part of the plan.

The undead rose from the river and charged the Tempest one at a time from different directions.

Heath took the opportunity to stalk slowly around the topiary. Satryn was a good ten feet away, five feet too far from the range of his springblades.

Jessa shouted, "Mother!" She unleashed a torrent of lightning that skittered off Satryn's body like water from a duck.

Satryn spun and charged her daughter. Jessa moved quickly but not fast enough to avoid getting punched in the face. To her credit Jessa slammed her elbow into Satryn's side. The women staggered in opposite directions, cradling their wounds before squaring off again.

"Ungrateful," Satryn spat. "The Coral Throne would have been yours."

"It already is," Jessa teased. "You just don't know it yet."

Heath sighed. The plan had been to provoke Satryn and lower her guard. But the Tempest never lowered her guard. Not even when it was her daughter. She and Heath had that kind of mistrust in common.

He crept across the grass as Jessa and Satryn circled each other. Above them massive tendrils of water swayed, ready to strike. Jessa couldn't override her mother's power, but she was more resistant to it than any of them. The water wouldn't drown her, and the lightning would only sting her.

Heath dived and glided toward Sword's body, remaining deathly still when he slid to a stop. He slowly moved his hand to Sword's, grasping his thin fingers in his hand.

"I did kill Father," Jessa said, "to put him out of his misery. I'm sorry I didn't recognize yours."

Satryn's hand exploded in a flash of light, manifesting a flickering blade of electricity. "You're a Stormlord. I'll grant you the death of a worthy rival."

"I deserve the throne," Jessa declared. "You're twisted by the diseases of the pureblood. They've made you mad and miserable." She twirled her wrist and conjured a saber of electricity.

Their blades clashed in an explosion of light. Satryn was quick and vicious, driving her daughter back with ease. Jessa parried frantically as she tried to fend off the attack. Satryn casually twisted her blade.

Heath sent his Light through Sword's body. There was a heartbeat, thin and weak. But it was there. He forced everything he had into Sword's body.

Satryn and Jessa clashed their blades. Jessa struggled to defend herself as Satryn mercilessly beat her backward. Jessa managed to just barely defend herself with clumsy parries; she offered a feeble riposte only to be driven back farther.

Jessa's timid, defensive stance, however, proved adequate. She had spent her life protecting herself from her overbearing mother, and a hidden competence lay behind her seemingly uncertain maneuvers.

Sword coughed. "The fuck?"

"Satryn's going to kill Jessa," Heath said. "You need to get in the game."

"Yeah, yeah, yeah." Sword leaned up from the grass and waved his hand.

The Razor of Setahari floated off the ground and floated behind Satryn as she sparred with her daughter. Jessa's reflexes were working frantically to provide defense. Satryn looked bored.

The dagger whipped into Satryn's thigh, slicing the femoral artery and unleashing a torrent of blood from the gash.

Satryn fell to her knees as Jessa grabbed her throat in her hands and squeezed.

Satryn laughed to herself, "I didn't think you had it in you. But if you kill me, you will be next in line. And I guarantee that you will *never* know a moment of peace/"

Jessa stared into her mother's cold silver eyes. "How is that any different?"

"You are my daughter." Satryn said digging her nails into Jessa's forearms.

Heath charged over, "Jessa, No! You don't need to do this. She'll bleed out in less than a minute."

Jessa released her mother and let her body fall to the ground.

Satryn smiled peacefully and said, "I loved you the only way that I knew how…"

Her eyes shut as the life fled her body. The rain fell harder.

Sparks flickered across Satryn's corpse and made their way to Jessa like a swarm of glowing eels. Satryn's body dissolved as lightning poured through her skin. Jessa jumped backward as they gathered at her feet. "Get back," she told Heath and Sword. "I don't want to hurt you."

Heath grabbed Sword's hand and pulled, but Sword pulled away.

Heath was about to say, "We need to get back," before he was ripped off his feet. *Oh, right. He's immortal.*

Sword's magic hurled them behind a shattered wall, his blade whirling behind him. It landed point first into the soggy earth. Heath rolled and absorbed most of the blow. His shoulder crunched painfully, but he saved his Light and glanced back.

Jessa doubled over as arcs of lightning crawled under her skin and into her veins, making them throb with blue power. Satryn's body disintegrated into a torrent of lightning. Jessa pulled at her hair and cried out desperately as the power funneled into her. Her body exploded in a corona of electricity. Her back arched upward, and she tossed a pulsing surge of energy into the sky, where it radiated in concentric bursts through the dark clouds.

The blast knocked Sword back, and a deafening peal of thunder rang out across the park. His body flailed from the shock and fell still. Smoke rose from his flesh even as the rains fell harder.

"He'll be fine."

Heath nearly jumped out of his skin when he saw the young Fodder from the DiVarian estate kneeling beside him. He was wearing a clinking bandolier of potions strapped over his chest. Crouched next to him was the ancient, leering face of Pytheria. At least a dozen shambling waterlogged revenants swayed behind her.

"Nice sword." Crateus reached out for Sword's blade.

"Don't touch it," Heath insisted.

"Shiny…" Pytheria's bony hands reached for the hilt. Heath was forced for one instant to imagine Sword in the body of a senile and, possibly undead, necromancer who had single-handedly ruined the reputation of Rivern's mages with her unethical experiments. The comic horror would almost be worth it.

"Never you." Heath glared, and she backed away.

"Sword!" Jessa shouted as she ran toward his inert body.

"Guard that blade with your life," Heath told Crateus. "But don't touch it."

"Yes, sir!"

"Your mother's dead. Why are the tentacles still here?" Heath gazed at the wavering tendrils of water as they reared back for a strike.

Jessa spun around and raised her hands, shouting, "Return to the Abyss, Kultea!"

The tentacles paused for a moment then retracted slightly into the canals surrounding Oiler's Park. But then they all lashed forward in unison. Heath felt the air rush toward them before the force of the strike.

A hand gripped his shoulder as the current washed over him. The water was clogged with the dead and the ruins of Rivern, but the looming murky shapes jaunted to the side moments before he collided with them. The water exploded into a splash, and he blinked his poorly made new eyes.

"I feel her power," Jessa said. "Kultea remains."

"Sword?" Heath called out, but there was no answer.

"Kultea knows I'm unworthy of her," Jessa muttered spitefully.

Heath grabbed her shoulders. "You're a Tempest. No one in Creation can match your power. You can do this. I believe in you."

Jessa laughed nervously. "And I thought my mother was the Queen of Lies."

Heath held Jessa's hands. "I believed in something once, and it turned to shit. The priests of Ohan used my mother's death to turn me into their assassin. I had no faith, when all I wanted was to believe in something. So when I say I believe in you, I fucking mean it."

She shut her eyes.

"What do you believe in Jessa?" Heath pleaded. "Even if it isn't true, what's worth believing in anyway?"

She gazed up at the turbulent clouds and scowled. "Not this."

Heath grabbed her hand. "Then make that real."

Jessa threw her head back. "There's truth to the claim that the world is a savage place. And perhaps it's a fiction that we tell ourselves it isn't. But there's beauty in those fictions."

Heath shut his eyes and prayed. "Ohan, I haven't asked you for anything in a long time, but…if you're real, now would a good time to show yourself."

"Kondole." Jessa whispered the blasphemous name of the Father Whale. It was a mere whisper, but it stirred on the wind.

An echo of thunder burst from the sky and knocked them to the ground.

A squarish, tapered mass of clouds plunged out of the sky. Two enormous glowing eyes of electrical power pooled together at the front of the cloud mass. A long, thin slit opened in the roiling cloud bank—dark and full of flickering electricity—and the clouds bound themselves together into a sinuous cetacean body. A whale made of storm and thunder.

The majestic creature let out a long, high bellow that shot to the ground.

Kultea's tentacles lashed toward the mighty beast but dissolved into drops of water as they struck the wall of sound. As the whale song spread over the city, the roiling storm clouds rolled back and dissipated into nothingness.

The Father Whale swam merrily through the clear, starry sky as the storm retreated. The sun was cresting the horizon in the north, and brilliant rays of light broke through the clouds, which lost their dark pallor and became white tufts as majestic as mountains. The sky was every color of red and orange and purple.

"Holy shit," Heath exclaimed.

Jessa grabbed his arm and pointed it toward Sword's broken body. The seal on his chest glowed gold and washed him in a flicker of aurous energy. His wounds were erased, along with the seal on his stomach, and his eyes blinked. He remained motionless as he stared up at the massive whale in the sky.

Heath ran over to him and shook his shoulders. "Hey, buddy. You okay?"

"Sword," Maddox mumbled. "Need Sword…."

"Dying must have broken the bond," Heath said.

"At least he's speaking," Jessa said.

Heath ran back toward Pytheria and Crateus, who were lost in wonder at the whale that swam in the sky. It nudged its head gently at cloud banks and thunderheads on the horizon, reverting them to harmless fluffy clouds.

Heath grabbed the sword by its blade, cutting his hand and avoiding the curse of the hilt, and ran over to Maddox's body. He slipped it under Maddox's hand, and in an instant his inexpressiveness was replaced with a smile. "Jessa," Sword said, "you should make him shoot a rainbow out of his blowhole."

She stifled a laugh. "I'm so glad to see you whole again."

"We won." Sword reared his legs toward his chest and brought them forward, using his momentum to gain a standing position. He nearly pulled it off, but after an initial stumble, he dug his blade into the ground to avoid falling flat on his ass. "I need to work out more."

"We did it," Heath smiled.

"Can we bring it in for a group hug?" Sword asked.

A Patrean soldier briskly marched toward them with a company of Fodders in tow. They were soaking wet, but if they suffered, they didn't show it in their stoic expressions. Their weapons were sheathed. Heath recognized Warmaster Jasyn as the leader of the company. His facial tattoos and age were distinctive enough to differentiate him as he approached.

"Empress Jessa," he stated, "the contracts of this city are yours under the rules of capture."

"I don't claim this city," Jessa explained, "or your contracts."

Heath leaned toward her. "Are you sure?"

"This was an invasion. The Protectorate is owed an apology."

Heath gazed over the ruins of the city. "No. It needs leadership."

"My soldiers and I need a contract holder to authorize any action of the military," Warmaster Jasyn said. "Otherwise we must report to Fort Reave for reassignment."

"You honestly…" Jessa moaned in exasperation. "Yes, I claim your contracts and authorize you to mobilize forces to rescue and secure the city. Don't engage the Red Army, and if Sireen moves her forces here, tell her I'll kill every last one of them."

"But…they're your forces now," the warmaster said.

"Then they can help!" Jessa snapped.

"Sure that's wise? Red armor doesn't look good coming into the city," Heath cautioned. "Maybe mix the patrols, with command falling to the Rivern officers to coordinate."

"I have no idea what I'm doing," Jessa admitted then turned to the warmaster. "Do as he says. Give aid where you can."

"It will be done." Warmaster Jasyn saluted then added, "I've worked for a lot of employers, Empress. You're doing better than most. Listen to your advisors, and never be afraid to say you don't know the answer."

"He was totally blowing smoke up your ass," Sword said, after Jasyn and his men had left.

Jessa started to pace. "We should meet with Sireen and the remainder of the government. We'll need to make plans. But the people need our aid. And the Razor of Setahari. We have to find that before we can do anything. If anyone picks it up…" She cast her eyes about frantically.

"It's probably in the river," Heath said. "Or the canal."

Jessa wrung her hands. "How can we be sure?"

"If only we had someone who had an affinity for water," Sword mused.

AFTERSHOCK (SWORD)

Conflict is essential to the human experience. Without principled opposition, strong beliefs are merely unquestioned assumptions.
-The Sentinel, Traveler Proverbs

Rivern had been demolished. The twin towers that spanned Trident Falls were nothing more than rubble. Homes, including Heath's, had been shattered, and the canals were choked with the broken remnants of daily life. And bodies.

Sword had seen a lot of death in his time, and this looked worse than it was. There had been far more survivors than casualties in the Overlook. Most of the buildings bore damage that ranged from superficial to major, but a few had been completely demolished. One half of a house remained intact, while the back and insides had been completely removed.

There was a mixture of mourning and celebration in the streets. The giant cloud whale, who was now white and fluffy, performed graceful backflips in the air. It distracted many survivors as they clutched their loved ones among the shattered remains of their homes.

Jessa solemnly walked atop the surface of the canal, deep in concentration, her hands extended to her sides. Periodically she waved her arm, and a dagger—or sometimes a person—bubbled up out of the water.

She seemed frail, but she dealt with tragedy better than Sword expected. She believed she was weak because her mother had fed her that horseshit—probably since the day she realized her daughter was made of sterner stuff than she was. Satryn's abuses only had made her more resilient; Maddox had been the opposite.

284

Whatever Jessa found, it was never the Razor.

Sword was doubtful they would find it. Sword himself had been thought lost countless times, only to mysteriously reemerge. The Sarn Arsenal had been crafted by the Artifex, so who knew what other theurgies he had built into his creations.

The trio came to the edge of the Saint Jeffrey Falls and stopped. Sword's heart sank as he looked out over the Backwash and saw nothing but ruin. The water was invisible beneath a crust of shattered wood, bodies, and junk. A small churning crescent of water from the triple falls was clogged with garbage and broken timber. In the distance the broken half of the Assembly tower jutted at an angle from Trident Lake below.

"Fuck," Heath said, gazing at the destruction. The ruins were swarmed with rowboats and survivors clinging to planks. Beaker Street was nothing more than a smear on the shoreline, and toxic runoff visibly dissolved the rubble into a bubbly brown foam.

Jessa hugged herself. "I can't bear this."

"There's no way we're finding anything in that mess," Heath said, always pragmatic.

"Oh, my Guides," Sword said, and pointed. "Look!"

Amid all the destruction, one building still stood. It was shabby and decrepit but no more than it had been. It was like a single flower growing from the ashes of a ruined city or a lone dove flapping its wings in the sunlight following a storm. It was a sight that warmed and exhilarated him.

The other two squinted.

"The Mage's Flask!" Sword exclaimed. "We have to go there."

"You want to go to a bar?" Heath said flatly.

"Look," Sword said, turning to Jessa, "you said we all have something to offer each other that the others lack. You two take yourselves way too seriously."

They both glared at him.

"Everyone I see—including both of you—is going to be dead. When I walk through a busy street, I see people living on borrowed time. I'll outlive everyone, until so many people have died that this catastrophe will be nothing more than a footnote in history. My best friend died during the Macerian purges, but that's not even part of the lore anymore.

"I know it's a big deal for you, but it's an eternal, inevitable fact of your existence that you'll die. Your friends, lovers, enemies, neighbors will all be dead and forgotten one day," Sword said emphatically, "but my fucking bar is the only thing that's still standing after the physical manifestation of fucking Kultea. If this isn't a good time for a drink and some levity, I don't know what is."

"Yes, people die, and it's sad for those who knew them," Jessa scolded. "But these people died before their time! This tragedy was a result of the senseless actions of my mother and family. Forgive me if I don't want to enjoy a congratulatory celebration amid the destruction we *failed* to prevent."

Sword admitted, "I'm immortal. If anyone has time to blame themselves for things that never can change, it's me. I just don't see a point to it. But the fact remains, that bar is still standing. That's not just convenient—it's significant… because nothing else down there withstood your mother. Don't you want to know why?"

He let the idea sink in.

"We should get back to Sireen," Jessa said.

Heath gazed at the ruins below. "The moment we go to her, we'll never get back."

"Exactly!" Sword chimed in.

"Fine," Jessa said. "We should investigate and look further for the Razor."

They made their way down the switchbacks against throngs of wet, desperate people winding their way up the side of the cliff toward dry land. The people of the Backwash were displaced, but they'd been displaced from the worst part of Rivern. Sword wondered briefly if that wasn't a good thing for these survivors, who would fill the vacancies in the abandoned residences of the upper city.

When they reached the edge of Trident Lake, Sword used his mind to build a stable bridge. He ripped out nails and boards, lashing them together to create a boardwalk in front of them as they walked. Where people were splashing helplessly in the water, he and Jessa brought them out. Heath walked behind, occasionally offering his fleeting Light to those in desperate need.

As they approached the Flask, they heard music and laughter. The decrepit structure stood untouched in a churning mass of utter destruction. Sword paused. "That's fucking creepy."

They walked through the door to find the place full of regulars and survivors alike, getting hammered at the bar. Bottles were being passed between piss-drunk people as they danced and staggered about. A brawny man was pawing a woman with his meaty hands, while another man danced on a table. The music was merry and lively.

"Maddox!" Cassie cackled happily from behind the bar. "Come here and give me a kiss."

"She hates me," Sword whispered. "Something fucked up is going on."

"It's your victory celebration," a short woman with bouncing golden hair pronounced theatrically. She wore a dancer's outfit, replete with colorful bows and ruffles. She was somewhat attractive, for a girl, but wore too much makeup. "Free drinks for everyone!"

She approached them, moving lithely through the patrons, as they slapped her ass. "Hi. I'm the Libertine, but just call me Libby. It's actually pretty close to my real name. I think that's how I ended up with it. How are you all doing? You were amazing up there. Just spectacular."

"How is this place still standing?" Jessa demanded. "Is this your doing?"

Libby smiled playfully. "Maybe…Look, I could go into all the boring details, but you don't want to hear me talk. You're the heroes of the city. We want to hear all about you—your anguish, your regrets, the hard decisions you've had to make."

"Wait," Sword said, remembering something from an ancient lifetime. "She's a Traveler, like the Harbinger, but with boobs and alcohol."

"Like the Harbinger but very, *very* different," she said. "We have a complicated, oppositional, but interdependent relationship. Don't worry—I'm friendly. I'm not here to give you any prophecy or cryptic riddles. I just want to throw a party. You can stay as long as you like." She winked.

"A pleasure to meet you." Heath offered a slight bow. "But why are you here? Is it your wyrd?"

"Wyrd? Wyrd. Wyrd…" She tossed the word around as if she were trying to chew it. "That sounds so…"

"Weird?" Sword offered.

Libby paused, placing a finger on her chin, then replied, "I was going to say 'formal.' But yes, we all do things for a reason, even if we don't always know what that reason is…or if it's even a good idea. Whereas the Harbinger's appearance is an omen of great misery, my presence offers consolation in the simple pleasure of the moment. Where there is suffering, there is no greater need for laughter in the face of it. Don't you agree?"

"I could think of a few things these people need more," Jessa said. "Graves for the drowned and medical supplies for the living, as a suggestion."

The Libertine placed her arm on Jessa's shoulder. "Those are just bodies. Death reminds us that all life is fragile and fleeting. Every moment wasted worrying about death is a missed experience in the present. Out there is past. What's happening here and now around you is the present."

"So we shouldn't care about any of it?" Jessa asked incredulously.

Libby smiled emphatically. "You don't have to. I can take away your pain, and you'll never have to feel sorrow again. Look at these people. They've lost their wives, their sons, their homes, but they've found true eternal happiness in this place."

"Never feel sorrow?" Heath echoed. "Even if they're injured or starving?"

"Even if," Libby said proudly. "No one chooses to be unhappy. Life chooses that for us, and we scramble to react. But fear begets paralysis. Rage begets regret. Sadness immobilizes us until we're unable to properly react to the situation life throws at us. These emotions don't guide us—they cripple us."

"What about motivation?" Heath asked. "If everyone were happy just existing, nothing would get done."

"That guy's getting a hand job at the bar," Sword said.

"Motivation? You mean like what paranoia and an unholy lust for power give you?" She motioned through the door to the shattered world outside. "I think we know what that can lead to. Theurgy is wonderful, but these malignant emotions are why we can't have nice things."

"Valid point," Sword said, "but she's still completely nuts. They all are."

"This is a waste of time," Jessa insisted, and spun toward the door. "I need air."

"The lunatics are running the asylum," Libby called after her. "There's a war happening all around us. The Harrowers were the beginning of something that threatens all of Creation. Satryn wasn't just a Stormlord—she was an Architect. This day will have massive ramifications, and your choices will affect the All-That-Is."

Jessa stopped and listened.

Sword froze. "Say more."

"Two Architects coming into their power at the same time." The Libertine looked him dead in the eyes. "The old magic is coming back. Satryn never should have been able to summon one of the primal aspects, and that power transferred to her daughter. Evan Landry shouldn't have been able to call the Harrowers. And you shouldn't have completed the Master Seal of Sephariel. These things never were supposed to happen again. And now they're happening, and the balance is shifting."

"You're scared," Heath told Libby. "There are a lot of bars in this town you could have set up in. The Broken Oar is bigger, and they have a much better wine list, which isn't saying much. You came here to tell us—to tell Maddox something because he's an Architect."

"If I were capable of fear"—her expression darkened—"I'd be huddled up and shaking in a corner. But lucky for me, I don't have to deal with that."

"What did you come to tell Madd—er, me?" Sword said.

"I have nothing against lushes with divine power, being one myself," Libby explained, "but he isn't the reason for my visit. You are, Valor of Crigenesta."

She reached behind her back and pulled out the Razor of Setahari by its hilt, took the blade in her other hand, and offered it to Sword. He wondered briefly whether Setahari was playing him, pretending to be a Traveler, but he knew she wasn't the Razor.

The blade floated in the air in front of him. The three of them stared at it as it twirled in the air, its sinister emerald-colored jewels twinkling in the light. Sword grabbed the blade and tucked it into his belt.

"Thank you, Libby." Jessa breathed a sigh of relief.

"We do help sometimes." She bowed slightly. "The Artifex made this and entrusted it to the great houses of Sarn. He was the only one of us to be both a Traveler and an Architect. I have no idea why the fuck he made such an ugly being, but he built it to last beyond his days. The thing is fucking indestructible, and like all his toys, it has a hidden purpose. Find out what that is."

"Aren't your people more qualified?" Heath asked.

"Studying isn't my forte, and we don't cooperate very well," she laughed, then added, "Anymore."

"Anything else you can tell us?" Heath asked.

"I'll do your fucking research if you fix his cancer," Sword said. If anyone could do it, a Traveler could.

"I can remove his fear, his sorrow," she said. "I can even limit it to the cancer growing in his stomach if he wishes to keep his other anguish. But I can't change what's meant to happen. He's going to die—"

"Don't say that." Sword grabbed her throat. "You can and you fucking will!"

Libby instantly vanished and appeared beside him. "Not cool, dude. When I say I can't do something, my words are the absolute truth. I don't prevent misery—I remove it—and for that to happen, there kind of needs to be misery. Our magic is nearly limitless in pursuit of our wyrd, but we have to follow its dictates to the letter. Now will you let me finish?"

Heath grabbed Sword's arm and gently lowered it. "Please. Finish."

"Heath is going to die because he's mortal. I didn't say how or when. The Archeans have a cure, and so do the Maenmarth witches. You might try asking them…ass." She rubbed her throat.

"Fuck you too," Sword said. "I knew that already. And stop pretending that hurts. You're barely human."

"I don't mean to offend you, but you're kind of harshing the vibe at my little soiree, so…" She flicked her wrist.

The world exploded into green and red. The ground seemed to rush up against Sword's feet, making him stagger. Heath stumbled beside him. Jessa remained upright, registering only mild confusion as she glanced at her surroundings. They were standing on grass inside a large red tent.

Soldiers in red armor drew their weapons and huddled around a group of people seated at a table. Sireen stood and spread her arms. "Jessa! You certainly know how to make an entrance."

Sword looked at the gathered dignitaries. Dame Woodhouse, Cameron, Turnbull, and Loran sat on one end of the table. The rest were clearly silver-eyed Thrycean nobles and their blood sages and warmasters.

"Satryn is dead," Jessa said.

Sireen nodded. "And Kondole once again rides the sky. Jessa, we've waited generations for you to return our people to the ancestoral traditions of our forefathers."

Heath asked, "So you're a heretic?"

Sireen smiled. "No. The heretics are the ones who followed Kultea, who preached oppression and deceit."

Jessa shrugged. "You didn't lack for talent, Aunt. The city of Rivern is in ruins."

"But in chaos is opportunity," Dame Woodhouse offered. "The old Assembly never would have allowed women a seat, but now we can have our own voice."

"The Protectorate did nothing to aid Rivern during the harrowings," Cameron said. "And as empress you can chart a new course for the Dominance."

Jessa shook her head. "Nasara is empress after Mother."

Sireen leaned forward. "You're equals in Heritage. The fight has just begun, and Nasara won't settle for peaceable negotiation."

Sword said, "Then we have to kill her."

"Easier said than done," Sireen replied.

Heath flashed an ivory smile. "No. Killing her is easy, and I have a perfect plan. But before we do that, I'd need to take care of some unfinished business."

UNFINISHED BUSINESS (HEATH)

Dear Scholar Baeland,

You have a tremendous gift.

We haven't shared the existence of the Master Seals with the world at large, and they're rare achievements among even our most skilled mages. The Master Seal of Sephariel hasn't been successfully inscribed since the Calamities, and only five mages have been known to possess one throughout all history. You are the youngest.

It brings me great delight to offer you a place at the Archean Academy. Historically Archea has always offered a place for people of exceptional talent. Over the centuries the bar has grown impossibly high as we isolate ourselves under the auspices of safeguarding our traditions. But even the staunchest among the senate could not deny your gift.

I wish we could share our knowledge for the benefit of Creation. Your accomplishment is an important first step in rolling back those restrictions. I hope you will say yes, for the good of my people as well as yours.

Make yourself ready, and speak the name of the Guide whose seal you bear into this parchment. The spell will do the rest.

Most humbly yours,
High Wizard Petra Quadralunia, Appropriations Committee
—Letter, received at the Lyceum four days after Maddox's expulsion

The ground beneath Heath's feet was soggy and strewn with bog filth. He despised being so far from the comforts of civilization, but this was something he had to do. He gave an envious glance to Jessa, who stepped across puddles and streams as if they were made of glass. She wore simple trousers and a hunter-green doublet.

"I don't suppose you can teach me that trick," he half joked, yanking his foot out of the mud.

"Stop being such a baby," Jessa chided. "I was born to a life of privilege, and I can assure you that refined sensibilities aren't categorically opposed to the enjoyment of the majesty of the untamed wilderness."

"Says the girl who can walk on water," Heath grumbled as he slapped his neck, "and electrocute mosquitoes. I'm being eaten alive. You know how many diseases they carry?"

"None of us has to worry about that problem. You can heal us all," Sword said, then turned to Jessa. "He's so prissy, though. He had a bad experience during his Inquisition survival training."

"I'll kill you to silence you," Heath said.

Jessa laughed. "It's so freeing to be away from all my courtiers, advisors, and generals. This might be the last time I enjoy such a luxury. Do try to be civil."

"Apologies, Your Majesty, but some things aren't appropriate to discuss in such esteemed company," Heath said. It was starting to sound less awkward, though to him she'd always be Jessa. She had become more comfortable in her imperial position, though not entirely. Her leadership skills were still weak, and she was idealistic to a fault.

"Kultea's cold tits." Jessa sighed. "Don't ever address me as if you were a subject. Please, both of you, swear to me that you'll always be candid and open with me."

"Careful what you wish for." Sword smiled. "But if I learned anything from Heath, it's that we need to get used to playing the part, at least in public. If people see us treating you like a normal person, they'll see it as a sign of weakness. Heath's good at this stuff."

"Thanks, buddy," Heath said.

"No problem, buddy."

Heath squealed when he saw the moldering corpse of a bog rat hanging from a tree amid the wispy hanging moss that grew on the branches. "That's disgusting. Why would someone do that?"

"Luck," Jessa offered. "In Amhaven some of the woodsmen tie offerings to trees to curry favor with the witches and Spirit folk. We're close to the border."

"I'm not going to enjoy my time in Weatherly, am I?" Heath asked.

"It will be brief," Jessa said. "I need to coronate a king, and then we can be on our way to the many-splendored city of Thelassus, where you'll live in a standard of luxury that all in Creation will envy. There you can enjoy hot baths, lithe man-servants, and of course, a murderous web of intrigue."

"I'll take your crazy family over a walk through the woods any day. That's how much I hate my life right now."

"You want a drink?" Sword pulled out a flask and offered it.

Heath stopped in his tracks. "Mad—Sword, you promised…no alcohol."

"Relax. It's just water." He tipped the flask back in his mouth and made a brief pained expression. "Really strong water."

Heath grabbed the flask and sniffed it. The smell nearly knocked him back. He tossed it as hard as he could toward a reed-infested pool of stagnant water. It froze midair and returned to Sword's hand. Sword grinned.

In some ways Sword represented the worst aspects of Maddox and Sword—he was impulsive, reckless, and defiant. Maddox never lacked confidence in his own abilities or superiority, but Sword's carefree humor made it almost charming. Almost sexy.

"I think we're close," Jessa whispered. "The water around us doesn't heed me as readily as it should."

"You can see it through the trees." Sword pointed past the gnarled roots of a swamp tree to a dead clearing.

Heath took Jessa's arm. "Your Majesty, whatever you see here…it will leverage your fears, your insecurities. It can appear as anyone in your life who's died, and it will use that appearance against you."

"I'm more than prepared," Jessa said. "My mother is the person who raised me to live in continual doubt of myself. She won't break my resolve. I'm just curious why you think this will work."

Sword explained, "The dolmens are old magic, corrupted by the Harrowers who use them them to murder people in this world. They can't be destroyed, and if they're contained, they move. Your magic is primal, which means it's older and stronger. If you can't blow this thing up, we're fucked."

"Summon the Father Whale if you have to," Heath added. "I'll pray to him as hard as I can."

Heath meant it. Since seeing Jessa summon Kondole from the clouds to defeat the avatar of Kultea, he had felt the stirrings of a faith he had long thought dead. There was no Ohan to come to the aid of mortals, only an ideal to encourage charity and cooperation—when it wasn't used to justify atrocities. But Kondole was real.

Jessa nodded. "I'm ready."

The trio marched into the clearing where the circular stone stood atop the mossy crumbling monoliths. As before, the clearing seemed unnatural, the wilderness silent, the sun somehow dimmer.

Jessa raised her palm toward the stones.

"Wait!" a familiar voice called from the stones.

A Fodder in sleeveless black leather armor stumbled out with his hands raised. He had a scar across his face and a jewel-encrusted bastard sword strapped to his back. "It's fucking great to see you again, mate."

"Scar," Sword whispered.

"Is he…?" Jessa paused.

Sword nodded. "It's my old self. Again."

"I was expecting Satryn," Heath said, "or your dad or my mom or…"

Sword chimed in, "Torin would have been an excellent choice. But I suppose if you want to get maximum effect, the manifestation should be someone all of us knew."

Scar clapped his hands slowly. "Bravo. You three have done a bang-up job. You ended Evan Landry. You saved Rivern. You've proven yourselves fucking champions. Cheers!"

"Rivern was destroyed," Jessa said coldly.

"And Riley was killed by his girlfriend," Heath corrected.

Sword added. "I'd call it a draw at best."

"But look at you all," Scar said emphatically. "Maddox got himself a better intelligence. Heath had a transformative epiphany that gave him faith, and Jessa…sweet, sweet Jessa. You finally found the courage to stand up to your evil mum."

Heath nodded to Jessa. "The Harrowers are scared. You should light this up…now."

"Full disclosure, mate," Scar said. "They're in fact very concerned that you'll do something rash. You see, these sites play an important role in the ongoing survival of humankind. The Memento Mori are the collected dreams, hopes, and memories of all people, preserved for all time."

Sword challenged him. "No, they're memory constructs patched together from the conscious effluvia of the dead, puppeteered by a malevolent alien consciousness with a hunger for human suffering."

"Still," Scar countered, "it's technically an afterlife. And it's not human suffering they hunger for. It's understanding. The pacts are a test. And you've passed with the highest honors."

Heath chuckled. "They're experiments, not tests."

"And what insight did the months of terror you inflicted on the people of Rivern and the refugees from my own homeland gain the Harrowers?" Jessa demanded.

"It helps them understand you, love," Scar explained. "They aren't conscious beings. They don't need to eat or shit or fuck or any of that. They aren't limited to seeing time happen in one direction or observing the world from a single perspective. It's as hard for them to understand the finite as it is for you to grasp the infinite."

"Why would anyone open the green door?" Sword explained to the others. "It was a question one of the Guides asked me in a vision I had. Behind the green door was infinite suffering."

"I don't understand," Jessa said, a confused look on her face.

Heath said, "How can a being not know they're opening a door to infinite suffering? That's the question behind every pact. An omniscient being can't comprehend what it's like to know nothing—no more than we could understand what it's like to see the future but not the past."

"I still don't understand," Jessa said, "and I'm not encouraged by this line of reasoning in the slightest. May I?" She readied her hands to deliver a blow against the dolmen.

Scar hastily said, "All right, all right! They have a deal for you. Five hundred and one years. For that amount of time, there will be no harrowings, no pacts. It's enough for you and your direct line of descendants to live in absolute peace. Additionally… we'll heal the priest's cancer. We'll also tell you the secret to destroying the Razor of Setahari. We can even reveal how to unbind the Seal of Sephariel, which keeps Maddox trapped in immortality. Hells, they'll even throw in…Catherine."

"Must be upsetting they wouldn't offer *your* life back, Scar," Sword said, "but you were a fucking asshole."

Heath urged, "No matter how good it sounds, it's always a trick. Nothing comes for free."

Jessa sighed. "This dolmen could truly represent an afterlife for all the people lost to Kultea's wrath."

"It *is* the home of millions of souls' memories," Scar encouraged.

"I wasn't finished," Jessa said brusquely. "This afterlife is worse than the five hells. I thank you for your role in saving my life, Scar. You and everyone else deserve better than to be the puppets of these dark forces."

Scar glowered. "You think you're so righteous, don't you? What bold new world will you create for mankind when your empire stretches to every far corner of the world?"

"I'm not my mother, and that isn't my ambition," Jessa countered.

"Sure you're not." Scar grinned. "But I'll give you one fun little secret before you take out your aggressions for Mommy on a derelict piece of ancient engineering. The three—and a half technically—of you…you're not the heroes in this tale. You're the bloody villains."

"Get somewhere safe," Jessa whispered to her companions.

Scar laughed. "You can't run from yourselves!"

Jessa raised her arms to the sky. "Kondole! I invoke you. Hear the prayers of your daughter and purge this world of blight!"

Clouds gathered in the sky above her, spilling out in a roiling vortex of thunderheads. Heath lowered his head in prayer—it felt strange to do, but he felt the presence of the divine.

Sword and Scar gazed up as the overcast darkened the sky. Flashes of lightning burst from within the cloud banks, illuminating them from within.

Sword enjoined with another incantation in an old language Heath didn't recognize—a summoning ritual perhaps.

Even Scar grudgingly admitted, "This is kind of badass."

As if the clouds were the surface of a vast ocean, the head of the Father Whale with his gaping maw of lightning surged toward the earth. The avatar was preceded by a shock wave of air pressure that nearly knocked Heath to his feet. He resumed his silent prayer.

Great Kondole, Creation needs you. The world is sick, and it has been far too long since the Gods dwelled among us. Grant us your protection and your mercy.

Kondole let out a high, mournful note that echoed over the sky as he floated toward the earth. His mouth was wider than the clearing and filled with a raging storm of lightning.

Kondole paused and let out a lower note, followed by something that sounded like an angry, guttural purr.

"Heath," Jessa cautioned, "you might want to step back."

Heath didn't move.

The Father Whale breathed a torrent of white light into the dolmen, blinding Heath. The air became electrified, and then the deafening crash of thunder shook the earth, toppling him to the ground.

He picked himself up and studied the clearing. The dolmen had vanished without a trace; only faint impressions in the earth marked its presence. Jessa knelt on the ground, and Sword was sprawled some distance behind her.

"Fuck," Sword said, rolling to his side.

"It is done," Jessa said, then quickly added, "Obviously. I don't know why I felt the need to say that."

"I'm afraid it may have just started. The Harrowers aren't going to take this lying down," Sword said. "At least we know they have a weakness—fuckloads of magic."

"We'll be ready." Jessa brushed her dress and stood.

"No, we won't." Heath struggled off the ground. "But we'll be capable."

Jessa stared at him, jaw wide.

Sword got off the ground and explained, "Achelon showed me another seal, and—" He stopped mid sentence, brow furrowed with confusion as he looked at Heath.

"Do I have something on my face?" Heath asked, feeling a bit exposed.

"Kind of," Jessa said slowly.

Sword walked over to Heath and drew his Sword. He shoved the mirrorlike blade in front of Heath's face so he could see his own reflection.

Heath's hand went immediately to his cheek. He recognized his handsome features, but his eyes—the eyes he'd partially healed during Satryn's attack—were whole. And silver.

"Fuck," Heath gasped.

"Does that mean what I think it means?" Sword asked Jessa.

"It can't be," she said. Heath saw his argent gaze reflected in Jessa's own.

"I'm not a Stormlord too, am I?" Sword asked, checking his reflection in his blade, only to shrug.

"Kondole has chosen you," Jessa said. "And I have no idea what that means. No one ever has acquired that power."

Heath flexed his hand as arcs of bluish light flickered between his fingers. He grinned with delight. "It's a sign."

"Of what, though?" Sword asked.

To Be Continued in Book Two

CODA: THE DAWN OF C8-N

FROM: astephens@qport.gov *(Astrid Stephens)*
TO: amaddox@qport.gov *(Audra Maddox)*
SUBJECT: It's raining frogs—another anomaly?

Hey,

This is weird. I've had three people bring me rocks that looked like frogs…because apparently I like frogs?

Dinesh swears up and down he's not punking me, and one of the rocks came from Tacker. Yeah, the director of Sentinel Security gave me a rock. He said he found it on a patrol and thought I might like it. What do you say to a nearly seven-foot-tall ex-Navy SEAL black-ops commando? I told him thanks.

There's just been a lot of coincidences lately, and I'm a little freaked out actually. A lot of things have been happening like that lately. Lily has lost and found her engagement ring on the beach three times now. It's a like a low-level mass hysteria back at Base Camp Two. Maybe there's something in the food supply. LOL. So far no witch trials.

Anyway if you find any frog-shaped rocks, kick them my way. I think they make cool souvenirs.

Love you always and stay safe,
A

Sagar and Skye were snuggling by a campfire on the beach. Their plastic pup tent looked like a glowing jellyfish from the light of the laptop screens inside. Strewn across the beach were matte-black cases of scientific equipment that

Astrid knew next to nothing about. The budget for this project had been exorbitant, and her role in approving things was more of a formality. Half of what the scientists had requested was probably unnecessary.

She carried a plastic water bottle filled with Lily's latest fermented concoction, something that tasted like an unholy cross between coconut water and moonshine. It was better than her last batch, however, and since the portal had closed, her mixtures were good for morale. She worried more about Tacker's team than the scientists.

"Astrid!" Sagar called happily. "How's it going?"

"I didn't mean to interrupt," Astrid explained, "but Dr. Valentine has offered us her latest creation—a fermented mixture of those edible fruits we discovered on C-17. It's going fast, so I thought I'd bring you something before it's gone. It's almost drinkable."

Skye laughed. "That's an improvement. Thank you, Astrid."

Astrid plopped down next to them and handed the bottle to Skye. She let her fingers sink into the sand as she gazed out across the ocean. It was full of bioluminescent plankton that outnumbered the stars reflected in the gentle water. "It's beautiful."

"It's the most beautiful thing I've ever seen." Sagar hastily added, "Except for my wife of course."

"Shut the fuck up," Skye teased, as she passed the bottle to her husband. "The only reason we got married is because neither of us can marry the sea."

The Janssens were two of the few people on the survey mission who knew each other from before and the only people who were family. An oceanographer and a marine biologist, they were the perfect couple. They even had matching tattoos on their calves; Sagar had a whale, and Skye had a squid.

Astrid sighed. "You two doing all right?"

"We'd be doing better if there were any edible fish to support a large population," Sagar said. "The plankton should have some sort of natural predator. The light they emit is normally a biological response to predators, but C8-N is like looking at Earth's history as it unfolds. The ecosystem isn't developed yet."

"Something has to be here," Skye said. "The water would exhibit much more acidity if the plankton population weren't somehow being contained or mitigated."

"The oceans here are exceptionally deep," Sagar countered. "There could be a much wider variety of life evolving down there. What if evolution happened at a lower depth on C8-N?"

"We really need a better name for this planet," Skye said.

Astrid interjected, "We've polled the teams, and C-8N has a ninety-nine percent disapproval rating, which is the closest we've had to a consensus. At least it's better than Nimrod."

"Nimrod was a hunter," Sagar countered.

Skye grabbed the bottle back. "The naming committee fucked that up, Sagar."

Astrid shrugged. "We didn't think we'd find a viable planet this quickly. The names were a randomized list, like the names of hurricanes. We actually put the worst ones at the top. And the government gets to decide the name anyway. Honestly I'm a big fan of ditching the whole mythology-to-name-planets thing. We should name this place after something that matters, so if our children grow up here, they'll know what it means. Like 'Promise' or 'Hope.'"

"Sorry. I forgot you were on that committee," Skye said, passing her the bottle. "I think 'Earth' is a good name. It's descriptive, historical, and…it actually is a planet. We don't need a fancy name for it."

"You can't call it Earth," Sagar said. "That's a dumb name for a planet covered with water."

Skye interrupted, "Which covers the—"

"Rock," Sagar stated. "And that rock contains more water than all the surface oceans."

"In microscopic amounts. The water below Earth's surface is basically blue rock."

Astrid handed the bottle to Sagar. "Jesus, get a room, you two."

Skye smiled. "This is what you and Dr. Maddox have to look forward to."

"No," Astrid said. "Her doctorate is in astrophysics. Mine is in business administration. We don't have these arguments because neither of us knows what the fuck the other is saying half the time."

"Any word on the Q-Portal?" Sagar said tentatively. He'd been through a couple of outages before, but it was a little nerve-wracking for everyone.

"Standard calibration," Astrid said. "We're rationing in case it drags out, but our last resupply left us enough to last at least three months. We're fine."

"Listen, we have something to tell you…" Skye started.

Astrid waited.

"We're pregnant," Sagar said, squeezing his wife.

"The first alien baby." Skye beamed as she rubbed her stomach. "We're thinking of calling him Noah, after the ark. Kind of appropriate. We want to have him here if that's possible."

Sagar added, "Or Heather if it's a girl."

"It's a boy," Skye said.

Astrid put a hand to her mouth. All the women on the team were given a birth-control implant, but the effectiveness rate wasn't 100 percent. "Skye, that's great news, but we don't have the facilities or the experts. When we move to phase six, I can put you at the top of the list for family habitation. But I can't advance the timeline on obstetric care—we haven't even vetted those experts."

"A full eighth of this survey team has some kind of medical degree," Skye protested. "Besides there are no pathogens here—it's safer than a doctor's office back home."

"What about day care?" Astrid countered. "And diapers. Do you seriously want to drop your kid off with Tacker's crew?"

"We were in the Peace Corps," Sagar said. "You'd be surprised what women in third-world countries—"

They heard a loud shriek from down the beach. "Woooo! What is up, bitches?" Dr. Lily Valentine ran through the sand, carrying a sloshing water bottle filled with cloudy liquid. "I brought reinforcements." She shook her bottle.

"Lily," Astrid said. "I thought you were partying with the tech ops."

She tossed her hair back. "I had to get the fuck out of there. Dinesh was, like, literally all over me. That guy is such a perv."

Skye and Sagar looked at each other and shared a giggle.

Astrid stiffened. The survey team had become a hotbed of sexual tension over the last few months. The fitness requirements for phase two meant there were a lot of brilliant—but young and by proxy impulsive—scientists and specialists.

"What happened?" Astrid said slowly. "You know I have to take these complaints seriously."

"It's fine." Lily waved her hand dismissively. "I blew him. We're good."

"Lily!" Astrid exclaimed. "Did he coerce you in any way? You know I'm required to report anything that potentially violates the code of conduct. Especially now, given what happened with Officer Harlowe."

Lily laughed. "You're so fucking serious. With your rules all the time…Jesus."

"How much have you had to drink?" Astrid asked her.

Lily shrugged. "A lot."

Astrid grabbed her shoulders and pulled her out of earshot from the campfire. "I need to know if you were forced or at any time withdrew consent."

"Shhhh. It's all good." Lily smiled happily. "I forced him if anything. But then he went into this whole speech about repopulating the planet. And I was all, like, 'Ew, I am not having your baby.' Even if we *are* stranded on this rock forever, this survey team is such a sausage fest—it could never support a viable birthrate. Like, duh."

"Lily," Astrid said firmly, "I'm taking you back to your tent and having Tacker assign a security detail. I'll speak to you and Dinesh tomorrow. If this is an issue, it could result in one or both of you being pulled off the mission. So you need to think long and hard about what you want to say."

Lily grinned. "You don't get it, do you? We're not going home. Ever. The portal's closed and won't reopen."

"So that's what this is about. It's just a routine calibration, Lily," Astrid reassured her. "We've been through outages before, and they rarely last more than a few days. This is your first time experiencing one, so I understand it can be upsetting, but we'll get through it. We can talk about your concerns tomorrow after you've had time to sleep it off."

"Whatever. *He* said we're all going to die here, so I figured, why not make the most of it?" Lily took a swig of her alcoholic concoction and ran toward the sparkling water.

"Dinesh said that?" Astrid said. "He's in IT, not quantum."

"No." Lily stripped her shirt off, baring her sports bra. She pointed. "*The Harbinger.*" Dr. Lily Valentine then turned and skipped into ocean, without a care in the world. Astrid was losing control of her team. There needed to be stricter psych evals, closer monitoring of fraternization. The board wouldn't be happy.

Astrid turned, and her face went pale. "Oh, shit."

Dr. Herschel Cohen, a gaunt elderly man with a slight limp and Coke-bottle glasses, walked up the beach. He was a mathematician who had predicted the collapse of Earth's ecosystem, to the year, back in the 1970s, well before climate change was a part of the national narrative. It had earned him a sinister nickname among his fellow scientists, who mocked his tendency for fatalistic predictions.

The Harbinger approached and he did not bring good tidings.

GLOSSARY

*T*ranslator's note: this book is translated from the original Thrycean, which was written in the Genatrovan dialect.

The Thrycean language has a rich tradition of obscure colloquialisms and a wide variety of dialectical idioms. The manner of speech and the idioms have been approximated to forms more familiar to English readers. High Thrycean, spoken by imperials, is an extremely exacting in its enunciation.

The Thrycean lexicon contains a robust corpus of suffixes and prefixes that facilitate the invention of new words and word concepts. Fluent speakers are able to do this artfully, and it's the prominent feature of much epic poetry. While it can be serviceably rendered to English, the art is lost in translation. More's the pity.

Abyss: The deep ocean kingdom ruled by the coelacanth. A water breathing civilization that lives miles under the ocean's surface in total darkness and beneath massive pressure.

Abyss: A civilization deep below the lightless depths of the ocean, ruled by the coelacanth

Achelon: the Desecrator, former ruler of the city-state of Minas Creagoria

Alessandria: the putative Queen of Lies, one of the most influential minds in Stormlord politics. She changed the tradition from rule by force to rule by manipulation.

Amhaven: a heavily forested nation to the west of the protectorate. Its capitol is Weatherly, and its primary export is exceptional timber from the Maenmarth woods.

Archea: a floating continent measuring ten square miles. Population is roughly half a million, with many living underground. Archea condones the use of slave labor and is ruled by a senate of its best and brightest citizens. Appointment is by merit, not popular vote. It is the last intact civilization from before the Second Era.

Artifice: the study of magic related to breathing life into enchanted objects and automatons. Masters of this discipline recently have learned how to transfer their minds to mechanical host bodies.

Asherai: a far-off kingdom on the other side of the world. This area is known for its shadow assassins, warriors who can teleport short distances.

Assembly: Rivern's elected government. The ranks often come from old money, but powerful guild interests also campaign for influence. They convene in the southern tower at the edge of Trident Falls.

Automaton: a clockwork construct of limited sentience. They're powered by heartstone cores that house their intelligence.

Backwash: the lower district of Rivern. The city's anarchic laws are often ignored, and a thriving black market is tentatively allowed by the Assembly.

Bamor: the de facto capitol of the Protectorate. With a population of more than a million, it's easily the largest city-state. The population and nobility are predominantly dark skinned, and the city has a reputation for iniquity. Saint Jeffrey declared a thousand-year jubilee when he defeated the Harrower Vilos. It is now year 568 of that celebration, which is held nonstop in one quarter of the city by revelers.

Barstea: a member of the Free Cities

Blood magic: the practice of reading and manipulating blood and other humors

Border Nations: impoverished monarchies with little access to magical power, including Amhaven, Veyal, Mythercia, and Gorin

Cameron: a firebrand assemblyman, representing the lower district of the Backwash

Dame Woodhouse: a woman of noble rank and an avowed rival of Muriel Silverbrook

Daphne: the leader of the Inquisition and Heath's estranged mentor

Dolmen: an ancient monument placed by the empires of the Second Era. Dark powers inhabit them.

Dominance: an imperial dynasty that stretches across the five oceans ruled by hereditary weather mages known as Stormlords. The nation is called Thrycea, and its capitol is Thelassus.

Duke Rothburn: A distant cousin of Jessa's who contests her claim to the throne of Amhaven,

Everstorm: A continuously raging storm centered above Thelassus that provides electricity to the city from its regular lightning strikes.

Fodder: an abbreviation of "cannon fodder," a derogatory term for the disposable nature of Patrean mercenaries. People who use this term are racially insensitive.

Free Cities: See Protectorate.

Geas: a compulsion magically imposed on a person. A favorite enchantment in the lost Sarn empire.

Genatrova: the continent upon which the Free Cities and border nations sit

Gorin: a border nation. Its primary industry is fishing.

Hamartia: a seal that has been inscribed incorrectly, creating a flawed result; typically manifests as a physical or mental affliction

Harbinger: member of the travelers. His wyrd is to preside over inevitable tragedy. Like all Travelers he possesses strong, mysterious theurgy. He can teleport and see any future that will never come to pass.

Harrower: one of thirteen mysterious creatures bent on sowing misery. Each night they claim a single victim while he or she sleeps.

Heath: a thirty-five-year-old mercenary, former Inquisitor, former criminal

Hierocracy: the primary organized religion of Rivern. Its followers preach the value of life, faith, and charity.

Ilyara: the Witch Queen

Inquisition: the part of the Hierocracy devoted to rooting out and destroying Dark Magic

Invocari: the void mages who have protected the city of Rivern for more than five centuries

Iridissa: the Tempest and empress of Thrycea

Isik: a necromancer who works as a coroner. Since necromancy no longer is taught at the Lyceum, he was born and educated in Volkov.

Jessa: daughter of Satryn and princess of Amhaven

Karthanteum: a far-off city where transmutation magic is practiced

Kondole (aka the Father Whale): a god worshiped by the peaceful ancestors of the Stormlords

Kultea (aka the Hungry mother): a goddess of cruelty and power worshiped in Thrycea

Libertine: a Traveler who just likes to have fun, regardless of the situation

Lidora: a distinguished seal mage, known for her caution and reserve; one of the first women to be appointed to the Lyceum's regents board since Pythcria

Lyceum: the arcane college of Rivern. It was once a premier institution until Dean Pytheria was convicted of unholy necromantic experiments. Its reputation is recovering; it is still considered the premier school for artificers.

Maceria: an ancient empire

Maddox: a twenty-six-year-old wizard

Maelcolm: Satryn's twin brother and Jessa's uncle

Maenmarth: An ancient forest inhabited by witches and spiritfolk, the bulk of which resides in the borders of Amhaven.

Mazitar: a settlement in the Dominance famed for pink-sand beaches and bioluminescent plankton

Memento Mori: a place to converse with echoes of the dead. See Dolmen.

Muriel Silverbrook: the richest, most influential woman in Rivern. She's also a countess and the matriarch of a family that holds many seats on the Assembly.

Mythercia: a border nation on the western coast

Nasara: Empress Iridissa's oldest daughter

Nash: a major Stormlord, father of Satryn and secret consort of Empress Iridissa

Necromancy: the arcane study of death and reanimation of the dead

Nerrax: Jessa's cousin and son of Nasara

Night wrestler: a homosexual Patrean, skilled in hand-to-hand combat

Ohan: the god of sunlight, life, and renewal

Orthodoxy: See Hierocracy.

Patreans: named for the wizards of the Patrean empire, who created them. A race of cloned people who serve in the world's armies as contracted mercenaries. They're stronger and faster than humans and don't dream or experience fear. They possess no magic. Every Patrean union results in a child who is a clone of his or her Patrean mother or father. Pregnancy lasts six months, and women can fight well into the third month without issues.

Petra Quadralunia: archwizard from Archea. Also a member of the senate.

Protectorate: a loose confederation of city-states that have thrown off the shackles of monarchial rule to be governed by the will of the people. Though each city-state has independence, the center of the Protectorate's collective government is in Bamor.

Pytheria: the disgraced former dean of the Lyceum who used her position to perform illegal necromancy experiments. She would be more than 100 years old today.

Quirrus: the head of the college of blood magic at the Lyceum. He creates strange hybrids by combining parts of different animals.

Red: the Patrean commander of the Twin Shields brothel

Reda: a fishing village

Riley: former student at the Lyceum

Rivern: one of the Free Cities of the Protectorate. It's known for engineering and steam works. The city is built around the split of three rivers known as the Trident which sits atop a great waterfall that spills into the lower city, a district known as the Backwash.

Sarn: an ancient empire

Satryn: queen regent of Amhaven

Seal: an inscribed design that grants its bearer certain powers, such as telekinesis, longevity, truth detection, and the ability to produce fire

Sireen: Jessa's aunt

Stormlord: a person born to Thrycean royalty who wields the power of storm and water

Stormraider: An ancient tribe of corsairs known for bloodthirst, who with the help of the coelacanth conquered the peaceful Wavelords and sired the current lineage of Stormlords.

Sword: An ancient weapon forged in Sarn, possessing an intelligence and capable of controlling it's weilders. Once bonded to the Sword the host body will be controlled by Sword's intelligence until death. Sword's personality and reasoning capabilities are limited or enhanced by the natural ability of its host.

Tertius: the dean of the Lyceum and Maddox's mentor

Thelassus: the capitol of Thrycea. Population is more than a million. The city has working electricity.

Thrycea: See Dominance.

Torin Silverbrook: a mage from the Lyceum; Maddox's classmate and Jessa's suitor

Travelers: a reclusive, mysterious faction of immortals. They vary widely in temperament and abilities. Each bears an epithet that describes their wyrd, a duty or obsession they pursue to the exclusion of all else. Examples are the Harbinger, the Libertine, and the Stargazer.

Turnbull: a mage at the Lyceum.

Veyal: a border nation with a failed government, ruled by a bandit prince. Nasara's father hails from here.

Volkov: Northern member of the free cities known for necromancy

Wavelord: A peaceful tribe of weather mages who lived on the beaches of Mazitar before being conquered by the Stormraiders.